COLD CASE REOPENED

CARIDAD PIÑEIRO

COLTON 911: UNDERCOVER HEAT

ANNA J. STEWART

MILLS & BOON

Cold Case Reopened © 2021 Caridad Piñeiro Scordato
Colton 911: Undercover Heat © 2021 Harlequin Books S.A.

Special thanks and acknowledgement are given to Anna J. Stewart for her contribution to the *Colton 911: Chicago* series.

ISBN: 978-0-263-28326-6

0221

MIX
Paper from
responsible sources
FSC
www.fsc.org
FSC™ C007454

This book is produced from independently certified FSC™ paper to ensure responsible forest management.

For more information visit: www.harpercollins.co.uk/green

Printed and bound in Spain
by CPI, Barcelona

COLD CASE REOPENED

CARIDAD PIÑEIRO

To my absolutely fabulous and amazing agent Michelle Grajkowski. Thank you for believing in me. Thank you for being such a beautiful person who can always bring a smile to my face and make me laugh. May we share many, many more slices of cheesecake together in the future!

Chapter One

It was hard to believe that such beauty possibly held unspeakable evil.

Rhea Reilly stood on the shore of the mountain lake where six months earlier her twin sister, Selene, had disappeared on a cold fall night.

Rhea's artist's eye took in the scene before her. The waters of the lake sparkled like diamonds beneath a sunny cerulean sky. At the farthest end of the lake, the waters tumbled over a spillway for the dam that held back a rush of water during a spring thaw or heavy rain. In the distance, ragged mountains leaped into the sky, still frosted with the remnants of winter snow at the highest elevations.

Normally she would have savored painting such a lovely sight, but not today, when it might be her sister's watery tomb.

Rhea hugged her arms tight around herself, closed her eyes and listened to the soft lap of the water against the rocky shores of the lake. Imagined Selene standing there that fateful night, tapping out the message she'd sent to Rhea.

I can't take it anymore. I can't. I'm finally going to do something about it.

The police had taken that text to mean that Selene had decided to end her life that night, right there on the shores of those stunningly beautiful mountain waters. But Rhea wasn't convinced.

Although her sister had been troubled the last few months, Rhea was certain that Selene would never take her life. If anything, it was more likely that Selene's husband had killed her, but the police in Selene's hometown had been unable to find enough evidence to charge him. No-body homicides were apparently very difficult to prosecute.

The police here in Regina, Colorado, where Selene's car had been found by the lake, were convinced that her sister had committed suicide, even though they also hadn't been able to find Selene's body.

But Rhea was sure her sister wasn't dead. There was something inside her, that special twin connection they had always shared, that had been saying from the very beginning that Selene was alive and hurting.

That was why she'd undertaken her own investigation once her sister's case had become inactive because the police had run out of leads.

Rhea dashed away the tears that had leaked from beneath eyes screwed shut.

Her sister was alive and, if she wasn't, her husband was responsible. She intended for the police to do something about it based on the information she had collected over the last six months. But for the truth to come out, she needed more corroborating evidence and only the police could provide the resources to accomplish that.

She whirled, stumbled a bit on the rough rocks beneath her feet. Righting herself, she marched to her car, which she had parked on the street near where Selene's sedan had been found. The street would have been deserted when Selene had texted her that night.

Rhea stopped to look around, examining the scene. Along the edges of the lake, a marina spread out across the shore. Dozens of boats were parked at the docks behind a large building that held a restaurant, a marina office and a shop that sold supplies for boaters, as well as tourists, partaking in the lake's many summer activities.

Across the way were a few homes and in one of those homes was a witness who had seen Selene park and walk toward the lake. The older woman hadn't thought much of it because people often stopped, even at night, to take in the splendor of the lake.

Rhea intended to speak to her, but hopefully with the police to back her up and add their own expertise to the interrogation.

The police.

It all kept circling around to needing their assistance, so it was time she got going and spoke to them about Selene's case.

She got in her car and headed to Main Street and the Regina Police Station. As she cruised down Main Street, she was once again struck by the loveliness of the town. It was postcard-perfect, with its charming downtown filled with an eclectic mix of shops that catered to locals as well as the tourists who would visit for skiing and water sports.

Rhea found a spot just a block shy of the police station, parked and grabbed the thick folder bulging with the information she had gathered over the many months. With it tucked under her arm, cradled as securely as a newborn baby, she walked to the police station and paused at the base of the steps.

Like everything else about this town, the police station looked like something off a movie set. The building blended harmoniously with the other structures along Main Street. On either side of the wide steps leading to the door, spring flowers in a riot of colors cascaded over the edges of the terraced garden. Bright pink, purple and blue blossoms waved at her in welcome as a slight breeze swept across the street, still a bit cold despite it being early spring.

The chill settled in her bones as if warning her that she might not be happy with what she found inside.

She dragged in air through her nostrils and then expelled it with a harsh breath.

Time to get going. She stomped up the stairs and to the reception desk.

The sergeant at the desk did a little double take, as if seeing a ghost, and Rhea understood. She and Selene were identical twins and Selene's case had caused quite a stir in the normally placid town. It was unlikely that the police officer hadn't seen a photo of Selene in the station or on the news.

"I'm Rhea Reilly. Selene's sister. I was hoping to speak to the chief if he had a moment," she said. She hadn't made an appointment because she wasn't sure of the welcome she'd get. Especially considering how poorly the meeting with the Avalon police chief had gone. What with rumors about the Blue Code, she hadn't wanted to take any chances; the Regina police chief might not see her if word of her mission had traveled to him.

"I'll see if he's available," the officer said and gestured for her to take a seat in the reception area, but Rhea had too much nervous energy to sit. She paced as the young woman called the chief. Heard the murmurs as the officer spoke to him before rising to say, "The chief will see you, but he has only a few minutes before another meeting."

The young woman gestured toward the back of the building where the police chief stood at the door to his office. He was dressed in a bright blue shirt the color of the lake waters and dark blue pants. The shirt strained against a bull chest and broad midsection. A shiny gold badge pinned to the right breast of his shirt identified him as the chief while on the left breast the town's emblem was embroidered on a patch. White, blue and gold colors on the badge-shaped patch showed the mountains in the background, skiers on a slope to the left and a swimmer in waves to the right. *Tourists. The town's lifeblood*, Rhea thought. Because of that, a murder in their town was the last thing the police and town officials would want. Easier just to call it a suicide.

The chief did a "come here" wave with his hand, but his weathered face was set in stern lines, his mouth a harsh slash that was clearly at odds with his gesture.

Despite his less than friendly demeanor, she pushed through the barrier the desk sergeant buzzed open and marched to the chief's office, her folder tucked tight against her.

As she did so, she passed one man who sat handcuffed on a bench by an officer's desk. Rough-looking with a heavily bearded face, he jumped, almost startled as she neared, and the color drained from his face. His hard eyes, dark and brooding, widened in surprise much like the desk sergeant's before he schooled the reaction.

Something about him sent a shiver of apprehension through her, but she tamped it down and proceeded to the chief's office.

"Miss Reilly," the chief said with a dip of his head and sweep of his hand to welcome her.

She sat in the chair across from him as he took a spot behind his desk. Like everything else about the town, the desktop and nearby bookcase were neat as a pin. So neat they almost looked staged, but then again, she remembered this chief being quite orderly and controlled. Compassionate even in the days after Selene's disappearance.

"What can I do for you today?" he said, as he laced his fingers together and leaned his thick forearms on the edge of his desk in a slightly friendlier posture.

The folder sat in her lap, heavy against her thighs. She shifted her hands across the smooth surface of it and said, "I really appreciate all that you've done for my family, Chief Robinson."

He dipped his head and his attitude softened a bit more. "Thank you. I know it was a difficult time for you. Rhea, right?"

She nodded. "Yes, Rhea. It was a difficult time and, again, I appreciate all that you did. What I'm hoping is that you'll reopen the case. I have new information—"

Chief Robinson held up his hands to stop her. "Miss Reilly, this isn't *Murder, She Wrote*. I'm sure you think you've unearthed some 'new evidence,'" he said, using air quotes for emphasis. "But we did a thorough investigation."

Anger built inside her at his dismissiveness, but she battled it back, certain it wouldn't help. "I know you did, but I've gotten more information—"

"Let me guess. From social media," he said with a rough laugh and wag of his buzz-cut head of salt-and-pepper hair.

She couldn't deny it. "Some of it. All I'm asking is that you let me show you what I've collected. Let me explain why I think…" She hesitated. The chief would never believe that Selene was still alive, but at a minimum she hoped that he would reopen the investigation and either find Selene or her killer.

At her silence, Chief Robinson leaned toward her again, compassion replacing his earlier disbelief. "Look, Miss Reilly. Rhea. I know this must still be difficult for you, but we have limited resources to…expend on this case."

She was certain he had really wanted to say "waste on this case" but she pressed on.

"Please, Chief Robinson. All I'm asking is that you look at this," she said and held up the bloated folder for him to see.

The chief stood. "I'm sorry. I have another meeting in a few minutes and have to prepare for it."

She'd been dismissed. Again, just like at the Avalon Police Department in her sister's hometown. But she didn't intend to give up.

"I'll be staying at the Regina Inn for a few days. Just in case you change your mind. And if not, rest assured I'll be reaching out to people in town to complete my investigation."

With that she shot out of her chair and escaped his office, her veiled threat hanging in the air. She was sure the chief would be less than pleased with her playing detective on his home turf. It would draw too much attention to the fact that not all was as perfect as it seemed.

She rushed through the pen of police officers and clerks, past the reception area and out the door, nearly running into an officer as he walked up the steps to the station.

"So sorry, miss," the officer said and caught her as she stumbled and dropped the folder. The rubber band around the folder snapped, and papers spilled out. She bent to collect them before the breeze swept them away.

DETECTIVE JACKSON WHITAKER kneeled to pick up the thick folder the young woman had dropped and round up loose papers. But, as he handed them to her and met her gaze, he felt gobsmacked.

Selene Davis. Her beautiful face was indelibly etched into his brain since he had been the one to find Selene's abandoned car by the lake.

Only Selene was dead, which meant this had to be her twin sister.

But before he could say anything, Selene's sister snatched the folder and papers from his hands and stomped off.

Whoa, so not happy, he thought and walked into the

office, wondering what had set off the young woman. As he entered, he said to the desk sergeant, "That was—"

"Rhea Reilly. She wanted to speak to the chief," Desk Sergeant Millie Rodriguez answered and jerked her head in the direction of the chief's office.

Speaking of the chief, he stood at the door to his office, his features a picture of upset. His lips were set in a tight line, and his beefy arms crossed against his thick chest. With a sharp wave of his hand, the chief summoned Jackson to come over.

Certain that he knew just what this meeting would be about, Jackson hurried to the chief's office but didn't take a seat. He stood before the desk, hands jammed into his pockets, rocking back and forth on his heels as he waited for the older man to sit. Once he had, the chief looked up at him and said, "That was Rhea Reilly."

Jackson nodded. "I gathered as much. She's a dead ringer for her sister. Twins if I remember correctly."

"You do. Rhea has been doing her own investigating and wants us to reopen her sister's case," Chief Robinson said and laid his muscled forearms on the edge of his desk.

Jackson considered the request, but only for a second. "It's hard for people to accept that someone they knew and loved would kill themselves. I imagine it's even harder for a twin."

The chief's eyebrows drew together in puzzlement, creating a deep furrow across his broad forehead, and Jackson quickly explained, "That twin connection some people claim they have."

"You believe that?" the chief asked, leaned back in his chair and steepled his fingers before his lips, scrutinizing Jackson as if he was a bug under a microscope.

Considering what he had seen of Selene's sister and her anger, she clearly believed something contrary to what their report had said. Because of that, Jackson shrugged. "Stranger things have been known to happen."

The chief continued to stare at him, as if sizing him up. "You know you're my choice to replace me when I retire next year."

Jackson nodded. "I do, and I appreciate your confidence in me. I promise that you'll be leaving the department in good hands."

"I think so. Maybe it's time I turn over some of the more difficult tasks to you, so that you acclimate to that position."

Jackson wasn't above hard work. His years in the military and on the police force had been filled with long days. Tough days, like the day he'd finally had to close Selene's case as a suicide. It had bothered him then because, much like Rhea, it had been hard for him to understand how a beautiful and vibrant woman with so much to live for could just walk into the lake and end her life.

"Whatever you need me to do, Chief," he said with a dip of his head to confirm his acceptance of any task his boss assigned to him.

"I want you to look at Rhea Reilly's information and then tell her she's barking up the wrong tree."

Chapter Two

Rhea had barely finished unpacking her things when the knock came at the door.

She hurried there and threw it open, expecting to find room service with the extra blanket she'd requested. That earlier chill hadn't left her, not that a blanket would end it, but it had been worth a try.

It wasn't room service. It was six-plus feet of lethal male, dressed in police blues, with a white Stetson held in hands that he shifted uneasily on the brim. He had shortly cropped sandy-brown hair that screamed former military and eyes the gray of lake waters on a dreary day. He clenched and unclenched his chiseled jaw as he stood there, obviously hesitant, before he finally said, "You should be more careful and check to see who it is before you open the door."

Anger ignited instantly at his chastisement. "I was expecting room service. Not the police."

He tipped his head, seemingly sorry, but he didn't strike her as the type to apologize. Not willingly anyway. And it occurred to her then that he was the officer she'd run into outside the police station. The one who'd helped her pick up her papers and whom she hadn't thanked.

"Rhea Reilly," she said and held out her hand. "I'm sorry I was so rude before. I was upset."

"I understand. Detective Jackson Whitaker. Jax to my friends." A ghost of a smile danced across full lips, and he enveloped her hand with his big calloused one.

His touch roused a mix of emotions. Surprising comfort. Unwelcome electricity and heat.

"We're not friends…yet," she said as he continued holding her hand, longer than expected. Longer than necessary. She withdrew her hand from his and wrapped her arms around herself. "And I doubt that you can possibly understand."

That slight dip of his head came again, as if accepting her statement, and he motioned inside her room with his Stetson. "Do you mind if I come in?"

She both did and didn't mind. Something about his presence was unnerving, but if he was here, maybe it meant that the chief had reconsidered her request.

"Please," she said and waved him in.

He entered and, as he did so, his gaze swept the room, assessing. Observant. A cop's eyes taking in the scene and immediately focusing on the thick folder sitting on a small bistro table beside French doors to a balcony facing the lake. The lake was a constant reminder of why she was here.

"May I?" he said and pointed toward the folder.

"Is that why you're here? Did Chief Robinson change his mind?"

JAX HATED TO burst her bubble so quickly, but he also didn't believe in lying. "The chief asked that I review your information."

Rhea narrowed her eyes, a bright almost electric blue that popped against creamy-white skin and dark, almost seal-black hair. "He just wants to shut me up, doesn't he?"

"Whatever he may want, I promise you that I'll be

objective when I look at your information," he said and meant it.

Rhea focused her eyes even more pointedly and then suddenly popped them open, as if surprised. "Detective Whitaker. You were the officer who found Selene's car."

He nodded. "I was. I also secured the scene and took part in the investigation afterward."

"And you agreed with the conclusion that Selene killed herself," Rhea pressed and laced her fingers together before her. An assortment of silver and gold rings decorated her slender fingers while a mix of bracelets danced on her delicate wrist.

With a quick, negligent lift of his shoulders, he said, "The evidence we had available indicated that, Rhea. I know that's a hard thing to accept—"

"Selene would not do that. She was too full of life to just throw it away," she said and shook her head, sending the shoulder-length locks of that dark hair shifting against the fine line of her jaw.

Jackson couldn't argue that it had seemed unlikely at first to him, as well. That her disappearance was likely foul play at her home prompted him to ask, "Why didn't you go to the Avalon police with your information?"

Rhea looked away and worried her lower lip and in that instant he knew. "You went to them and they didn't believe you, did they?"

She shook her head again, a softer almost defeated motion, and as she glanced his way, her gaze held the sheen of tears. Damn, but he couldn't handle tears. They were his kryptonite. He held his hands up and said, "I'm sorry, Rhea. But you have to understand that we're both small towns with limited resources."

"And what's one missing woman, right? Do you have any idea how many women go missing every year? How many women deal with domestic abuse every day? End up dead because no one believes them?" she said, her voice husky with suppressed tears and anger.

He nodded and juggled his Stetson in his hands. "I do. My sister…" He hesitated, the reality all too real for him still. "She was lucky. She got out."

"I'm sorry, Detective," she said and walked over to stand hardly a foot from him. She was so close he could smell her fragrance, something flowery and clean, like the scent of a spring day. The top of her head barely came to his chin. She was fine-boned beneath the gauzy floral fabric of her blouse. So slight, and he imagined Selene must have been built much the same. It bothered him to think any man would beat on her.

"We had no indication of domestic abuse when we investigated," he said as Rhea removed some papers from her folder and laid them out for him on the smooth mahogany table.

With a shrug of her slight shoulders, she said, "She never told me, but I had sometimes seen bruises on her arms. She always had an excuse for them. After she…disappeared, I found out that Selene had gone to a domestic violence support group. Just once. Only once…"

Her voice trailed off, and she fixed her gaze on the papers, avoiding his.

Jackson placed his thumb under her chin and applied gentle pressure to urge her to face him. "It's hard for people to admit they're being abused."

"And it's even harder to admit that someone you love killed themselves," she shot back, clearly anticipating what he would say, but Jackson didn't want to fight with her right now. You had to pick your battles, and he intended to save his ammunition for what would happen after he looked at her evidence. For when he might have to tell her that she was "barking up the wrong tree."

"May I take this information? Take a look at it?" he

asked, intending to review the materials later that night after he had finished his shift.

Rhea hesitated, almost like she'd be trusting a stranger with her only child. It bothered him, but he tried not to show it. "I'm the one shot you have to reopen this case, Rhea. You've got to trust that I'll look at this objectively."

She laughed harshly and twisted away from him. Her loose blouse swirled around her slim midsection and then she faced him again with a heavy sigh. "I bet the chief told you to bury this. Am I right about that, Jax?" she said, emphasizing his name in a way that said they were anything but friends.

Since he believed honesty was the best policy, he said, "He did, but I'm not the chief. If I give you my word that I'll look at this with an open mind, you can bank your money on it."

"The Code of the West? Or the Blue Code? Which will it be?" she challenged, one dark brow flying up like a crow taking wing.

Exasperated, he blew out a heavy sigh and jammed his hat on his head. "I gave you my word. So what will it be?"

She settled her gaze on him, assessing him again. Then in a flurry of motion, she gathered all the papers and stuffed them into the folder. Grabbed it and handed it to him. "Don't disappoint me, Detective."

He cradled the binder to his side like a fullback cradling a football, put a finger to the brim of his Stetson and nodded. "Like I said, I give you my word."

He pivoted on his cowboy-booted heel and marched out of the room, intending to make good on his promise no matter what the chief had said.

The little voice in his head pestered him with, *What will you do if Rhea is right?*

I'll fight that battle when I get to it, he responded.

RHEA WAS TOO wired to finish unpacking after the detective's visit. So she did the one thing she always did when she needed peace. She drew.

She grabbed her knapsack, which always held a sketch pad, pencils, erasers and a blanket she could spread out to make herself comfortable while she worked. She snatched a jacket against the spring breeze, slung her knapsack over her shoulders and hurried out of the inn and onto Main Street.

The inn was at the farthest end of the street, away from the nearby highway that ran all the way from where her sister lived in Avalon to Denver, where Rhea had her home and art gallery. Her pace was hurried at first since she was in a rush to sketch, but there was a peacefulness about the town that was impossible to ignore. It seeped into her body, replacing the earlier chill she'd experienced. Slowing her headlong flight, she took the time to window-shop, appreciating the eclectic mix of shops.

By the time she reached the end of Main Street, her itchiness to draw because she was upset had been replaced by a desire to capture the charm of the quaint town nestled beneath a cloudless sky and the jagged snow-frosted peaks of the mountains in the distance.

A low stone wall with a wide granite ledge ran across the end of the block, marking the entrance to downtown. She opened her knapsack, pulled out the blanket and her materials and began to sketch. With swift determined strokes, an image of the town took shape on the paper. The trim and neat shops with their wooden signs and shiny windows. The many pots of flowers and shrubs before the shops. The wooden posts with streetlights that looked like old-time gas lanterns.

Beyond that, the slopes leading up to the nearby mountains, thick with evergreens in shades ranging from deep green to the bluish-gray of the spruces. Here and there big clumps of spring green identified groves of aspen that in the fall would turn golden, making for a spectacular display against the darker evergreens.

It popped into her brain that dozens, sometimes even hundreds, of aspens were often joined underground by a single root network, making them a massive living organism.

It made her wonder if the loss of one of those intertwined trees caused pain to the others. If they felt the connection the way she did with Selene. A connection that hadn't diminished despite Selene's disappearance. It was the reason she believed with all her heart that her sister was still alive, not that she would tell the detective that. He would dismiss it without question, so she had kept it secret to avoid dissuading him from reopening the case.

But she knew that eventually she would have to tell him, because if they couldn't confirm that Selene's husband, Matt, had killed her or that Selene had killed herself…

She shut her sketch pad abruptly. She'd finish the sketch later, when her mind wasn't as distracted. Packing everything away, she put on her knapsack and marched to the side of the street she hadn't visited yet.

Little by little peace filtered in, but it was tempered by the reality that her sister's last steps might have been down these streets. That these were the last images she might have seen.

Or that maybe they were the images she still saw if she was alive.

As she neared the spot opposite the inn where she was staying, she paused and turned, feeling as if someone had been following her. But there wasn't anyone there who seemed to have any interest in her. Shoppers went from store to store, or just strolled up and down the quaint downtown streets.

She rolled her shoulders, driving away the uneasiness, and did a quick look around to once again confirm she was just imagining the sensation. Satisfied, she returned to the inn to drop off her knapsack and relax before going in search of dinner.

Not that she could really relax with Detective Whitaker's decision hanging over her head. A decision that would make all the difference to her sister's case and maybe even help find Selene if she was still alive.

She hung on to that thought and the hope that Detective Whitaker would keep his promise. That he would keep an open mind to look at the evidence she had diligently gathered over the last six months.

An open mind that would help her find her missing sister.

Chapter Three

It had been a tiring day, filled with the kinds of routine things Jackson had come to expect in Regina.

A fender bender when someone had pulled out of a parking spot without looking.

A couple of tickets for speeding or running a red light. Another for someone failing to leash their dog in one of the public parks.

At a pub located close to the highway, which sometimes hosted a rougher crowd, he had been forced to issue a warning about a minor public disturbance.

Mundane things. Some might even say boring, but Jackson relished it after the many years he'd spent in the military. He'd seen too much death and destruction in Afghanistan, which was why he'd turned down jobs in other areas for the peace and tranquility of his hometown of Regina.

Selene's disappearance six months earlier had upset that serenity. From the moment the BOLO had come in and Jackson had discovered her car by the lake, it had been days of nonstop action. Securing and scrutinizing a possible crime scene. Coordinating with the Avalon Police Department and, after, searching the lake for Selene's body. A body that had never been found and maybe never would be if the spillway had been open, allowing her body to go over the dam and down the river.

It had taken a few weeks for things to die down. For the press to stop pestering the police and people in town about Selene's disappearance.

Things had gone back to normal, but now Rhea was here and determined to ask questions, possibly upsetting that peace.

But Jackson had never refused any mission in the military, no matter how scary or dangerous. He'd led his team on assignment after assignment and was proud to say he'd kept them safe with a level head and preparation.

He would do that with Rhea's request.

Much like he had prepared for a mission, knowing all he could about the terrain and the enemy, he intended to do the same with Rhea and find out more about her.

He put up a fresh pot of coffee, poured himself a big mug and sat down at his hand-hewn cedar kitchen table. Grabbing his laptop, he logged on to his police department account and searched through their resources for any information on Rhea Reilly. No criminal record of any kind. Not even a speeding ticket.

Hitting that dead end, he shifted his focus to a search of public information on the internet and quickly had hundreds of hits. Rhea Reilly was apparently a critically acclaimed artist who worked in several different disciplines. Oils, watercolors and mixed media. She owned the building where she lived and had a number of tenants who rented apartments, and a shop, from her.

The building was located on the 16th Street mall in Denver, a popular location for both locals and tourists. She also had an art gallery at the location, and he surfed to the gallery's website. From the portfolio on the site, it was clear that Rhea sold not only her work, but that of local artists, and not just paintings. Photographs, jewelry, pottery and other art pieces were proudly displayed on the site.

He scrolled through the images but was pulled back to Rhea's work time and time again. He understood why Rhea was so successful. There was so much…life in her work. Passion. The images jumped off the screen with their vibrancy, much like the woman he had met earlier that day.

Filled with life. Filled with passion for finding out what had happened to her sister. Stubborn, too. He had to throw that one in, as well, and he suspected that she wouldn't back down even if he refused to reopen the case.

The case, he thought as he set aside his laptop and pulled over the bulging folder with Rhea's evidence.

Opening it, he found it as neat and organized as any case file he'd ever prepared. The pages held timelines of Selene's husband's possible movements from Avalon to Regina and back, and then up to his client's building location in the mountains just outside Avalon.

The timelines she had documented, if true, deviated from the account Selene's husband, Matt, had provided in the days after his wife's disappearance.

Matt's testimony about the bonfire in his backyard was also contradicted by Rhea's evidence. According to the neighbors she had spoken to, Matt had kept the bonfire going almost overnight and not just for a short time to dispose of some leaves and branches.

Had he done it to dispose of Selene's body? Jackson wondered. *Was it even possible to cremate someone so completely in a home bonfire?*

Rhea had also reviewed the state of Matt's SUV the morning after Selene's disappearance. She had combined photos of his newly detailed SUV with those of his client's building location and the road leading to it, graveled and in relatively good condition. Not a dirt road that would have muddied his SUV, as Matt had claimed.

Not to mention the nighttime trip to a building location. It had hit him as implausible when he had heard that detail from the Avalon police, but they had investigated and found that the alibi held water.

But as Jackson went through all of Rhea's detailed notes, photos, maps and more, it was impossible for him to ignore the discrepancies that were piling up, deeper and deeper, like the winter snows when they came.

He leaned back in his chair, cradled the now almost-empty coffee cup and scrutinized the materials. Sucking in a breath, he shot to his feet and poured himself another cup. He searched through the junk drawer for a pen and pad and sat down once again, taking notes as he went through the papers a second time. He added his own questions to those that Rhea had raised until he had filled a few pages in his pad.

An ache blossomed in his back, and he tossed his pen onto the paper. He rose slowly, unfolding his large frame vertebrae by vertebrae into a stretch until the ache died down. Pacing around his kitchen, he ran his hand through his hair as he considered all the questions jumping around in his brain. Once the ache had been relieved, he returned to the table, leaned his hands on the top rung of the chair and examined all the materials again. Stared at his own pad of growing notes and questions.

With a sharp shift of his shoulders and a jagged exhale, he realized that there was only one thing he could do.

THE HAMBURGER SHE'D eaten hours earlier sat heavily in her stomach, keeping her awake.

It had been a large burger and quite tasty. Since she hadn't eaten all day, she'd scarfed down the burger and fries, but was paying the price for it now.

She was about to give up on sleep when the thump against the French door frame drew her attention.

Is someone trying to open it? she thought and held her breath, listening intently for any other sounds.

A rattle and another slight thump came again, louder. As if someone was jerking the door handle, trying to enter.

Her heartbeat raced in her chest as she carefully reached for the smartphone beside her bed, telling herself she was mistaken about what she was hearing. But the rattle came again and was followed by a scratching sound against the frame of the door.

She had no doubt now that someone was trying to break into her room.

She leaped from the bed, her phone in her hand and held it up, shouting as she did so.

"I'm calling 911! You hear me! I'm calling 911!" she shouted, while also engaging the camera and snapping off a burst of shots of the French door, hoping to capture an image of whoever was on the other side of the glass. For good measure, she raced toward the fireplace and grabbed a poker from the andirons. She held it up and said, "I'm armed! I'll use this!"

Heavy footsteps pounded across the balcony and down the fire escape, confirming that she hadn't been wrong. Someone had been out there.

Her own heart pounding as loudly as the footsteps, she raced back to the night table and snapped on the light. She pulled out Detective Whitaker's business card and dialed his number, hands shaking as she did so.

He answered immediately, almost as if he had already been awake. "Detective Whitaker."

"It's Rhea. Someone just tried to break into my room."

JACKSON RACED OVER to the Regina Inn, where a police car sat in front, watching the building.

He pulled up behind the cruiser, got out and approached the officer behind the wheel.

"Good evening, Officer Daly. Have you seen anything since I called?" he said.

The young man shook his head. "Nothing except the innkeeper coming out to ask what was happening. She's upset that someone might have tried to break in, but also that we're drawing too much attention."

Jackson understood. "Do me a favor and pull around the corner where you're not as visible. That might help if someone was here and decides to come back. They won't spot you on the side street."

He pulled his flashlight from his belt and walked the grounds around the inn. At the fire escape there were clear signs of footprints on ground softened by yesterday's rain.

To avoid any further upset, he dialed Rhea to advise her that he was coming up and also dialed the innkeeper.

The innkeeper met him at the door in a bathrobe she had tossed on, her face filled with worry. Lines of tension bracketed her mouth and her hair was in disarray, as if she had repeatedly run her fingers through it.

"Mrs. Avery. I'm so sorry to drag you out of bed at this late hour," he said with a tip of his head and swept his Stetson off as he entered.

"Is everything okay? Do we need to worry?" she asked, clutching the lapels of her robe with age-spotted hands.

He hated to cause upset but had no choice. "There's evidence someone was in the area of the fire escape. I need to check Rhea's room and balcony just to confirm and will let you know once I finish my investigation."

"Investigation?" she hissed and glanced up the stairs to the guest rooms.

"If something happened, I don't think you have to worry about the other guests, and we'll try to keep things quiet," he said, understanding the older woman's concern.

Jackson went up the stairs, careful not to make noise

so as to not wake the other guests. He tapped softly on her door, and it flew open.

Like the innkeeper, Rhea had a robe wrapped tightly around herself, dark hair tousled. Her face was pale and she worried her lower lip for a second before she said, "Thank you for coming so late at night."

"Just doing my job," he said, although he had already started thinking of Rhea as something other than just a job. "May I check the door?"

She nodded, and he hurried over. He opened the French door and looked out. Muddy areas on the balcony appeared to be footprints. He slipped onto the balcony, avoiding the footprints, and noted that some paint had been scratched off the frame close to the latching mechanism. Someone had clearly been trying to pry it open.

He slipped back in, closed the French door and locked it shut. For good measure, he engaged the security bolts at the edges of both doors that would prevent it from sliding open even if someone broke the lock.

When he faced her, she stood hugging herself, obviously fearful. "Please tell me I was imagining it."

He shook his head. "You weren't. Someone tried to get in. When you called you said you snapped off some photos. May I see them?"

She nodded, slipped her hand into the pocket of the robe and removed her smartphone. She unlocked it and handed it to him.

The blurry shots of the doors didn't show much. If you looked closely, there was a shadow on the balcony, but the photos were too dark to reveal much about whoever had been out there.

He handed her the phone. "I'm sorry. There's not much to work with, but someone was there. Did the person look familiar?"

She quickly shook her head. "I couldn't see much. I was too scared. I'm sorry."

Jackson walked over and laid a comforting hand on her forearm. "No need to apologize, Rhea. You were understandably frightened. If you had to guess who—"

"Matt. Selene's husband. He's angry that I'm pushing for Selene's case to be reopened," she immediately said.

Her response was possibly a little too quick. "How do you know?"

She swiped her screen again and held it up for Jackson to read Matt's message.

I've had enough of your lies and the trouble you're making for me. Leave me alone.

"You think he knows that you want to reopen the case?" Jackson asked.

Her answer came quickly again. "Yes. I think he has a connection on the force. Someone who works for Matt when he's not on duty."

Since it wasn't unusual for officers to have second jobs for when they had multiple days off on their shift, it didn't seem unlikely that there was some overlap between the police force and a local contractor. But it was something he'd have to check out, if his chief agreed to let him proceed with the investigation.

"I'll speak to the Avalon Police Department and have them see if Matt's at home. In the meantime, I can stay—"

"I'm okay. There's no need for you to stay," Rhea said, thinking that while the detective's presence would be comforting in one way, it would be disturbing in another. He called to her too strongly in a physical way. Even with tonight's upset, he was hard to ignore.

Jackson narrowed his gaze, considering her, but then

he heaved his shoulders up in a shrug. "If you're sure, but I'll arrange for an officer to stay outside and keep an eye until the morning."

Only until the morning, Rhea thought. "What happens after that?"

Jackson hesitated, but finally said, "After that, we'll decide what to do."

"With an open mind?" she reminded him, still worried about what he thought about the evidence she had gathered.

"With an open mind," he confirmed and then gestured to her front door. "I have to get going. If you need anything, don't hesitate to call."

She dragged a hand through her hair and blew out a harsh breath. "I won't. Thank you for coming tonight."

He tipped his head. "Just doing my job, Rhea."

But as his gaze met hers, Rhea suspected that he was thinking of her as more than just a job. Her heart sped up at the thought, but she tamped it down.

Her one-and-only involvement with the handsome detective had to be finding out the truth about Selene's disappearance.

Anything else was out of the question.

Chapter Four

"You want to do what?" Chief Robinson said, eyes wide in disbelief.

"I want to reopen the Selene Davis case, Chief." He sat in front of the older man's desk, leaned toward him and argued his case before his boss totally shut him down.

"I looked at all the materials Rhea gathered."

"It's Rhea now, is it?" the chief muttered.

"It is because I was trying to establish a rapport with her in order to determine if she was a crackpot or genuine," he said and plowed on. "She's genuine, Bill."

His chief sniggered and shook his head. "Never figured you'd let a pretty face sway you."

The heat of anger burned through his gut, but he tempered the flame. "If that's what you really believe, then maybe I shouldn't be your choice for police chief when you retire."

His boss's big body shuddered with a rough laugh and he wagged his head again. "I'm sorry, Jax. You know I trust you—"

"Then trust me on this, Bill. I looked through all her materials. Did a thorough review just like you asked. There are major discrepancies in Selene's husband's alibi and his actions the night she disappeared. And neither us nor the Avalon Police Department were aware of the fact that there might have been domestic violence going on," he said, arguing his case the way a lawyer might before a jury.

Chief Robinson laced his fingers together and placed his hands behind his head. He leaned back and his chair creaked from his weight. "I know that's a hot-button topic with you on account of Sara."

"It is, but you have to admit that if we'd had that info we would have looked at Matt Davis much more closely since—"

"Most murdered women have previously been victims of domestic violence," his chief finished for him.

With a chop of his hand against his palm for each item, he said, "There's evidence he abused her. His business was in trouble. The life insurance payout would keep that business afloat. He had a bonfire going almost all night. Who keeps a bonfire unattended for that long and takes a trip up a mountain at night to look at a building site?"

The chief swung back toward his desk and laid his forearms on the edge, steepled hands held before him. "What about a body, Jax? Hard to charge someone without a body."

With a dip of his head, Jackson agreed. "True, but we didn't find a body in the lake and were still prepared to label it a suicide."

When his boss didn't respond, he forged ahead. "I know it's all circumstantial, but we may be able to make a case. Maybe that's why someone tried to break into Rhea's room last night. Either to silence her or to get their hands on the evidence she collected."

Chief Robinson scrubbed his face with his hands. "This could be embarrassing for both departments, Jax. And if it is, you can forget ever becoming police chief here or anywhere for that matter."

"I know that, Bill. But again, none of us were aware of

the abuse. If we had known we would have handled the investigations differently."

With a sweep of his hand, the older man said, "Go ahead, Jax. But if this all goes south—"

"I'll take responsibility for it, Bill. Count on that. I won't dishonor the department no matter what."

RHEA HADN'T BEEN able to sleep after what had happened. She'd snapped on the television and snuggled on a couch with a clear view of the French doors and windows, the heavy brass poker resting by her side. In the early morning hours she'd dozed off, but woke as the sun rose and bathed her room with light.

She'd made a cup of coffee and sat impatiently, waiting for the detective's call, even if only to arrange for the return of her folder. She was surprised when he suggested that they meet for lunch to discuss her materials and last night's intruder.

She tried to tell herself not to be too optimistic. Not to believe that the detective might actually be reopening her sister's case. She didn't want to have her hopes dashed, as they had been when she'd gone to the Avalon Police Department.

But then again, that police department hadn't even taken a moment to review her evidence. The Regina Police Department had.

Or at least she hoped the detective had done as promised.

At the restaurant, Detective Whitaker had already taken a seat at a table by a window. As she entered and met him, he straightened his long, lean form and wagged his head in greeting.

"Miss Reilly."

"Detective Whitaker. Thank you for meeting with me, and thank you again for last night."

"I wish I could say it's my pleasure, but we both know this meeting isn't about pleasure." He pulled out a chair for her.

She sat and clutched her hands together tightly in her lap. "Have you made a decision?"

A momentary flicker of some emotion, indecision maybe, flashed across his face. "I have, but first, I'd like to know more about Selene. About you."

It was her turn to hesitate. With a quick shrug, she said, "We were very close as you can imagine. Inseparable until Selene got married."

"What happened then?" He angled his big body toward her as if to hear her better. His gray gaze, steely with determination, fixed on her face. Slightly unnerving professionally and personally. Her body responded to him in a way it never had to any other man, maybe because she wasn't used to being around such physically powerful and lethally potent men.

She shifted her chair back a little. "We grew up in Boulder but moved to Denver for school. Roomed together during college and after. My career took off like a rocket while Selene was getting her master's."

"She was a teacher?"

"She's a music teacher, but also a very talented pianist and singer. She often performs in Denver when she visits," she said and her voice grew husky with emotion.

He stroked a hand down her arm to offer comfort. "Take your time, Rhea."

She nodded, dragged in a breath and released it with a rush of words. "She got a teaching job in Avalon and moved there. Met Matt and they married. After that we would have regular girls' weekends, mostly in Denver. Matt didn't like having me around."

"Maybe because you saw more than you should," Jackson said, sympathy alive in his tone.

With a shrug, she continued. "Maybe. When I first saw the bruises, I asked Selene how she'd gotten them. She told me she had fallen while on a hike. I forced myself to believe it, but then it happened again. A few times, but Selene had an excuse each and every time."

"You can't blame yourself, Rhea."

"But I do. I tell myself that if Selene's dead…" She stopped short, well aware of the slip and that the detective had caught it. For a long moment she sat there, trying to decide whether to be honest, but if she was anything, she was honest.

"Something was off that night after the text. I knew Selene was in trouble. I still feel her—" she tapped her chest "—in here. I know she's still alive."

Long moments passed, but as she peered at the detective's face, she had no clue what he was thinking. His face was as stern and stony as the summits of the mountains in the distance.

The waitress approached at that moment, but sensing the tension between them, and at Jackson's raised hand, she walked away.

As he had before, the detective leaned toward her and, in a low voice, he said, "Selene is gone, Rhea. We both wish it was different—"

"She's alive. I know it," she insisted, and his features softened as he sat back. She worried that she'd blown whatever chance she had of his reopening the case. But then he said, "Promise me one thing, Rhea."

Relief speared through her. "Whatever you want."

He arched a brow. "I know you're not normally that agreeable. If you were, we wouldn't be sitting here discussing this."

She couldn't argue with him. When it came to finding out what happened to her sister, she'd fight him tooth and nail if she had to. "You're right. What is it you want so that you'll reopen the case?"

"Promise me that you'll accept Selene's gone if that's what all the evidence says."

Accept that her sister was gone. Forever. That they'd never have another girls' weekend. Never share another laugh. Or cry. Never see that face that was like looking in a mirror. Something that anyone who wasn't a twin could never understand.

"That's some promise," she said and swiped away the tears that spilled down her cheeks.

The detective looked away and muttered something under his breath. *Kryptonite*, she thought he said before locking his gaze on her again. "Well? Rhea?"

"I promise."

JACKSON SUCKED IN a deep breath, held it and in a rush said, "I spoke to the chief, and we're reopening the case. Especially after last night."

Rhea's face paled, and she leaned away from the table. "It was Matt, wasn't it?"

He looked away for a moment, but then focused his gaze on her. "The Avalon police went by his house. It doesn't seem as if he was home."

"And if he wasn't, he was here," she said as she dragged a hand through her hair, making the thick locks dance around her face.

"Possibly. It's something I'll have to investigate."

She gestured between the two of them. "We'll investigate. I want to be a part of this investigation."

Jackson shook his head vehemently. "No way, Rhea. This is a police investigation."

Rhea shifted toward him, the blue of her eyes icy cold. "There wouldn't even be an investigation without me." She tapped a finger to her chest. "*I'm* the one who got all this evidence. *I'm* the one who knows the information inside and out."

"And *you're* the one who is too close to this. Too close because it's your twin, your mirror image. The person who is a part of your soul," he shot back.

A pregnant silence hung in the air, heavy with emotion, but then Rhea broke that silence in words barely above a whisper, as her gaze sheened with tears yet again.

"You made me a promise and you kept it," she said, voice husky with feeling.

He nodded. "I did."

"I made you a promise, as well. But the only way I can keep it, that I can know Selene is gone, is if you let me be a part of this investigation."

Silence reigned again as Jackson considered her request. As he skipped his gaze over her features, taking in her pain and her determination. She wouldn't rest until she had an answer. And she would never believe that answer unless she was certain that he had turned over every stone, even the tiniest pebble. Because of that, there was only one thing he could think to say.

Chapter Five

"Okay."

She jumped, startled by that one-word answer. "You mean that? You'll let me help you?"

He nodded. "I hope I don't live to regret this, Rhea."

"You won't, Detective. You won't regret it," she said.

Jackson had no doubt that she meant every word. But his gut told him that this investigation was going to test him. He hoped he didn't fail the test.

The waitress slowly approached once again and, at Jackson's nod, she came over to take their orders, even though they'd been so busy they hadn't really looked at the menu.

"The soup and salad combo here is really good. My favorite is the grilled cheese and tomato soup. But if you're hungrier, the French Dip is good, as well," Jackson said.

Rhea nodded. "I'll have the grilled cheese and tomato soup combo. A little comfort food is always good."

"I agree. I'll have the same, but the full version, Sheila. Some pop also," Jackson said.

"Diet pop for me, thank you," Rhea added, which earned a long look from the detective and a raised eyebrow. The look sent butterflies into flight in her stomach and ignited warmth at her core.

"I've been missing my regular workouts," she offered in explanation.

"What kind of workouts?"

"Is this some kind of interrogation?" she parried, eyes narrowed as she considered him.

He shrugged those broad shoulders. "I just like to know more about the people I'm working with, Partner."

Partner. Rhea liked the sound of that but, other than Selene and a few, very few, close friends, she wasn't used to sharing details of her personal life. But as her gaze locked with his, it occurred to her that the detective wouldn't be satisfied if she didn't answer his questions.

"I normally do a yoga class or two each week, plus some strength training. I also like to take really long walks or hikes when I can."

"In between painting and running the gallery?"

The waitress brought over the sodas at that moment, but once she'd gone again, Rhea answered, "I paint in the early morning and late afternoon when my studio has the best light. I have a full-time manager for the gallery, although I'm the one who decides what to show there."

"I've seen some of your paintings on the website. They're beautiful. Did you always like to paint?"

Rhea nodded and with a laugh said, "My mother said I used to paint myself and Selene with our baby food."

"Is your mom—"

Rhea shook her head. "She and my dad passed a few years ago in an automobile accident. I'm glad, because the worry over what happened to Selene would have killed them."

But Rhea didn't want to revisit Selene's disappearance right now and luckily the waitress arrived with their meals at that moment.

Hunger for the food replaced his hunger for information for the next few minutes, but then he began again.

"I understand. My parents always worried when I was deployed," Jackson said in between bites of the grilled cheese.

"Where did you serve?" she asked and murmured in appreciation of the sandwich, "Delicious."

Jackson smiled and it transformed his face from that of the stern-and-stoic police officer into an almost boyish dimpled grin that made him look much younger.

"I'm glad you like it," he said, but didn't answer her question.

She pressed. "So where was it? Iraq? Afghanistan?"

"Afghanistan. Marine just like my dad."

"Are your parents still alive?" she asked, wondering about her "partner" and his life.

He spooned up some soup, ate it and nodded. "They live in Florida now, close to some of my cousins. Got tired of the Colorado cold, but they come back in the summer to visit."

"Must be nice," she said, thinking of her parents and how much Selene and she had loved to spend time with them.

He nodded and polished off the last of his meal. "It is. I miss them."

"You're lucky to have family," Rhea said wistfully, and Jackson quickly picked up on it.

He raised his glass of soda and peered at her over the rim. "Is it just you and Selene?"

"It is. My parents were both only children, and my grandparents are all gone. It's why it's so important to find her," she said, and Jackson winced as she said it. He didn't believe Selene was alive and didn't want her to get her hopes up, but she'd keep hope alive as long as she could. Because of that, she said, "So, Partner. When do we start this investigation?"

AFTER THEY'D FINISHED LUNCH, Jackson had suggested that they go to his office at the police station, where he'd taken all the materials Rhea had gathered and locked them in his desk for safekeeping. Especially after what had happened at the inn the night before.

If Matt had been the perpetrator, he might have not only intended to do harm to Rhea, but to also destroy the materials so that the police would not use that information against him.

In the police station, Jackson got Rhea settled in one of their conference rooms so they could discuss her evidence. Normally he would set up a board with all the pertinent information, but since Rhea and he would have to move from Avalon and back, he had created a notebook in the cloud to hold the info, questions and any answers they gathered.

He grabbed his laptop and her evidence and joined her in the room, where he displayed the digital information on a large monitor. As he laid out the hard copies, he said, "I locked these up to keep them safe, but I also plan on scanning everything and adding it to my notes."

"Thank you. I appreciate all your hard work," she said. She splayed her long, elegant fingers, with their teasing rings of gold and silver, against the tabletop, almost as if to still any nervous motion.

As he would with any board he made for an investigation, he talked through the info in the digital notebook, filling in Rhea as he worked.

"There are three possible scenarios. The first is that Matt Davis murdered your sister. The second is that Selene killed herself. The third is that an unknown suspect murdered your sister."

"And another scenario is that Selene is still alive, and we need to find her," Rhea added. Even though Jackson had only known her for a couple of days, he knew not to argue with her. At least not yet. In time the evidence would eventually rule out that possibility, but he wasn't going to press the issue at that moment.

Pick your battles, he reminded himself.

He went through Rhea's evidence, entering the information into his notes. As he did so, she jumped in with her thoughts to add to the materials. When they finished, it added up to a lot of questions and doubts about the story Selene's husband had provided to officials, making him Number One on Jackson's list of suspects. Which he should have been from the very beginning since the spouse was generally the prime suspect.

But there were also questions about the other scenarios and overlaps. "If there was an SUV by Selene's car that night, and if it wasn't Matt, it's possible that the owner of that vehicle may have something to do with Selene's…disappearance," he said, biting back the murder reference in respect of Rhea's beliefs.

"It *is* possible that SUV is tied to Selene's…disappearance," Rhea agreed, likewise holding back. "What do we do now?"

Jackson rifled through the papers and pulled out her notes on the insurance policies that had been issued barely weeks before Selene's disappearance. Holding up the papers, he said, "How was it that you found out about the policies?"

"I got a call from an investigator from the insurance company. They were doing their own review about Selene's disappearance since the policies were so new," she said and gestured to the bottom of the page. "That's his name and number."

Jackson thought about it for a moment. "Normally most policies are paid out very quickly. At the most, maybe sixty days after the death, but since they had questions, maybe we'll get lucky." He pulled over the conference room phone and dialed the investigator.

"Winston Summers," he answered after a couple of rings.

"Good afternoon, Mr. Summers. This is Detective Jackson Whitaker with the Regina Police Department. You're on speaker and I have Rhea Reilly with me, as well."

"Good afternoon, Detective. Ms. Reilly. How can I help you today?"

Jackson shared a look with Rhea and plowed on. "I understand you were investigating the insurance policies issued to Matt and Selene Davis."

"I was, but we're getting ready to close our case and pay out the policy on Mrs. Davis," the investigator said.

Jackson detected something in the other man's tone. "You don't sound too happy about that, Winston."

A rough laugh came across the line. "I'm not. I can't prove a thing, but this just doesn't smell right to me."

With a quick sidewise glance at Rhea, whose face had paled with those words, Jackson said, "It doesn't feel right to us, either. That's why we've reopened the case here in Regina."

"Well, you've made my day, Detective. No offense meant, Ms. Reilly. Now that you've done that, I'll tell my superiors to hold off on the payout," Winston said.

Jackson laid his hand over Rhea's and squeezed reassuringly. "I'd appreciate that. If you don't mind, I'd like to tell Matt Davis myself about that decision."

Summers chuckled. "I understand, Detective. I'm sure he won't be happy. I hope that helps your case."

Jackson provided Summers with his contact info and hung up.

Rhea was confused by the investigator's statements. She shook her head and said, "Why will it help the case?"

"It'll make Matt angry and angry people act rashly. They make mistakes, and those mistakes may help us find out what really happened to Selene."

Rhea blew out a breath. "Matt will be pissed, especially if his business is still having problems."

Jackson flipped through her papers again. "You say Matt was having financial issues at the time Selene disappeared?"

She nodded. "Selene had told me business had fallen off and his bills were mounting. That was creating a lot of tension in their marriage." She hesitated, remembering how upset her sister had been, as well as something troubling. "I think that's when I first spotted the bruises on Selene."

"The pressure blew off his lid. Revealed his true nature. Hopefully our visit, and the news about the insurance policy, will do the same. Are you up to going to Avalon?"

Am I up to it? she thought, but then an image of Matt's smug face flashed through her brain. He hadn't even tried to deny the abuse when she'd confronted him shortly after her sister's disappearance.

"I am *so* up for it. If Selene is dead, I'm sure Matt did it, and I want to prove that," she said, her throat tightening as she said the words.

Jackson's touch came against her hand again, comforting and secure. His palm rough, but soothing. "We'll go in the morning."

Which meant she had to spend another night at the inn. Another sleepless night, watching the doors and windows for signs of an intruder.

"You'll stay with me tonight," he said, almost as if he'd read her mind.

She peered at him, weighing the risk he presented to her in a very different way, but if they were going to see Matt tomorrow, she had to be sharp.

"Thank you, Detective. That's very kind of you."

He raised a hand to stop her, like a cop directing traffic. "Just part of the job," he said, but she doubted that it was standard procedure to take partners home.

When he rose, he grimaced, grabbed his back and stretched, as if to work out a knot. She realized then that they'd been sitting for hours reviewing the case. A second later, his stomach emitted a loud rumble that he tried to hide by covering his lean midsection with his big hand.

"Sorry," he said with a chagrined smile.

"No, *I'm* sorry. I didn't realize how late it was. How about I treat you to dinner?"

He did another stretch of that long lean body and grimaced again. "Actually, I have a nice big steak I was going to cook tonight. How about we pick up your things and we throw the steak on the grill? It's enough for two."

Since she felt like she was already imposing on him, she deferred to his request. "That sounds nice. Thank you."

"Don't thank me just yet. My cooking skills leave a lot to be desired."

She doubted that. Detective Whitaker struck her as someone who was likely quite capable in many ways, which brought a rush of unwanted heat as her mind drifted where it shouldn't. To hide her reaction, she turned her attention to organizing the papers scattered around the table while Jackson scooped up his laptop.

She handed him her notes, and he stood before her uncertainly, his gaze traveling over her face, examining her. But surprisingly, he seemed to misunderstand what she was feeling. "It'll be okay, Rhea. Everything is going to work out."

She went with it, not wanting to clue him in to how uneasy he made her on a personal level. "I know it will," she said and tilted her head in the direction of the door. "I guess it's time for us to go."

Chapter Six

It *was* time to go, and Jackson hoped he wasn't making a big mistake by taking Rhea home with him. But he'd barely gotten any sleep the night before thanks to the intruder at the inn. He needed a clear head tomorrow when they spoke to Matt Davis, which meant he needed to get some rest.

But as he caught sight of Rhea's slim but enticing figure as she walked out the door, his gut tightened with desire, and he wondered just how much sleep he was actually going to get.

In no time they had checked Rhea out of the inn and were at Jackson's home on the outskirts of town. The log cabin home was on a large wooded lot that provided gorgeous views of the lake below and the dam's spillway in the distance.

"This is lovely," she said as she set down her suitcase, walked through his home and out to the large deck that faced the lake.

He shrugged. "Thanks. My dad and I built the place when I got back from Afghanistan."

"You did an amazing job," she said, leaning against the railing and glancing back toward his home.

"Let me show you to the guest room," he said, walked back in and snared her suitcase. He took her upstairs to a room a few doors down from his and set her things by a queen-size bed. With a flip of his hand, he said, "The bathroom is across the way if you need it. I'm going to get started on dinner."

"Let me help," she said, and they returned to the ground floor where the open-concept space held the kitchen, dining room and living room with a wall of glass that opened to the deck and offered views of the lake, mountains and Regina.

They prepped a salad and sliced up some potatoes and onions to cook on the grill beside a large steak. Since it was still nice outside, they decided to eat out on the deck.

Rhea stood by Jackson as he laid the potatoes, onions and steak on the grill. Contrary to what he'd said earlier, he was quite a capable cook and the meal they ate was simple, but delicious.

Unlike lunch, dinner was a quieter affair, maybe because they had already done a lot of talking during the day. Although Jackson offered an after-dinner coffee, Rhea was eager for some time alone to think about all that had happened the last few days and what would happen in the days to come.

She helped Jackson clean up, but when she offered to help him wash, he demurred. "It's okay. I can handle this."

He could. He seemed to be able to handle a lot, from cooking to building a house. She told herself to have faith that he would handle the investigation of her sister's disappearance as capably.

"Thank you for everything," she said as she inched up on her tiptoes and brushed a kiss across his cheek before making her escape. She noticed his home was almost spartan, but had fabulous bones and stunning views. There were a few bedrooms upstairs, hinting at the fact that the detective hadn't planned on living there alone.

Which made her wonder if he'd built the home with someone special in mind.

She forced that thought away and went to her room. Although it was early, she was tired and wanted to be at her best when they confronted Matt. Closing her door, she changed quickly and got into bed, hoping to make it an early night.

JACKSON STOOD AT the sink, listening for the familiar creak of the floorboards just inches away from the landing and in front of the first bedroom. More than once he'd thought about fixing it, but it served as a very reliable alarm system.

The creak came as Rhea went across the hall to the bathroom and then back, telling him it was safe to head up once he finished the dishes. He took his time, thinking about the materials they'd reviewed earlier, as well as planning an approach to Matt Davis tomorrow.

If Davis was as Rhea had said, he'd be less than pleased about their reopening the case and holding up the insurance payout. He'd push the other man in the hopes of either eliminating Matt from that prime suspect spot or collecting enough evidence to be able to charge him for Selene's murder.

Selene's murder.

Rhea wouldn't handle it well if that's what the evidence proved, but it would at least bring closure. Even if that closure brought pain.

He finished the dishes and went upstairs, careful to step around the creaky floorboards to not wake Rhea. Once he was in bed, he returned to his earlier thoughts, planning tomorrow's mission. The approach and what would follow if Matt's alibis failed to satisfy the many questions he had.

He was just starting to drift off, the plan running through his brain, when he heard the warning squeak that someone was in the hall. A second later, a soft footfall, someone barefoot, alerted him that Rhea was coming down the hall.

His door was open, and he rose up on one elbow as the shadow of her petite figure came into view. She leaned her hand on the doorjamb and, in barely a whisper, she said, "I can't sleep."

JACKSON SAT UP, revealing a broad bare chest with a smattering of chest hair angling down…

Rhea wouldn't think about where that happy trail led, and was reconsidering her visit when he said, "Bed is plenty big, and I've got lots of pillows." He grabbed a couple and laid them down the center of the king-size bed, creating an effective bundling board.

"Thank you. I promise not to be a bother." She hurried to the side of the bed where he wasn't, slipping beneath the sheets. They were smooth, but slightly warm from where he'd been lying earlier.

The bed dipped a little as he settled down again. "Good night, Rhea," he said, his voice husky.

"Good night… Jax."

RHEA WOKE TO an empty bed and the smell of coffee and bacon.

Hurrying, she washed, dressed and met Jackson in the kitchen, where he was forking perfectly crisp bacon slices onto a plate.

"How do you like your eggs?" he said.

She didn't have the heart to tell him she normally didn't eat breakfast. "Whatever is easiest."

In no time, he was cracking eggs one-handedly and scrambling them like a pro.

She poured cups of coffee and asked, "Milk and sugar?"

"Cream and two sugars, please," he said, and she smiled.

"Just like me," she said, earning her a heated look and a laugh.

"Light for sure. A good wind could blow you away, but sweet?" he teased.

She laughed and shook her head. "I can be difficult at times," she admitted.

He lifted an eyebrow in challenge, but she ignored him easily, especially when he laid a plate of eggs, bacon and toast before her and the smells awakened her hunger. She dug into the meal with gusto.

In truth, she was much lighter than she had been six months ago because she hadn't been sleeping or eating well, worrying about what had happened to Selene. Hoping against hope that the feeling inside her that Selene was still alive wasn't wrong.

She was so famished, she finished her plate well before Jackson had finished his, prompting his laughter. "Girl, you sure can put it away."

"And you can sure cook. Thank you."

"You're welcome, but we should get going. Avalon isn't all that far away, but we've got a lot to do."

In a rush, they cleaned up and were on their way to Selene's hometown, which was only about forty-five minutes away from Regina and two hours from Rhea's home and gallery in Denver.

Rhea had done the drive many times before tensions between her and Matt had cropped up and the trips had become one-sided, with Selene only visiting Denver for their girls' weekends.

As they drove, Rhea went over the discrepancies in Matt's alibi. "He said he was gone for only about an hour to check out his client's building location, but I spoke to the neighbors and they said that he was gone for a lot longer. At least three hours if not more."

Jackson shot her a quick glance as he drove. "That gives him more than enough time to do the round trip to Regina."

"And still supposedly 'check out his client's location,'" she said, emphasizing his explanation with air quotes.

Jackson shook his head. "Who goes to a building site at night? I didn't believe it then, but the Avalon officers confirmed the alibi."

"They did, but how much of that was influenced by the officer who works with Matt?" she asked, questioning it the way she had from the very beginning.

Jackson clenched his jaw, clearly not liking her assertion. "I'd rather not think that an officer let a murderer go free on account of a personal relationship."

Rhea scoffed. "You think that's never happened? That it's possible it didn't happen this time?"

Jackson sucked in a deep breath and held it, recalling his chief's words about embarrassing either of the two police departments. But if losing the police chief's job was the price to be paid for the truth, he was willing to pay that price. "Let's not go there until we've run out of options. First thing I'd like to do is talk to Matt and hear what he has to say. After, we'll take a run to the building site. See how long it takes us to get there and then back to Avalon."

"And we can check out the road there also. Matt said he detailed his Jeep the morning after Selene disappeared because it was muddy and he was meeting a client."

Jackson mentally reviewed the evidence Rhea had gathered. "You said the road was paved with gravel."

"It is," she insisted.

"Maybe it wasn't paved six months ago," he offered in explanation, and she shrugged her slim shoulders.

"I'm no expert, but it didn't look like a new road to me. You saw the photos, right," she reminded.

"I did. If things don't add up… I have a friend in the area who has trained dogs," he said, omitting that they were cadaver dogs in deference to Rhea's emotions. But, as he peered at her out of the corner of his eye, it was obvious she'd guessed exactly what kinds of dogs. She worried that full lower lip and glanced away, her gaze shimmering with tears.

"And what then? What if we get nothing from it?"

"We keep on looking, Rhea. I made you a promise and I intend to keep it. We'll go over every fact and every discrepancy. We'll talk to the Avalon police. I called to let them know we were reopening the case," he said.

She shot him a quick look, eyes wide with surprise. "How did that go?"

"They weren't happy. Felt like I was interfering in their jurisdiction, but I reminded them that the Regina Police Department had been involved in the investigation, as well." He reached over and laid his hand on hers as it rested on her thigh. "We have an appointment to talk to them this afternoon."

A deep furrow raked into her brow as she considered what he'd said. Long moments passed until she said, "I appreciate all that you're doing."

He brushed his hand across her cheek and said, "No need for thanks. It's my job." A more difficult one thanks to what he was starting to feel for Rhea.

Returning his attention to the road, he continued the drive to Avalon and the discussion about the case. "Matt started a bonfire that night. It was one thing that struck me as really odd back then. Who starts a fire and then leaves it unattended for any length of time?"

"And he kept it going almost all night, according to the neighbors," Rhea added.

Jackson nodded, wondering what that might mean. "Matt may have been trying to dispose of…" He hesitated again, sensitive to Rhea's feelings, but that was only making things harder and not easier, so he plowed on. "I'm not sure you can fully cremate a body in a bonfire, but it's something we'll have to check out."

A tired sigh, as if Rhea was carrying the weight of the world on her shoulders, escaped her. "And what if it doesn't prove Matt killed my sister?"

"If it doesn't, we have other scenarios to consider and resolve," he said without hesitation.

"The turn's just in a few miles," Rhea said and gestured toward the highway exit. "Is Matt expecting us? Did you call him?"

Jackson smiled and shook his head. "Matt is in for a surprise. We've got to rattle him, remember?"

Rhea blew out a breath and wagged her head. "Get him angry. Get him to make mistakes."

He jabbed his finger in her direction to confirm it. "You got it. If he's guilty, we will unravel that supposed alibi and get enough evidence to build our case."

MATT DAVIS'S JEEP WRANGLER sat in the driveway, hinting that he was likely at home.

Jackson parked his police cruiser directly in front of the Davis home in a clear line of sight to a big bay window. He cut the engine and shifted in his seat to peer at Rhea. "Are you ready?"

Face a sickly pale, lips pressed tight, she nodded.

"Let's roll," he said as he sprang from the car and around to open the door for her.

Her hand was ice cold as she slipped it into his and they walked to the front door.

He scrutinized the home as they did so, taking in the recently mowed spring green grass. The landscaping was well-kept, and the home spoke of someone who took care of it.

He had barely raised his hand to knock when the front door flew open and Matt Davis stood there, his face mottled with angry red blotches that grew larger as his gaze settled on Rhea. "What are you doing here?" he said, his voice trembling from the force of his rage.

"Matt Davis?" Jackson said and angled himself so that Rhea was partially behind him.

Matt jerked his head up in challenge. "Yes, and who are you? You're not with the Avalon Police Department."

Jackson reached into his jacket pocket, removed his business card and handed it over to Matt, who snatched it away with a swipe of his hand.

Matt shot it only a quick look and said, "What do you want?"

"Detective Whitaker, Regina PD. We've reopened the Selene Davis case," he said calmly, sensing that the more controlled he remained, the more upset Davis would become.

Matt glared at Rhea. "Why won't you leave this alone? I told you I had nothing to do with Selene's disappearance."

"Just like you had nothing to do with those bruises she had?" Rhea challenged, her voice steady even though Jackson felt her trembling beside him.

Matt angrily jabbed a finger in her direction. "I never touched her. If Selene told you that, she lied."

"She never told me, Matt. I saw for myself. I saw the way you treated her. That's why you didn't want me around," Rhea challenged.

Matt made a move toward her, fists clenched, but Jackson swept up his arm, blocking his access to Rhea. Calmly, Jackson said, "Seems to me you've got an anger problem, Davis."

Matt whipped his head around to nail Jackson with his gaze. "You'd be angry, too, if you were being accused of something you didn't do."

There was a sincerity in the man's response that was unexpected. But sociopaths could be quite convincing,

Jackson reminded himself. "If you didn't do it, I assume you'll be willing to answer a few questions."

Davis deflated before his eyes, his shoulders lowering as he took a step back. But then he looked toward Rhea again and jabbed his finger in her direction. "If it means I never have to see her face again, I'll answer any questions you want."

"Where were you two nights ago?" Jackson said.

"Home. Asleep," he said with a nonchalant shrug.

"The Avalon police came by and said no one answered," Jackson pressed.

He shrugged, but met Jackson's gaze head-on. "I sleep with earplugs, and I'm a heavy sleeper. I probably didn't hear them."

The Avalon Police hadn't seen Matt's SUV, unlike today, where it sat in the driveway. He gestured to the Jeep. "Do you normally park in the driveway?"

Matt shook his head. "I normally pull it into the garage, but I'm custom-building something in the garage. I started the project yesterday afternoon."

"Mind showing it to me?"

With a harrumph, Matt pushed past him and to the garage, where he entered a code and opened the door to reveal a number of sawhorses covered with plywood and pieces of a woodworking project.

"Thanks," Jackson said, but pressed on. "Let's talk about the trip to your client's location. You say you went the night Selene disappeared? At night, Matt?"

The other man shrugged and looked away this time, a telltale sign that someone was lying. "I had been at a site all day and, when I came home, Selene and I had a fight. I needed to blow off some steam and went outside to do some yard work."

"You had lots of scratches and cuts on your hands. You

told the officers you got them doing the yard work," Jackson said.

Matt nodded. "There were lots of brambles, but I was so mad, I didn't pay attention and got cut up while I piled them in the firepit."

"And then you started the bonfire?" Rhea asked.

Matt glared at her again, but nodded. "I did. I like to keep things looking neat, and it was the easiest way to get rid of them."

Jackson peered all around the house once more and said, "I see that you care, which makes me wonder why you left a live fire to drive up a mountain."

Matt dragged his fingers through unruly waves of blond hair. "Stupid, I know, but I was still too wired after doing that and decided it was as good a time as any to check out my prospective client's building site."

"Up a mountain? In the dark?" Rhea pressed. She had never believed Matt's alibi from the very beginning and nothing had happened that would change her opinion.

Matt glared at her, and spittle flew from his lips as he said, "Maybe if Selene had earned more at that stupid school I wouldn't have had to bust my ass just to keep a roof over our heads."

Rhea was barely controlling her anger. Her body shook with the force of it, but Jackson laid a hand on her shoulder. Gave a reassuring squeeze.

"I understand you were having some financial difficulties," Jackson said.

Matt's gaze narrowed to almost slits and settled on her. More bright splotches of red erupted on his cheeks and down his neck as he said, "I was working out of it. That's why I drove up the mountain. It was a big job and really helped me get things back on track."

Me *and not* us. *It had always been about Matt*, Rhea

thought, but kept quiet to let Jackson continue the inter-rogation. But he surprised her with his next statement.

"That's good to hear, Matt. Especially since I told the insurance company we had reopened the case. They're holding up the payout on Selene's policy until we close the case."

Matt's barely leashed anger turned toward Jackson. "You had no right to do that. No right," he shouted and leaned toward Jackson, his pose threatening. But he was no physical match for Jackson, who had several inches on him in height and width.

Jackson met him dead-on, his nose barely an inch from Matt's. "I had every right, Davis. A woman is missing. Likely dead and, from what I can see, you had a hand in it."

As he had before, Matt backed down. Bullies couldn't handle being challenged, and it made Rhea realize why Matt hadn't wanted her around. Unlike Selene who hated confrontation, Rhea wouldn't have put up with the way that Matt treated Selene.

"I didn't kill Selene. I don't know what happened to her after she left here that night," Matt said, a defeated tone in his voice.

"If that's true, you'll have no issues with helping us prove that," Jackson said.

Matt gazed away again and nodded. "Whatever you need. I just want to get on with my life."

"Great. We'll be back," Jackson said and exerted gentle pressure on her shoulder to guide her toward his cruiser.

"He just wants to get that insurance money," Rhea said under her breath, not believing a word of Matt's explanation.

"For sure, but he won't get it if he doesn't cooperate to clear his name," Jackson said.

Rhea stopped dead and glanced at Jackson. "You think that's possible? That he didn't do it? That she killed herself?"

"Or that she's still alive, like you hope." His gaze was a

dark gray, like a troubled sky, when it settled on her. With a harsh breath, he said, "Anything's possible right now. But, fact by fact, we'll determine what really happened."

Although he had voiced her hope as a possibility, Rhea was certain he didn't believe it likely. But she'd take it for now.

"What's the plan?" Rhea asked, impatient to continue their investigation.

"A trip up a mountain."

Chapter Seven

Rhea had visited Matt's client's site barely a week after Selene's disappearance. She directed Jackson down the highway for several minutes until the turnoff for a narrow gravel-paved road.

Jackson pulled the cruiser off the smooth highway and onto the rougher gravel. The car dipped deeply before beginning the rise to the building site on the ridge.

"This road had gravel when you came up," Jackson said as he drove, navigating past a rut here and there on their journey up the mountain.

Jackson had given her a link to the digital notebook they had created the day before. She pulled her tablet out of her bag and, in no time, she had opened the notebook and navigated to the pages that held the photos she had taken shortly after Selene's disappearance. She held the tablet up so Jackson could see it.

He stopped the car to take a better look at the photos. "Definitely gravel, but not as deep as right now. Do you remember how deep it was?"

Rhea shook her head. "I wasn't thinking about that at the time," she admitted, wishing she had been more observant.

Jackson ran the back of his hand across her cheek. "Don't blame yourself. What you've put together is amazing."

She appreciated his words and braved a smile. She scrolled to other photos of what the site looked like before any construction had taken place. "There was a lot of land cleared along the ridge. Plenty of places and time for him to…"

She couldn't say it and left it at that.

Jackson clearly got it. "Let's go see what's up there now."

They bumped their way up the road to the wide hilltop ridge where Matt was building his client's custom home. A truck was parked before the home's double garage doors. One of the garage doors was open, and a large stack of siding sat there, waiting to be installed.

"Looks like they're almost done with the build," Jackson said.

The home was a large contemporary structure, situated to provide views of the valley below, the town of Avalon and the mountains in the distance.

As they got out of the car, one of the laborers walked over, a puzzled look on his face. "Can I help you?"

"Detective Whitaker with the Regina PD. We're just here to take a look at the site. Is that a problem?"

Obviously uneasy, the man held his hands up in a stop gesture. "Above my pay grade, Detective. I'll have to check with the contractor." Without waiting, he walked away, whipping out his cell phone as he did so. A short, clearly upsetting conversation ensued, but the man returned and said, "Matt says look away, but don't bother the workers."

Jackson dipped his head and touched the brim of his hat. "Thank you. We appreciate your cooperation."

The man said nothing, only pivoted and returned to work, shouting out instructions to his people who were busy installing the siding.

Rhea brought up the photos again to show Jackson how the ridge had looked before the construction had begun in earnest, since there had already been some digging going on.

Jackson looked around, comparing the site to the photos. With a shake of his head, he said, "The home takes up most of the flat land at this point."

He walked toward the home and backyard, Rhea following. With a sweep of one hand, he held up the tablet with the other and said, "This was all woods. They cleared a good bit to make this open space for the house, the deck and the grass area beyond that."

Rhea nodded. "It was. I remember wondering how big a house they could build without taking down some of the aspens." The thought stormed through her brain again about the aspens being one and feeling the loss.

Jackson tightened his lips and tipped his hat back. "It didn't take that long to get here. When Matt made this round trip, he had plenty of time at this location, but… I can't imagine him burying Selene anywhere on this ridge. Most of the land here would be touched during construction. It's too risky."

A numbing chill erupted inside Rhea at the thought of her sister buried here or somewhere else, and she wrapped her arms around herself. Rubbed her hands up and down her arms to chase away the chill.

Jackson immediately noticed and hugged her. "I want to check out the ridge," he said, and they walked, joined together, to the edge of the property where the land dropped off sharply to thick woods at least a hundred feet below.

"It's more likely he would have dropped her over this edge. The woods down there are dense and probably not well traveled."

Jackson paused and whipped off his hat. He dragged a hand through his hair in frustration. "I don't remember anyone searching that area."

Rhea nodded. "As far as I know, they didn't. They searched all along the ridge up here, but not below."

"Well, that's where we start tomorrow," he said with a quick nod and urged her in the direction of his cruiser. He paused by the edge of the build site.

Bending, he ran his hands across the gravel. "It's pretty thick. Enough to keep an SUV from getting too dirty," he said as he rose and brushed the dirt off his hand.

She was satisfied by that assessment, but not about any possible delay. "Why tomorrow?" she asked, eager to do the search as soon as possible.

Jackson pulled her door open and she sat, but he didn't join her right away. He leaned his arms across the top of the door and peered away from her as he said, "Today we see Matt again—"

"Why?" she asked, wondering at the reason for another visit.

Jackson met her gaze. "We press on why he spent so much time up here and why he says his car was dirty. Maybe even push him to let us examine his SUV again."

"They found Selene's blood in the house. On the sofa in the living room. Matt claimed it was from a nosebleed," Rhea said and tried not to picture Matt hitting Selene. Hurting her.

"I know it's hard but try not to think about that. We have to stay objective," Jackson urged.

Rhea expelled a sigh. "Objective. She's my sister. A part of me I still feel in here." She laid a hand over her heart.

"I get it. When my sister finally told me about what was happening to her, I wanted to rip the guy apart, but that wouldn't have helped her," Jackson said. "We can help Selene by keeping calm and following all our leads."

He was right, but it didn't make it any easier. However, she would do as Jackson said. Well, for now. She wasn't about to roll over if she didn't agree with what he planned.

"So Matt first. Then Avalon PD. And tomorrow?"

"I arrange for my friend with the dogs to help us scope out the base of the ridge."

He shut the door, walked around and slipped into the driver's seat. Executing a K-turn, he started the drive back down the road. They had only gone about halfway when a shot rang out and pinged against the metal of the cruiser.

"Get down!" Jackson shouted and pushed her down with his hand.

Rhea's heart thumped loudly as she struggled with her seat belt. Another shot and ping rang out. She finally got her belt free and sank even lower, burrowing against the dash and hoping it would provide cover.

Jackson had thrown his door open and knelt behind it for protection as he scoured the area for signs of the shooter. Another shot rang out, coming straight at them. Jackson grabbed his cellphone and called 911.

"Shots fired! Shots Fired! Aspen Ridge Road."

"Say again," the dispatcher responded.

"Shots fired. Aspen Ridge Road."

Another bullet pinged against the door by Rhea.

"Identify yourself," the dispatcher asked.

"Detective Whitaker. Regina PD. I'm on Aspen Ridge Road. We're pinned down. Shots fired."

"Sending backup," the dispatcher said.

Jackson reached for his own weapon and shouted out to their assailant. "Police! Backup's on the way!"

The response was the roar of a car engine starting up and the squeal of tires as they took off.

Jackson peered at her. "You okay?"

She nodded, unable to say a word, throat tight with fear. Heart pounding so loudly it was almost all she could hear.

Jackson rose, and she screamed out, "Jax, no! He could still be there."

"He's gone, Rhea. It's okay." He held his hand out to help her up.

Jackson swallowed up her delicate hand with his, and it was impossible to miss the violent trembling of her body. She was shaking so hard her teeth were chattering and he yanked off his jacket, leaned in and covered her with it. "It's okay, Rhea," he said again and tucked the jacket around her.

"Thank you," she said, teeth knocking together.

The screeching sound of a siren approached, followed by the crunch of gravel as a cruiser shot up the road until they were in sight of his car.

He held his hands up in the air and walked into plain sight. "Detective Whitaker. I think the shooter took off down the highway."

One of the Avalon police officers exited the car and called out, "Did you see what they were driving?"

Jackson shook his head. He'd been too busy making sure Rhea was safe and taking cover himself to see the vehicle. "Sorry. I didn't."

The officer said something to his partner, who also got out of the car. The duo approached and Jackson greeted them. "Detective Whitaker. Regina PD."

"Officers Watson and Hughes," Officer Watson said, and the other officer added, "You're a long way from home, Detective."

Cops could be territorial, and he got it. No one liked someone else stepping on their toes. "I am. I'm meeting with your chief later about the Davis case. I've got her sister with me," he said and gestured to his cruiser.

The two officers shared a look, and then Watson took a small notebook from his jacket pocket. "How many shots fired?"

"Four. They all hit the cruiser. I was just going to check it out," he said with a toss of his hand toward the vehicle.

They walked to Rhea's side of the car where two shots had hit the passenger door. The road angled at that point, exposing Rhea's section of the vehicle.

"He had a clear shot at your passenger," Officer Hughes said as he knelt by the bullet dings in the door. "Low caliber, as well," he added.

Jackson examined the damage and couldn't disagree. He glanced at the impressions on the door and imagined where the bullets may have ricocheted. He walked to his side of the car and noticed a mark along the dirt wall on his side of the road. He went there as the two officers examined the opposite area and a stand of trees.

He smiled at the glint of metal in the dirt wall. "I've got a bullet here," he called out to the officers.

"We have some damage to the bark but finding anything will be tough. Lots of duff in this area," Officer Hughes said while Watson came over. He took a small evidence bag from his pocket, and Jackson gestured to the bullet.

Watson dug out the slug with a pen knife. Deposited it into the evidence bag. He held it up for Jackson to see. "Definitely a .22. Small caliber, but it could have gone through the doors."

Jackson nodded. "He would have hit Rhea if that had happened. I wonder why he didn't go through the window or the windshield."

"You think she was the target?" Watson asked, one eyebrow raised in emphasis.

Jackson had no doubt about it. Between the intruder at the inn and now this, someone clearly wanted to scare Rhea off the investigation. Or worse.

He nodded. "She is, but they're going to be sorely surprised. Rhea isn't going to give up until we figure out what happened to her sister."

"We cleared Davis," the officer said, but there was something in the other man's tone that hinted at more.

"Seems like you're not buying the official story," Jackson said.

The officer looked toward his partner, who gave him a "Go ahead" jerk of his head.

"We both always thought the story stunk, but we just couldn't get enough evidence. If you've got it, we're all for you putting that bastard behind bars," Watson said.

Jackson tipped his hat in thanks. "Appreciate it. Right now I think we're going to see that bastard, ask where's he's been the last hour and if he owns a rifle."

"We'll meet you there for backup," Watson said.

Chapter Eight

It had been well over an hour since they'd gone up to the site and returned. Davis wasn't at home when they first arrived but got there within a few minutes.

He appeared confused at the sight of the two police cruisers, but then immediately grew defensive as Officer Watson called out, "Hands on the wheel, Davis."

"I haven't done—"

"Hands on the wheel!" Officer Watson repeated and laid his hand on his holstered weapon.

Matt's gaze skipped across all their faces quickly and then he complied. He looked straight ahead as he said, "What is this about?"

"Do you have a firearm in the car?" Officer Hughes asked.

"No. I'm coming from one of my job sites," Matt explained, his jaw tight and mottled spots of color on his cheeks. His hands clenched and unclenched on the wheel.

"But you own a rifle," Rhea jumped in, and Matt whipped his head around to nail her with a cold stare. Filled with hate, it sent a shiver down her spine.

"Owned. I had to sell it to pay off some bills."

"I'm sure you did all the appropriate paperwork," Jackson said, and at that, the color on Matt's cheeks deepened and a nervous tic erupted along his jaw. He turned away from Jackson and faced forward again.

"Davis? You got the paperwork?" Officer Watson pressed.

Jaw muscles jumping nervously, Matt said, "No. It was a client, and I didn't want to hassle them."

"I guess you won't mind us checking with him," Jackson said.

Matt's head whipped around again and said, "Her. I'd rather you not bother her. I can't afford to lose a good client."

"Where were you the last hour?" Officer Watson said.

"Like I said before. At one of my job sites. You can ask any of the guys there," Matt advised.

"Trust us, we will. How about you give us the info so we can confirm your story," Officer Watson said, while Hughes jerked his head toward their cruiser to indicate he wanted to talk to them alone.

Rhea walked beside Jax to the car, where the three huddled together as Hughes asked, "Is there anything else you need right now?"

Jackson glanced at Rhea, who said, "If we can, a look in his trunk would be great."

"You want to look for the rifle?" Hughes asked, but Jackson quickly said, "Blood. I know your office checked earlier, but I'd like to see the trunk for myself."

Hughes shot a look toward his partner and gestured to the back of the Jeep. "Ask him if he minds opening up the trunk."

Watson leaned in toward Matt, who shook his head, but a second later the glass went up and the hatch unlocked with a *kerthunk*. Watson stepped away to let Davis exit the SUV and open the back so they could inspect it.

"I'm going to lodge a complaint. This is harassment," Matt said as Rhea, Jackson and Officer Watson approached.

"This is an ongoing investigation, Davis, and you are the prime suspect," Jackson explained.

Rhea was so thankful for the presence of the officers. She could never have accomplished any of what had happened so far without them.

Matt shot her another withering look, but she refused to let him cow her. She met his stare head-on and raised her chin a defiant inch. Seeing that they weren't going to back down even with his threat, he swept his hand across his open trunk.

"Look away," he said.

Matt and Rhea walked over, and Rhea immediately noticed the difference. "You used to have a liner in here."

A belligerent shrug was his answer until Jackson said, "Where's the liner?"

"Tossed it about a month ago. It got damaged at a job site," Matt said.

Jackson shook his head. "Convenient. Mind if we take a look anyway?"

"Look away," Matt said facetiously.

Rhea watched as Jackson did, using a blue light to check for blood, she assumed. He did it thoroughly, examining every inch of the trunk area and then the ceiling, as well. But nothing showed up.

As Jackson stepped away from the trunk, Matt smiled smugly and crossed his arms. "Satisfied, Detective?"

Jackson tipped his hat back in a relaxed way, but Rhea couldn't fail to notice the tightness along his jaw and the way he clenched his other fist, as if he was barely restraining himself.

"I wouldn't be so smug, Davis. I'm like a dog with a bone and, right now, you're that bone. I'm going to chew you up and spit you out in pieces to get to the truth about

Selene's disappearance," Jackson said, voice calm. Maybe too calm.

Matt clearly understood. "I didn't do anything to Selene. She ran away to her," he said and flipped his hand toward Rhea, but didn't stop there. Spittle flew off his lips as he said, "You were always in the way. Always putting foolish ideas in her head. Making her think she was something special. That she was too good for me."

The heat of anger burst into flame in her gut. She stepped toward Matt and eyeballed him, barely inches away. She sensed Jackson and the two officers behind her, ready to move if Matt did, but if anything, she suspected it was Matt they'd have to protect if she lost her control.

In a deceptively neutral tone, she said, "Selene is something special. Something way too good for the likes of you. You never appreciated just how unique and wonderful she is, and I'm glad she finally realized that. And if you think Jax is determined—"

"Jax, is it? Did you charm him into doing this or did you do something else?" Matt said with a snigger.

Jackson stepped toward him, fists clenched, but Rhea laid a hand on his chest to stop him. "We will get to the truth, Matt. And when we do, you'd better hope that you have been telling the truth all along, otherwise…"

She couldn't finish, because she couldn't imagine what she might do to him. She'd never pictured herself as a violent person, but…she wanted to hurt him the way he'd hurt Selene. She wanted him to pay for everything he'd done to her sister.

Afraid she would lose control, she whirled, grabbed Jackson's hand and dragged him back toward his cruiser. At the passenger door, Jackson opened it and then leaned on it, a hint of a smile on his face.

"You got…spunk, Rhea. I kind of like it," he said, surprising her and, before she could respond, he walked to his side of the cruiser, got in and started the car.

"Are we going to see the Avalon Police Chief?" Rhea asked.

"We are. I'm sure by the time we get there he'll know someone shot at us and have heard from Matt," Jackson said. With a strangled laugh he added, "I'm not sure he'll be happy to see us."

For once, Rhea couldn't argue with him.

"THAT WENT WELL," Jackson said and blew out a sharp breath.

"Not," Rhea added with a roll of her eyes.

Jackson leaned against the bumper of his cruiser, tucked his arms across his chest and peered at the Avalon Police Station. With a shake of his head, he said, "At least he promised to check out Matt's story about the rifle."

"Convenient, right?" Rhea asked and likewise took a spot against the vehicle, her gaze also on the stationhouse.

"Especially since it was a .22. The same caliber as whoever was shooting at…us," Jackson said, careful of his words since he didn't want to worry Rhea that someone was targeting her.

Rhea shifted her gaze to him. Her blue eyes were dark, clearly reflecting her concern. "You mean me, don't you? Someone was shooting at me."

With a slight dip of his head, he acknowledged it. "I can't deny that it seems like someone wants you to drop this."

Rhea's gaze skipped over his face, questioning. Almost challenging before she said, "Do you think I should drop this?"

His answer was immediate. "No. The fact that someone wants to shut you up confirms that they're trying to hide something."

She looked away and sucked in a deep breath. In a voice tight with emotion she said, "I'm not afraid of pushing for the truth, Jax."

He ran his hand up and down her back, trying to soothe her upset. "I'm not, either. And to get to you, they're going to have to come through me. I won't let that happen."

She surprised him then by turning into his side, her head tucked against his chest, the gesture so trusting his heart constricted. He splayed his hands against her back and he almost spanned the width of it with one hand, reminding him of how petite she was. How vulnerable.

"I won't let that happen," he repeated and brushed a kiss across her temple.

That action propelled her into moving away from him. She tucked her hands under her arms and shook her head. "This is confusing, Jax."

He had no doubt she wasn't referring to Selene's case. He held his hands up in surrender. "It is, and I'm sorry. It's time we got back to Regina. I've got some calls to make and some more research to do before we return to search beneath the ridge."

"I've got some things I want to go over, as well," Rhea said.

With a nod, he opened the door and waited until she was sitting. "It'll be dinnertime by the time we get back to Regina. How about we get some take-out barbecue?"

"I'd love that. Thanks."

JACKSON'S DINING ROOM table was covered with a mix of spareribs, brisket burnt ends, cornbread, beans, coleslaw, and the photos and papers from Rhea.

Rhea sat at one end with a plate piled with food she had barely picked at, not because it wasn't tasty, but because she was too focused on reviewing materials she had already seen dozens of times in the last six months.

Jackson was at the other side of the table, a nearly clean plate sitting there while he read the papers. As Jackson set the materials down, he took note of her watching him, and of her virtually untouched dinner.

"You need to eat something. We didn't eat all day, and you're going to need the fuel tomorrow for that hike beneath the ridge."

With a quick lift of her shoulders, she said, "I'm not really hungry."

He shot to his feet then, wincing as he straightened. Grabbing his back with one hand, he stretched before coming to her side of the table.

"You okay?" She'd seen him suffer with his back more than once in the last couple of days and wondered if it was from an old injury.

"I am." He gathered the materials at her side of the table and shifted her plate of food directly in front of her. "Eat. Once you do, we can go over this. Again."

Rhea stared at the food and then shot a quick glance up at Jackson. The hard set of his jaw and steel gray of his gaze said he wouldn't budge.

She dug it into the brisket and ate the perfectly cooked meat. It was tender with a delicious barbecue sauce. The taste awakened hunger, as did Jax's promise…or maybe it was better to say his threat that they wouldn't look at anything until she had eaten.

She forked up more meat and, after, beans and coleslaw. Before she knew it, she had cleaned her plate and, as promised, Jackson spread out the materials he had taken away earlier.

Jackson gestured to the police photos of Matt's SUV the afternoon after Selene's disappearance. The Jeep was pristine.

"It rained that afternoon," Jackson said, prompting her for a response.

"It did, but you saw that the road was paved with gravel. There was no reason for Matt to clean it. And why did he get rid of that liner? Because he was afraid someone would find evidence the Avalon Police missed?" she pressed.

Jackson hesitated, obviously uneasy, forcing Rhea to push on. "I'm not afraid of the evidence, Jax. It makes me sick in here," she said and tapped her chest. "It makes me sick to think of Selene dead. Of *how* she died, but we need to be able to talk about it openly."

Jackson pursed his lips and inclined his head, scrutinizing her as if to judge her sincerity. Apparently convinced, he said, "If Matt had Selene in the back of the Jeep, on that trunk liner, it would be hard to get rid of blood evidence."

"Unless she was wrapped in something. A tarp maybe."

He nodded. "Maybe. Or unless he put her in that bonfire instead and didn't take her up the mountain."

"But there were no bones there."

Another slow nod. "And we don't know if it's possible to do that in a bonfire. I'm researching that in addition to the timeline of Selene's trip from Avalon to Regina." Jackson grabbed a map where Rhea had written in the approximate time Selene had left and been seen by the lake and the exact time that Selene had texted her sister that night.

Rhea ran her finger along a route on the map and said, "Selene had to have stopped somewhere. Maybe more than one place. I did the route a few times to time it, but I'd like to do it again and see what's along the highway."

"First, we search the ridge. And then, depending on what we find, we investigate what's possible with the bonfire. Hopefully by then we'll have something from the Avalon PD about Matt's rifle and the cell phone location information I requested from both Matt's and Selene's provider."

Puzzled, Rhea narrowed her gaze. "Don't you need a subpoena for the cell phone data?"

"Not under ECPA," he began, but paused at her continued puzzlement.

"The Electronic Communications Privacy Act. I don't need probable cause, just sufficient facts to support making the request, and I think you gave me what I needed," Jackson explained.

"Thank you," she said, appreciative of his recognition of all that she'd done.

"We should be thanking you. I feel guilty that I didn't do more at the time, only… Once the Avalon PD cleared Davis, the most plausible explanation was that Selene committed suicide," Jackson said, real apology in his tone.

She laid her hand over his as it rested on the map she had marked up. "I get it, but Selene wouldn't do that. She just wouldn't."

Jackson had had his doubts in the weeks after they'd closed the case and was ashamed that he hadn't done more. But he'd been told to leave it alone and, by then, the winter crush of tourists had kept him busy with an assortment of problems and crimes. Mostly minor incidents, but enough of them that he'd been too busy to give any time to a case his department had closed.

"I understand," he said and turned his hand to take hers into his. He squeezed it tenderly and offered her a compassionate smile. "We will get to the bottom of this. I won't stop this time."

He cupped her cheek with his free hand and ran his thumb across the dark smudges beneath her eyes. "We're both tired. It's time we got some shut-eye."

"Let me clean up." She started to round up the plates, but Jackson stopped her by laying a hand on her forearm.

"I'll get this put away. Go get some rest," he said, intending to not only clean up their dinner, but do a quick walk around his property to make sure all was well.

Rhea was too smart not to realize there was more to his

request, but she complied, and he was grateful for that. He was too tired for another argument, although in the last couple of days they'd seemed to agree more than disagree.

He quickly loaded the dishwasher and went to the sofa, where he'd laid his service belt. Grabbing his flashlight and Glock, he exited his home, careful to lock the door as he did so. Aiming the flashlight, he first searched the woods close to the front door and then did his walk-around, vigilant for signs of any intruders.

Nothing.

Relieved, he went back inside. He turned on a small lamp on the first floor and softly tread up the stairs, careful to avoid the squeaky floor at the landing.

Rhea's door was closed. Jackson hesitated there, wondering if she was okay, but then he hurried to his own bedroom. After showering and slipping on a pair of pajamas, he got into bed and grabbed his tablet. He had reached out to some experts on body cremation and luckily he'd gotten a response. Rhea would not be happy with what the expert had to say.

He added the expert's response to his digital notebook and then skimmed through the remaining emails. His friend with the cadaver dogs had answered that he could assist them the next day. Confirming that the time his friend had proposed was acceptable, he finally set the tablet away for the night.

Time to get some rest because the hike along the base of the ridge would not be easy, both physically and emotionally.

No matter what they found tomorrow, it was going to upset Rhea. He was certain of that. He only wished he could be as certain of what had happened to Selene that night.

Nothing they'd found so far had eliminated her husband

in her disappearance. If anything, he remained the prime suspect in Jackson's book.

But with no body, a circumstantial case would be hard to prove. Based on what they had so far, no district attorney would bring the case before a grand jury.

If they couldn't find anything more on Davis, they'd have to push on with the other scenarios.

He just hoped Rhea would be satisfied by whatever they discovered.

Chapter Nine

The sounds and smells of breakfast dragged Jackson from bed. He'd already been up, mentally reviewing last night's response from the forensics experts, as well as what they'd need for today's hike. But whatever Rhea was whipping up smelled just too good.

He threw on clothes and hurried down to find Rhea at the stove, already dressed for the day. He hadn't known what to expect given what she'd worn over the last few days. Loose and very feminine blouses and hip-hugging capri pants.

This morning she was wearing faded jeans and a light sweater that hugged those curves he'd noticed more than he should. Well-used hiking boots, and he recalled that she'd mentioned that she and Selene had regularly gone for hikes. A different side to the talented artist, and one that was more in his wheelhouse. One that was more dangerous for sure, because it was too easy to picture the two of them taking long walks through the woods together.

"Good morning," he said and headed straight to the coffee maker to pour himself a cup. She already had a mug on the counter beside her as she worked at the stove.

"Good morning. I hope I didn't wake you by making too much noise," Rhea said and peered at him over her shoulder.

"I was awake, but those amazing smells forced me to move my butt," he said and ambled to her side to see what she was making.

"I just pulled some things from the fridge. Do you like Mexican food?" she said and, once again, glanced at him, a little apprehensive.

"Love it," he said and passed a hand down her back to comfort her. "It smells amazing."

"Thanks. I figured we'd need something substantial for today's hike." She opened the oven and removed a pan holding corn tortillas filled with eggs and chorizo.

"Take a seat and I'll finish these up." She tilted her head in the direction of the table she'd already set.

He did as she asked and, in a few minutes, she served him a plate with the corn tortillas topped with a red sauce. His stomach rumbled in anticipation, and he barely waited until she was seated to dig in. The flavors exploded in his mouth, and he murmured an appreciative sound. "Delicious. Thank you."

Rhea smiled, her blue eyes alight with pleasure at his compliment. "You're welcome. It's my small way of showing how much I appreciate what you're doing."

"It's my job, Rhea. But I wish we'd done more at first. Known more, like about the domestic abuse," he admitted.

She did the tiniest shrug that barely moved her shoulders. "You couldn't have known. Even I didn't really know, and Selene and I were like this," she said and crossed her middle and index fingers in emphasis.

Despite her all-action clothes for hiking, her elegant fingers and wrists still bore her rings and bracelets. Those feminine touches tightened his gut and had him imagining things best left alone. Especially considering why Rhea was in his home.

"That won't happen this time. We will not leave any

stone unturned, but even with that, we may not have enough to charge Matt. You realize that, right?"

The blue of her eyes darkened, and she paused with her fork halfway up to her mouth. "I do, Jax. Trust me, I do."

"Good," he said, hating that he'd dimmed her earlier joy and possibly caused her pain, but he didn't want to set her up for even greater pain by not being realistic.

The exchange created a pall over their meal, and they finished it in silence. Since she was already dressed, Rhea offered to clean up, and Jackson hurried to dress. In no time, he was ready and headed out to his shed to grab a machete. They might need it to clear their way through the underbrush at the base of the ridge. But as he neared, he noticed that the shed door was open.

He reached for his weapon and called out, "Police! Come out with your hands up!"

No sound came from the shed. He approached warily, ready for action as he pulled the door open. He immediately noticed that several items had been moved around, but other than that, everything was as it should be.

He wanted to believe that he'd merely forgotten to shut the shed, but he was the kind of person who had a place for everything, and things were clearly not in the place he'd left them.

Someone had been in the shed.

Matt Davis? he wondered. *Had he followed them back from Avalon to see where Rhea was staying? Had he also been the one at the inn?*

He grabbed his machete, but didn't touch the tools that had been moved. With a quick call to the station, he arranged for his colleagues to dust the tools for prints.

When he returned to the house, Rhea was standing on the back deck, arms tucked tight across her chest against the slight nip in the morning air. "Everything okay?"

"Fine," he lied, not wanting to worry her.

She seemed to see through his ruse, but didn't challenge him.

It took only a few minutes for them to grab some water bottles and their jackets for the hike and hit the road.

RHEA SAT IN silence beside Jackson, wondering what he wasn't telling her. She'd seen the look of concern on his face as he'd returned from his shed. Had he seen something unusual, or was he just worried about what would happen on their hike today much like she was?

She'd been up half the night imagining Selene out in the woods beneath the ridge. Trying to hold on to that belief that her sister was still alive, but even that vision brought despair. If Selene was still out there, what was happening to her? Was she being abused? Was she losing hope that she'd be found?

Rhea would never lose hope, but in that way Selene was the weaker of the two of them. Her mother had often used a Shakespeare quote to describe Selene's spirit. *Swear not by the moon, the inconstant moon, that monthly changes in her circle orb, Lest that thy love prove likewise variable.*

Selene's love had never been inconstant, but she'd been easily swayed at times. Rhea was convinced that was why Matt had deluded Selene about his real character. A character that had convinced Selene to abandon her dreams of being a singer for a more stable profession as a music teacher.

When they found Selene, Rhea would do her utmost to make sure Selene was able to follow those dreams and escape her abusive husband. In a way, Rhea was a lot like the goddess after whom she'd been named. She'd always been a mother figure for Selene and others and would do anything to protect her, much like the goddess Rhea had hidden away Zeus to keep him safe.

She'd been so lost in her musings, she didn't realize

they were already close to Aspen Ridge Road until Jackson pulled over just past the turnoff for that street. Parked ahead of them on the shoulder was a pickup with a dog box in the bed. As they stopped, the pickup door popped open and a man in hunting gear stepped out. A second later, two dogs also leaped from the vehicle and followed him to Jackson's door.

The two men shook hands, and Jackson's friend leaned down to peer through the window. He was a handsome Latino with a dimpled smile and eyes the color of hot cocoa. "Good morning, Miss Reilly."

Jackson said, "Rhea, this is Diego. We served together in Afghanistan."

"Good morning, Diego. Please call me Rhea," she said.

"Rhea," he said with a deferential dip of his head. He glanced toward the woods by the turnoff. "Am I in the right place?"

Jackson nodded. "Our suspect claims he went up to a building site at the top of the ridge. Too easy to find a buried body with all the construction, so we think he did the next easiest thing."

"Tossed her over the edge," Diego said and straightened to scrutinize the area. After he did so, he said, "Let's get going. It may take some time to hike to the spot beneath that ridge."

"I agree," Jackson said and looked at her, his gaze sympathetic. "You ready, Rhea?"

Am I ready for what might lie ahead?

"I'm ready."

THEY HIKED BENEATH the rising wall of the ridge for close to an hour, Jackson ahead of her, hacking through vines and thick underbrush. Yards behind her, his friend Diego gave the dogs free rein to check the area for signs of any decomposition. For signs of Selene. They didn't hit on anything, which was both a disappointment and a relief.

Sweat dripped down the middle of her back and her temples from the heat and humidity in the forest. Sweat lines were visible down Jackson's back and armpits as he cut their way through the forest. In another half an hour, they finally reached a spot directly beneath the building location.

Jackson stopped, sucked in a deep breath and wiped away sweat with a muscled forearm. He shot a quick look at her. "You okay?"

Her legs were trembling, she was a little out of breath and a lot hot, but she shook her head and said, "I'm okay."

Jackson peered over her shoulder at Diego. "How about you, *amigo*?"

Diego smiled. "A walk in the park," he teased. With a hand signal, he set the dogs into action. They scurried into the nearby woods, sniffing here and there, jumping over fallen logs and beneath tangled vines. As time passed, it was clear they weren't hitting on anything.

With a low whistle, Diego summoned the dogs back. "*Nada* here. Maybe we should press on a little more."

Jackson sighed and looked at her. "You okay with that?"

"I'm ready to do anything we need to do." She was determined not to waste this opportunity.

They pushed on, and then in an even wider circle in the area closest to the custom home's location up on the ridge.

But despite all their hard work in clearing the underbrush and hiking through the rough terrain, the dogs failed to locate anything.

It was impossible for Jackson not to see the mixed emotions spiraling through Rhea. Despair. Relief. Disappointment. Hope.

He laid an arm around her shoulders and drew her near. Brushing a kiss on her temple and ignoring Diego's surprised look, he said, "Don't let this get you down. We'll find her."

She turned into him and murmured, "It's just… I don't know. I'm upset, but also relieved, you know."

He knew, boy, did he know. "Let's go grab a bite and regroup. Decide what else we have to do in Avalon before heading home."

Home. His cabin had always felt like home, but with Rhea there now it felt more…complete, worrying him.

It was too much, too soon and, as Diego shot him another questioning look, he realized his friend was likewise wondering what was up.

Rhea nodded, and he released her so they could trudge back through the path they had blazed earlier. By the time they reached their cars, his entire body was bathed in sweat, and his arm was beginning to ache from swinging the machete to cut through the underbrush.

At his cruiser, Rhea stopped and offered a smile to Diego. "Thank you so much for doing this. We really appreciate your help."

"Anything for an old friend," Diego said and clapped Jackson on the back. *Maybe a little too hard*, Jackson thought and grimaced as pain swept across his lower back.

"We do appreciate it, *amigo*," Jackson said, but sensed his friend wanted a private moment. Especially when Diego jerked his head in the direction of his pickup.

He got Rhea settled in the cruiser. "I'll be back in a second."

She nodded, and he joined his friend as Diego rewarded his dogs and then loaded them into their boxes.

With a quick glance in Rhea's direction, Diego said in a low whisper, "Do you know what you're doing?"

Jackson didn't dare look toward Rhea, afraid he'd reveal too much. He also wasn't sure what to tell his friend. "I know we're trying to investigate her sister's disappearance."

"But that's not all, Jax. It's obvious you have feelings for her," Diego said and finished securing the latches on the dog boxes. He leaned on the tailgate. "Is that going to compromise your investigation?"

"No. I won't let whatever is happening between us change what I have to do."

Diego arched a brow. "Which is?"

"Find out what really happened to Selene Davis."

Chapter Ten

After grabbing a quick bite at an outdoor café, they decided it was worth a go at the building location. They also wanted to look around Matt's home, but Matt refused to allow any inspection without a warrant.

Matt's client was not as reluctant. In fact, he welcomed it.

"I want this all behind me, and would feel better knowing there's nothing going on at my home," he said on the phone.

With that approval, Jackson, Rhea and Diego went to the ridge and allowed the cadaver dogs to roam the property. They were just about finished when Matt pulled up in his SUV and jerked to an angry stop in front of the home.

He jumped from the SUV and came at them, jabbing his finger in their direction. "You have no right. No right," he shouted.

Jackson tucked Rhea behind him protectively and braced for Matt's attack, but at his glare, Matt stopped dead in his tracks. But apparently Rhea wasn't about to hide behind him.

With the spunk he'd come to love, she shifted from behind him and said, "We have every right. We have the owner's permission, because he has nothing to hide."

"I have nothing to hide," Matt said and jabbed his chest angrily.

"Seems to me that if you had nothing to hide you'd let us search your yard," Jackson said and gestured to the dogs who had returned to Diego's side.

"You're six months too late. I'm done with this. I'm done with being harassed. You can bet I'm going to file a formal complaint."

Without waiting for a response, Matt whirled and stomped back to his SUV. Gravel spewed from beneath the tires as he whipped around and raced away.

"Someone's got anger issues," Diego said as he watched the SUV bounce down the road.

"It hurts to think of Selene suffering from that anger," Rhea said, the sheen of tears brightening her gaze. "What do we do if he files a complaint?"

While Jackson liked that it was a "we," he didn't want Rhea to worry. "Let him file a complaint. It won't go far. We'll put together all our evidence for the Avalon PD and see if they can't get a warrant to search the property with the dogs. Especially the bonfire area."

Rhea peered at the animals. "They can identify remains if there's been a fire?"

Diego nodded. "Their sense of smell is strong enough to detect human remains in ashes. Especially if they have a scent to pick up on. Do you have anything with Selene's smell on it?"

With a quick nod, she said, "I do, but back in Denver. Do you want me to get it?"

It was nearly a two-hour trip to Denver, but totally worth the time if Diego's dogs could rely on the scent. "Are you sure about the ashes?" he asked his friend.

Diego nodded. "It's possible, Jax. I can come back once you get the warrant."

With a nod, he looked at Rhea. "I guess we're going to Denver."

IT WAS DARK by the time they started the trip back to Regina from Denver. Rhea had picked a number of items that Selene had left behind in her apartment, and then they stopped for dinner since it was getting late.

It has been an emotional day, Rhea thought as she sat in silence beside Jackson. She'd been filled with dread as they'd hiked through the woods. Not finding Selene's body had been a mixed blessing.

When they were almost on the outskirts of Regina, Rhea said, "Thank you for arranging for Diego to help us today."

Jackson shot her a quick look, then immediately glanced in the rearview mirror. "He's a stand-up guy. I knew he'd come if I asked him."

"He served with you?" she asked and, as Jackson again checked the rearview mirror, Rhea likewise looked over her shoulder and saw something way behind them. The lights on the vehicle were off, making it difficult to see it on the dark roadway.

"What is that?" she asked, eyes narrowed as she examined Jackson's face to gauge just how worried he was.

"Nothing good," he said and swept his arm out to press her back against the seat. "Hold on."

He increased his speed, trying to put distance between them and the vehicle that was racing toward them. In front of them, a slow-moving lumber truck blocked the road, and they were on a section of highway that made it difficult to pass.

Jackson muttered a curse beneath his breath and slowed. He shot another look in the rearview mirror, and she did the same. The unknown vehicle was advancing on them. Too quickly.

Inching into the lane for opposing traffic, Jackson whipped back behind the truck at the sight of lights coming toward them.

He splayed his hand across her upper chest and said, "Brace yourself."

The first hit against the back of the car sent her reeling forward and back, while Jackson battled to maintain control, working the steering wheel to stay on the road. Hitting the brakes to stay away from the back of the lumber truck and the logs that would break through the windshield and kill them.

A second jolt had the cruiser swerving, fighting against the momentum sending them toward the truck and a fatal collision.

Jackson swung the wheel into opposing traffic, searching for an escape, but the threat of lights coming toward them drove him back behind the truck again.

He shifted to the open shoulder and hit the gas. Gravel pinged against the underside of the cruiser. Another ram almost sent them off the shoulder and into the woods beside the road.

As soon as Jackson cleared the truck, he swung in front of it, earning a loud blare of the truck's horn as he cut if off. He used the truck as a shield for their rear, but the vehicle that had been chasing them switched tactics.

While riding on the shoulder, the vehicle smashed into the side of their car, sending them into the opposing traffic. It swung into the lane, blocking their way back onto the right side of the road, leaving Jackson little choice but to race onto the far shoulder. It was much narrower and, as he did so, the cruiser sideswiped a number of trees until he jerked to a rough stop.

Their attacker sped away, any view of them blocked by the slow-moving lumber truck.

"You okay?"

Am I? she wondered, finally taking a deep breath. Her heart pounded so powerfully in her chest it echoed in her ears.

"I'm okay," she said, forcing calm into her voice even though she was anything but.

The lumber truck had stopped, and the driver exited the cab and came racing over. Jackson lowered the windows on the cruiser to speak to him.

"You folks okay?" he asked, leaning in through Rhea's window.

"We're okay. Did you get a plate number on the vehicle that hit us?" Jackson asked.

The trucker shook his head. "No, sorry. I was too busy trying to control the truck. All I can tell you is that it was a Jeep Wrangler. Red, I think."

Jackson and Rhea shared a look. "How about the driver?" Rhea asked.

The trucker tossed his hands up in apology. "No, sorry. Didn't see him."

"Mind if I get your contact info before you go?" Jackson asked and, without hesitation, the trucker pulled out his wallet and handed Jackson his license. Jackson snapped a photo and handed it back to the man, who ambled to his truck and took off.

Jackson grabbed his radio to call in the incident, but they were in a dead zone. Same for their cell phones.

Grumbling, Jackson said, "We'll have to drive closer to town to get a signal. Are you sure you're okay?"

Rhea blew out a rough laugh. "As okay as you can be when someone tries to kill you."

Jackson brushed the back of his hand across her cheek. "Davis is obviously angry that you're not letting this alone."

"I won't let it alone until we know what happened to my sister," Rhea said, no doubt in her voice despite the fear that had filled her barely moments earlier.

Jackson smiled. "That's my girl."

She wanted to say she wasn't his girl or anyone else's,

but in truth, it felt good. She felt good. Protected despite all that had happened in the last few days. Jackson would keep her safe, but she was no damsel in distress. She'd keep him safe, as well.

The cruiser, damaged and worse for wear, could be driven, and Jackson pulled back onto the road.

In less than fifteen minutes they had arrived at the Regina Police Station where Jackson had to file various reports regarding the attack. While he did so, Rhea sat beside his desk, sipping on a coffee someone had been nice enough to bring over. Despite the heat of the liquid, a chill had settled into her center as she considered that someone had tried to kill them.

Matt? she wondered again, despite the call to the Avalon police who had confirmed that Matt's Jeep was sitting in his driveway with a cold engine and nary a scratch on the vehicle.

A gentle hand on her knee pulled her from her thoughts. "I'll only be a little longer," Jackson said.

She nodded. "It's not a problem. Take whatever time you need." She didn't think she could sleep anyway once they got home. Cradling the coffee mug in her hands, she let it warm her cold fingers and still the slight tremble.

Less than five minutes later, Jackson shuffled all the papers he'd been working on into a neat stack, shot to his feet and held his hand out to her.

Without hesitation, she slipped her hand into his and rose unsteadily from the chair. He grabbed hold of the coffee mug from her other hand and set it on his desktop.

A gentle tug on her hand urged her close, and he wrapped an arm around her. Hips bumping as they walked, they left the station and walked to a different cruiser. The first one was now evidence.

Once she was seated, she wrapped her arms around herself, shock still filling her center with cold. "We're going to find out who did this," Jackson said and rubbed a hand across her shoulders.

"I know," she said, confident that Jackson would keep his promise.

Jackson started the cruiser, turning up the heat and, little by little, the cold left her thanks to a combination of the warmth blasting from the vents and Jackson's presence.

Another police cruiser sat in the driveway of his home.

Jackson waved at the young officer behind the wheel and the officer waved back, confirming he had their attention.

"He'll be there all night," Jackson advised, and it offered some comfort.

"Thank you for all that you're doing. I know it wasn't easy for you to buck your chief."

Jackson cupped her cheek. "It wasn't easy, but everything that's happened just confirms there's more to Selene's disappearance."

Rhea wouldn't read more into his use of *disappearance* instead of *murder* or *suicide*. There still wasn't enough to substantiate her belief that Selene was alive. But there was certainly enough to prove that whatever both police departments had believed might be wrong.

"Do you think Matt had anything to do with what happened tonight?" she asked, certain that her sister's husband had to have been the one who'd driven them off the road.

Jackson blew out a breath and swiped his thumb across her cheek. "He's my prime suspect, but if he did it, it was with another SUV. If he does own another one, we'll find it."

With another gentle caress, he said, "Let's get some rest."

She nodded and met Jackson at the front bumper. She tucked herself against him, wanting to not only draw comfort from his presence, but to offer it, as well.

When they entered, she had no doubt where she'd be sleeping that night.

Beside Jackson.

Upstairs they separated only long enough to change, but she went straight to his room and slipped into bed beside him. Turning, she laid a hand on his chest. His skin was hot beneath her palm, and she cuddled close, laying her head against him. But despite that, she felt restless with too many thoughts racing through her brain.

He eased his arm around her and splayed a hand across her back to hold her close. He soothed it up and down and said, "You need to shut it down and get some rest. Tomorrow is going to be a long day."

She raised her head to peer at him. At the strong, straight line of his jaw, stubbled with his evening beard. "I can't stop thinking about all that's happened. All we still have to do."

He shifted until they were almost eye-to-eye. Until his nose bumped hers and his breath warmed her lips. His body was hard beside hers. Strong. The body of a warrior with the scars to prove it, she realized, noticing the shine of old scars along his shoulder and upper arm.

She raised her hand and ran the tips of her fingers along it, her gaze on those injuries before skipping up to meet his.

"Shrapnel from an IED. Kandahar province."

He said it matter-of-factly, but there was no missing the tension that crept into his body.

"Did you lose anyone?" she said and stroked her hand across the scars, wanting to soothe him the way he had her so often in the last few days.

"We avoided the worst of the blast and didn't lose anyone. Didn't lose anyone on my tours of duty and brought everyone home," he said, pride evident in his tone.

She had no doubt his leadership was part of the reason.

That kind of leadership would have been coveted anywhere, which made her wonder why he had chosen Regina.

"Was Regina home for you?" she asked, wanting to know more about the man who was unexpectedly becoming a part of her life. A man who was tempting her at a time when she needed to be focused on only one thing: finding her sister.

He nodded. "I grew up in Regina, and my parents lived here until they moved to Florida. It's a safe place that I want to keep safe so I can raise my kids here."

Kids. She wondered if there had ever been anyone he'd wanted to have his children and the question escaped her before common sense could silence her.

"No one special," he said. "Before now," he quickly added and locked his steely gray gaze on her. He cradled her cheek and traced the outline of her lips with his thumb.

Her heart skipped a beat, and her breath trapped in her chest. The rough pad of his finger was a powerful caress and jolted her core alive.

"Jax," she eked out past the knot in her throat.

"Relax, Rhea. It's too soon, and we have too much to do," he said and tempered his touch, releasing her gaze and shifting his hand to the back of her skull to draw her close. He massaged her head tenderly, easing past the charged moment. Bringing some peace as her mind traveled from thoughts of the past and Selene to those of a happier future. One possibly spent exploring whatever was going on with Jackson. Maybe kids. Maybe a little shop along the quaint street in Regina. A Matt-free Selene finally doing what she loved.

Rhea's light snore and the softness of her body along his confirmed she had fallen asleep. It brought a smile and relief to Jackson.

It had been a difficult day and night with all that had happened. Tomorrow would be no less stressful.

Even though they had picked up clothing from Rhea's apartment that hopefully had enough of Selene's scent to examine the bonfire ashes, unless Matt consented they'd have to wait for a search warrant. Regardless of that, he'd done enough research to recreate the bonfire Matt had kept going all night.

Hopefully that recreation would provide the information they could use to either charge Matt or get the search warrant they needed.

And if not…

Jackson refused to consider that possibility. One way or another, he'd find out what had happened to Selene that fateful fall night.

Chapter Eleven

Jackson examined the circle of pavers that his friend Declan had recreated from the crime scene photos. A large pile of wood sat a few feet away, ready for a fire.

"What do you think?" Declan said, arms crossed as he also scoped out his work and shot a quick look at Rhea.

"It looks like Matt's firepit," Rhea said and strolled around the circle, likewise scrutinizing Declan's work. "Thank you so much."

"Anything for my friend Jax," Declan said and clapped Jackson on the back, making him wince from the force of the blow.

"Easy, dude," Jackson warned and eyeballed Rhea, hoping she hadn't caught his pain, but she had.

"Sorry, dude. I forgot," Declan said. He gestured toward the back of his restaurant. "I'm going to go get the hog, okay?"

Jackson forced a smile. "That would be great, and thanks again for helping us with this. Let me know what I owe you—"

"No way, dude. I owe you big time," Declan said, raising his hands to stop Jackson from insisting on his request.

"Well, thanks," he said and watched as his friend returned to his building to fetch the pig carcass they were going to cremate.

"You okay?" she asked. Laying a hand on his shoulder, she gently skimmed her hand from his upper arm to the middle of his back, as if trying to soothe his pain.

He nodded, his lips tight against both the slight sting that lingered from his friend's exuberance and admitting weakness to Rhea. "I'm okay. I still have pain sometimes from the shrapnel damage."

Turning into him, she surrounded him with her arms and hugged him, providing comfort and peace he hadn't felt in quite some time. Not since before Afghanistan.

The moment was shattered as Declan and one of his workers returned, arms wrapped around a large hog that roughly weighed the same as Selene. They wrestled the carcass to the center of the firepit and dropped it. It landed with a thud, kicking up dirt. Making Rhea jump with the sound.

He returned her embrace, hugging her close. Peering at her, he said, "Are you ready to do this?"

She shook her head. "No, but there's no choice is there? Not if we want to know if Matt did this to Selene."

Before he could warn Rhea not to get her hopes up, she was in action, making a pile of brush and kindling above the hog. As she started to expertly stack the logs, he joined her and said, "I see you've built campfires before."

"Selene and I were Girl Scouts. We started a lot of campfires in our day," she said, adding more wood to the tipi atop the hog.

He helped her, adding logs and tinder until the body of the pig was almost completely covered.

Jackson stepped back, hands on his hips as he scrutinized their prospective campfire. Rhea joined him, staring at the pile and then up at him. "What do you think?"

"I think it's ready." He reached into his pocket for the box of matches and, once the match was lit, tossed it into the tinder material. The first hint of flame quickly flared into more. Smoke came from the pile along with the crackle and snap of wood igniting. The fire had taken.

Satisfied, he headed to the trunk of the police cruiser where he'd stowed two portable camping chairs. Rhea and he set them up several feet away from the campfire. The heat quickly built from the intensity of the flames, but they still had to keep it going for several hours, much like Matt had done the night of Selene's disappearance.

Rhea was silent as they sat there, staring into the flames as they consumed the pig. The smell of the meat roasting was awkward. While there was no denying it was pork, it made her wonder…

No, better not to wonder, she told herself.

Jackson shifted from his chair to add more logs and keep the fire going. It had barely been an hour, but the greedy flames were quickly eating up the wood on the pile, as well as the carcass beneath the ash and embers. Because of that, Jackson walked over to an area with wood waiting to be split, grabbed an ax and went to work.

He swung the heavy ax with ease the same way he had chopped with the machete the day before. He was clearly a man used to physical labor, despite the injuries that still seemed to bother him. Over and over he swung the ax, the thunk of it hitting the log loud in the quiet of late morning.

Feeling guilty, she rose and went over to collect the split wood and add it to the pile by the fire. Tossing more logs into the firepit as well to keep the flames going.

The physical labor helped to keep her mind off what was happening in the firepit, but it also whet her hunger. Especially as Declan's restaurant opened for lunch service and the smokers that they'd loaded up that morning were opened, spewing the tasty smells of barbecued meats into the air.

Almost as if he'd read her mind, Declan exited from the back of the restaurant with a large tray loaded with food and drinks. He brought it over and placed it on a stump by their chairs. "I thought you might be hungry by now."

"Thank you. That was very thoughtful," she replied.

Declan did a side glance at the firepit as Jackson approached. "I know this is a tough thing for you."

She nodded. "It is, but your help has really made it easier."

Declan shrugged. "Like I said before. Anything for Jax…and for you since…well, you and Jax." He stopped, clearly uncertain and possibly uneasy as Jackson returned from splitting logs.

With a laugh, Jackson wagged his head. "Deck, you always manage to talk too much."

"And before I stick my foot in my mouth even deeper, I'm going," he said as he jerked a thumb in the direction of the restaurant and backed away.

Rhea smiled at the friendly and jovial exchange between the two. "I guess you've known each other a long time."

Jackson chuckled, sat and reached for one of the plates that Declan had brought out. "You might say that. We grew up together, but then I went off to college and Deck stayed to help his family with the restaurant."

"Have they had it for long?" The building was well-kept and had that look of age that hinted at permanence.

"A few generations." Jackson took a big bite of the brisket sandwich Declan had provided.

"Where did you go to college?" she asked, wanting to know more about the man who was intriguing her on so many levels.

"Annapolis," was his one-word answer around a mouthful of pulled pork.

She picked up her own sandwich, grateful it was beef and not pork. She nibbled the burnt ends, murmuring her approval. "Delicious."

With a nod, Jackson took another big bite. After swallowing, he said, "His pops taught him well, and Deck really upped his game. He's won quite a number of competitions over the years."

Rhea admired the pride that Jackson had in his friend, as well as the fact that they had been friends for so long. Much like the permanence of the restaurant, it spoke to Jackson's character and the fact that he was a man you could count on. But then again, he'd more than proved that over the last few days.

"You were a Marine?" she said, resuming her earlier quest for information.

"I *am* a Marine. Once a Marine always a Marine," he said with a smile.

Yet more proof of his ability to commit. "And then you came home and became a cop?"

With a small shrug, he swallowed the last of his sandwich. "I wanted to serve, and it seemed like the best place to do it."

In a town the size of Regina, she imagined crime was usually limited to minor incidents, which was why Selene's case had been such a big deal at the time. "It must be pretty quiet in Regina for the most part."

He placed his plate back on the tray and did another shift of his shoulders. "It is. Problems with people partying too much. Noise complaints. Shoplifting. Occasionally a burglary or assault."

"Cat up a tree," she teased, imagining him dealing with a dowager and her felonious feline.

Jackson laughed as she'd intended. "More like bear up a tree. Those suckers can really climb," he said, but then he grew a little more serious. "I like it. I like dealing with people. Solving problems. If I become chief…"

There was something in the way his voice trailed off that warned there was an issue there.

"Are you next in line?" she asked, wondering about his hesitation.

"I was…am," he said with a little more confidence, but she sensed his concern. When he shot her a hurried, almost furtive glance, she realized she was the cause of that worry.

"Your chief was going to blow me off, wasn't he?"

"Let's just say he wasn't sure there was enough evidence to reopen the case." Jackson rose and tossed more wood on the bonfire before returning to his chair.

He was in major avoidance-mode, but she wasn't going to give up until she had her answer. "But you decided differently, and he didn't like that."

Heaving a sigh, he nailed her with his gray gaze, now almost charcoal with his upset. "You know you would have made a great interrogator."

She met his gaze. "I suspect you think I'm more like a Grand Inquisitor. But I don't give up, which is why we're sitting here, trying to cremate a hog."

"It is," he admitted with a slight dip of his head.

"But that put you in hot water. Maybe even enough to affect you becoming chief?" She hated that she might be the reason Jackson's career was at risk.

His demeanor was deadly serious as he said, "If it gets to the truth of what happened to Selene, it's worth it, isn't it?"

She nodded. "It is."

"And you remember your promise, right?" he pressed, turning the tables on her.

She remembered, as much as she might not like accepting that Selene was truly gone. "I do, Jax. I remember it every time we hit another brick wall."

Jackson nodded and worried that today's experiment would turn into another disappointment for Rhea. With that in mind, he said, "I reached out to people who might know more about cremating bodies."

She tilted her head and focused on him, her gaze both questioning and challenging. "Does that mean you don't think this is going to prove anything?"

He hesitated, but had to be truthful. Especially since he'd already kept his problems with the chief secret. "It may prove something you don't want."

"Which is?" she urged and gripped the arms of the seat with hands white with pressure.

Gesturing with his hands, he mimicked the path of the flames in the bonfire. "With those low paver walls, we're getting a lot of flames, but the energy of the fire is being expended upward."

A deep furrow marred her brow. "What does that change?"

He once again used his hands to illustrate what he'd learned. "If the fire was contained, like in a barrel or a pit with higher sides, you'd get more heat in a concentrated area."

Her eyes opened wider and she nodded, getting what he was saying. "We may not have enough heat to cremate..."

She couldn't finish, and he didn't push on that point. "Bingo." He reached into his pocket and pulled out his smartphone. He opened up his digital notebook with the crime scene photos of Matt's bonfire. Leaning close to Rhea, he held the phone so she could see, although he suspected they were tattooed on her brain.

"There's a lot of ash here, but nothing else."

"He could have taken away anything that was left."

He couldn't deny that. "He could possible remove larger bits of bones, but getting rid of other—"

"What other?" she countered.

"Body residues. Teeth," he said, but she held a hand up to stop him, the sheen of tears glistening in her gaze.

"I don't want to upset you—"

She cut him off again with a quick wave of her hand. "I get it, Jax."

He had no doubt she did, but just in case, he reviewed what Matt had done that night. "He started a bonfire and went up to the ridge location."

"Supposedly. He could have also followed Selene to Regina."

Jackson drilled back to the pages in his digital notebook on the timelines Rhea had worked out. Analyzing them, he said, "He could have. It's only about forty-five minutes to Regina, and the neighbors say he was gone for a few hours."

Losing some of her earlier upset, Rhea jumped right into helping him work through the materials. "We have two witnesses who place an SUV near Selene's car."

With a nod, he ran a finger across his screen, scrolling through the notes and then thought out loud. "Let's say he and Selene did fight. She storms off. He's pissed and needs to literally burn off his anger. He starts the bonfire. But he's still really pissed at Selene and needs to do something about that."

Rhea joined in. "He goes after her to give her a piece of his mind. There's really only one way to Denver, and it runs right through Regina. He finds her. They fight again and something happens."

Jackson wagged his head. "But it's possible Selene took longer to get to the lake than everyone originally thought. We'll have to investigate that. But let's assume he ran into Selene right away. Why not just toss her body in the lake?"

"We'd find Selene right away in the lake, wouldn't we?"

Jackson immediately knew where she was going. "Which is why you think she may still be alive. Because otherwise we'd have found her body in the lake." He paused for a moment and then quickly added, "Unless the spillway was open to keep the lake levels in check."

She whipped out her phone, and her elegant fingers danced over the smartphone screen. With a satisfied dip of her head, she held it up for him to see a report she'd obtained.

He'd only done a quick glance at it before, but now he took her phone, used his thumb and forefinger to zoom the image. Rhea had filed a Freedom of Information Act request to obtain information on spillway activity from the department that managed it.

"Spillway was closed that night and for days after. If Matt put Selene in the lake—"

"Or if she killed herself—which she didn't—we would have found her body," Rhea finished.

The crackle and thump of logs collapsing in the fire drew his attention. Embers shot up and danced in the air as more wood fell in the center of the pit. "Time for more logs."

Together they piled on even more wood and, as they did so, it was obvious to Rhea that there was a little less of the pig carcass beneath the ash and embers.

She snuck a peak at her watch. "It's been about four hours since we started."

Jackson likewise did a quick look at his phone to confirm the time. "About. We'll need to keep it going a while longer to match what Matt did."

"Which means more time to get to know each other," Rhea said, wanting to find out all she could about Jackson.

"First, more firewood," he said and walked over to split more wood.

She recognized avoidance when she saw it, but she refused to let him avoid that talk. He was becoming too special to her in just the few days they'd spent together. Too hard to resist, even though becoming involved with a man was low on her priority list. Both before and after college she'd been focused on establishing her career. Once it had taken off, her emphasis had shifted to her gallery. In the years since then, she'd made a number of friends and spent time with Selene, but a relationship...nonexistent.

That she was giving the "relationship" label to what she was feeling for Jackson was a scary proposition. He was connected to too much hurt. He was also nothing like the artsy men who inhabited her life. But maybe that was why she found him so interesting. He was the epitome of the strong, silent hero type, but beneath that hard surface was a powerful and compassionate man.

Instead of sitting, she walked to where he was working and, as he split the logs, she picked them up and carried them close to the firepit. They had just finished making a nice pile when Declan came out of the restaurant with another tray, this time loaded with what looked like slices of pie and tall glasses of lemonade.

"Dude, if you're in the mood to keep on chopping, I could use some hickory for the smokers," Declan called out and motioned to a far pile of wood with the tray.

Jackson nodded. "Sure thing. Least I could do to thank you for all your help and the food."

And to avoid talking to me, Rhea thought, but bit her tongue. He could run, but he couldn't hide.

When Jackson moved to the pile of hickory logs, she tagged along, picking up the pieces he'd split to add them to the neat pile Declan had beside the uncut logs.

"You've known Declan forever," she said, hoping to start the discussion on what was hopefully a safe topic.

Jackson raised the ax and sent it flying down onto the log, splitting it in half. "We grew up in the same neighborhood. Went to school together."

"I bet you were a jock," she said, picturing him on a football field.

Jackson grinned and shook his head. She thought she

heard him murmur, "Grand Inquisitor," but then he said, "I was. Baseball, not football."

It was too easy to imagine that powerful and lean body in a tight baseball uniform, igniting heat at her core. But he was more than just a pretty face.

As she picked up a pile of cut hickory logs, she asked, "Why does a landlocked Colorado boy decide to go to Annapolis?"

Jackson set the ax on the ground and stretched, arching his back and wincing slightly. But before she could offer to help, he picked up the ax and went back to work.

She pressed him for an answer. "Why Annapolis?"

He finished quartering the log and set the ax aside, obviously in pain. But he finally answered her. "I didn't want my parents to have to pay for college since they still had my sister and brother to worry about. Dad is a Marine and I wanted to follow in his footsteps. Annapolis made sense."

She stacked the last of the logs he'd split and followed him back to the fire. Together they tossed on more wood, then sat to eat the slices of pie Declan had brought out. But that wasn't going to keep her from her goal.

"Are you always so sensible and responsible?"

Chapter Twelve

He paused with a forkful of apple pie halfway to his mouth and glanced at her. His steely gray gaze glittered with a heat she hadn't thought possible. "Not always."

The warmth that had kindled in her core earlier grew ever higher, like the flames in the fire a few feet away. It was so intense, she had to cool off with a few sips of icy lemonade.

"What about you, Rhea? I know you're talented. Determined," he said, the latter word followed by a playful chuckle.

She considered him over the lip of the glass, thinking about how to answer. After a pause, she said, "I know some people think artists can be temperamental and flighty. You probably did."

He smiled as he scraped the last of his pie from the plate and then licked the fork clean. "I plead the fifth," he joked, but then quickly added, "But you probably thought I was uptight and by-the-book."

She felt the urge to shake him up a little. "I still do, but I look forward to you proving me wrong."

His glass rattled against the tray as he set it down and, when he fixed his gaze on her, it seared her with its fire. "I look forward to that also."

She gulped down the rest of her lemonade to cool the

blaze he'd ignited and turned her attention to her pie. Another collapse of the logs in the bonfire had them both bolting from their chairs to the wood pile. They almost collided there, forcing Jackson to reach for her to keep her from falling over.

Electricity sparked between them, and Rhea rushed back to her seat.

Jackson took his time feeding the fire, needing to control what he was feeling for Rhea. Banking the flames burning inside because he worried that if he released them, it might consume him. He was unused to such feelings, being, as Rhea had said, normally uptight and by-the-book.

But Rhea had loosed those bounds he'd lived with all his life, first as an athlete, then as a Marine and finally as a cop.

It couldn't have happened at a worse time, he thought. Rhea's emotions were too fragile, and he had to stay focused because so much was at stake, including his career. But more importantly, he had to keep Rhea safe.

His Crime Scene Unit was working on the cruiser, trying to get paint and metal samples in the hopes of identifying the vehicle that had attacked them. They were also trying to locate any CCTVs along the route that might also yield more information. The Avalon police were determining if Matt owned any other SUVs that fit the bill and still trying to get a warrant to search his property.

With a cruiser parked in front of his own home, he hoped that would be enough to safeguard Rhea.

The vibration of the cell phone in his pocket warned that they'd hit the time limit for their bonfire.

"Is it time?" Rhea asked.

He nodded. "We need to let it die down and see what we have."

"I'm ready, Jax. No matter what happens, I'm ready,"

she said and met his gaze, hers unwavering and filled with the kind of determination he'd come to expect from her.

"We'll be ready, Rhea. And if this doesn't work out, we'll move on," he said, wanting to reassure her.

"I know." She reached across the short distance separating their chairs, holding her hand out to him.

He grasped her hand and twined his fingers with hers. The comfort he offered her with that touch rebounding to bring him peace, as well.

It took another hour for the fire to die down enough for them to check out what had happened.

Jackson grabbed a shovel that Declan kept for feeding and controlling his smoker fires. Carefully, he shifted the still red-hot embers in the firepit, moving them away from the center to try to expose what, if anything, was left of the pig carcass. It was hot work, and sweat bathed his body from the heat.

As he moved the embers toward the edges, he had to take a step back to cool off.

Rhea was immediately there with another tall glass of lemonade.

"Thank you," he said. He swiped his forearm across his brow to wipe away the sweat and chugged down the drink.

After a few deep breaths, he resumed shoveling the embers until he had revealed a large portion of the carcass. Or at least what remained.

He stood beside Rhea, hands on his hips, staring at the pile of bones in the center of the pit. A dark residue, probably from the animal's fat, stained the area around bones that were relatively intact. Some spots near the edges, where the fire hadn't been as hot, still had minute remnants of flesh. Ashes and embers circled the pig remains close to the pavers.

Maybe if they allowed more time for it to cool down, the central section with the bones might be closer to the crime scene photos that the Avalon Police Department had taken in the days after Selene's disappearance. *But is it close enough?* Jackson wondered.

"It's not similar, is it?" Rhea said, dejection obvious in every line of her body. Her shoulders drooped, and deep frown lines were etched beside her lips. The blue of her gaze was dark, like the lake waters during a storm.

He eased his arm around her shoulders and tucked her close. "Let me get the embers back in place, add another pile of logs and then let the fire die out naturally. We'll come back later to check it out and, if that doesn't do it, we move on, right?"

She nodded and, in a tiny, hardly audible voice, she said, "We move on. I'll get you another drink."

Rushing away, he watched her go, aware she was barely holding it together. He quickly returned to work, piling the glowing embers back into the center of the pit. He added another mound of logs and hoped that by doing so the end result might support continuing their investigation of Matt because the other alternative…

Rhea didn't want to believe that Selene had killed herself. He found it hard to believe, as well, but no one knew why someone would choose such an end. Why they didn't ask for help and kept it bottled up until the emotions were just too much to handle.

The sound of a footfall drew his attention, but it wasn't Rhea. It was Declan, with another tall glass of icy lemonade and deep furrows across his brow.

"Your…friend is… Maybe it's time you guys went home. Took a break. I can finish up here," he said with a flip of his hand in the direction of the fire.

Jackson hated to leave their experiment unfinished. But as he looked at Declan's face, his friend was obviously as worried about Rhea as he was. "Do you mind us leaving it here until later?"

"Until tomorrow, Jax. You need to take a break. A long one," he said and clapped him on the back, gently this time.

In truth, whether later or tomorrow it wouldn't matter. Not to mention that the ache he'd been feeling off and on in his back all day was blossoming into major pain. "Tomorrow," he said and followed his friend into the restaurant where Rhea was sitting in one of the booths.

The lunchtime crowd had died down, and Declan's staff was getting ready for the dinner rush.

He eased into the booth across from her and their knees bumped beneath the table. He laid a hand on her knee. Squeezed reassuringly. "How about we head home?"

She nodded, but remained silent, her face flat. Shoulders still fallen.

Declan hurried over and laid a pizza box on the table. At Jackson's questioning look, his friend shrugged and said, "Figured you might not want to cook dinner."

Jackson rose and bro-hugged his friend hard. "Thanks for everything, Deck."

His friend dipped his head in Rhea's direction, urging Jackson into action.

Jackson held his hand out, and she slipped her hand into his, but peeled away for a moment to hug Declan. "Thank you. We really appreciate all that you've done."

"Anything for friends," Declan said as he embraced her.

"Let's go," Jackson said, and Rhea seemed only too eager to leave. He understood. Their experiment was leading them on a path to other scenarios.

One of which included Selene's suicide.

Normally he'd be relieved when he eliminated one scenario during an investigation and moved closer to solving a case.

He felt no such relief today.

The short ride to his home was quiet, but Rhea's disappointment was almost palpable. In just two short days, they'd eliminated the idea that Matt had disposed of Selene's body at his client's location and probably the possibility that he'd cremated her in his firepit.

But that didn't eliminate Matt or their other scenarios, including the one where Selene was still alive.

"Matt could still be a suspect," he said, but as they pulled past the police cruiser stationed in his driveway, instinct said something was wrong.

"Stay here," he said and opened his door while unclipping the thumb strap on his holster. As he did so, the smell of smoke drew his immediate attention. A slight breeze carried smoke from beyond his home.

He leaned down and drew his backup Glock from his ankle holster. Bending, he held it out to Rhea and said, "Do you know how to use this?"

Rhea took the gun from him and pushed the button to remove the magazine and check it before slipping it back in. "I've got it."

"Good. Stay put."

Rhea eased the safety off the Glock and watched as Jackson walked toward the police cruiser. When he got there, he immediately acted, reaching in for the radio and calling for an ambulance.

The hackles rose on the back of her neck, and she hoped the officer wasn't badly injured.

She searched the area in front of the home, but the fading light of dusk and the tree line around the home created too many shadows. But her gaze caught on a brighter swirl of white above the home. Smoke.

No, not Jax's home, she thought and opened the door. The smell of smoke was impossible to miss now and, as Jackson rushed around the edge of his home, gun drawn, Rhea couldn't just sit there doing nothing.

Ignoring Jackson's instructions, she dashed from the cruiser, gun in hand. Following the path Jackson had taken, she ran into him as he stood on his deck, pulling a garden hose from a reel. He ran with it toward the shed. Licks of flame were just beginning to escape from a broken window at the front of the structure.

Jackson turned the hose on the shed, trying to keep the fire tamed. He had holstered his gun and was radioing with his free hand. She walked over and took the hose from him, and he mouthed a "Thank you." With his hands free, he drew his weapon again and finished calling for the fire department since the garden hose was barely keeping the flames at bay. If they spread to the deck or to the pines behind…

She didn't want to think about the fire destroying Jackson's home because of her. *Because of me.*

Keeping the hose aimed on the flames, she also kept her eyes and ears open for signs of anything out of the ordinary. Like the scream of sirens approaching and the lights flashing through nearby woods. Reds and blues escaped through the underbrush and tree branches as police cars, an ambulance and a fire truck raced up the road.

The crunch of gravel and pounding footsteps signaled that help was on the way. Jackson joined her a second later and said, "Whoever did this is long gone."

"I'm sorry, Jax. How is the officer?"

"Awake. He thought he heard a noise, opened his window to investigate and got cold-cocked. EMT is with him, and it seems like he'll be okay," Jackson explained and held his hand out for his backup weapon.

She returned it, and he strapped it back into his ankle holster. As he did so, he asked, "How did you know how to use the Glock?"

"Dad was a cop. He taught us how to safely handle a weapon," she explained and began to hose down the edges of his deck as the heat of the shed fire warned it was in danger.

Luckily, a crew of firefighters dragged a fire hose from the front of the house and turned a burst of water on the shed, beating back the flames. But the fire had done major damage to the structure, and it collapsed with a loud crash, sending embers flying all around.

The firefighters moved closer to douse the burning remnants, as well as the area all around, to avoid the spread of the fire.

Rhea stood there, more worried about Jackson losing his home than the likelihood the fire had been set because of her. Jackson came up behind her, wrapped an arm around her upper body and drew her against his chest. She went willingly, the comfort and security of his arms welcome.

The firefighters shut off the water and walked over to inspect the remnants of the shed. One of them shook his head, tipped his hat back and walked to where they stood. He glanced at Jackson and said, "Can't say for certain yet, but I think an accelerant was used."

"I kept gasoline in there for the chain saw and mower," Jackson advised.

The firefighter took a look back toward the shed and nodded. "Probably used that, since it was handy. We'll know more once the arson investigator has his look at it."

"Thanks, Max. You guys did an amazing job," Jackson said and leaned over to shake the man's hand.

"Appreciate it, Jax. Sorry this happened to you," he said and shot a look at Rhea, as if wondering if she was the cause. Rousing her guilt again about what had happened.

Jackson and she followed them to the driveway, where the EMTs were pulling away and Jackson's colleague was standing by his car, chatting to the police chief.

"Stay here and, this time, do it," Jackson said and reinforced his instruction with a slash of his hand.

Since the chief shot her a look that was both annoyed and concerned, she decided to stay put as Jackson had instructed.

Jackson spoke to his injured colleague and the police chief in hushed tones, making it impossible for her to overhear what was being said. The chief waved to officers standing by another cruiser, who joined them as discussion resumed.

Not long after, the injured officer got into his car and pulled away, and the police chief did the same, leaving the one cruiser with the duo of officers. Jackson spoke to them for another few minutes. With a series of handshakes and some backslapping, the conversation ended, and Jackson returned to her side.

"Are we good?" she asked, wondering at what they'd planned.

"We're good. They'll stay all night and run hourly checks on the grounds," Jackson advised and opened the door on his cruiser to remove the pizza Declan had given them.

At her questioning gaze, he said, "Dinner. A man's got to eat."

Despite his comment, he handed her the pizza box at the front door and said, "First, a quick check through the house, although I doubt whoever did it is in here."

"Why?" she wondered aloud.

"If they really wanted to do damage they'd have torched the house. The shed was intended to be a warning," he said and, once again, drew his weapon.

He didn't need to say the words. His warning glance rooted her to a spot by the door, pizza box in hand.

She waited, patiently, as Jackson did a sweep of his living room, dining room and kitchen, and then went up the stairs. Long anxious moments later he came bounding down the stairs, his gun holstered once more.

"All clear," he said and took the pizza from her. But as they entered the house, the smell of smoke on them was powerful.

She wrinkled her nose and said, "I think I'd like to shower and change."

Jackson sniffed the air, as well, and said, "Me, too. I'll get this in the oven while we shower."

"Thanks," she said and rushed up the stairs and through her shower.

She beat Jackson to the kitchen, scrounged through his refrigerator to make a salad and set place mats and cutlery on the breakfast bar, trying to stay busy. Keeping busy was definitely a way to keep from thinking about the fact that someone was trying to stop their investigation.

Was Matt that desperate? she wondered, but didn't have time to dwell on it too much as Jackson came into the kitchen in a T-shirt and sweats. The T-shirt hugged hard muscle, and the sweats hung loose on his lean hips. Her brain went somewhere dangerous, especially as he came by to snag a piece of lettuce from the salad and brushed against her.

He smelled of soap and man. All man, but she had to contain that awareness of him. It was just too dangerous, too distracting, considering all that was happening. But try as she might, it was impossible to ignore his presence. Powerful. Comforting. Tempting in a way that no man had ever tempted before.

And surprisingly, despite all that had happened that day, hunger awoke as Jackson pulled the pizza from the oven. He cut the slices with a big knife, his movements competent. Almost elegant, which made her itch to sketch him. She'd been so crazed in the last couple of days she hadn't even touched her sketch pad, but maybe she'd try tonight.

If Jackson would model for her, that was.

Working together as if they were an old married couple used to routines, she served the salad and he brought over the pizza and sodas. A glass of wine might have been nice, but they had to stay alert, not to mention that a little wine might make him even more dangerous to her control.

The pizza was delicious and unusual. "I've never had grilled pizza with barbecued chicken before."

"It's one of Deck's specialties. People love that he turns things on their heads," Jackson said and stuffed the last bit of crust into his mouth.

"He's been great. Please thank him for me," she said, grateful for all that Declan had done.

Jackson leaned back in his chair and focused his gaze on her, his eyes locked on her face. "Your dad was a police officer?"

She nodded and nibbled at the pizza crust. "He was. My mother was a music teacher, like Selene."

Jackson dished out the last two slices onto their plates and said, "I guess that explains the information you gave me. It was as neat and complete as any case file I've ever read."

"Dad was a stickler for being orderly and for doing the right thing," she said with a lift of her shoulders.

"That also explains why you're so determined to make things right for Selene," he said, grabbed his slice and took a big bite.

Although she picked up her own slice, she held it before her, unsure how to answer without having him worry. But he'd been nothing but honest with her, even admitting that assisting her might cost him the position as chief. So she charged on. "The only thing that would make things right is to have Selene home again, Jax. That's what I want more than anything."

Jackson set down his slice and this time when he gazed at her, the gray of his eyes was almost charcoal with worry. "I know you want that—"

She raised her hand in pleading. "Let's just leave it at that. Please."

He did as she asked, finishing the rest of his slice in silence while she nibbled at hers.

They washed dishes much the same way, standing side by side in silence, Jackson washing and Rhea drying. When they were done, Jackson leaned against the counter. "It's not that late. What would you like to do?"

It came out of her mouth before she could stop it. "I'd like to sketch you."

Chapter Thirteen

Jackson lifted a brow. "Sketch me?"

She mimicked drawing on paper with her hands. "It helps me relax."

It might help her relax, but being the object of her attention would do little for his peace of mind. Still, it had been a challenging day for her, far more than for him, so if it would help her, he'd suffer it.

"If it'll help." He pointed toward his living room. "Mind if I start a fire?" he said, even though between the bonfire and the shed destruction he'd almost had enough of flames and wood smoke. But, as night had fallen, a chill had settled in the air and in him.

One of her dark brows flew upward, as if questioning his sanity, but seeing that he was serious, she acquiesced with a tilt of her head. "I'll get my sketch pad and pencils."

She rushed out and, if Jackson was reading her right, she was anything but relaxed. Despite that, he intended to go along with her request, no matter how dangerous it might be to his self-control.

He marched to the living room, determined to get this over with as quickly as possible. Since he always kept the fireplace ready, it took little time for the tinder to catch and spread flames to the logs neatly stacked above it. Much like Rhea's dad, he was also a stickler for being orderly and doing the right thing. Which meant, no matter how tempting Rhea might be, he had to control himself.

At the wall of windows facing the deck, he hit a switch to engage the privacy blinds built into the panels. He didn't normally use them, preferring to see the woods and stars beyond, but the last thing he wanted was for a colleague doing his rounds to see him modeling for Rhea. He'd never live it down with his friends at the station.

She returned to the living room with her sketch pad and pencils, and took a spot in a chair directly opposite his big leather couch. "Would you mind stretching out there?" she asked, peering at the couch.

He stretched out there often after a hard day at work, the fireplace lit and the television turned on to one of the fix-it channels or a baseball game. But doing so for her…

Sucking in a breath, he lay down and spread out on the couch, his toes touching one arm while he tucked a pillow against the other arm and set his head down on it.

Half-facing her, he tried to inject comfort into his voice as he said, "Here I am. Draw away."

A half smile, the smile of a siren luring men, graced her lips while she flipped open the pad and grabbed a pencil. "Would you mind…?" She didn't finish, only did a little wiggle of her finger that communicated her wishes.

Despite being filled with trepidation, he pulled off his T-shirt. She rose and shut off the light on the table beside him, leaving only the firelight for illumination. It created intimacy in the room. Maybe too intimate since desire seemed to catch and flare like the tinder and logs in his fireplace.

Instead of returning to her chair, she sat on the edge of the coffee table and skimmed her hand over his shoulder to adjust the position of his body. But her touch changed as she ran her hand along the muscles on his arm and down his side, getting lighter. Even hesitant, but it did nothing to quell the passion rising within him.

He grabbed her hand to stop her, but found himself twining his fingers with hers and drawing her close. "I thought you wanted to sketch me?"

With a big swallow, she said, "I did. I do."

"The wisest thing would be for you to sit back in that chair and draw," he said, his voice husky to his ears from the strain of not pulling her close.

A light huff escaped her before that siren's smile drifted across her lips again. "That would be the right thing to do. So would this."

She leaned down and covered his mouth with hers, her lips mobile against him. Wet. Warm, so warm.

He cradled the back of her head to keep her near as they kissed over and over until they were both breathless. And while he wanted to urge her down beside him on the couch, he mustered his last bit of self-control.

Sweeping his hand around to cradle her jaw, he applied gentle pressure to shift her away. He locked his gaze on hers, a turbulent navy blue with desire. "I want this… I want you."

She nodded, clearly understanding where he was going. "You do the right thing. *We* do the right thing."

Clapping her hands on her thighs, she shot to her feet and sat across from him. She snatched her sketch pad from where she'd laid it earlier, picked up her pencils, crossed her legs and leaned the pad on her knee.

Rhea worked furiously at first, pencil scratching against the paper as the initial lines of the drawing took shape. The rough shape of the sofa. The long lines of his strong body, lying there with tension in every muscle. The power nestled in the shadows between his thighs…

"Relax," she said and inhaled deeply to do the same, slowing the stroke and pressure of her pencil to add dimension to the drawing. She normally did landscapes and still lifes, rarely portraits, but she was pleased by the image slowly coming alive on paper.

"You look…pleased," he said, a sexy huskiness in his tone.

She was and flipped the pad so he could view the drawing.

He raised an eyebrow. "Is that how you see me?"

She turned the pad around and examined her work. The man in her sketch was passion personified, his gaze heavy-lidded. A sexy smile on his lips that promised the pleasure she had experienced barely minutes earlier.

"Yes," she answered without hesitation.

He shifted to sit, fingers laced together, forearms leaning on his muscled thighs. His features were troubled, his brow furrowed and his gaze nearly black. "I think it's time for me to do another walk around the property and check in with my colleagues."

Without waiting for her response, he grabbed his T-shirt and jerked it on. Pushed to his feet and marched off. After the snick of the front door opening and closing, Rhea leaned back in her chair and sighed.

What am I doing? It was crazy to get involved with Jackson, and not just now, when all their focus and attention had to be on the case. She had her life in Denver that she loved. The gallery, her apartment and the vibrant city life. But she couldn't deny that despite Selene's disappearance in Regina, the town called to her with its beautiful downtown, homes and the surrounding countryside. And, of course, Jackson. She wanted to explore what she was feeling for Jackson, both emotionally and physically.

And he clearly felt the same.

He wanted her and she him, but it would have to wait.

She collected her drawing supplies, determined to avoid Jackson. Determined not to crawl into bed with him. This time it wouldn't be because she was afraid or needed comfort. When she did join him the next time…

Driving that image from her brain, she bounded up the stairs and to her room. As she did so, she heard the front door open and close again, as well as the grate of the lock. Glancing toward the stairs, she caught sight of Jackson and closed her door. It was the coward's way out, but she didn't trust herself not to give in to what she wanted.

Jackson.

Leaning against the door, she took a bracing breath and listened for his footsteps as they came near and stopped by her room. A long pregnant pause followed, but then the footsteps moved away, down the hall to Jackson's bedroom.

The breath rushed out of her. Arms wrapped around her sketch pad, she walked to the bed and quickly changed into her pajamas. As she slipped into bed, she took hold of her sketch pad and opened it to the drawing of Jackson. Ran her fingers over it, imagining it was his skin beneath her hand, but not tonight.

Closing the pad, she grabbed her tablet, too wired to go to sleep.

With a few quick strokes, she was in Jackson's digital notebook. As she did, the program notified her that Jackson was likewise reviewing the information, and she shook her head.

In some ways, we're too alike, she thought and gave herself over to considering the evidence. Again.

THE LITTLE ICON at the top of the menu indicated that Rhea was likewise logged on to the notebook with the case file.

It seemed almost silly that they were both working on the materials separately, yards apart, but Jackson understood. Being together right now was too dangerous.

With the evidence they'd gathered in the last few days, it pointed to the possibility that Selene's death may have happened in Regina and not Avalon. He opened the file with the information that detailed the witness accounts of Selene's visit to the lake and the possible presence of a second vehicle.

First, he reviewed the approximate times against the spillway activity logs Rhea had obtained. The spillway had opened for a short stretch of time early that night, but even with adjustments for possible witness error as to the time Selene had been at the lake, the spillway had likely been closed when Selene had been killed.

If she'd been killed, the little voice in his head challenged.

Despite that being one of the possible scenarios, it just didn't seem plausible. If she had run away from Matt, Jackson had no doubt she would have run to her sister.

And then there was the text she'd sent.

I can't take it anymore. I can't. I'm finally going to do something about it.

What had that "something" been? he wondered. Had it been ending her life? If it had, the timing of that text would put her by the lake. Wouldn't she just have walked into the lake to take her life? Especially since her purse and cell phone had been sitting in her car, supporting that supposition. And if so, they were back to the fact that her body should have been found in the days after her disappearance.

He and his colleagues had searched the lake and surrounding shores with a fine-tooth comb and had not found her nor any evidence of her.

Blowing out a frustrated sigh, he opened his nightstand and pulled out the pad and pen he kept there because he often got ideas about cases at the oddest times.

He switched to the page in the notebook with information on the timeline for Selene's trip from Avalon to Regina. Setting aside the laptop, he took the notes and transferred them to his pad of paper, confirming what they had discussed before, namely, that Selene had spent way more time on the road between leaving Avalon and arriving at the lake in Regina.

Since he was well familiar with the route, he listed a few places Selene might have stopped that night. Since Selene had rushed off according to Matt, she might not have been prepared for a trip to Denver. That possibly meant a stop for gas.

There were two different gas stations near Regina to check in the morning.

She might have also been hungry or thirsty. Maybe tired and needing a pick-me-up, like a cup of coffee. There was a general store and coffee shop right off the highway, as well as two different restaurants on the street leading to the lake.

He jotted down those names and, for good measure, grabbed his laptop and searched the route using one of the online mapping services. That had him adding a chain pharmacy location, as well as a local pub. It was the kind of place a single woman might go for a quick hookup, but Selene would not have known that. She also would not have known that on occasion a rougher crowd frequented the location.

A chirp on his phone alerted him to a message.

She had to have stopped somewhere along the route to the lake. Maybe the coffee shop. She's a caffeine fiend.

He texted back, I agree. I made a list of spots we can check in the morning.

A long pause followed before she texted, Thank you. I appreciate all that you're doing.

He wanted to say that it was his job, but it had become more than that to him. *She* had become more to him.

Fingers over his phone screen, he hesitated, but then finally wrote, We will find out what happened. Together.

Breath held, he waited for her response and smiled when it came.

Together. Good night, Jax.

Good night, Rhea.

Chapter Fourteen

Morning came way too quickly.

Jackson woke just as the first rose-and-purple fingers of dawn were clawing their way into the sky. He dressed in his uniform, strapped on his service belt and chatted with the two officers in the cruiser.

"Nothing happening, Detective," said the one young officer.

"Thanks, Officer Troutman. I'm going to take a walk around the property, just in case."

He reconnoitered the grounds, but everything was in order, except of course for the burned shed, including the charred remains of his favorite chain saw and ax.

When he went back inside, Rhea was also dressed and putting up a pot of coffee.

"Good morning, Jax," she said, glancing over her shoulder at him.

He walked to her and laid a hand at her waist, urging her around. "Everything okay with us?"

She peered up at him, her blue gaze skimming over his face, as powerful as a caress. "We're…okay." With a flip of her hand in the direction of the stove, she said, "I was just going to make breakfast before we checked out some of those stops."

"One of the places, the general store, has a 24-hour cafeteria. Since you're up, how about we get breakfast there? The food is really good."

"That sounds great. We could also poke around. See if anyone remembers seeing Selene," she said and went to leave, but he tightened his hold at her waist to keep her close.

"Don't get your hopes up. Luckily, we'll have that cell phone information I requested later today. That should help us pinpoint Selene's and Matt's whereabouts on that night."

"I get it, Jax. Don't get disappointed that nothing we've done so far has helped us know more about what happened to my sister. I get it," she said, the threat of tears obvious in her voice and eyes, which shimmered with angry tears.

He wasn't going to push anymore. "I'll wait for you outside." He eased his grip, and she raced away to get her purse.

He went out to his cruiser to wait for her. When she approached, he held the door open and waited until she was settled to get behind the wheel for the drive to the general store.

Rhea tried to stay patient as Jackson drove, even though her insides were as turbulent as water boiling for tea. She hadn't meant to sound condemning but knew it had come out that way. But it wasn't Jackson's fault that they hadn't made any progress on the case. Well, not unless you counted ruling out scenarios as making progress.

But she was sure of one thing: If Matt had killed Selene, he hadn't taken her back to Avalon. Everything at the ridge construction site and the bonfire seemed to point to that. But everything inside of her continued to say that Selene was still alive. Rhea still felt her presence strongly and maybe in the next few days they would get the evidence needed to prove that.

The general store was on the road immediately adjacent

to the highway. If Selene had taken the exit for Regina, she would have driven down that road on her way to the lake.

Much like everything else in Regina, the general store was a quaint throwback to earlier times. Way earlier times, like the 1800s. It had that old Western feel to it with a retail area where you could buy an assortment of items. Right beside the retail section was the restaurant area, complete with waitresses in neat candy-striped aprons that screamed 1950s instead of 1850s. Both areas were neat, clean and busier than she had expected at such an early hour.

As soon as they walked into the restaurant, one of the waitresses, a pretty twentysomething with dark brown hair, doe eyes and a brilliant smile hurried over to greet them. Well, greet Jackson.

"Nice to see you again, Jackson," she said and literally batted her eyelash extensions at him while barely flicking a glance in Rhea's direction.

"Nice to see you, too, Melissa. Table for two please," he said and smiled at Rhea. For good measure, he laid a possessive arm around her waist.

Melissa's smile immediately faded as she stared at Rhea and at Jackson's gesture.

"Right this way," Melissa said and, with jerky motions, pulled menus from a nearby holder.

They followed the young woman to a booth. After handing them the menus, Melissa rushed off with a muttered, "I'll get you some coffees."

Rhea stared after the waitress and raised an eyebrow. "Old flame?"

"Unwanted crush," he answered without hesitation and buried his head in the menu.

As handsome as Jackson was, she suspected he was the object of quite a lot of crushes, including her she had to admit. Although it was well past the crush phase and into the "What do we call this now?" point in a relationship.

To distract herself from where those thoughts would go, she perused the menu, which reminded her of one from a diner she had visited during a trip to New York City. There were dozens of menu choices, from a variety of omelets, pancakes and waffles to assorted breakfast wraps. Maybe too many choices, but Jackson had said the food was good here.

The noisy clatter of china and cutlery heralded Melissa's return as she set their cutlery and coffees down before them. She whipped out a pad and pen. "What can I get you?"

"Cream. Sugar. Huevos Rancheros, please," Rhea said and handed the menu to the waitress.

"Rocky Mountain wrap for me. Thanks, Melissa," Jackson said and likewise returned the menu. Before she could walk away, Jackson said, "Do you ever work the nighttime shift?"

She shook her head. "Going to night school, so I'm always on either the morning or afternoon shift." She jerked her head in the direction of another of the waitresses. "Judy over there sometimes works late night."

"Would you mind asking her to come over?" Jackson said and offered up a smile that seemed to restore some friendliness to the waitress.

"Sure thing, Jax. Anything for you," she said, stevia-sweet, but with a frown in Rhea's direction.

She sped away to place their orders and talk to another waitress, who was just hanging up her apron behind the counter. The older woman glanced in their direction, but seeing that it was Jackson, smiled and waddled over. She was at least six or seven months pregnant.

When she approached, Jackson popped up from his seat and offered it to her, but she waved him off. "If I sit down, I may never get up again," she said with a tired laugh, laid a hand at her waist and stretched.

Jackson chuckled and slipped back into the booth. He reached into his shirt pocket and pulled out a photo of Selene, which jerked a puzzled look to Judy's face. The pregnant waitress looked from the photo to Rhea and back to the photo. Rhea explained.

"She's my twin sister. She disappeared six months ago."

Judy nodded. "I remember. Her photo was all over the papers and on the news."

"Were you working that night?" Jackson asked.

Judy nodded. "I normally work those late shifts. Lets me be home for the kids during the day. She wasn't in any night that I was working."

"You sure?" Jackson pressed and slipped the photo back into his shirt pocket.

Judy tightened her lips and wagged her head. "Very sure. We don't get that many people late at night during the fall months. More in the summer and winter. If I'd seen her, I would have contacted you back then."

"Thanks, Judy," he said.

Rhea parroted his words. "Thank you. We appreciate it, and good luck with the new baby."

"Thank you, and hang in there. You're in good hands," Judy said with an incline of her head in Jackson's direction.

"I know," she said as Judy waddled out of the restaurant.

At that moment, Melissa returned with their orders, and Rhea understood why Jackson's dish had been called the Rocky Mountain wrap. The wrap was huge and piled high with french fries, gravy and cheese. Not that her eggs were much smaller. A big pile of scrambled eggs were topped with fresh salsa and cotija cheese, and the smells…

Her stomach rumbled from the aromas of spice, fresh cilantro and the earthiness of the coffee.

"These are gut busters," she said, but dug into her eggs.

"Perfect," Jackson said with a wink and likewise forked

up some of his wrap because it was way too big to eat with his hands.

Hunger tamped down any discussion for several minutes, but Rhea realized she'd never be able to finish. There was way too much food, no matter how tasty it was.

Jackson seemed to have no such problem as he continued chowing down. She hated to interrupt his enjoyment of the meal, but after Judy's comments, she'd been wondering where else Selene might have stopped the night she disappeared.

"My sister loves her coffee. If she was in a hurry, but tired, she might have stopped for a shot of caffeine to keep her going."

Jackson nodded. "It is another hour and a half to Denver, so that makes sense. We'll try the coffee shop next while we wait for the cell phone location information."

Rhea leaned back into the booth cushion and rubbed her belly, which she was sure was at least an inch bigger thanks to the delicious breakfast. "I feel like I need a nap and we just woke up," she said with a laugh.

Jackson grinned and chuckled. "I know what you mean, but I can't say no to the Rocky Mountain wrap," he said and kept on eating while she sat there, watching him and thinking about where else her sister may have stopped.

If Matt had attacked Selene, had she had fought back? If she had done that, had she been hurt? Had she stopped at an urgent care facility or a pharmacy for some supplies? Rhea wondered. All places for them to check, and she knew Jackson had placed the big chain pharmacy on his list. She felt confident that Jackson had things under control. That she was in good hands, as Judy had said.

And such nice hands, she thought, as he laid down his knife and fork when he finished his meal. She was a sucker for hands, and she had to admit that his touch, so comforting and strong, stirred intense emotions within her.

He raised his hand and signaled for Melissa to bring over the check.

"Let me," Rhea said, and Jackson was about to argue with her, but apparently seeing her determination, he demurred.

"Thanks, Rhea," he said and laid his hand over hers.

Comforting and strong, she thought again and took hold of his hand. "I should be thanking you for offering your time. Your home. Your protection."

JACKSON WANTED TO say again that it was his job, but that would be a massive lie. It had become so much more than that. But he had to maintain his objectivity, which had slipped more than once in the last few days. Because of that, he tried to adopt a neutral and professional tone as he said, "It's what I had to do to help solve this case."

Her hand jerked in his, obviously stung by his words and tone. She awkwardly drew her hand away and hid it beneath the tabletop. When Melissa brought over the check, Rhea barely glanced at it before placing her credit card on the plastic tray. Melissa swept by and snatched it off the table, clearly still in a huff.

Great, two women pissed at me, he thought. His cell phone vibrated and chirped in his pants pocket, and he drew it out to see a message from the desk sergeant.

Just emailed you info from cell phone company.

He texted back, Great. Thanks.

He swiped to open his email and smiled at the data the cell phone company had provided. Not only was there a spreadsheet for the week Selene had disappeared, the company had assigned one of their engineers to interpret the data.

Rhea was tucking her credit card back in her wallet

when he said, "We have the info. I suggest we head to the police station to review it."

"That's good news," she said and slipped out of the booth.

He followed Rhea to his cruiser. It took only a few minutes to reach the police station and settle themselves in the conference room. With a few commands, Jackson had the spreadsheet and analysis on a large monitor.

His police chief strolled by the room, then backtracked to enter. The older man gestured to the information. "Is that the cell phone data?"

Jackson nodded. "It is, and we also have a report that pinpoints where Selene and Matt were that week."

With the laser pointer and mouse, Jackson reviewed the data and maps with Rhea and his boss. The information confirmed exactly when Selene had left Avalon, but more importantly, where she had stopped that night. The tracking continued after Selene's message to Rhea, but since the cell phone had been left behind in the car, it told them little about what had happened after the text.

Still, the data showed that there had certainly been enough time for Matt to follow Selene and then return to Avalon.

"The Avalon police didn't ask for Matt's cell phone info because he supposedly forgot it at home that night," he said, recalling the information they'd provided from their case file. He pulled up the report on Matt, which confirmed that his phone had been in Avalon the entire night.

"Too convenient," Rhea said, and the police chief echoed her comment.

"The kind of thing someone does if they don't want to be tracked," he said.

"But his Jeep has a navigation system," Rhea reminded them, only Jackson shook his head.

"Most NAV systems use a positioning system that's

only a one-way stream of data. But if he has something with a cellular connection, that provider might have that info. It's something we'll have to investigate further if this info doesn't pan out," he said and went back to the data on the screen.

"It looks like Selene stopped for gas right before she got to Regina," he said.

"Just like we thought, since she left her house in a rush," Rhea said, recalling their conversation of the day before.

"That's our next stop. We'll see who was working that night and reach out to them." Jackson moved on to the next stop that the cell phone company engineer had identified.

"She was at the pub for a good half an hour. Probably to get dinner," Jackson said and frowned. "Not the best place for a woman alone."

"Not unless she's looking for a hookup. That is what you call it now, right?" the police chief said and glanced toward Rhea. "Sorry, ma'am. No offense intended."

"None taken, but Selene isn't that kind of woman. It makes me wonder why she would have stopped there."

The police chief snapped his fingers and screwed his eyes upward, as if searching for something at the tip of his memory. "Isn't the guy who owns that gas station buddies with the pub owners?"

Jackson searched his memory. "I think you're right, Bill. They may even be related. Cousins, I think."

"If the cousin was working he might suggest the pub if someone asks for a recommendation," Rhea added to the discussion.

"Or he may tell his employees to suggest the pub," the chief said. With a smile and a point of his finger at Jackson, he added, "Good work, Jax. Just remember what we discussed."

With that, the chief pivoted and marched out of the room,

leaving Rhea with a puzzled look on her face. Her eyes narrowed and settled on him, clearly expecting an explanation.

He hesitated, but Rhea deserved to know. "Nothing that embarrasses us or the Avalon PD."

"And what if it does that? Are you willing to bury the investigation—"

"Have I done anything that would make you think that?" he challenged, a wildfire of anger rushing through him.

Demurely, seemingly chastised, she said in a soft tone, "No. You haven't."

"I made you a promise and I intend to keep it, Rhea. If you don't trust me—"

"I do, Jax. I'm sorry that I suggested otherwise. It's just…emotional for me, and I can't be as objective as I should."

"Neither can I, Rhea. You make me feel…" He jammed his hands on his hips and sucked in a breath. "We've finally got a solid lead and we need to keep our focus on this." He circled the pub on the map with the laser pointer and then moved it to a location by the lake, the last spot on Selene's journey.

Subdued, head slightly bowed, Rhea said, "I guess we hit the road to talk to some people."

"We do. Are you ready?" The words seemed simple enough, but they were filled with many more questions. Was she ready to learn more about that night? Ready for possibly more disappointment?

So many questions, but at least now they had the data to continue to ask those questions. *Thanks to Rhea*, he thought.

She met his gaze directly, her chin tilted defiantly. A tight smile on her face. "I'm ready."

Chapter Fifteen

The gas station was a no-frills no-name location that survived due to a lack of competition. For anyone who had underestimated the distance to either Denver or any of the ski resorts to the west, the gas station was a last resort.

Jackson parked in front of the tiny market the station boasted. *A patron can pick up some sodas or snacks, in addition to the gasoline,* Rhea thought. The far side of the station housed several mechanic's bays. As they stepped out of the car, a large mountain of a man clothed in grease-stained overalls ambled out of one of the bays. He wiped his hands with a cloth that wasn't much cleaner and frowned as he saw Jackson.

"Detective," he said when he approached, but didn't hold his hand out. Instead, he held them up to show they were just too dirty for a handshake.

"Hannibal. Good to see you. How's it going?" Jackson asked, totally at ease despite the hostile vibes she was sensing from the man.

"Got work and customers, but I don't think you're here to talk about that," the man said. His voice was deep and with his longish brown hair and beard and large size, he reminded her of a bear, but not the cuddly type. The kind with sharp claws and teeth to tear you apart.

Jackson held his hands up as if in surrender. "Not here to create any problems. Just to ask a few questions."

Hannibal shrugged. "Ask away. I've got nothing to hide."

Which was just what she would expect someone to say if they did have something to hide.

"This is Rhea. Her twin sister, Selene, disappeared about six months ago, and we've got info that says she stopped here for gas," Jackson said.

A careless shrug of Hannibal's wide, thick shoulders was followed by, "I get lots of people stopping here for gas. I'd have remembered a looker like that." His stare in her direction, very much a leer, left Rhea feeling dirty.

"Watch it, Hannibal," Jackson warned. "Do you work the night shift?"

Hannibal shook his head. "Too old for that. Couple of local kids work the late shifts."

Jackson nodded. "What about the pub? Doesn't your brother own it?" he asked, puzzling Rhea, since she thought Jackson had said it was a cousin.

With another shake of his head and wipe of his hands with the dirty cloth, Hannibal said, "My cousin Drew, but he doesn't do that at the pub."

Do what? she wondered at the same time as Jackson asked the question.

"Girls. Slavery. That kind of stuff," Hannibal answered, sending a shiver of fear through Rhea. While she hoped Selene was still alive, the thought of her having been trafficked...

"If someone asked for a recommendation for a restaurant—" Jackson began, but Hannibal quickly cut him off.

"I'd recommend the pub. Tell my boys to do the same. Family sticks together."

Jackson paused, but then challenged Hannibal. "Does family stick together enough to hide a murder? Or a kidnapping?"

The other man obviously didn't like the insinuation. "We're done here, Detective. You want to talk to me or my boys again, call my lawyer." Without missing a beat, the man walked away and back to the mechanic's bay. A second later, the sound of metal striking metal told them he was back at work.

Jackson peered at her. "Time to hit the pub."

THE OUTSIDE OF the pub was not quite what she expected for a place of supposedly ill repute. The parking lot and grounds surrounding the building were clean and the landscaping welcomed with colorful flowers and neat bushes. The cedar shake siding, trim and doors had a fresh coat of paint.

When they entered there were very few patrons, but a couple of people were eating a late breakfast. The biggest feature in the space was a large horseshoe bar that separated the dining area from a section boasting cocktail-height tables, a dance floor and an upraised stage.

The place smelled faintly of yeasty beer, fried eggs and bacon, with a lingering hint of disinfectant, as if the floors and other areas had just been cleaned.

They had no sooner entered when a thirtysomething bearded man approached, a broad smile on his face. He stuck his hand out to Jackson and said, "Jax, dude, how are you doing?"

Jackson took the man's hand and pulled him in for a bro hug. "Marcus. What are you doing here?"

As the man stepped back from the embrace, he eyeballed Rhea and Jackson, as if to trying to figure out what they were doing together. "And you're…?"

She offered her hand to the man, and he shook it, politely and almost gently. "Rhea Reilly. Jackson and I are investigating my sister's disappearance."

Marcus lost a little of his earlier effusiveness and dipped

his head respectfully. "Sorry to hear about that, but what brings you here?"

"We have some questions, Marcus. Is there some-where—" Jackson peered all around the restaurant to see who might be listening "—more private."

Marcus nodded and swung his arm wide. "My office."

Marcus led the way, with Jackson and her following. As they walked, Jackson said, "Your office? You're work-ing here?"

Marcus looked over his shoulder and shrugged. "After those fights you busted up last summer, the owner decided he needed to restore some law and order, so here I am."

Jackson explained for her. "Marcus used to be on the Regina police force, but decided to retire."

They had reached the door to a back office, and Marcus unlocked it. They followed him down a hall past storage areas and a kitchen to an office at the farthest end of the hall. As he sat and invited them to join him, Marcus said, "Let's be honest, Jax. I had an alcohol problem, but thanks to you I've been sober for over a year and I have a new chance at life. I've been the manager since last September."

"I'm glad to hear that, but isn't it hard for you to work here?" Jackson asked and held his hands wide in emphasis.

A quick, tense shrug answered him. "Not easy at times, but this was a great opportunity, and it's been working as you may have noticed."

Jackson nodded. "Haven't been called out here for any-thing major."

"Good. Let's hope it stays that way. So how can I help you with your investigation?" Marcus leaned back in his chair, which creaked with the motion.

Jackson glanced at her, and she understood. "My sister may have been here the night she disappeared. We're try-ing to figure out if she met anyone that night."

Marcus shared an uneasy glance with Jackson before

blurting out, "We get lots of women here, especially on the weekends. They come in for fun. Maybe meet someone."

"Selene, Rhea's sister, probably just stopped for dinner. She wasn't here for more than about forty minutes," Jackson said.

Marcus raised a brow as if to say it didn't take long for what most women in the pub wanted, but he was gentleman enough not to say it. "I don't know how we can help with more."

Rhea pointed out his door to another office where she had noticed a number of monitors flashing images. "You have security cameras. Do you keep recordings from those cameras?"

Marcus leaned forward to track where she was pointing. He nodded and leaned back again, totally casual. "We do, but we only hold them for about two weeks. Unless there's some kind of incident. Then we label and store them."

"Would you possibly have any from November of last year? November 7, actually?" Jackson said.

Marcus immediately answered. "No, sorry."

"Are you sure?" Rhea asked, worried they were going to hit another dead end.

Marcus nodded. "I am. The PC for the recording system died on us right around then. Tech said it was toast and took it away. Set up a new system."

"Is it possible he still has that failed system?" Jackson asked.

"Possible," Marcus said and pulled open his desk drawer. He scrounged around, yanked out a wrinkled business card and handed it to Jackson. "Here's his info. I'll let him know you're coming."

"We truly appreciate that, Marcus. Thank you," Rhea said, grateful that the man hadn't been an obstructionist, which was what she'd been expecting after their earlier meeting with the gas station owner.

"My pleasure. Like I said before, we're trying to clean this place up, so anything to support our local police department," Marcus said as he rose and held his hand out to Jackson again. "I mean that, dude. You saved my life."

Jackson clasped the other man's hand in both of his. "I'm glad to see you're doing well, Marcus. Just remember we're all here for you."

"You always were. If you don't mind, I've got some things to do before lunch," Marcus said and grimaced at the pile of papers on his desk.

"Totally get it and thanks again," Rhea said and hurried from the office to the restaurant, picturing Selene there. Wondering if someone had approached her. Someone who had decided to take her.

"Penny for your thoughts," Jackson said as they stepped outside and looked back at the pub. He smoothed a finger across the furrow in Rhea's forehead.

"Maybe something happened to her here. Someone who thought she was here for a hookup and decided to make that happen," Rhea said, worried that such an encounter may have turned into something violent.

"It's possible, Rhea. Although we've never had that kind of problem here," Jackson said.

Rhea crossed her arms and rubbed her hands up and down her arms. He hugged her close, offering comfort. Aware that, little by little, Rhea might be losing hope that Selene was still alive.

"Let's hit the road and see the tech."

The silence as they drove to the tech's offices weighed on him heavily, because Rhea was hurting. Luckily the office was just a block off Main Street and, as promised, Marcus had called ahead. The tech greeted them with no hesitation.

"Marcus says you want to look at their old system. I pulled it off the scrap pile for you." The tech walked to a large worktable in his back room. A computer tower sat there, a little dusty and worse for wear.

Jackson scrutinized it and then peered at the tech. "No chance of it working?"

The tech shook his head. "Tried, but there was a head crash. Head plinked around that disk like a marble in a pinball machine," he said and mimicked something bouncing around with his fingers. "That's why it was on the scrap pile. I keep the older units around in case I need power supplies, motherboards. That kind of thing."

"Mind if we take it?" Jackson said, earning a puzzled look from Rhea, and he explained, "My cousins in Miami are tech savants. Maybe they can get something off the unit."

"I'd be happy to pull the drive for you," the tech said and went into action, removing it from the system and packing it up.

"Good luck with it," the young man said and handed the box to Jackson.

"Thanks for all your help," Rhea offered, and Jackson echoed her sentiments.

"We appreciate the assistance."

Outside the tech's office, Jackson paused by his cruiser and whipped out his cell phone, wasting no time to call his cousins. Robert answered on the first ring. "Cuz, long time no hear," he said.

"Sorry, Robbie. I've just been a little busy. How are you and Sophie doing?"

"We're doing well. Let me put you on speaker," Robbie said and, a second later, the tone grew a little tinny as the speaker kicked in.

"I'm putting you on speaker also, Robbie. I have Rhea Reilly on the line with me. We're working on a case together."

"Hi, Robbie. Sophie," Rhea said.

"Nice to meet you," Sophie said. "What can we help you with?"

"You always cut to the chase, Sophie," Jackson teased and plowed on. "We have a hard drive with a head crash that may have information we need."

Robbie let out a low whistle. "Head crash is bad, man. That head hitting the disk probably took out some data."

"Some, but not all I gather," Jackson said, feeling optimistic that if anyone could get information from the disk it would be his cousins.

"Not all. Can you send it to us?" Sophie said.

"We can courier it to you for morning delivery," Jackson said, and his cousins clearly understood.

"We'll work on it immediately. Anything in particular?" Robbie asked.

"The hard drive was on a security system. We're looking for camera images from November 7. Anything from about 7:30 p.m. to 9:00 p.m.," he said.

"We're on it, Jax. If we can't get it for you, no one can," Sophie said.

"Thank you. It means a lot to me, since it may help us find out what happened to my sister," Rhea said.

"Family is important. Remember that, Jax," Robbie said, guilt heavy in his tone.

Miami was so not his style, but he understood. "I get it. When I have a vacation coming up I'll come visit my parents and swing by South Beach to see you."

"We'll hold you to that, Jax," Sophie said, and then the line went dead.

Rhea narrowed her eyes and glanced at him. "Somehow I can't picture you in South Beach."

Jackson sighed. "A little too city, hot and humid for me, but my parents have a place not far from there, and my uncle married into a Cuban family in Miami."

"And your cousins are there?" Rhea asked.

Jackson nodded. "Robbie and Sophie have their own tech company that develops apps and software, but my aunt's family has this high-powered private investigation and security company. The Liberty Agency. Robbie and Sophie often help them."

"I guess law enforcement runs in the family," Rhea said as Jackson opened the door to the cruiser.

Jackson slipped back into the driver's seat and, as he did so, he said, "And the military. Several of the members of the Gonzalez family that runs the Liberty Agency also served. Plus my Aunt Mercedes and Uncle Robert work for the NSA in D.C."

"Wow. Super-secret shadowy types," she teased.

He was about to start the car when a chirp announced he had a text message. With a quick look, he said, "Declan sent the photos of the bonfire." He held the phone so she could see the first photo. But as they swiped from one to the other, it was clear that the results of their experiment were not close to the crime scene photos of Matt's bonfire.

"There's a lot of dark residue and…bones," Rhea said with a frown.

Jackson nodded. "The experts pretty much told me to expect the residue from the body tissues."

With a rough breath, Rhea said, "I guess the cremation theory is out, isn't it?"

Jackson laid a hand on her shoulder and squeezed. "Tabled for now. Once we get this package off to my cousins, there's not much for us to do. Maybe review the materials again? Call Avalon PD for updates."

RHEA WASN'T SURE she could spend another night looking at the information and worrying about being disappointed or whether whoever was after her would try something else.

"I'd like to take the night off and return to Denver. Check in at my shop and maybe just get away from…everything," she said, and at his crestfallen face, she realized he'd interpreted it to include him. Speedily she added, "You're welcome to come with."

Peering at her, gray eyes squinted, awakening lines at the corners, he said, "It makes sense, because I want to make sure you're okay, but are you sure?"

She was and wasn't and hated that she couldn't figure out what she wanted with him. She punted and said, "You can use my guest room. Selene normally stays there."

He hesitated, but then nodded. "Let's get this package mailed and swing by my house to get our things."

"Sure," she said and sat there, anticipating what it would feel like to have him in her home. He was so big and masculine. Country. Her apartment was a lot like her. Artsy. Feminine. City.

In no time, they had run to the courier service and dropped off the hard drive, as well as made the trip to his house to pick up things for an overnight stay in Denver. Jackson also changed out of his police uniform into street clothes, and her heart did a little jump at the sight of him. The faded jeans hugged his powerful legs and trim waist. A pale blue button-down shirt brought out shards of blue in his gray eyes. But a loose denim jacket barely hid the bulge that told her he was wearing his holster and service weapon.

As they drove, she stayed silent, her thoughts bouncing around like the marble in the pinball game the tech had mentioned earlier.

She hadn't really expected to be staying in Jackson's home and the time spent there with him had provided her a whole new view of the detective she had nearly barreled over just a few days ago. He was a man who loved his family and obviously wanted one of his own, judging from the home he had built himself. He was honorable, even if it might cost him personally. And a leader, judging from the way Diego, Declan and even Marcus had assisted with the investigation. They clearly respected him, but he obviously cared about them, as well.

She was so lost in her thoughts that she hadn't realized they had entered the city limits until Jackson parked. They did the short walk to her building and she guided him toward the elevator at the back of the lobby. "I'm on the top floor."

Jackson took the time to appreciate Rhea's building. It was done in art deco style, with speckled black terrazzo floors and marbled walls. Sconces and other accents in shiny steel lightened all those dark colors as did the ornate wooden doors of the elevator.

As they stepped into the elevator, Rhea stuck a key into the panel to unlock the penthouse access and once they reached that floor, the elevator opened right into her home. A very feminine home filled with neutral-colored furniture with plush cushions and brightly colored accent pillows. The walls boasted an assortment of artwork, including some of Rhea's pieces. He recognized them immediately based on what he'd seen on her website. The paintings had that passion and life that jumped off the walls and called to him to take a closer look.

"Do you like?" she asked, hands clasped before her. A nervous seesaw from side to side while she waited for his opinion.

"I love it. You make the image come alive," he said and smiled. He turned and held his hands wide. "This is very nice. Full of life. Color."

"Thank you. It's taken some time to get it here, but I'm happy with it," she said and visibly relaxed, holding out a hand to him, which he took in his.

"I can see why. I know it's early, but how about a walk and dinner?" he said, splaying a hand across his stomach to hide the hunger grumble he felt building inside.

"I'd like that. One of my favorite places is just a few blocks away."

"I want to get to know what you like. How you live." She had intrigued him on multiple levels, from her determination and work on her sister's case, to her strength while in harm's way and the art on the walls that spoke of her passion for life. And, of course, the steel hidden beneath her delicate exterior that said she was the kind of woman he could have by his side. A woman who didn't wilt when faced with adversity.

"Great. I think you'll really like it." She tugged on his hand gently to steer him toward the door. He went willingly, eager for Rhea to have a distraction from her sister's case and the attacks against her, if only for the one night. Eager to get know more about her and how she lived.

Outside, they hurried away from the mall area and toward the Larimer Square historic district with its heritage buildings, eclectic shops and restaurants. With the warmer weather a number of the restaurants had created al fresco dining areas on the sidewalks. Edison lights had been strung overhead and across the street, creating a festive feel especially when combined with vibrant banners touting an upcoming music festival. Beneath trees boasting bright spring green leaves rested planters with vibrant blooms and small bushes that softened the urban feel of the buildings.

Rhea dragged him to the entrance to a steak place and, at his questioning look, she said, "I love a good piece of beef as much as you do."

He swung her arm playfully. "I'd tell you I'm vegan, but you already saw me chow down at Deck's."

"I did, and I hope you'll love this place also," she said, and with another tug, urged him into the restaurant.

The host at the podium, a youngish man in his late twenties, raised an eyebrow as Rhea came in with Jackson. The man swung around the podium to give her an effusive hug. "Rhea! So good to see you! And who's this?" he asked, shooting a warning glare in Jackson's direction.

With a playful shove, she pushed the host away. "Easy, Randy. This is Detective Whitaker. He's helping me with Selene's case."

Jackson shook the other's man hand and tried not to be too stung that Rhea hadn't said he was a friend. But then again, he wouldn't be too happy about being friend-zoned, either, since he wanted more from her.

"Your favorite table is free," Randy said, grabbed some menus and guided them to a spot right by the windows where they could have dinner and people watch, as well.

After they were seated, Jackson leaned close and over the top of his menu whispered, "If you and Randy—"

Rhea chuckled and skimmed her hand across his forearm. "He's just a friend. A friend who's probably way more interested in you than me."

Jackson peered at the man, who smiled at him.

"Oh, okay. I was worried he might think I was competition or something."

Rhea smiled, and it was the smile of a seductress. Her crystal blue gaze darkened and her voice was husky, sexy, as she said, "No one can compete with you, Jax."

Wow, definitely not friend-zoned. "I can say the same about you, Rhea. My one wish is that we hadn't met the way we did, but I'm glad we've met."

"Me, too," she said and set her menu down.

The waiter approached at that moment and said. "Good to see you again, Rhea. The usual?"

"The usual, Sam," she answered and handed him the menu.

"What about you, sir?" the waiter said, his tone not anywhere near as friendly, warning that Rhea had another possible protector.

"The porterhouse. Medium rare," he said. As the waiter rushed away to place their orders, Jackson picked up his water glass and glanced at her over the rim. "You have a lot of defenders."

Rhea grinned and shook her head. "They're just not used to me bringing a man here," she said and then covered her mouth. He thought he heard her mutter, "Stupid, stupid, stupid." It brought a smile to his face, since it made him special and since it confirmed that Rhea lacked guile.

He took hold of her hand. "I'm glad I'm special. I am special, right?"

With a chuckle, she twined her fingers with his. "And dense, if you don't know that yet."

Sam, the waiter, returned with a wine bottle and made quite a show of opening it. "Courtesy of Randy. One of our best cabernets."

They both offered their thanks, and Jackson took the first sip. "Excellent."

Sam filled their glasses and walked away to give them privacy. Jackson raised his glass and toasted. "To friendship."

She tapped her glass to his and surprised him again with her boldness. "To friendship and more, Jax."

With a dip of his head, he said, "To more."

Chapter Sixteen

Jackson lounged on Rhea's sofa, his muscled arms resting along the top of the cushions. He'd taken off his denim jacket and carefully folded it to cradle the holster he also removed. The pile of the jacket and holster sat off to the side, a very masculine contrast to the brightly colored pillows tucked all around him.

Her belly was full with the fabulous filet mignon and wine she'd had for dinner, as well as the cheesecake slice she'd shared with Jackson. In truth, she was a little sleepy and, dare she say it, at peace for the first time in months.

Hard to believe, considering she still didn't know what had happened to Selene and someone was trying to either kill her or drive her off the investigation.

But with Jackson there…

So many different emotions raced through her in addition to the peace. Comfort. Need, especially as he settled his gaze on her. His gray eyes were dark, almost black as he invited her to join him on the couch. Invited her to more.

She didn't hesitate, taking hold of his hand and snuggling into his side, her head pillowed against his chest. His heartbeat loud and beginning to race beneath her ear.

He skimmed his hand across her hair, smoothing it. Slipping beneath the hair at her shoulders to her neck, where he massaged her muscles and then shifted his hand downward again to hug her close.

She snuggled in tighter and higher, until her lips were barely inches from his. Laying her hand on his chest, she pressed upward to trace the edge of his jaw with her mouth. Beneath her hand, his muscles tensed.

She looked up at him. Found the question in his gaze. "I'm sure, Jax. I've never been more sure of anything in my life."

Her words released his control. Urgently he slipped his hands to her waist and urged her upward. Their first tentative kiss, one of invitation and acceptance, quickly flared into one of heat and passion. They kissed over and over, mouths meeting ruthlessly, hungrily.

As Jackson brought his hand around to cup her breast, she moaned and moved to straddle his thighs. His body was hard everywhere. Strong. So strong and insistent against hers.

She shifted on him, needing him. Needing to release her control and savor what this amazing man could provide.

Jackson groaned as Rhea moved on him. He clasped her hips with his hands and urged her to still. "Rhea. Are you sure?"

"Yes, I am. Come with me." She eased from his lap and tugged him off the sofa.

He willingly followed, needing Rhea like he had no other woman. Wanting to explore the complex woman he'd only known for a few days. Humbled that he could feel so much for her in so short a time.

In her bedroom, she went straight to the bed and offered him a smile that was both welcoming and hesitant. He bent and tasted that smile. Accepted the invitation and hoped to ease her sudden reluctance, because if he couldn't...

He wouldn't pressure her.

He turned to sit on the bed, bringing her face-to-face with him.

Cupping her cheek, he gentled her and welcomed her into the V of his outspread legs. Gently he strummed his thumb across her cheek. Soothed his other hand up and down her side.

She laid her hands on his shoulders before leaning close and kissing him again. The kiss tentative at first until passion ignited need so intense, it was impossible to stop.

Kissing was interrupted only to remove clothes until flesh was against flesh, and Jackson slipped on protection. He covered her with his body, joining with her. Breaths caught with the union. Exploded as Jackson moved within her, pulling her ever higher. Pushing them closer and closer to the edge until, with a final thrust, they tumbled over the edge together.

Rhea cuddled tight to Jackson's side, her thigh tossed over his. Her head pillowed on his muscled chest. He draped his arm down her back, holding her near. He laid his other arm across hers, pinning it against his chest. His touch soothing as he grazed his hand along her upper arm.

"That was…nice," she said, unable to find the right word to describe what she was feeling. Satisfied. Peaceful. Expectant.

"Ouch. Just nice," he teased, laughter in his tone and in the shake of his body beneath hers.

She leaned an elbow on his chest and glanced up at him. "Okay, maybe more than nice. But don't let your ego get out of hand."

He inched a dark brow upward. "A lot more than nice?"

Chuckling, she settled back onto his chest and drifted her hand down his midsection and lower. "Maybe. Want to try for way more than nice?"

He rolled her beneath him. "Definitely."

THEY WERE HEADING back to Rhea's apartment after visiting her gallery the next morning when the call came from his cousin Sophie.

"I hope this is good news," Jackson said as he answered and paused by the entrance to the building.

"So nice to talk to you, too, *primo*," Sophie teased.

"Sorry, cuz. It is nice to hear from you. How are you?" he said and looked in Rhea's direction. With a dip of his head, he confirmed it was the call for which they'd been waiting.

"I'm fine, and so are you. Robbie and I managed to get some images off the hard drive of that woman whose photo you sent. It wasn't easy. We had to get the corrupted data off the drive, rebuild the FAT table and—"

"Sophie, English please," he said, teasing her about the geek speak.

Sophie chuckled and said, "I'm sending the photos via email, and I'll text them to you, as well." He heard the click-clack of keys to confirm the dispatch of the images.

"I owe you big time."

"You do, so how about you come visit and bring your lady friend, as well?" Sophie said, laying on the guilt.

"My mom told you to say that, didn't she?"

Sophie's husky laugh confirmed it. "Call us if you need anything else, *primo*."

"I will, Sophie. Thank Robbie for me," he said and hung up to peer at the images she had sent.

Jackson angled the phone so Rhea could see the grainy black-and-white photos. The first was of Selene inside the pub, sitting and eating. There were other patrons nearby, including two heavily bearded and long-haired men who seemed to be looking in Selene's direction. The second photo was similar to the first, but in this one there was no doubt that the men were staring at Rhea's sister. The last three images were from the exterior of the pub. Selene near her car and, after, another one showing her pulling away, but in the background, the two bearded men again. They were leaning against what looked like a Jeep. The final photo created a blast of memories through Jackson's brain.

The Jeep was backing out, providing a glimpse of its front bumper.

It was that bumper that had piqued his interest, since it was way too similar to what he'd seen only moments before they'd been rammed and almost driven into the back of the logging truck.

"Is that—"

"The SUV that hit us? I think it might be," he said and used his thumb and forefinger to zoom the photo and enlarge the bumper section.

"A definite maybe," he said.

Rhea wiggled her forefinger at the phone. "Go back to the earlier images. I think I've seen that man before."

He did as she asked, and she nodded. "He was in the police station when I came to speak to the chief."

Jackson zoomed the image to focus on the faces of the two men. Their heavy beards and long hair hid many of their features, but there were some similarities in the shapes of their eyes, noses and lips. "They could be brothers," he said, tracing those features with his forefinger.

"They could be. And I had a witness who said she drove by and noticed another Jeep by Selene's car that night. We've been thinking that it was Matt's Jeep, but maybe it wasn't. Maybe it was this Jeep."

"There's only one way to find out. You have contact info for that witness, don't you?"

Rhea nodded and skimmed through the info on her phone. "I do. I guess we go see her."

"We do, only..." He wanted to tell her not to get her hopes up, but that would be unrealistic. The photos and connection to their attackers was beyond coincidence. It was a solid lead, and one they had to follow.

"Let's go," he said and held his hand out to her.

Her smile was grim as she slipped her hand into his. "I'm ready. Let's go."

GAIL FRAZIER WAS a sixtysomething LPN who worked at an assisted living facility in Regina and volunteered with an organization that provided meals and companionship to seniors. She had been coming home from one of those volunteer assignments when she had seen Selene's car and the unidentified SUV.

"What time do you think you left Mrs. Wilson's home?" Jackson asked as they sat with the LPN in her workplace's cafeteria.

"Much later than normal. Mrs. Wilson was a little despondent that day since it was her husband's birthday. He passed several years ago," Gail explained.

Rhea nodded. "That was so nice that you stayed to cheer her up."

Gail sniffled, and her eyes filled with tears. "I lost my own husband two years ago and started volunteering to fill the empty hours. My assignments help me as much as I help them," she said and picked up her coffee mug that said "#1 Nurse." She took a sip and after said, "I think I was there until about nine. Maybe a little earlier. I got Mrs. Wilson settled in bed, cleaned up a bit and then drove home. That's when I saw the cars by the lake."

Jackson pulled out a photo of Selene's sedan. He laid it in front of Gail. "Is this the car you saw that night?"

Gail nodded, her head shifting up and down emphatically. "I think so. I didn't think anything about it that night since people stop to look at the lake at all hours."

"What made you reach out to me and not the police?" Rhea asked.

Gail shrugged and pointed to the photo. "At first I didn't think it was unusual. But then I ran across your posts on Facebook asking for any additional information. It got me thinking about that night."

Jackson considered the older woman, judging her sincerity. "So you suddenly remembered a second car months later."

Another emphatic nod answered him. "I did. I wish I had made the connection earlier, but I didn't. Like I said, nothing seemed off until I saw Rhea's post and started thinking about it."

Which would make her testimony in court totally vulnerable to challenge. Any good defense lawyer would chip away at it to attempt to prove she imagined the second car as a way to help Rhea. She was a caregiver by nature and liked to volunteer to help others. Giving Rhea that info totally fit her nature, even if the veracity of the information might be doubtful.

Jackson tried to push her some more. "You thought the other car by the lake was a Jeep. One like this?" He slipped a photo of Matt's Wrangler in front of the LPN.

She laid her hand on the photo and drew it near for a closer inspection. With a shrug and a small frown, she said, "Like this one, but not this new or nice. The one I saw looked older. More beat-up."

Jackson shared a look with Rhea. If Gail was right, Matt was moving further down on the suspect list with each new bit of information they gathered. Opening his folder, he drew out a photo that his cousins had provided. "What about this SUV?"

Gail peered at the photo, squinting at the image. She picked up the glasses hanging on a bejeweled chain around her neck. Slipping on the cheaters, she said, "I don't really need them, but use them just to be sure of the directions on some of the patients' medications. The print is just too small and this photo… Well, it's quite grainy."

With the cheaters in place, she perused the photo for a too-long minute before she set it down and gestured to it. "Like that one."

Rhea leaned toward the other woman and placed her hand on the photo. "Like that one? So you don't think this is the SUV you saw?"

Gail got snippy. "I didn't say that, did I, young lady?"

Rhea inhaled deeply, held her breath and then in a gentler tone said, "I'm sorry, Gail. I truly appreciate that you came forward so we can find out what happened to Selene."

Seemingly chastened by Rhea's statement, Gail picked up the photo once again and reexamined it. When she set it down, she said, "I think this was the car. I remember it having that weird bumper thing."

The same weird bumper thing that I saw just before we were rammed, Jackson thought.

"That's important, Gail. Thank you," Rhea said and shot Jackson a look, as if saying, *Tag, it's your turn.*

He ran with it. "Did you see anyone near the cars? Selene? Anyone else?"

She shook her head. "Just the cars. I didn't think to look at the lakeshore. Like I said, it didn't seem anything was out of the ordinary and truth be told, I was tired. I just wanted to get home and get some rest."

"We understand. You do hard work here and with the volunteering… You must be exhausted late at night." Rhea laid a hand on Gail's, offering her thanks with the touch.

"I am, but like I said before, it helps me, as well. If there's anything I can do, please let me know," Gail said and glanced at her watch. "I really should get back to my patients. It'll be lunchtime soon and I have to get their medications ready."

When she rose from her chair, Jackson and Rhea did the same. Jackson shook her hand and said, "We appreciate the time you took. If need be, would you be willing to testify to what you saw?"

Gail peered at Rhea and said, "I would and I'm so sorry for your loss. It must be difficult for you."

Rhea's lips were in a tight line, her voice choked with emotion as she said, "Thank you again, Gail. I appreciate you coming forward. It's been truly helpful."

With a quick nod, Gail slipped away to return to her patients, and Jackson and Rhea left the facility. At the cruiser, Jackson crossed his arms and leaned against the fender, facing Rhea. She stood before him, arms wrapped around herself defensively. "I know this is upsetting."

Rhea shook her head and her dangling silver earrings danced against her neck. "It is, but I can deal."

"Can you deal with the possibility Matt wasn't the one who killed Selene?" Jackson pressed, hating to hurt her, but needing her to acknowledge he was likely not their suspect any longer.

"She's not dead," Rhea said, which shouldn't have surprised him, but it did.

"Rhea, please," he urged and reached for her, but she brushed off his touch and stepped away from him.

Chin tilted up and ice in her crystal blue gaze, she said, "If we've eliminated Matt, then we move on to the other scenarios, and they include the possibility that Selene is alive, Detective. So what do we do next?"

Chapter Seventeen

Ugh, detective-zoned. Far worse than friend-zoned, but he understood that Gail's information had upended what had been the most plausible explanation for what had happened to Selene. The others, including that Selene was alive...

He pushed off the bumper and opened the door for her. Meeting her gaze, he said, "We head back to the pub and speak to Marcus. Maybe he knows more about those two men."

Without waiting for her reply, he walked around and eased into the driver's seat. They were at the pub in no time. Quite a number of vehicles were in the parking lot, since it was almost lunch hour. Jackson parked, and Rhea and he entered. They located Marcus, who once again took them into his office to avoid prying eyes and gossip about Jackson's visit.

"How can I help you again?" Marcus asked with a tired sigh as he plopped into his chair.

"Rough morning?" Jackson asked, inching a brow upward in emphasis.

"Totally, dude. One of the chefs burned himself pretty bad, and we had a problem with one of the freezers, but I'm handling it," Marcus advised and skimmed his gaze from Rhea to him and back.

"You two look like your morning was as bad," Marcus said.

"You could say that," Rhea blurted out.

Marcus trained his gaze on Jackson, as if asking for his confirmation. Instead, Jackson took the photos from his folder and handed them to his former colleague. "What can you tell us about those two?"

Marcus shuffled through the photos and then gestured to Rhea with them. "This is your sister in the photos?"

Rhea nodded. "It is."

Marcus let out a low whistle. "You really are identical, aren't you?"

"Marcus, focus," Jackson said, and it brought back memories of working with the other man on the force. Although he'd been a good cop, he'd also been easily distracted.

"Easy, dude," Marcus warned and glanced at the photos again before handing them back to Jackson. Fingers laced, he laid his hands across his midsection and said, "They apparently come in every few months."

"Have you seen them lately?" Jackson asked.

Marcus tilted his head to the side and looked upward, searching his memory, and then shook his head. "Come to think of it, no. The staff calls them the 'Mountain Men.'"

Rhea jumped in with, "Why is that?"

With a shrug, Marcus said, "When they first came in, I got bad vibes. I asked the old-timers who gave me the skinny on them. That they seemed like recluses who only came down every few months. Kept to themselves. Creeped out some of the female customers."

"In what way?" Rhea asked, her gaze narrowed as she trained it on Marcus.

"I'm told they'd stare at them. Make comments. I wasn't around at the time, but they were asked to leave one night and got in the old manager's face. Pushed him around."

"Did you call the police? Is there a report possibly?" Jackson said, hoping that there would be so they might identify the men.

Marcus shook his head. "Sorry, but they didn't. It got handled, and no one was hurt."

"Do you mind if we ask your staff about them?" Jackson said.

Marcus frowned. "Dude, we're just about to start the lunch service. Can I send them to the station later?"

He glanced in Rhea's direction. She was bouncing her feet nervously, expectantly. She clearly would prefer to deal with it now as he would, but Marcus had been open and helpful, and he didn't want to push. Besides, they had things to do at the station anyway.

"We'll be there," he said, earning a quick hard glance from Rhea, but she remained silent.

"I appreciate that, Jax. I'll speak to my guys and ask them to go over after their shift. I'll make a list of who might have info also, just in case." Marcus stood as if to reinforce it was time for them to go.

"Just in case?" Rhea asked and stood, her face puzzled.

Marcus did a quick shrug. "Some of my guys… Let's just say they're not fans of the police. But I'll get them to you, I promise."

"Appreciate the help, Marcus. We truly do," Jackson said.

Once they were out in the restaurant, Jackson played it up as if to make it seem like their visit had been only a friendly one, since several eyes had turned in their direction. "Thanks for that donation to the PAL fund, Marcus. We truly appreciate it," he said, his voice loud enough to be overheard by those in the area.

Marcus smiled and chuckled. "You're welcome, Jax. Anything for a friend."

Rhea went up on tiptoes and brushed a kiss across his cheek, truly grateful for his assistance. "Thank you."

With a wink and a broad smile, Marcus said, "Anything for you, pretty lady."

Rhea returned the grin and suddenly felt the possessive press of Jackson's hand at the small of her back. Still angry, she glared at him and pushed away, eager to return to the police station. As she had told Jackson earlier, she thought she had seen one of the men at the station.

She hurried from the pub, the soft soles of her espadrilles creating a dull thud with each quick step. She shoved through the door to the cruiser and didn't wait for Jackson to do the gentlemanly thing. Grabbing the handle, she waited for the *kerthunk* to signal that he'd opened the lock, but when it didn't happen immediately, she turned to find him standing there.

"What?" she asked, wondering at his delay.

"I know you're angry," he began, but she shut him down with a sharp raise of a brow and the crossing of her arms. She lifted her face to stare at his, her chin tilted in defiance.

"My possibility is as plausible as any that remain."

Jackson jammed his hand on his hips, looked away from her penetrating gaze and sucked in deep breath. Blowing it out sharply, he said, "It is, Rhea. But it's the one that will bring you the most pain if it proves false. I don't want you to experience that kind of pain. Again."

His words mollified her anger, filled as they were with concern. "I'm a big girl, Jax. While it may be painful if I'm wrong, it brings me comfort to think she might be out there somewhere. To think we might be able to save her from suffering if she's alive."

He nodded, and while she sensed he had more to say, he bit his tongue. Literally, because she could swear she saw him wince before he unlocked the doors and walked around to his side of the cruiser.

She eased into her seat and buckled up, and Jackson took off for the police station. The trip was short, since Regina wasn't all that big. As they crossed Main Street, its beauty struck her once again and made her itch to finish the sketch she'd started the other day. When her gaze skimmed to Jackson, the sharp lines of his handsome face stole her breath and roused passion, both to finish his sketch and to be with him again.

At the station house, the desk sergeant who had been on duty the day Rhea had first come to see the chief was guarding the entrance again. Rhea smiled at her, and at the dip of Jackson's head, she buzzed them through.

But Jackson paused right past the barrier and turned to Rhea. "Do you see the officer here who had brought in one of our possible suspects?"

Rhea gazed around the various desks, looking for the middle-aged officer she thought she had seen with someone who looked like one of the Mountain Men, but she didn't spot him. But then two officers emerged with coffee from what must have been a break room. She pointed in their direction. "I think that's him. The one to the left."

Jackson nodded and called out to his colleague. "Officer Bellevue. Do you have a moment for us?"

The officer hurried over. "How can I help?" he said as he shook Rhea's hand and dipped his head in Jackson's direction.

Jackson opened his folder and handed a photo to Officer Bellevue. "Have you seen either of these men before?"

The man examined it and tapped on the face of one of the men. "Had this one in earlier this week."

Jackson shared a hopeful glance with Rhea. "Can you pull your report for us?"

A bright stain of color erupted across the officer's face. "I'm sorry, Jax, but I didn't file one. I brought him in for some minor shoplifting, but the owner said that if he paid for the items, she wouldn't press charges. He did, so I let him go with a warning."

Jackson dragged a hand through his hair in frustration. "You didn't get a name or address?"

"I did get a name, although it took some doing. Guy kept on muttering about how his brother would be so mad at him for getting in trouble. He did have a wallet, but no ID. " Officer Bellevue said and pulled a small notepad from his shirt pocket. Flipping through the pages, he stopped at one and said, "Wade Garrett."

"Thank you, officer. That's really helpful," Rhea said with a smile, trying to ease the officer's earlier upset about not filing a report.

"If you need me to run him down—"

Jackson held up a hand to stop the other man. "Thanks, but we'll do it. If there's anything else you can think of, please let us know."

"I will, Jax," he said and walked away to his desk.

"A name. I guess that's a start," Rhea said.

Since they'd almost made peace after that morning's upset, Jackson didn't want to tell her it wasn't much of a start, especially if the man had provided a fake name. "Let's go to my office, so we can try to track him down."

He laid a hand at her waist and was grateful she didn't shy away as she'd done before. With gentle pressure, he guided her to his office. Tossing the folder with the photos on his desk, he sat and explained to Rhea what he was doing on his computer. He couldn't let her see the screen once he logged on to the various police databases since she wasn't authorized, but he did turn the screen slightly as he added the photos his cousins had retrieved to their digital notebook and also updated the information from Gail Frazier.

"I'm going to run Wade Garrett through the state and

federal databases to see if we get a hit," he said and moved the screen out of Rhea's line of sight.

"Do you think you will?" Rhea asked, worrying her lower lip, her look expectant as she leaned toward him, almost as if urging him to get going.

Jackson shrugged. "Maybe."

He tapped away on the keys while Rhea sat there, almost bouncing up and down in her chair. The records he searched brought up several hits in various court cases, but as he skimmed through the available details it became clear a few of the cases dated to the early 1940s and involved an adult male.

"Got a few hits involving criminal cases, but the person would be way too old," he said, but quickly added, "Although it could be a parent."

After reviewing the last few entries, he leaned back in his chair and said, "Nothing here, and in Colorado vital records are considered confidential and not online. Plus, that assumes they're locals, and we don't know that. I'll search the DMV records, even though Bellevue said he didn't have a license. It might mean he just didn't have it with him."

But the DMV search didn't produce any hits and he advised Rhea of that. "Since that was a bust, I'm going to search through the national criminal databases that are available."

"Like which ones?" Rhea asked, craning her neck toward the screen, clearly wanting to be involved.

While Jackson entered his username and password into the first system, he said, "A whole alphabet soup of databases. NCIC. NICS."

A BRIGHT GRIN and chuckle relieved her earlier intensity. "Definitely alphabet soup. Which reminds me that we haven't had lunch yet." As if to reinforce her comment, her stomach grumbled noisily and she hastily laid a hand over her midsection to quiet the noise.

Jackson smiled and with a flip of his hand at the monitor, he said, "This may take a while. There are some chips and things in the break room, but also a nice sandwich shop just a few doors down on Main Street." He reached into this top desk drawer, found a take-out menu and handed it to her.

Rhea accepted the menu. The edges were ragged, and the paper was soft, as if it had been handled many times. "I guess you order from there a lot."

With a chagrined smile, Jackson said, "You have a lot of late nights in this job. Sandwiches make it easier to eat and work at the same time."

"But not healthier, mentally or physically. I'll take a walk and go get us something."

She placed the menu on his desktop, but as she moved away, he raised an index finger. "No salad. I'm allergic to green things."

She chuckled as he had intended and shook her head. "Got it. No salad."

Hurrying out to the street, she walked toward the center of town, where most of the stores and restaurants were located. She remembered seeing one place that sold pot pies with various fillings. They'd be a nice hearty lunch and force Jackson to take a break from the tedium of searching through the databases.

The shop had quite an assortment of fillings, from one mimicking a Cuban sandwich to the more traditional chicken and turkey pot pie variations. She chose the chicken for herself, but a chili-style filling for Jackson.

She had barely gone a block when she got that feeling she was being followed. Turning quickly, she caught a glimpse of someone ducking into a small alley between two of the buildings.

The hackles rose down her neck and back, and she quickened her pace almost to a run. Turning every now and then to see if she was still being followed. She thought she caught another glimpse of someone as she hit the stairs for the police station, but safety was just a few steps away.

She stumbled on the last step, almost sending herself tumbling into the glass doors for the station, but she righted herself and managed not to drop their lunch while doing it.

Bursting through the doors, she immediately drew the attention of the desk sergeant who jumped to her feet, eyebrows knitted with worry. "Are you okay, Rhea?"

Rhea peered back over her shoulder. No one outside on the steps. Lifting her gaze to glance across the street, she thought she saw a big, bearded man again, one who looked too much like the one in the photos from the pub, but then he vanished.

Maybe it was all in her imagination. Her mother had told her on more than one occasion that she had a vivid imagination and, of course, it came part and parcel with being an artist.

"I'm okay. Just a little spooked."

The officer glanced past her and out the door, as well. "I'll buzz you through," she said after apparently determining that everything was in order.

"Thanks," she said and hurried to Jackson's door.

He was at work, but looked at her as she walked in. He was immediately in action, coming to her side to take the package and guide her into a chair.

As he wrapped his arm around her, she realized for the first time that she was shaking.

"What happened, Rhea? You look like you've seen a ghost," he said, drawing her closer and brushing a kiss across her temple.

She wiggled her head, embarrassed. "Nothing, only... I thought someone was following me."

Jackson muttered a curse. "I'm sorry. I should have told you that I had one of our officers trailing you to make sure you were safe."

"Maybe that's why I felt I was being followed," she said with a shrug, wanting to alleviate the obvious guilt he was feeling.

"Maybe," he said, hugged her hard again and skimmed another kiss on her cheek.

A rough, overly loud cough, drew them apart.

She peered over her shoulder to find Jackson's boss staring at them intently. His face as hard and rough as the stone outcroppings on the mountains around Regina.

"Am I interrupting something?" the chief said and arched one bushy gray eyebrow.

"I just had a scare," Rhea said and slid to one side of her chair to create some distance from Jackson.

The chief crooked a finger in Jackson's direction and he rose, then stepped outside his office to speak to his boss. Bodies tilted toward each other, voices low, the two men spoke and, while she was unable to hear, their posture and the few chest pokes the chief gave Jackson said it all. He was clearly not happy with what he had just seen.

When the other man left, Jackson laid his hands on his hips and looked upward before entering his office and shutting the door for privacy.

"He's angry, isn't he?" she said as Jackson busied himself with removing the pot pies and cutlery from the bag. He ripped the bag open and spread it across the surface of the desk to act like a place mat.

"Jackson, talk to me," she said and placed her hand on his forearm to still his angry motion.

"Chief says I need to wrap this up. We're wasting too many man hours and resources. I'm letting it get too personal." His words were clipped and chilly.

She laced her fingers together and laid her hands in her

lap. Peering at them, she said, "I'm sorry, Jax. I know how important becoming chief is to you—"

"But not more important than justice, Rhea. We're close. I can feel it," he said.

His body was stiff, and he had clearly shut himself off from her, so she decided not to press. They ate in silence, and while the food may have been scrumptious, she didn't taste a thing thanks to the emotions roiling inside.

Jackson gobbled his pie down in record time and swung back to his computer. Barely a second later, he returned to his two-fingered pecking at the keyboard. His brow furrowed as he paused, probably to review the information on the screen. That process was repeated over and over while Rhea picked at her pot pie, keeping herself occupied with counting the peas and carrots as she ate to keep from bothering Jackson.

A good hour went by like that until Jackson blew out a rough breath and pushed away from the computer. He leaned his elbows on the arms of his chair and steepled his fingers before his mouth, clearly unhappy.

"Nothing, right?" she said, reading his signals.

He nodded, his frustration apparent despite his earlier optimism that they were close to finding something. "Nothing. Nada. Zilch. Zero."

She was about to say something, she didn't know what, when he slapped his hands on his desk and said, "But that's not stopping me. Us. I'll be right back."

He rushed from his office and came back with a large roll of paper. She quickly cleared off the remnants of their lunch and threw them away so Jackson could unfurl the paper across his desk. A map of Regina and the adjacent mountain areas. He jabbed at the mountains and said, "Marcus said that it seemed as if the men had come down from the mountain. What if they did? What if they live in one of these nearby areas?"

"But these are all protected lands, right?"

"That doesn't stop poachers or squatters." He traced his index finger along the highway that ran along the base of the mountain peaks and near the lake where Selene had last been seen.

"They could have grabbed her here." He jabbed at the map by the lake. "And taken her somewhere on one of these mountains."

Rhea peered at the map. "That's a lot of territory to cover."

"For sure," Jackson said, but then grabbed his desk phone and tapped out a few numbers. "Dillon. Do you have a few minutes to help me?"

His smile confirmed Dillon would be over quickly, and within seconds, another officer was at Jackson's door. "You needed me, boss?"

Jackson nodded. "You're an expert hiker, aren't you?"

The other officer nodded and grinned. "I am. You need some advice on hiking trails?" he said and approached the desk. He barely looked old enough to be a cop, making her feel suddenly old, even though she was only twenty-eight.

Jackson gestured to the two mountains closest to Regina. "How hard would it be to hike up either of these peaks? Maybe even build yourself a little cabin. A private one."

Dillon let out a low whistle. "Depends on the time of year."

"Fall. November," Jackson said.

Dillon shot a quick glance in her direction and with a shrug said, "If there isn't snow on the ground, it's not so hard on this peak. There's actually a small road that goes up about halfway. You get some hikers who drive and then head to one of the lower peaks on foot. It takes more experienced climbers to actually reach the summit."

"So it gets enough traffic that it might be hard to hide?"

Rhea asked. If she was trying to hide, she wouldn't want a lot of people traipsing nearby.

Dillon considered her comment and then nodded. "Enough traffic. Plus, there's a ski resort here," he said and gestured to the far side of the mountain, the area closest to where Selene disappeared.

Jackson stood, arms akimbo, perusing the map. He gestured to the other mountain. "What about this area?"

Dillon mimicked Jackson's pose and examined the map. With a nod of his head, he said, "That's a tougher hike for sure. Not many people do it."

"How would you get up there if you wanted to?" Rhea asked, leaning over to look at the map.

Dillon scratched his head. "Rumor has it there's an old logging trail, but it's been closed to the public for ages." He leaned his hands on the desk and shifted closer to the map, inspecting it more carefully. Running his finger along one stretch of highway, he said, "Somewhere around here."

"Satellite image might confirm it," Jackson said and hurried back to his computer. In no time, he had a map of the area up on the screen and turned it around so they could all see it. He zoomed in on the image and gestured to one section. "This looks like a trail, doesn't it? We could search in that area."

Dillon did another shrug of shoulders that still needed to fill out. "Maybe, but you're still talking a lot of area to search, boss. Acres and acres. It would take a lot of people to find anything in that wilderness."

Jackson laughed and leaned back in his chair. "I'm not talking people, Dillon."

Rhea narrowed her gaze and searched Jackson's features for some sign of what he was thinking, but failed. "What are you talking about, Jax?"

Chapter Eighteen

"LIDAR."

"LIDAR? What's that?" Dillon asked.

Jackson clapped the young man on the back. "I thought you young guys were all about the tech," he teased and then explained, "It's like RADAR, but using laser light to make 3D images of an area."

"3D images of lots and lots of trees," Rhea said dejectedly.

"Actually not," Jackson said. "I've been reading about how you combine LIDAR images with software that can actually strip away vegetation to reveal any hidden structures."

Dillon mimicked opening the pages of a book. "Reading, like on paper."

"On paper and on the net. My cousins have been trying to keep me from becoming a Luddite," Jackson quipped.

"Can your cousins help us with the software part of it?" Rhea asked, losing a little bit of the glumness that had filled her tone a moment ago.

"I'm sure Robbie and Sophie can help us with the software. Maybe they even know someone in the area with drones equipped with LIDAR. Depending on what the images show, Dillon here can help us hike into the area.

Maybe the forest service, as well. It is in their jurisdiction after all," Jackson advised.

Jackson's desk phone rang and he hit the button to engage the speaker. "What's up, Rodriguez?"

"I have a visitor for you. He says Marcus sent him over," Millie said.

"Perfect. Please put him in the conference room. We'll be over in a second," he said and disengaged the speaker.

"That's good news, right?" Rhea said, suddenly feeling more optimistic than she had barely minutes before.

Jackson nodded. "For sure." He turned to Dillon and shook his hand. "Thanks for the help. We'll let you know when we need you again."

Dillon did a little salute. "Anytime, boss."

He exited, and Jackson gestured for Rhea to follow him. Once in the hallway, he laid a hand at her back in a way that was becoming achingly familiar. It offered immediate comfort and a sense of protection.

He guided her toward the conference room where an older man sat, waiting for them. He looked familiar, and as she dug through her memory, she recalled that she'd seen him tending the bar at the pub.

He stood as they entered, and Jackson held his hand out for a shake. She guessed that his use of the conference room and friendliness were intended to put the man at ease and not make him feel as if he was being interrogated. "Bradley, right?" Jackson said.

The man dipped his head in greeting in her direction and said, "That's right. You have a good memory, Detective."

"Jackson, please. Thanks for coming by," Jackson said and sat kitty-corner to the man. Rhea sat beside Jackson, opposite the bartender.

"New manager says to come by, I come by. I don't want no trouble," the man said, hands clasped before him on the tabletop. His fingers were gnarly, arthritic. He also had assorted scars on his hands, nicks, cuts and even a larger silvery shape, like from a burn. Clearly the hands of a man who worked hard for his living. But also obviously a nervous man as he bounced those clasped hands on the surface of the table.

"I guess you know something about the two men we're interested in?" Jackson asked.

A slight lift of his shoulders was followed by, "Some, but not much. They come now and again. Usually when we're not as busy."

Which confirmed what Marcus had told them earlier, Rhea thought.

"Anything else?" Jackson pressed.

"They're rough. Not people persons. Mostly keep to themselves except…they've harassed some of the women," Bradley said.

"Marcus said they were booted from the place for that," Jackson said, trying to elicit more with the open question.

"They were. Not recently. After that they seemed to clean up their act, but they still creeped us out. The one brother seemed to be the leader and was just plain mean."

"Mean in what way?" Jackson said, obviously wondering as she was what had prompted that impression.

Bradley bounced his hands on the tabletop faster and, as if realizing what he was doing, suddenly pulled them down beneath the edge of the table. "He almost growls his orders. Never a smile. Never a tip, but I got the feeling they didn't have much money. Their clothes were raggedy and sometimes they smelled. Bad. If the girls didn't put out the pretzels and nuts in front of them fast enough, we'd hear it."

Jackson cupped his jaw and rubbed it thoughtfully. "Marcus said you all called them the 'Mountain Men.' Do you think they live up there?"

Bradley laughed and wobbled his head of salt-and-pepper hair back and forth. "It wouldn't surprise me if they hole up in a cave somewhere and, like bears, only come out of hibernation a couple of times a year."

Jackson continued with his questioning. "Anything else? Any names?"

The man shook his head, but then snapped his fingers. "I think the mean one called his brother 'Wade.' The older one was always warning his brother to stop one thing or another."

As if to confirm, Jackson said, "You think they're brothers?"

Bradley nodded vigorously. "I have an older brother, so I know how it goes. Totally brothers. And they look alike, I think. Hard to tell with all that hair."

Jackson peered in her direction for the briefest moment before returning his attention to the bartender. He rose and held his hand out to the other man. "Thank you so much for coming by, Bradley. You've been really, really helpful. If by any chance you remember anything else or see these guys—"

"You'll be the first person I call, Jackson," the man said as he shook Jackson's hand and once again dipped his head in Rhea's direction. "Miss. I hope you find out what happened with your sister."

With that, the older man exited the room.

"What do we do now?" she asked, wondering, but Jackson clearly had no doubt about their next steps.

"We call Avalon PD and suspend what they're doing about Davis. Then I'll check with our Search and Rescue guys to see if they have LIDAR and if not, time to talk to the cousins again."

"I HOPE THOSE images we got for you were helpful," Robbie said.

"They were, cuz, but the thing is…they've taken us in a

new direction in the investigation," Jackson admitted and did a quick look at Rhea to gauge how she was handling that new direction.

"Wow, okay. I guess you need more help. Let me get Sophie on the line," Robbie said.

"Afternoon, Jackson," Sophie said as she came across the speaker.

"Our investigations are pointing to two suspects who may be squatting on federal lands. But it's a problem to do a traditional search on foot. Too large an area and too much underbrush and vegetation," Jackson explained.

Robbie let out a low whistle. "Tough luck, but there are ways to search using drones."

"And LIDAR," Sophie added.

Jackson smiled, and Rhea jumped in with, "Jackson thought we might be able to do it that way."

"You definitely can. First, you survey the area with drones equipped with LIDAR, and then you process that imagery to see what's beneath trees and other foliage," Sophie confirmed.

Jackson shared a look with Rhea. "We're hoping you can connect us to someone who can do the drone work."

The murmur of low voices drifted across the line. "We can do that, *primo*," Robbie said.

"And we have software to process that imagery for you," Sophie quickly added.

"Thank you so much! That would be fantastic," Rhea said, her tone excited and grateful.

"We need to call a couple of drone specialists to see who's free, but hopefully we can get back to you by later tonight," Robbie said.

"Appreciated, cuz. Your help has been invaluable. I don't know how we can repay you," Jackson said and prepared for what he was sure would come next.

"Bring your lady friend to Miami!" Sophie said enthusiastically.

Rhea glanced in his direction, and the heat in her look could have ignited a forest fire. It was easy to picture the two of them, holding hands and walking along Ocean Drive in South Beach.

Voice husky with desire, he said, "I'll definitely think about that. Thanks again, and we'll talk to you later."

He ended the call and peered at Rhea, hoping he hadn't misread her earlier signals. "I'm sorry my cousins involved you in the Miami thing."

Her gaze narrowed and grew a little more somber. "I guess you don't like that idea?"

He raised his hands to stop her from going somewhere negative. "I do like it. I'm just not sure where we're headed. I mean, we've kind of been forced together."

"Forced? Is that what happened last night?" she said, her tone getting harsher by the second.

"Hell, no, Rhea. Last night and this morning were amazing. But you're vulnerable right now, and I've got to think about—"

"Becoming police chief?" she said with an arch of her brow, the blue of her eyes becoming as chill as the ice on a winter lake.

"The investigation. And you. I never expected what's happening between us, but I don't regret it."

"I don't, either, Jax. But maybe we need to take a step back until this is all over," Rhea said.

He hated that she was right, but it made sense to bring things back into perspective until the investigation was done. And if his cousins could basically work a miracle and find something on the mountain that would lead them to their two new suspects, the investigation would quickly be coming to a close.

"I just want to update the digital notebook and reach

out to my local contact at the Park Service and see how she wants us to handle this. I can have someone drive you home if you want," Jackson said.

Rhea shook her head. "I'll just hang out here and do some sketching."

She didn't give Jackson time to argue with her, since she grabbed her ever-present knapsack and pulled out her sketch pad and pencils. Balancing the pad on her knee, she went to work and he did, as well, adding all the information they'd gathered to his notes.

Rhea flipped to the sketch of Jackson that she had started just two days ago. It had the barebones lines of him lying on the sofa, but needed so much more to do justice to the man sitting across from her. Especially since she now had intimate knowledge of that body. The hard muscles sheathed in smooth skin. The scars of a warrior along his shoulder and back, making her wonder if that accounted for the pain she'd seen on occasion.

And his face. Lord, it was the face of a fallen angel, tempting a woman with his full lips, dimples and the slight cleft in his chin. Those features were balanced by the strong line of his jaw and sharp straight nose.

She worked on those elements, since she had an unfettered look at them as he worked, a slight furrow in his brow as he concentrated and pecked information into the computer. At one point he leaned back, rubbed his jaw with his hand, as if puzzled, but then he was back at work.

Smiling, she shifted her pencil lower, adding definition to the broad expanse of his chest and lean midsection. Capturing with her pencil and paper the details her hands had explored last night and this morning. Understanding, but regretting, that she wouldn't explore more of him tonight.

Caught up in her sketching, she was jolted back by the loud ring of Jackson's cell phone. He answered and said, "Hi, cuz. That's good news. Thanks."

With a swipe, he ended the call. "They've reached out to their contact and copied me on the email. Hopefully we'll be able to arrange to have the drone survey tomorrow."

"That's good news," she said, grateful and expectant, but also worried. As long as the investigation wasn't done, she'd be with Jackson and Selene was still alive. The next few days could change all that, but would it be for the better?

"Ready to go home?" he said, lacing his hands behind his head to stretch. A slight grimace skipped across his features, but he controlled it and brought his hands down to the arms of his chair to push to his feet.

"Back hurting?"

It was obvious he didn't want to appear vulnerable as he shrugged and said, "Just a kink. Too much sitting. They say sitting—"

"Is the new smoking," she finished for him with a chuckle. "We're both in professions where we do a lot of sitting."

"Too late for a hike, but maybe we can think of something else to do." His gaze met hers, the gray of it smoky, warning of the fire that might soon ignite.

"For sure," she said, despite her earlier reservations, and held her hand out to him in invitation.

As he slipped his work-rough hand in hers, she told herself not to worry about tonight or tomorrow. Whatever was meant to be was meant to be.

Even if it brought heartache.

THE TENSION HAD been building ever since they'd left the police station and grabbed a quick bite for dinner in one of the restaurants along Main Street. Night had fallen as Jackson let them into his home, the ever-present police cruiser sitting in the driveway to warn off whoever had burned down Jackson's shed.

Inside, they paused at the base of the stairs, the tension so thick it felt like a presence shimmering between them.

With a wave of his hand, Jackson pushed away that sensation and said, "I have some things to do in my office. Why don't you go up and get settled?"

Coward! Rhea wanted to scream, hating that he'd put the onus on her to decide where she'd spend the night because, well, she was feeling as craven as he was. With a curt nod, she stomped up the stairs, annoyed. Anxious. Needy. Despite knowing what was happening between them was so uncertain, she still wanted him. She wanted to not waste a minute with him because once the investigation was over...

She wouldn't think about that.

She wouldn't think about what she would do if Selene...

No, I won't think that. She's out there. Somewhere, she told herself and walked to the guest bedroom to get her nightshirt. A nice hot shower was bound to relax her and buy some time until Jackson came up and then...

She hurried into the shower, but took her time luxuriating beneath the rain showerhead, working shampoo into a thick lather. Soaping up and running her hands across her skin. Letting the heat of the water sink into her bones. Thick steam gathered in the room, warning her she'd been in there for quite some time.

Reluctantly she shut off the water, grabbed a towel and dried off. Her skin seemed sensitized as the touch of the terry cloth across her body roused memories of the feel of the sheets beneath her, and Jackson above her, his big body driving into her.

The warmth on her skin from the water morphed into a different kind of heat deep within.

Rushing into Jackson's bedroom, she didn't even waste a moment to turn on the light. She slipped beneath the sheets and pulled them tight about her, the bed feeling empty without him. Her senses hyper, tuned to the slightest noise until she heard the first footfall on the steps.

She held her breath, waiting for him. Eager for his body next to hers.

The footfalls came closer and paused at the door. A breath seemed to burst from him, almost as if he'd been holding it in anticipation. A rush of steps came before his weight settled on the edge of the bed.

"Rhea," he said softly. Hesitantly.

She glanced at him. His face was in partial shadow, the only light that from the hallway. It made it hard to gauge what he was thinking. But then he cradled her jaw and tenderly ran his thumb across her cheek. Drifted it down to her lips, where he traced the edges of it, as powerful as any kiss. Stirring awake desire.

"Touch me, Jax," she said and covered his hand with hers. Urged it to her breast where her nipple pebbled beneath his rough palm.

"Rhea, this is crazy," he said, but he strummed his thumb across the hard tip and then reached beneath the sheets to find the hem of her nightshirt and draw it off her body.

With eager fingers she undid the buttons on his uniform shirt, baring his chest to her. Sitting up to drop kisses across the expanse until she tongued his masculine nipple and he groaned and held her head to him. With a little love bite, she brought her hands to his sides and urged him down to her, wanting his skin against hers. Wanting his hands on her.

"Please, Jax. Please," she pleaded.

Jackson moved away from her only long enough to remove the rest of his clothes and slip beneath the sheets with her.

She had her hands on him instantly, cupping him and stroking his hard length.

"I want you in me," she said and pressed him close.

"Bossy, aren't you?" he teased, drawing a chuckle from her as he fumbled in the nightstand for a condom. He had barely taken it out, and she was shifting, urging him to his back and taking it from him. She tore it open, took out the condom and, with delicious leisure, rolled it down over him, and now it was his turn to plead.

"Rhea. I need you," he said, and she didn't disappoint. She straddled him and sank onto him, slowly.

He laid his hands on her hips. Guided her to move on him, riding him. Thrusting into her forcefully, driving until the release washed over them, stealing their breaths.

Rhea wrapped her arms around him and laid her head against his chest. His heart beat rapidly beneath her ear, and his skin was damp. He smelled of man, leather and Jackson. She inhaled that aroma to commit it to memory. To remember it long past when this moment was done. He made her feel loved, but she told herself not to think too much about that.

There was still too much to do. Too many unknowns.

And when the morning came, it might be the beginning of the end depending on what the drone footage revealed. Much like the end of the investigation would reveal if whatever she was feeling for Jackson was real.

Chapter Nineteen

The drone sitting on the ground before them in the bright morning light was nothing like the small drones Rhea had seen at various events in Denver. The drone was easily a good three feet or more across, with large propellers to lift it high into the air. It sat on two upraised legs and nestled at the center was something that looked like a camera, but she guessed was the LIDAR device, whatever that was. Projecting above the body of the drone, almost on antennae, were some pod-like pieces.

Jackson and the drone operator had gathered by the police cruiser, where Jackson had spread out the map of the mountain area above. He instructed the other man on what they wanted to survey. As she approached, she heard the drone operator issue a low whistle, look up toward the mountains and rub his head.

"Lots of dense vegetation, but hopefully the laser will be able to get through to get the data we need for Robbie and Sophie," the man said.

"What if there isn't enough data, Rick?" Jackson asked, taking the words right out of her mouth.

With a shrug, Rick said, "Robbie and Sophie are miracle workers. They can probably download topographical maps of the area and work them into any analysis to fill in gaps."

"Will it take long?" Rhea asked.

Rick peered up at the mountains again and said, "Your cousins sent me the specs for several flight plans. I've programmed them into my tablet, and once we send up the drone, it will fly those plans on its own to collect the data. My guess is a couple of hours."

"And then you send the data to my cousins?" Jackson said.

Rick nodded. "I'll transmit it to them, and they'll use their programs to get whatever images you want." Knowing what question would come next, Rick added, "With their supercomputers, it shouldn't take too long to process the data. You'd probably have it tomorrow if they jump right on it."

"Sounds good, and thanks again for doing this," Jackson said.

"Anything I can do. I can only imagine how hard it must be for you, Rhea. Hopefully we'll be able to help you find your sister," Rick said and walked to his tablet and remote controls. He picked up the controls, and a second later, the propellers whirred to life. With some swipes on the tablet, the drone lifted off and sped toward the mountains.

Jackson and she leaned against the cruiser and watched the drone disappear up the mountain, but the hum of the propellers gave testament that it was still there, working its way along the first of the flight plans that Jackson's cousins had programmed. Rick walked back toward them, his gaze locked on his tablet. As he neared, he held it up for them to see the images that the drone was capturing.

"Lots and lots of trees," Rhea said, slightly worried that was all the imagery would capture.

Rick nodded, but seeing her concerns, he explained. "That's what our eyes and the camera see, but the LIDAR is getting a lot more. Trust me."

"We do," Jackson said and laid his arm over her shoulder to draw her near with a reassuring squeeze.

"We trust you, Rick," she added, almost in apology for having any doubts.

"Great. Let me get back to watching, just in case," he said and walked away to keep an eye on the drone's footage, the remote control nearby. She assumed that was just in case there was a problem with any of the flight plans.

The chill of morning faded as an hour passed, and then another, as the drone flew flight plan after flight plan. Jackson and she sat on a blanket spread beneath the shade of a large aspen, sipping coffee from the large thermos they'd brought with them. Taking over some coffee and breakfast pastries to Rick while he monitored the drone.

It was almost lunch hour when the drone came whirring back and landed just yards away from them. They approached as the blades stopped whirring, and Rick walked over to the machine. He worked quickly to remove the LIDAR device and store it in its protective luggage.

Jackson helped him with packing up the rest of the equipment, and once they were done, Jackson said, "What do you do next?"

Rick gestured to the luggage with the LIDAR device. "I'm going to connect that to my computer and get the data uploaded to the cloud. Once that's done, I'll let Robbie and Sophie know so they can generate the information for you."

Jackson nodded and shook the man's hand. "Thanks again. If there's ever anything we can do for you—"

"I'll let you know. Maybe help me score some BBQ from Declan's place. I hear it's the best in the area," Rick said.

Jackson smiled. "It is. Whenever you want to head over there, I'll let him know you're coming and it's on me. Whatever you want."

"Thanks, Jax. And good luck with everything. Rhea," the man said with a deferential nod.

Jackson and Rhea helped Rick load all the equipment

containers in the back of his van. After another handshake from Jackson and hug from her, Rick drove off.

Rhea hoped that they'd gotten what they needed. With Matt virtually eliminated as a suspect, they had to focus on whether the two men at the pub had possibly had a part in Selene's disappearance, the attacks against her and the destruction at Jackson's home.

Jackson laid a hand on her shoulder and drew her near, comforting her. "This will work," he said with a playful nudge, trying to lighten the mood.

"It will," she said with more confidence than she was feeling and with anticipation. His cousins' supercomputers couldn't work fast enough as far as she was concerned, but she knew everyone involved would work as quickly as possible.

But in the meantime, they had little to do and she was too antsy to just sit around. She was even too antsy to sketch, which rarely happened. Jackson must have sensed her mood, since he said, "It's a beautiful day. Feel like a walk around town?"

She'd love a walk, but didn't want to deal with having other people around. She wanted something more private where it just the two of them. "Anywhere it can be just the two of us?"

Jackson peered at her and nodded. "I know just the place. How about we pick up a picnic lunch?"

She smiled. "That sounds nice. Thank you."

In just over fifteen minutes, they had a picnic lunch from one of the restaurants in Regina and were back on the road. Not far past the lake and nearby spillway, Jackson turned off onto a side road that ran parallel to the lake. Every now and then he'd look back, as if to check if anyone was following, but apparently satisfied they were alone, he continued on their trek. To the right of the paved road was what looked like a hiking trail that ran for some distance.

Less than a quarter mile from the turnoff, they pulled up in front of a large cabin that faced the lake. It reminded her of Jackson's home, and when they pulled into the driveway, she noticed the mailbox with the owner's name: Whitaker.

"Is this your family's place?" she asked as Jackson parked the cruiser.

"Mom and Dad's place. While they're in Florida, I come up here every week or so to make sure everything is in order. It's got nice views of the lake. I figured we could have lunch up on the front porch and then do a short hike along the trail. If you want, that is."

"I'd like that," she said. She also liked that he asked and didn't assume, unlike her last boyfriend. An artist like her, it had started off well at first, but then he'd become more and more demanding. More controlling until she had finally put an end to the relationship. In the couple of years since then, she'd stayed out of the dating game, focusing on her artwork and building her business.

She wasn't sure she could call what was happening with her and Jackson dating, or call him her boyfriend. It was way more than that.

He grabbed the bag with their food from the back seat and swung around to open her door, ever the gentleman. The comforting touch of his hand came at her back, the pressure gentle as he guided her up the long set of steps up to the generous front porch for the cabin.

The porch wrapped around the cabin. In the front there were two large rockers and between them a small circular table where he set the bag with their lunch. As Rhea swept past him to one of the rockers, Jackson removed their sandwiches, chips and soda from the bag and laid it all out on the table.

They settled on the rockers to sit and eat, their words few as they satisfied their hunger, but maybe also possibly because they were both thinking about what had happened that morning and where it might lead.

For Rhea, there was no doubt the end was near. If the images found nothing, the investigation would go cold again. If there *was* something on the images…it would help them find her sister, and she refused to give up hope that Selene was alive.

Jackson took a last bite of his sandwich, scooped up a handful of chips and popped a few into his mouth. He chewed thoughtfully, swallowed and said, "I think it went well this morning."

"I think so, although I'm not really into tech. Not a Luddite, mind you, but I like doing things hands-on."

He raised an eyebrow and fixed his gaze on her. It was hot, so hot. "I like that you like that."

Rhea's cheeks burned with the heat ignited by his look. She shook her head and chuckled. "I'll have to remember that."

"And me? Will you remember me?" Jackson said, his mood growing more somber.

Remember him? How can I ever forget him? She reached over and laid her hand on his forearm. With a tender stroke, she said, "I could never forget you, Jax. What we have… it's complicated, isn't it?"

"It is, but you're very special to me, Rhea. Whatever happens…" He wagged his head in an almost defeated gesture, laced his fingers with hers and offered her a sad smile. "How about that hike?"

"Sounds nice," she said, eager to move away from a discussion that could only bring sadness.

Hand-in-hand they walked down the steps and across the one-lane road to a small path that led to the trail by the lake. Sunlight frolicked on the surface of the lake, glittering like silver and ice-blue confetti against the cerulean blue waters. Waters that lapped softly along the reeds at the lake's edges.

Ducks and geese swam here and there on the surfaces, dark shapes against the light dancing on the lake. Far ahead of them, wading in the grasses on long sticklike legs, a great blue heron stood still, patient. Waiting to snare a meal. They carefully walked past so as not to disturb the bird and pushed on, voices silent. Thoughts loud, but calming slowly thanks to the beauty of the nature around them. A little farther up the trail, the sudden and loud flap of wings alerted them to a large bird taking flight.

A bald eagle soared into view over the lake, majestic and immense. With a few flaps of its wings the eagle climbed ever higher, then glided on a burst of breeze, reveling in its freedom.

JACKSON WATCHED THE regal bird soar and dance on the wind. Its flight graceful, but filled with strength. In some ways, Rhea was like that bird. Elegant. Powerful. Free.

He had to remind himself of that. Free to choose her own path. Free to leave when the time came, but much like the bald eagles who left in late winter, sometimes a pair would stay behind to nest and build a family.

They walked together for a good hour, enjoying the many sights along the lake. The spring weather was perfect for their walk, with a slight breeze to combat the heat building from the bright sunlight. In the shade of the trees on the trail, it was almost a little chilly and when Rhea shivered, he wrapped an arm around her shoulders and drew her close.

Hips bumping, they finally turned around and strolled back toward his parents' home, peace filling him. Funny, really, if you thought about it. He was in the middle of an active investigation. Someone was trying to hurt her, maybe even kill her, and yet what he felt was a peace that he hadn't experienced in years.

His heart was huge with that peace, with love for her, as they got back into the cruiser to head back to the police station for another look through their notes and to see if anyone needed his help on any other cases. The chief had warned him about how the investigation was taking too much of his time and the town's resources. With some downtime until his cousins came through with the information from the LIDAR footage, he had to give his attention to other cases his colleagues might be working on.

Back at the police station, he did just that, leaving Rhea comfortably tucked away in his office sketching while he checked in with the other officers on the force. He assisted one with recreating the scene of a hit-and-run. At another desk, an officer asked for advice about a burglary and that officer's version of the entry into the building.

Pleased with being of help to his colleagues, he was returning to his office when his police chief walked back into the station. If he remembered correctly, his boss had had a meeting with the mayor and some members of the town council about the police budget for the coming year.

"How'd it go, Bill?" he asked, hoping for positive news.

The police chief lifted his meaty shoulders in a careless way. "It's too soon to know, but at least it wasn't an immediate rejection."

Jackson heard the tone of worry in his chief's voice. "Which might happen if they get a whiff of any issues. Like Selene's case, right?"

His boss glared at him. "Like that, Jax. I told you that when you first decided on this lunacy. Have you made any progress?"

Jackson clenched his jaw, biting back his anger. With a cleansing breath, he said, "We have. We've pretty much eliminated Matt Davis as a suspect. I've called Avalon

PD to let them know that. We have photos of two possible suspects and a witness who saw their vehicle by the victim's sedan the night of her disappearance. Once we have the results of some drone imagery, we may know their whereabouts."

Taken aback, possibly shamed, the chief blustered, "Well, that all sounds good, Jax. Keep me posted."

The older man hurried away and Jackson returned to his office, where Rhea was still bent over her sketch pad, drawing.

"It's almost six. Are you ready to go? Maybe get dinner?" he said, but as he walked toward her his smartphone chirped. He grabbed it off his desk and realized it was his cousin Robbie calling.

"Hey, Robbie. Do you have good news for us?"

Rhea's head popped up at the sound of his cousin's name.

"Putting you on speaker," he said as he walked over to Rhea and sat in the chair beside her, the smartphone held between them.

"Okay. I've got Sophie here with me, and like I said, good news. We were able to process the LIDAR data and get some images for you. How about a video call and a bigger screen, so we can explain the information?"

"I'll arrange that. I'd also like to include one of my colleagues who is familiar with the area," he said.

"Great. I'll send a link to the meeting. Fifteen minutes?" Sophie asked.

"We'll be ready," Jackson said and hung up. He shared a look with Rhea and hoped she would be.

Chapter Twenty

Jackson had set up a large projection monitor in the conference room and sat next to her, a laptop before him ready to make the video call. Officer Dillon sat across from them at the table, poised with pen and paper to take notes if necessary.

Following the link Sophie had sent, Jackson began the video call. The almost musical beep-bloop-beep chime ended quickly as Robbie and Sophie answered and their smiling faces jumped onto the big screen in front of them.

Even if she hadn't been told that they were Jackson's cousins, she would have seen the family resemblance. They both had the same square jaw, straight nose and thumb-print cleft in their chins. Broad dimples bracketed their mouths, and like Jackson, they had light eyes, although it was hard to tell what color thanks to the quality of the video combined with the projection.

Jackson's hair was a light brown, but Robbie and Sophie both had coffee brown, slightly wavier locks. Robbie was handsome. Sophie beautiful, but not in a classic way. More like a warrior goddess, strong and sure of herself.

"Happy to see you, *primo*," she said.

"Happy to see the both of you, and thank you again. I've got Rhea and Officer Dillon with me," he said, although he was the only one visible on the video call thanks to the angle of the laptop's camera.

"Like I said before, we've got good news for you," Robbie said and, a second later, a photo replaced their smiling images.

"We took the LIDAR images, and this is the raw photo," Robbie said, describing the first image. "There's lots of forest on both mountains, except for the ski resort to the extreme right and an obvious trail near that area."

As Robbie spoke, the mouse highlighted the areas his cousin was describing. When he shifted to the path close to the resort, Dillon spoke up. "That's the trail that most hikers use."

After that, Robbie continued, pointing toward the middle of the photo. "Here there appears to be slightly less vegetation, but then it's quite dense to the left of it."

Dillon rose from his spot and walked toward the screen. Gesturing to the area where the forest was less dense, he said, "I think this is the old logging road I told you about. I'm not sure just how passable the road is nowadays, and I don't think many people use it."

"Thanks for that info, Officer Dillon," Sophie said. "There was clearly something there even before we processed the image with our software."

When she finished, another image immediately popped up on the screen, surprising them with the look of it. All vegetation had been cleared away, revealing the contours of the mountainside, as well as what appeared to be other features.

Robbie came back online and continued with his explanation. "We downloaded a topographical map so we could have reference points to assist us in determining what was natural and what was man-made. Beside the resort area that was visible before, the processed image reveals several buildings beneath the tree line close to the resort and the path of the nearby trail."

"Wow, way cool," Officer Dillon said.

Very, Rhea thought as Sophie took over, explaining the other features revealed by their work. "There is clearly a break of some kind on the second mountain. I think Officer Dillon mentioned it was an old logging trail. But fairly high up on the trail, there's a small structure. Maybe a lean-to of some kind."

"Would that be big enough to hide a vehicle?" Jackson asked.

"For sure," Sophie answered and pressed onward. "About two miles away there's another structure. A cabin. See this square at one side? Probably a chimney."

"You're sure that's a cabin?" Jackson asked.

"Without a doubt," Robbie said and then shifted to an image zoomed and enhanced to show the details of the structure. After that, he displayed several other photos, from slightly different angles, which helped to define the path of the logging trail, as well as a possible trail from the lean-to toward the cabin.

When he finished, he said, "We've sent you these photos via email. If you need us to testify to them, we'd be happy to do that."

"We totally appreciate all you've done," Rhea said, suddenly feeling very optimistic about what the photos had revealed.

"We never say 'No' to family," Sophie said, which prompted a rough laugh from Jackson.

"Hint duly noted, as well as massive guilt, Sophie. I love you guys, and I hope to see you soon," Jackson said.

"Hope to see you soon *in Miami, primo*," Robbie said and ended the video call.

"They sure know how to lay on the guilt," Rhea teased, and Jackson laughed. He shot to his feet to turn on the lights in the conference room, leaned against the wall and crossed his arms. Peering at Dillon, he said, "You mentioned that logging road might be tough to traverse."

Dillon nodded. "Might be. We'd obviously need 4x4s and additional manpower. Those guys are probably armed."

Jackson nodded. "I spoke to the Parks Service, and they're leaving it up to us to take action. I'm thinking two other officers, SWAT possibly, if the chief approves of course."

"I agree. Weather tomorrow is supposed to be good," Dillon said.

Almost too eagerly, Rhea thought.

"I'll speak to the chief and ask him who will be our backup, but remember this, Dillon. These men are likely dangerous. Possibly murderers, or kidnappers if Selene is still alive," Jackson said in warning, likewise sensing the young officer's almost misplaced enthusiasm.

"Alive? It's been over six months, boss. Sorry, miss," Dillon said with a guilty look in her direction.

"It's okay, Officer Dillon. I understand." She peered at Jackson as he continued to lean against the wall.

As her gaze met his, determination filled his gaze, but also pain. They were possibly almost at the end of their journey. It might end at a most dangerous place tomorrow, after they made their ascent up the mountain and to the structures the images had revealed.

"I'm going with you tomorrow, Jax. Make no mistake about that," she warned.

"We'll discuss this later. Right now, I have to get the chief's approval for this operation."

He didn't wait for a reply from either her or Dillon. He rushed out, his face dark with worry and hurt, gray eyes as stormy as rainclouds. His lips a thin line in a face as stony as granite. Closed off from her, and she understood. He wasn't just preparing himself for the danger to come.

He was preparing for her to leave.

HE MOVED IN HER, his big body driving her toward release. His gaze locked on her, wanting to see when she went over and to hold that moment close before he lost control.

Her blue eyes had darkened, were almost black with desire. A soft moan escaped her with one thrust, and he worried he might have hurt her until she dug her fingernails into his skin and arched her back, deepening his penetration. He thrust again and she urged him on, wrapping her legs around him.

Inside pressure built, his heart pounding harder and louder. Almost as if calling out what he was feeling. *Love you, love you, love you,* but the words never left his mouth, trapped by fear.

Beneath him, her body shuddered and tightened, and she called out his name, her release washing over her. Spilling onto him as he drove into her one last time. Her name escaped his lips and he fell over with her.

He held his weight off her, but then she reached up and cradled his shoulders. Invited him to rest on her, their bodies still united. But after a short minute, he rolled onto his side and took her with him, tucking her close.

They lay there in silence until Rhea stroked a hand across his chest. "It's going to be okay."

A rough laugh escaped him. "Funny. I thought that was supposed to be my line."

She didn't respond, she just moved closer, her hand resting over his heart.

He understood. As much as he had searched for the words since they'd left the police station earlier, he hadn't found them. Hadn't been able to figure out how to tell her that he loved her. How that had happened in just a few days. What he hoped for the future with her. If there even was a future.

Rhea rested beside him, her hand tucked over his heart, listening to the beat as it settled into a steady rhythm. She felt his tension growing. The muscles beneath her hand were tight, unyielding. The arm resting down her back, keeping her near, didn't exude that feeling of comfort or protection that his touch usually did.

It made her wonder if it would be okay, as she'd said earlier. If after tomorrow, no matter what happened, they could make this relationship work. If they could explore the love that had somehow blossomed between them at such an unlikely time. But it had taken hold and sunk its roots deep in her heart.

Has it done the same in him?

She refused to think that it hadn't, but tomorrow would tell. No matter what happened, they might have to go their separate ways.

But can we find our way back together?

Chapter Twenty-One

The turnoff to the logging road was blocked by a wall of underbrush, but the tire tracks in the soft dirt confirmed it had been recently used. Jackson and Dillon got out of the SUV and, after examining the tumble of vines and brush, pulled it away to allow them to pass.

They bumped their way up the uneven road, which was fairly navigable despite the large boulders and soft loose dirt at numerous spots along the path. At one point, the SUV behind them carrying the two members of the Regina SWAT team got bogged down in one of the softer ruts. Jackson got out, cut down some branches with his machete and tucked them under the tires, providing the traction to get them out of the rut.

Inside their SUV, Dillon manned a tablet with software that Robbie and Sophie had provided, which visualized exactly where they were based on the LIDAR images. As Dillon lifted the tablet, a 3D rendering of the area around them sprang to life. But as they got closer to the first structure identified by the drone imagery, they didn't need a tablet to tell them what was right before their eyes: the SUV from the photos at the pub.

Jackson got out of the car, stood on the running board and gestured to everyone to hold their positions with his upraised fist.

He hopped off the running board and carefully approached the lean-to, which housed the SUV, worried that anyone who had taken the time to hide the turnoff for the road might have created a booby trap to protect the vehicle.

He inched his way all around the area, searching for trip wires or hidden traps.

"All clear," he said and gave the hand motion to go.

Everyone exited the vehicles and came over to examine the SUV against the pub photo.

"Definitely the same car," said the one SWAT officer as he stood in front of the Jeep, his rifle slung across his chest.

Jackson squatted to examine the custom bumper. There were rough gouges and scratches in the thick steel, a testament to when they'd used the vehicle to ram them. There were even still some hints of white paint from the police cruiser's bumper.

"This is the vehicle that attacked us." He straightened and faced his team.

"These men are dangerous. They are likely armed. We need to use extreme caution on our approach and you—" he gestured to Rhea "—you hang back and stay close."

Jackson hated that she was even with them, but Rhea had insisted, and he knew it wouldn't have done any good to argue with her. They had come so far together, and it would end with them together. He walked over to her, cupped her jaw and said, "You understand, right? I don't want to see you hurt." For good measure, he checked the bulletproof vest and helmet she wore, making sure she'd be secure.

Rhea cradled his face. "I understand. I'll stay close, because I don't want to see any of you hurt."

He nodded and went to the head of his team. Gave the Move-out symbol.

There was a narrow trail from the SUV lean-to westward, and they hiked on it cautiously, watching for booby traps or alarms. Checking the tablet to see just how close they were to the cabin, which had been revealed by the LIDAR.

Jackson figured the structure was a good two miles from the logging trail. Not a long hike normally, but he and the other officers were in full protective gear. It was hot and sweaty beneath the body armor and helmets. Still they pressed on, navigating the trail until the cabin came into view, just where the LIDAR had said it would be.

He gave the Hold command and examined the clearing around the structure. Off to one side, there was an area with a woodpile and log with an ax buried in it.

One less weapon for them, Jackson thought.

Crude chairs fashioned from branches graced an equally crude and rustic porch, clearly an add-on to an otherwise solid log cabin. Curtains in an indiscriminate color hung on the windows, blocking his view into the building.

Wood smoke escaped the chimney, and the smell of it drifted over to them along with the scent of bacon. Someone was making a meal. Maybe a late breakfast.

A good thing. It meant they were home and maybe not paying too much attention to the exterior of the cabin.

He gestured to his team members to come close, and once they had gathered around him, he spoke to them in a low tone, directing each member to a different side of the structure. With a quick glance at Rhea, he said, "You stay down and close to me. Understand?"

Rhea nodded, comprehending Jackson's concerns. But there was no way she was going to miss this moment after all that they'd been through to get here.

She hung back, as close as she could so as not to hamper Jackson, and watched as the other team members fanned out. They had only gotten about halfway to their positions when a clanging sound rang out. A cow bell, warning anyone in the cabin that someone was outside.

The SWAT member who had tripped the alarm dropped to the ground, trying to avoid detection, but a second later came the sound of glass breaking and a shot rang out in his direction. Bark flew off a tree in his general direction.

A curtain shifted in the front of the cabin, and the glass shattered as a second rifle barrel poked out.

Jackson muttered a curse and shook his head. With a backward sweep of his arm, he tucked Rhea behind the protection of his back. Having been discovered, he had no choice but to shout, "Police. Drop your weapons and come out with your hands up."

A round of gunshots came in their direction, smashing into the trees and brush around them. One of their team returned fire, but Jackson radioed them and said, "Hold your fire. They could have a hostage in there."

He again called out to the men in the cabin. "We don't have to do this the hard way. Surrender, and I can speak to the DA to keep the sentence reasonable."

In response, a female face suddenly appeared in the window, but then was hauled back abruptly. "We'll kill her," someone shouted.

Selene. Alive. Selene's alive, Rhea thought and stood up slightly, her gut reaction to run to her sister.

Jackson hauled her back down and looked over his shoulder at her. Blood dripped from a cut on his cheekbone and a bit of bark stuck to his helmet. Eyes hard, he said, "Steady, Rhea."

Without missing a beat, he turned back toward the cabin and screamed, "You can make this easier for yourselves. Let the woman go, and I'll talk to the DA."

More gunfire erupted, but it was followed by shouting from inside the cabin. The thick log walls were enough to muffle whatever it was they were saying to each other, but Rhea hoped they were talking about surrendering. Her hopes were dashed as bullets tore into the underbrush and ground all around the SWAT officer who had tripped the cowbell.

A volley of gunfire erupted from the officer toward the side of the cabin. The dull thud of bullets striking wood reverberated through her.

Once again, Jackson reined in the response. "Hold your fire. Repeat, hold your fire."

"Copy that," echoed from all the officers.

The creak of the door drew their attention. It opened, almost in slow motion, providing a partial view of the interior of the cabin. But then suddenly, Selene stood in the doorway, hands held on top of her head.

She paused, a little wobbly. *Way too thin*, Rhea thought. The tattered shirt hung on her slim shoulders and was stained in various spots. Rhea had given her the shirt two Christmases ago. Her jeans were worn and torn, likewise dirty as if from soot or soil.

"Come forward slowly, hands up," Jackson shouted.

Selene took another hesitant step toward them onto the front porch. She squinted, as if the sunlight was too much for her, making Rhea wondered if it had been months since she'd been outside the walls of her prison.

"Walk forward slowly," Jackson said as another burst of shouting came from within the cabin.

A bearded face became visible in the window, and the man called out, "You have her. Now leave us alone."

More fighting followed that declaration, and with the door open, the words were a little more discernable. One voice, stronger and obviously in command. "Shut the door. Shut the damn door."

The second, weaker, almost stumbling. "B-b-b-ut—"

"Shut it," boomed the first person, and the door slammed closed.

Selene jumped, almost as if shot, and it was all Rhea

could do not to run to her sister. But Jackson had his arm stuck out, a barrier keeping her back.

The shouting resumed inside the cabin, and Jackson took advantage of that to stand, exposing himself to gunfire. He held out his hand and motioned to Selene. "Here. Come here, Selene."

Her sister's eyes widened, but then she ran toward them and dropped to her knees, into Rhea's arms, when she got there.

Rhea kissed her sister's face and wrapped her arms around her, unable to believe she was really there. That she was alive.

"You've made this easier for yourselves, but you've got to surrender. Come out, hands up," Jackson commanded.

More yelling came from the cabin, followed by an assortment of crashes, as if someone was trashing the place. More shouts, and then silence. Finally, surprising all of them, the sound of a single gunshot.

Jackson sucked in a breath, trying to fathom what that single gunshot might mean. Especially as the door slowly opened again and a hesitant voice called out, "D-d-don't shoot. Please don't h-h-urt m-m-e."

There was almost a nervous quality to the voice, warning him that it might be the younger brother. A gentle hand on his forearm drew his attention back to where Rhea and Selene huddled, arms around each other. It was Selene's hand, and as he met her gaze, so much like Rhea's, he was taken aback for a moment. But only a millisecond in this life and death situation.

"It's Wade," Selene confirmed.

Jackson nodded. "Come out slowly, Wade. Hands on your head. We won't hurt you."

Finally, someone appeared in the doorway. One of the men in the photos. One of Selene's kidnappers.

"Slowly, Wade," he repeated as the man faltered on the

front porch, clearly afraid as his gaze darted all around, seemingly uncomprehending.

Wade took a few more uncertain steps into the clearing in front of the cabin.

Over his shoulder, Jackson asked Selene, "What's his brother's name?"

"Earl," she said harshly, as if it pained her to say his name.

"On your knees, Wade. Where's Earl?" Jackson said, rising slightly so Wade could see him, but keeping behind the trunk of the tree for safety.

"Dead. Kilt himself," Wade said and whipped his head in the direction of the cabin.

Jackson radioed his team. "Visuals? Can anyone confirm?"

Dillon spoke up first. "I can see into the cabin. Looks like a body on the floor."

"Are you sure, Dillon?" Jackson pressed, wanting to avoid any additional bloodshed.

"I'm sure, boss."

Jackson commanded the two SWAT officers. "Levine. Anderson. Move in. Dillon, hang back and secure our suspect when possible."

"Copy that," all the officers confirmed.

Jackson waited, protecting the two women while his counterparts hurried toward the cabin, guns drawn. The SWAT officers paused at the door. Entry areas like that could be a fatal funnel, but as the one officer peered inside, he lowered his weapon slightly.

"Shot himself in the head. Going in to check on him. Cover my six, Anderson," Officer Levine said and entered the cabin. He emerged a second later and gave the All-clear motion.

Jackson stood and helped Rhea bring her sister to her feet. Together, they supported her to walk to a stump, where she sat and gazed up at them, tears streaming down her face.

"I thought I'd die here...like the others," she said, and her gaze skittered back to the cabin for a second and then back to them.

"Others?" Jackson asked, hands on his hips as he focused on Selene's face, so much like Rhea's, but so much thinner from her captivity. The remnants of a bruise, going yellowish and purple, lingered along her right cheek. He clenched his jaw with anger at the thought of anyone striking her.

Selene nodded. "Wade let it slip that they'd taken other women, but I already knew. There were other feminine things in the cabin. Combs. Jewelry. Clothes. I think they killed them."

"Anderson. Dillon. Levine. Secure the area. I'm going to call in the Crime Scene Unit, since we may have other victims here," Jackson instructed and then stepped away to phone his chief and advise him on their status and the possibility they had multiple kidnappings and homicides.

"I have to say I'm surprised, Jax. That's just not the kind of thing that happens here," the chief said.

"I'm with you, Bill. I'm hoping Selene is wrong, and it was just Wade shoplifting things, like he did in Regina, but if not..." If not they had serial killers on their hands.

"I'll get them up there ASAP. How's the woman? Do you need transport to take her to the hospital?"

Jackson glanced back toward where Selene sat, Rhea kneeling beside her. "She's shaky, Chief. We may need transport, but give me a little more time to talk with her and see what she wants."

Jackson returned to the two women and was once again struck by how identical they were. Same intelligent crystal-blue eyes and full lips. The dark, almost black hair, although Selene's was far longer and dull. As he neared, they both looked toward him, the motion of their bodies in unison.

"CSU will be coming up to search the scene and preserve evidence. I'd like to take you to the hospital—"

"No, I want to go home," Selene said, shaking her head furiously.

Jackson looked toward Rhea, who did a little dip of her head. "I think that would be best."

Blowing out a rough breath, Jackson said, "We need to take some photos of you and get a statement. Are you up for doing that?"

Selene nodded. "I am. Anything you need me to do."

"I'm grateful for that, Selene. I can call for a transport chopper—"

"I can walk. I just want to get out of here," she said, wrapped her arms around herself and began to rock, like a child trying to comfort itself during a nightmare.

Rhea hugged her sister and kissed her temple, trying to calm her. "It's okay, Selene. It's over. You'll be home soon."

"With you. I want to go with you," Selene cried and grabbed hold of Rhea's arm.

"With me, sis. Don't worry. You can stay as long as you need to," Rhea said.

"Let me just give my men some other instructions and then we'll head back to Regina," Jackson said.

He returned, leaving Dillon to guard Wade in the hopes he would provide more information to the CSU. They read him his Miranda rights, using Dillon's body cam to preserve it and anything else he said as evidence. He worried that if they didn't record it, it might not hold up in court, but his top priority, beside getting Selene home, was discovering if Wade and his brother had kidnapped and killed other women.

Together, Rhea and he supported Selene for the hike back to their vehicle. As they walked, she seemed to grow stronger, her back straightening and her head lifting from its earlier cowed droop. Halfway through the walk, she began her story.

"Matt and I had another fight, and he hit me again. I ran, afraid of him. Scared of myself and what I was becoming. I was driving to you, Rhea, but it was late and I got hungry. I stopped for gas and when I asked the clerk about a place to eat, he recommended the pub." She stopped to draw a shaky breath and then continued, "I ordered a burger and was eating when Earl and Wade came by. They started making comments. Eyeing me. When I left, they followed me out and catcalled me again, but I ignored them, got in my car and drove away.

"When I got to the lake, it called to me, so I parked and walked toward the shore. Stood there thinking about my life and decided it was time to leave Matt. Time to follow my dreams like you had, Rhea." She glanced at her sister and offered her a smile.

Like Rhea, Selene is even more beautiful when she smiles, Jackson thought.

"Is that when you texted me?" Rhea asked.

Selene nodded. "It is. I was going to come to you that night, but as I turned, someone grabbed me and covered my mouth. Someone else took hold of my feet to haul me back toward the road. I was kicking and trying to scream, but I couldn't breathe and passed out."

"Earl and Wade took you to the cabin?" Jackson said.

"They expected me to service them and if I didn't…" Selene's voice cracked then, and tears came to her eyes and spilled downward, but she swiped them away furiously. "They'd rape me once or twice a week. Wade really didn't want to, but Earl would bait him and say that he wasn't a real man if he didn't."

Walking beside Selene, Rhea was likewise crying, obviously thinking about everything her sister had suffered in the months she'd been held captive. The two sisters held each other, offering support. Offering comfort to each other as they finished the hike and reached the police SUVs.

Jackson helped the women into the back and got behind the wheel. It was time to return Selene to civilization. Back to her real life.

Away from Regina, he thought, but reined in his emotions. Selene was alive and free, but there might be other women who had not been so lucky.

Now it was his job to speak for them and to give their families relief. Everything else would have to wait.

Chapter Twenty-Two

Rhea had sensed his withdrawal with every mile that took them away from the cabin and to Regina. Upon their arrival, he was the consummate professional, arranging for one of the female officers to take photos of Selene and afterward getting her statement on video while he took notes. While she understood he had a job to do, it only reinforced her earlier fears that once this case was over, they'd be over.

But her pain was dimmed by the joy that Selene was alive. *Alive*, she thought and hugged her sister hard. Gazing at her, Rhea examined Selene, taking note of how she'd changed in the many months she'd been gone. There was something in her gaze that was older somehow, and there were tiny scars, the remnants of scratches and cuts, in addition to the very-visible remnants of a bruise along her cheek.

As Rhea continued her perusal, she noted additional bruising along her collarbone and bruises that looked like fingerprints on her upper arms.

Selene's gentle touch came to Rhea's jaw, urging her gaze away from the bruises. Selene was smiling, a sad smile that didn't quite reach her eyes. "I knew you wouldn't give up. I knew you'd come for me."

Rhea's gaze grew hazy with unshed tears and emotion

choked her throat. She fought past it and said, "I knew you were alive. I felt it, in here." She tapped her chest.

Selene nodded. "Me, too, and I feel your pain now," she said softly and peered toward Jackson as he stood outside the interrogation room, speaking with his chief. "He's special to you, isn't he?"

Rhea closed her eyes to fight the tears and wagged her head. "He is. Very special."

"It will be all right, Rhea. Believe that," Selene said, but fell silent as Jackson returned to the room.

He laid the file in his hand on the table. It contained Selene's statement, his notes and the photos they'd taken of her various injuries. With a heavy sigh, he said, "I think we're done here, but I hope that if we need more information, you'll make yourself available."

"I will," Selene said and skipped her gaze between Jackson and her. "Do you two need a moment?"

"Yes," Rhea said at the same time that Jackson said, "No."

Rhea's heart plummeted with that, but she refused to show it. "I guess we should go now."

Jackson nodded, but didn't look at her. Instead, he focused on Selene and said, "I think you should go to the hospital."

Rhea was looking away, but she caught sight of Selene peering between them as she said, "If you think so, but what about you two—"

"Rhea wants to make sure you're safe and sound also," he replied and grabbed hold of his file. "If you don't mind, I have to head back to the cabin. The CSU team has found other victims there."

He hurried from the room, but before he did so, he gazed at her like a hungry man at a king's feast, igniting hope that he really did care. That he really wanted more for them despite his behavior.

And then he was gone to do his job, and she had her own responsibilities to fulfill. She needed to get her sister to the hospital and make sure she was fine. Once they were home, she needed to help Selene rebuild her life and get on with her own.

THE POLICE STATION still looked picture perfect, the craftsman building nestled harmoniously with the other shops along Main Street. The flowers on either side of the wide steps leading to the door had grown larger in the month since she'd last been there. As a warm breeze swept past, the petals waved at her in welcome as they had a month ago.

She only hoped she would be as welcome inside, because so much had happened in the last few weeks.

Jackson and his team had found the bodies of three other women buried a short distance from the cabin. The jewelry and other items had helped to confirm their identities. One of the women had been missing for nearly four years, and based on the date of her disappearance, as well as the others, it seemed as if the brothers had taken a new woman every year. The other victims had been taken from farther away, which was why neither the Regina nor Avalon police departments had noticed a pattern. It had kept them from being criticized in the press. If anything, Jackson and his team, as well as her, had been praised for the police work that had brought closure to the other cases and families.

Wade had confirmed that it was Earl who had been at the inn, wanting to grab Rhea so they'd have both sisters under their control. When he'd realized Rhea was no pushover, he'd decided to scare her away or kill her if need be.

Entering the building, the familiar sight of the desk sergeant was a relief. Millie would know who she was, and she suspected the other woman would know who she was there to see. She wasn't wrong, as the young police officer smiled and buzzed her through the barrier. Rising, Millie said, "It's good to see you again, Rhea. Or, at least, I hope it's a good thing."

She nodded. "It is, Millie. Wish me luck."

Millie smiled and gestured toward the back of the station. "I think you know where his office is."

"I do," she said and, without waiting, headed to see Jackson.

As she neared the door, she passed Dillon who said, "Better be careful, Rhea. He's as cross as a bear with a thorn in its paw."

Jackson's door was closed. She knocked and heard his grumbled "I'm busy" through the door.

She'd come too far to be ignored that easily. She pushed through the door and shut it behind her.

A look of surprise filled Jackson's face before he schooled his features and stood.

He took her breath away, much like he had the first time she'd seen him. His police blues seemed a little looser around his body, and his face was thinner, as well. His shortly cropped brown hair had grown out a little and the gray of his eyes was muddled, like the sky during a rainstorm. He clenched and unclenched his jaw as he stood there, clearly uneasy.

She charged on, "It's good to see you again, Jax."

"Nice to see you again, Rhea," he said, although nothing about his tone and stance said he was happy to see her.

"I know we left things on a weird note," she began, and he laughed harshly, rocked back and forth on his heels.

"That's an understatement. How is Selene? How is she doing?" he asked and relaxed a little. He invited her to sit, but she was too nervous. And too anxious about what she intended to say to him.

"She's doing well. She divorced Matt and has been seeing a therapist and going to a support group. She's also been singing at some of the local clubs."

"Sounds good." He paused, jammed his hands in his pockets and said, "How about you? You okay?"

This was the moment she'd been waiting for and she didn't hesitate to grab it with both hands. "I'm miserable. I miss you. I hated how it ended with us because… I don't want it to end, Jax. I'm in love with you."

He reared back as if he'd been struck, but then he rushed toward her and embraced her in a bear hug. "You can't imagine how many times I dreamed you'd come back and say that."

She laughed, dropped a kiss on his jaw and said, "You dreamed of me?"

"Every night, Rhea. But when we started you were so vulnerable, and I felt so guilty that I might have taken advantage. That's why I forced myself to make you leave that day. You needed space. So did I."

She playfully elbowed him and then urged him to sit with her in the chairs in front of his desk. "I was so hurt that day, but once I was back in Denver, helping Selene, I realized I needed to find out if what we had was real."

He arched a brow and took hold of her hand, lacing his fingers with hers. "And did you?"

She nodded without hesitation and squeezed his hand. "I did. I want to be with you, Jax. That is if you want to be with me."

He leaned close and laid his forehead against hers. Kissed her cheek. "I want to be with you, but your life is in Denver."

"It *was* in Denver," she said. She broke away from him only long enough to remove a key from her purse. She dangled it in front of him and, at his questioning look, she said, "I rented a storefront on Main Street for a new gallery."

"Are you sure?" Jackson asked, unable to believe that

what he'd dreamed of for the last month was actually coming true. That Rhea was back. For good this time.

Rhea smiled and said, "I'm sure. I love you, Jax."

As he perused her features, her love beamed from her crystal-blue gaze, dispelling any remaining doubts he might have had.

"I love you, Rhea. I can't wait for our life together to begin."

"Why wait?" she said and pulled him up from the chair and toward the door.

Jackson laughed, but stopped at the door to kiss her. Hard. Demanding. But he tempered the kiss, worried they might not make it out of the station. As they broke apart, he cradled her face and said, "Have I ever said how much I love that you don't give up?"

"I think you called me stubborn, but that's okay, because I won't ever give up on us, Jax."

He smiled and kissed her again. "I think I can live with that. Forever, Rhea."

"Forever, Jax," she said and pulled him out the door and into the rest of their lives.

* * * * *

COLTON 911:
UNDERCOVER HEAT

ANNA J. STEWART

For Patience. For asking.

Chapter One

Controlling fire came as easily to Tatum Colton as breathing.

The arc of the flame, the quick flash of pristine blue giving way to brilliant orange as it brushed its heat in time with a quick wrist flick of the sauté pan in her hand. Warmth caressed her arms through the white chef's jacket she wore. The familiar beads of sweat coated her forehead as she moved from the stove to the workstation, where she plated the butter-rich pasta and fresh asparagus. A quick swipe of the towel tucked into the apron string around her waist, and the plate was set on the service table.

"Spring primavera up!" She glanced at the order screen, already mentally sorting out the ingredients as one of her chefs took the prepared bowl to the garnishing station before service. "Simon, how're we doing on the special orders for table nine?"

"Finishing now, Chef." Simon "Chester" Chesterton, one of her newest line chefs, worked magic with the vegan offerings at True, Tatum's restaurant. True was a lifelong dream of hers, and just last year, only their third since opening, she'd earned a James Beard nomination. The framed certificate hung on the press wall of the kitchen where they celebrated the accomplishments of all their staff. The nomination hadn't been her achievement alone. It was theirs. This year she was determined to take even bigger leaps and make the restaurant a food haven destination in the North Center neighborhood of Chicago.

The white-noise roar of the gas grills and burners, along with the scraping of a pizza peel as it slid freshly kneaded dough topped with imported cheeses and meats made in-house into the custom-built oven, soothed whatever nerves she might have had when it came to feeding her full house. Garlic, roasted spices, and the ever-present promise of a delicious, perfect European-inspired meal hung in the air and invigorated her. Her team moved fluidly and effortlessly through the kitchen as wait and cleaning staff bustled in and out of Sunday dinner service.

The employees at True had helped bring her vision to life. They were the blood that kept the heart of True beating. This place was her life. She'd put everything— all her finances, all her energy, all her focus into making it what it was becoming. And it had repaid her in kind by giving her a place of refuge and solace these past few weeks.

Grief and anger mingled low in her belly as tears of frustration and loss burned behind her smoke-filled eyes. If she didn't have this place she'd have been lost in the weeks since her father and uncle had been killed. No, she reminded herself as sternly as her sister Simone would have. They hadn't just been killed; they'd been murdered.

A murder the police still didn't seem to have a decent lead on.

One minute here, the next minute gone.

She grabbed a clean pan, dropped a fresh serving of pasta into the simmering water on the back of the multi-burner stove and got back to work.

"Tatum?" Susan Ford, Tatum's assistant front-of-house manager, dodged two of her line chefs. "There's a customer at the bar requesting to speak with you."

Tatum glanced up at the clock. "I'm not scheduled for my round of greetings for another forty minutes. Who is it?"

Susan shook her head, the unfamiliar expression of befuddlement clear on her face. Normally Susan was unflappable. "He didn't give me his name, just said he needed to speak with the owner as soon as possible."

Meaning Susan didn't know who the man was. And given Susan knew just about everyone in the food industry—from critics to owners to busboys—Tatum continued cooking. "Tell him I'll be out as soon as I can. And give him a drink on the house."

"He's not drinking."

Tatum's eyebrows arched, but she didn't comment. For all she knew, the man could be in recovery. "All right, then, a free appetizer. Provided you're certain he's not a salesman looking to hit us up on a buy."

"Definitely no salesman vibe with this guy." The grin on Susan's face had Tatum biting back a smile of her own. "He is seriously *h-o-t* hot. Just so you know ahead of time."

"Noted for future reference." Tatum chuckled and reached for the bowl of fresh tomatoes one of her prep chefs had placed nearby. Adding a stop at the bar to her mental list of the usual table rounds, Tatum refocused and worked her way through the continuous run of orders.

Whoever the man was, he was just going to have to wait.

DETECTIVE CRUZ MEDINA of the Chicago Police Department nursed his club soda with lime in what had to be a glass made from actual clear-cut crystal. From his seat at the bar, he admired the pristine, oversize cubes mingling about the sparkling liquid. The interplay of clear lines and vibrant colors was reflected in the decor of True, Tatum Colton's upscale, trendy and somewhat pricey restaurant.

Glass and silver fused with displays of lush greenery that brought in a feel of the outside. Clearly a renovated warehouse, he thought, as he surveyed the high ceilings and walls covered in geometric greens and gold that added to the relaxed atmosphere currently on display in the packed house.

Normally he'd have turned down the hostess's offer of a free appetizer while he waited. He was more a pizza and wings kind of guy, but that was because of convenience and a lack of time. After perusing the menu she handed him, he figured he may as well experience what the other half did, and ordered the fried calamari and lemon garlic aioli.

If his normal attire of slacks and loose-fitting T-shirt were out of place, he wasn't made to feel that way. The bartending staff was polite and welcoming, as were the servers who moved as if they had wings on their feet.

Their uniforms looked surprisingly comfortable. Dark slacks, white shirts under tasteful floral ones in the same natural tones as the decor. Deep-pocketed aprons held everything from small tablet computers for order taking, and biodegradable straws upon request, to packets of crayons for the few tables where children were handed their own miniature coloring books.

As far as Cruz could tell, True ran smoothly, effortlessly and without drama.

Which made it the perfect cover for illegal activity.

He sipped his soda, shifted around on his stool and scanned the crowd behind him in the mirrored shelves of the bar. He had yet to decide on what tactic he was going to take when it came to talking to owner Tatum Colton. It wasn't going to be an easy conversation, however he approached it. Also, the timing could be better. Given everything the Colton family was going through right now, with the still unsolved killing of Ms. Colton's father and her uncle, this wasn't the best time to present her with his suspicions about her business. But he had a case to solve, and every day he didn't, more addicts stayed on the street and more people became victims of overdose. More families suffered.

The murder of twin brothers Alfred and Ernest Colton had rocked Chicago to its foundation. There were plenty of wealthy residents in the city who wielded their power and finances like weapons, but not the Coltons, and certainly not the brothers. While Cruz had never met either man personally, he was acquainted with plenty of people who had, and their impressions went a long way in telling Cruz what kind of people they really were. The Colton brothers had been good people. Solid people.

And their loss was felt well beyond the borders of their family and friends.

Still... Cruz couldn't turn his cop brain off long enough to avoid considering if Tatum Colton was involved with the drug trade in the city, and whether she was somehow responsible for her loved ones' deaths. The idea sounded as ridiculous as it had the first time it slipped through his mind, but it still left a thread, however thin, of doubt. Until they were cleared, he didn't consider anyone free of suspicion.

Right now the Coltons were a grieving family, and while Cruz didn't want to pile on to an already difficult situation, he had an investigation to finish. An investigation that had already cost people he cared about far too much.

"Ms. Colton should be out in a few minutes." The elegant-looking hostess who had set him up at the bar returned with his appetizer. She was tall, on the curvy side, and wore her copper-highlighted red hair plank straight down her back. "Are you certain it's something I can't help you with?"

"I'm certain, thank you." He offered his most charming and understanding smile to the pretty young woman before glancing at her name tag. "I know she's busy."

"Busy is her eternal state," Susan said with a friendly laugh. "She'll be checking in on her dinner guests first, but she knows you're here. Is there anything else I can get you?"

"No, thanks," Cruz said. "I think I've got enough to feed a small army." One thing was for certain, he thought, as he focused on the plate brimming with golden, crispy-fried goodness in front of him. True fed to impress. He was not a fan of those "art meals" where the presentation looked as if it took a special design degree to construct. The portions here weren't stylishly scant, but bountiful and appealing and served on heavy, substantial, pristine white plates which made the food the star of the show. The restaurant's dedication to fresh, farm-to-table provisions was more than evident and a testament to why this place had helped revitalize a once forgotten area of the city.

One taste set his taste buds to singing. Any longing he'd had for a cheese-laden cardboard box delivery vanished as he ate. Enjoyed. And watched.

CURIOSITY, TATUM HAD to admit, got the better of her by the time she took her front-of-house break. Break was such a misnomer. She wouldn't stop until after she got home well after midnight. Most nights she wasn't in bed until after two. While her happy place was in front of the stove, with a knife in her hand, or creating new recipes, she knew that interacting with her customers was just as important as the food she served them.

"Showtime," she whispered as she let down her hair, changed into a clean jacket and headed out the swinging doors into the main dining room. Faces familiar and new moved in and out of focus as she greeted those who chose to spend time in her creation, feeding both their bodies and their souls with her food. The feedback on the meals was valuable of course, but this was also a way for Tatum to check and make sure everyone was having a good time and to put a face behind the experience. She wanted them all to feel as if they were at home.

When she had worked her way to the tables by the front door, she glanced at Susan, who inclined her head toward the bar. Tatum gave a short nod, and letting her gaze drift to the upper platform, scanned the line of stools and their occupants with practiced ease.

She'd have noticed the man even if he hadn't requested a conversation. Who was she kidding? She resisted the urge to pat her suddenly warm cheeks. She'd have noticed him if he'd been standing in the middle of a crowd.

In Tatum's experience, there were men who commanded attention. There were men who captured a woman's gaze as ferociously as a hunter caught his prey. And then there were men like the one sitting at her bar: the kind of man who turned a woman's normally locked-down, practical mind toward spinning images of very intimate, almost erotic encounters.

She shook her head as if trying to dislodge the thoughts. Not an easy task, considering those dark, fathomless eyes had found her as if she'd been a beacon he'd instantly honed in on.

Tatum let out a long, slow breath, bade good evening to the last group of guests and made her way toward the bar.

Everything around her faded into silence. He lowered his feet to the floor, stood to his full six-foot height and had her inching her chin up to meet his eyes. Shaggy dark hair brushed against his shoulders. His brown skin was accented by a neatly trimmed beard and mustache that outlined full, rounded lips and camouflaged a jawline indicating not only stubbornness, but determination. His body was trim, streamlined and inappropriately tempting beneath his dark slacks and shirt, which showed off biceps that spoke of an attention both to fitness and a woman's intimate desires.

He was, Tatum thought in the moment before he took her hand, a man who could make a woman forget everything about her life before he walked into it.

"Ms. Colton?" His voice was as smooth as the imported cognac she kept in stock for her most discerning customers. "Cruz Medina. I appreciate you taking some time. I know how busy you are."

"Always happy to speak with one of my customers." She motioned for him to take his seat, then slid in between him and the empty stool beside him. Resting her arm on the edge of the bar, she gave him her full attention. "I see you chose the calamari. Did you enjoy it?"

"I haven't had better since I was in San Francisco," he said, his eyes twinkling with something akin to mischief. No doubt he was well aware of the effect he had on women. Or, Tatum thought, her specifically. "I appreciate the service and the experience."

"That's what we are here for." Pride had her steeling her shoulders. "Is there something I can help you with, Mr. Medina?"

"There is." He wiped his mouth, pushed his empty plate away and reached into his back pocket. When he flipped open his wallet, Tatum found herself looking down at a shiny gold badge. Her heart did an odd *kathump* in her chest as the breath left her lungs. "It's Detective Medina, actually. I'm here to ask you about the drugs being run through your restaurant."

Chapter Two

It would forever remain a mystery, Tatum would later think as she closed herself in her kitchen office after closing, how she'd made it through the rest of her shift. Her anger threatened to bubble over, and the ringing in her ears even now grew louder as she paced the upstairs space she used as a refuge.

She tried to lose herself in the faint, cacophonous, almost frenetic noise of the nightly cleanup echoing up the staircase. The dishes being washed, pots and pans being run through the industrial fast-working washer. Tables being pre-set for their next open night's service. The down-to-business but still good-natured ribbing that ricocheted through the kitchen. She looked down through the wall of windows that gave her an eagle-eye view of her pride and joy and, for a moment, felt as if she was about to lose everything.

While she might not sleep at True, it was her home. Her center. The people who worked here were her family. She loved them. More important, she trusted them.

The idea anyone would come into her home slinging accusations, accusing people she cared about of… drug trafficking?

"It's absolutely ridiculous." She grabbed the rubber stress ball her sister Simone had given her and smacked it off the desk, sending it soaring across the room. There was a short rap on the door before Susan poked her head in.

"Everything okay?"

"Yeah, fine," Tatum lied before she centered herself. She couldn't let one completely unfounded allegation throw her. Yet. Her future demeanor would depend on the conversation she planned to have with the good detective now that the doors were closed. "Just needed a couple of minutes of relative quiet."

"Hmm." Susan's eyebrow arched in that lie detector way she had. "I'm thinking something else drove you in here. Is he about six feet, has devastating eyes and looks like he should be sipping tequila on the Riviera?"

Tatum turned her back and removed her chef's jacket, tossed it onto her chair with her purse, then unclipped her hair. "He's definitely made an impression," she managed, barely keeping her temper in check. "You ready to take off?"

"Yeah. I've got the day's printouts and cash bundled up. You want to take them or should I leave them for Richard for tomorrow?" She held out the bank bag she'd filled from the two in-house registers. Normally she'd let Richard Kirkman, her manager, deal with it. He took Sundays off and did all the "office" work on Mondays, when they were closed to customers.

"I'll take them with me." Something told her she wasn't going to be sleeping much tonight. And not because of anything Susan might be thinking.

"Okay, then, I'll be heading out." Susan gave her a quick if not confused smile.

"Hey, Susan?"

"Yeah?"

Choosing her words carefully, Tatum walked around and leaned back on the edge of her desk, her arms crossed. "I'm a pretty good judge of people, right?"

"Well, you plucked me right out of business school graduation, so I'd say yes." Susan's gentle laugh almost made Tatum smile. Almost. "Sorry. I would say yes. You're an excellent judge. The people you've hired, we all fit. And believe me, that's not an easy thing to do in any business, let alone a restaurant."

Susan's answer should have been a relief. "So there's no one you'd say doesn't work right or seems…out of place."

Susan frowned, stepped back inside and closed the door. "No one I can think of. Why? What's going on?"

"I don't know." Tatum rubbed a hand across the back of her neck. "Maybe nothing. Just…do me a favor and let me know if anything looks, sounds or feels…" She waved her hand in the air, struggling for the right word.

"Hinky?" Susan supplied.

"Yeah, hinky."

"All right. Well, to be honest, my boss is currently sounding like something's bothering her, and it sounds like she both does and doesn't want to talk about it." Susan inclined her head. "That's a bit hinky."

Tatum couldn't help it. She laughed, and the pressure that released in her chest allowed her to breathe for the first time in hours. "That might just be exactly what I needed to hear."

Another knock on the door had Tatum standing up straight once more. "Yes?"

"Sorry to interrupt." Detective Medina leaned in, looked between the two of them, his dark-eyed gaze completely unreadable. "You said to come up once you closed."

"Come on in." She waved him in, moved around him and shooed Susan toward the door.

"You know you're going to have to tell me everything, right?" Susan mock-whispered.

"Go home, Susan." It was all Tatum could do not to roll her eyes. "Enjoy the day off."

"Right." Susan leaned back, craned her neck and grinned over Tatum toward Detective Medina. "It was nice to kind of meet you."

"Nice to meet you, too, Susan."

Tatum glared at him as he took her spot, propped himself against the edge of her desk and stretched out his legs. He looked, she thought, like a cat who had finished off the last bowl of cream.

"He knows my name," Susan whispered with a grin before Tatum shoved her the rest of the way out the door and closed it.

When she was certain privacy was in place, she swung on Detective Medina, hands planted on her hips, the anger burning a hole in her chest. "What the hell do you mean coming into my restaurant and accusing me of being a drug dealer?"

He barely moved. The only indication he gave he'd even heard her was a twitch of those lips that not so long ago she'd had serious fantasies about. When he spoke, she could tell it was with deliberate care, which only scraped on her frayed nerves. "I didn't accuse *you* of any such thing," he said finally. "I do, however, think True is being used as part of a drug distribution chain in the city."

"That's the most ridiculous thing I've ever heard," she snapped. "What on earth led you to that conclusion?"

"Six months of investigation." He sounded so casual, as if they weren't talking about something that could destroy her life. "I've got players in this from all over the city, including the restaurant business, and funnily enough, a lot of the paths I've followed lead right through your doors."

"Who are these players? I want names. If I've got criminals working for me—"

"You have two ex-cons on the payroll, actually." He inclined his head as if imparting information she didn't already know. "Sam Price and Ty Collins."

"Three," she added with a smirk. "You missed Bobby Quallis. All three were nonviolent offenders, and all three have served their time and fulfilled their probation obligations. They also attended culinary training at community colleges and haven't been in trouble since." She'd wanted to be able to give back to the community in some way, to offer her employees chances other businesses might not. "I'd stand up for any one of them."

"Noted." He shrugged. "You're the trusting sort. Good to know."

"I know people," Tatum said. "More important, I like them. Well, most of them. You certainly aren't on the top of my list right now. What actual evidence do you have that True is involved in whatever case you're investigating?"

For the first time since she'd seen him in the bar, she saw him tense. Not a lot. Just enough to let her know she'd hit some kind of target.

"Actually, it's evidence I'm hoping to find. Right now all I have is a hunch."

Relief surged through her and had her shoulders sagging. "A hunch." The word tasted like cheap vinegar on her tongue. "I've been breathing fire for the past three hours because you have a hunch?"

He held up his hands as if she were going to attack. "*Hunch* is maybe the wrong word. I have very good intuition about these things and my gut is telling me there's something here. Not necessarily with you."

"You mean I'm not a drug dealer?" She pressed a hand against her heart and sighed dramatically. "Oh, that's such a relief." She stalked around the desk and dropped into her chair. He stood, but slowly, so that she got a very up-close-and-personal look at his very fine butt. Irritation sizzled through her veins. She pursed her lips and shoved her mind back on track. "You can take your hunch and your intuition and everything else you brought with you and get lost."

He sat in the one empty chair across from her, the entertained expression fading from his face. "I can't do that, Ms. Colton."

"Why not?" She should have poured herself a glass of wine before she'd come in here. Hell, she should have grabbed a whole bottle.

"Because." He waited until she looked him full in the eyes again. "My hunches are never wrong. True is being used in the distribution of narcotics in and around Chicago. I wouldn't be here if I didn't believe that. I also wouldn't be talking to you about it if I thought you were personally involved. We'd be discussing it down at the station with you under caution."

"Down at the station." Tatum rested her elbows on the desk and lowered her head into her hands. "Suddenly I'm in an episode of *Law and Order*." He didn't laugh. He didn't respond. And when she met his gaze again, she felt her stomach pitch at the sympathy she found on his handsome face. "What do you want from me? Access to my books? Employee files? Phone records?" She could hear their family attorney screaming in protest. "You can question my employees, but I won't hold it against them if they request a lawyer."

"Since you're offering, I'll say yes to all of that. But that isn't why I'm here." He leaned forward, clasped his hands between his knees and offered a smile that had her heart skidding to a halt. "I want you to give me a job."

CRUZ HAD TO give Tatum Colton credit. He'd thrown a lot at her in a short amount of time and she'd taken each hit like she was wearing a bulletproof vest. Every bit of information struck home and had no doubt stung and even bruised her, but she'd barely flinched.

And that, Cruz thought as he watched her process his request, told him more about her than the dozens of media and news features he'd read about her. He knew the stats—her birthday, her very single marital status, and where she lived. He also knew after his first glimpse that she was a knockout—from that rich honey-blond hair to those stunning, sparkling blue eyes of hers, down her very fit figure to the tips of her cushioned, black-sneakered feet. The definition in her arms, along with the sweat-kissed tendrils of hair surrounding her face, told him she wasn't just the pretty public face of the restaurant: she was the constantly humming engine behind it. But from the way she absorbed the information he shot at her, the play of tense emotions that first dulled then sharpened that pinpoint gaze of hers, he knew his gut instinct was right.

Tatum Colton wasn't a drug trafficker. She wasn't a criminal.

What she could be was useful.

His request for a job wasn't completely impulsive. It was an option he and his lieutenant had discussed as a possibility. Not the first option of course, but that would have only happened if Tatum had somehow collapsed immediately and confessed.

Cruz watched Tatum blink her way through his words as if spitting out Morse code. He'd been a cop long enough he could have a second career as a lie detector. He'd bet his future pension she had no involvement in the drug activity he was convinced was being conducted through True. No one, not even Academy Award winners, could act so convincingly. He didn't pick up on nerves or guilt. But he definitely felt a surge of anger shimmering through the air.

He also felt a spark of attraction. One big enough to set this whole building on fire. But that wouldn't get him anywhere but in a whole lot of trouble.

"Would you excuse me for a moment? I'll be right back." Tatum pushed out of her chair and headed for the door. He winced as she gave the knob a particularly nasty twist before stepping out. He heard every single foot-pounding step she took downstairs, then a few minutes later, every single stomp back up. She stormed back in and, as her hands were now full with a bottle and two of those pristine cut-crystal glasses, kicked the door shut behind her.

She sat again, all but ripped the cap off the bottle and poured two healthy portions before pushing one toward him. She tossed back a shot and slammed her empty glass on her desk, arching a perfect brow at him. "Are you joining me?"

He felt his lips twitch as he reached for the glass, followed suit and downed what he now realized was one of the smoothest aged tequilas he'd ever ingested. Cruz grabbed the bottle, nearly balking at the label that would have set him back a good couple of weeks' pay. "Well, hell." He sat back, enjoying the burn as the alcohol made its way down. She reached for the bottle. "Are you sure you want to do that?"

"Oh, yeah." She poured again, a bit more generously this time, but he covered his glass with his hand, shook his head.

"I have to admit," Cruz said with more amusement than the situation called for. "This wasn't exactly the reaction I expected."

"I'm a constant surprise to people." She toasted him, then tossed the second drink back, poured a third. This time when she looked back at him, her eyes were swimming with tears, but she blinked them away and let the anger shine through. "Tell me something." She pressed the back of her hand to her mouth. "Is this theory of yours about drugs being run through my restaurant common knowledge among your fellow cops or is this something you're sharing with me first as a courtesy?"

"I wouldn't say it's common knowledge," Cruz said. "My lieutenant is aware, as are a few other detectives in my squad. Why?"

"Why?" She blinked again. "Because the second word gets out you're investigating True, everything I've worked for will disappear. Even just the hint of illegalities will shut the doors to this place faster than I can toss a pizza. I might never get them open again."

Cruz knew he should have felt like squirming under that heated, penetrating gaze of hers, but he didn't. He couldn't. He had a job to do. An important one. Stopping the flow of drugs into the city had been his sole focus from the time he joined the department seven years ago. He wasn't going to back off now because his investigation might inconvenience a few business owners here and there. He'd promised his partner. His brother-in-arms. A brother whose life would never be the same again. And Cruz never, ever gave up on a promise. "Hurting your business is not my intention."

"Intention or not…" She capped the bottle and sat back in her chair, filled glass clasped between her hands, and looking, Cruz had to admit, a bit more relaxed and even sexier than before. "That's what's going to happen."

"Look." Cruz, not known for his diplomacy, found himself choosing his words carefully. "Contrary to how this looks, I've approached you quietly. Off the radar. Because my gut is telling me this is where I'm supposed to be. I'm good at my job, Ms. Colton. Very good at it.

Part of the reason I am is that I don't let anything stand in my way. We could have done this officially, called you into the station house for questioning, asked to see your books, your records, your employee files…" He held up his hands when she opened her mouth to speak. "All of which you just offered me free and clear. But I didn't do all that. I'd like to do this clean, where it would cause you and your business the least amount of damage and publicity." It wasn't a lie.

But it also wasn't the truth.

She considered him with a narrowed gaze. "What if I say no?"

"No to what?"

"No to giving you a job." She rested her cheek in her palm and looked at him, not with the resentment and anger he'd seen before, but with a barely shrouded gaze of desperation. "No to cooperating with you. What if I tell you to conduct your investigation as you have been? From outside. And before you answer, remember you haven't shown me anything to prove anyone here is involved with the drug trade. All you've done is tell me who you are and that my business is a front for drugs. Why should I believe you?"

"I don't think it's a front," Cruz said. "I have no doubt your business is exactly what you mean for it to be. A successful, neighborhood-rejuvenating restaurant that serves some pretty incredible food." Once again, he found himself pulling back from his normal bulldozing ways. He needed an in. He needed more evidence to convince his lieutenant he was on the right track. He didn't have nearly enough for warrants, court orders or even surveillance. Which meant he needed to find another tactic.

And from what he could tell, the best way in was through Tatum Colton.

"Someone is using your business, Ms. Colton. Someone is using what you built to bolster their own criminal enterprise. I'm sorry to have to tell you this, but those are the facts."

"The facts as you see them," Tatum challenged as she downed the last shot. "The facts as I know them tell me you're wrong."

"Then let me prove it one way or the other." He inclined his head. "If I'm wrong, I'll back off and you'll never see me again. But if I'm right…" He shrugged.

"If you're right, your investigation could destroy everything I've worked for in my life." She eyed the bottle of tequila, seemed to shake off the idea, as if she realized that wasn't going to solve anything. "I need to think about this."

"I thought you might." Feeling as if some progress was being made, he stood, reached for his wallet and pulled out one of his cards, set it on her desk. "When you've decided, give me a call. Day or night. My cell is always on."

She let out a short laugh. "I bet you say that to all the girls."

"Tonight I'm saying it to you." He found himself smiling. He liked her. He hadn't expected that. He liked her a lot. "I don't always mean it, though."

"Yeah, well, I bet not all your ladies can help you investigate drug running in Chicago." Instead of putting his card away, she pocketed it. "I'll let you know."

"I do have one other question before I leave." He faced her at the door. He was close, not too close, but close enough to catch the faint hint of olive oil and smoke wafting off her skin. "This one's a bit more personal."

"Can I plead the Fifth if I choose not to answer?"

She really did have a way of making him smile. "Why tequila?" he asked.

"Because it gives me the most bang for my buck and never disappoints." When her face relaxed and she leaned against the doorframe, he found himself suddenly reluctant to leave. And not just because when she crossed her arms over her chest he caught a significant glimpse of cleavage beneath her tank top. She caught his eye when he lifted his gaze back to her face, and her grin widened. "But I also chose it because I figured you could match me shot for shot. It was nice to meet you, Detective Medina." She held out her hand. "One way or the other, I'll be in touch."

"I look forward to hearing from you." He shook her hand, gave it an extra squeeze just to test the waters. When she squeezed back, he felt that bolt of attraction hit him dead square in the chest.

As he left her office and headed downstairs to the kitchen and then the front door, he found himself wondering when he'd last been on anything resembling a date. He couldn't remember. When he reached his car, he tried to recall the name of any woman who had captured his interest over the past... It didn't matter how far back he went, the list didn't exist.

But he had one now.

And it began with Tatum Colton.

AFTER LETTING THE rest of her staff know she'd be sticking around to close, Tatum locked herself back in her office and stashed the bottle of tequila in the bottom drawer of her desk for what she assumed would be a need later on. She pulled open her laptop and began skimming through the last six months of her business accounts.

Assessing the numbers had, until recently, been a nightly ritual. These days, she left most of the office work and number crunching to her manager, Richard. He'd been a godsend from the start, popping up right after the unexpected resignation of her last manager, who had sadly been killed in a car accident a few days later. And then since her father's death, he'd stepped up and in, eagerly accepting the challenge of expanding True's catering options even as he took over food and supplies ordering, employee schedules, and payroll. All of which freed Tatum to do what she did best: cook.

Looking at the network-shared spreadsheets, accounts and banking statements, she didn't see anything amiss. It was a cursory check, but she knew her business well enough to spot red flags. Revenue was up considerably, but they'd had a full list of reservations for nearly two months now. An uptick in cash made sense. She clicked open the catering spreadsheet, noticed that currently the expenses were definitely outweighing profit, but that wasn't wholly unexpected. As of now they only had a few bookings and only two recurring clients. Time to start pushing for more. She jotted down a note to discuss the catering with Richard ASAP.

Not for the first time tonight, she picked up her cell, her fingers itching to reach out to the one man who had always been her shoulder to cry on, her confidant. Her protector. She tapped open the number pad before she remembered her father wouldn't answer. He was gone.

She bit her lip, pressed the phone against her forehead and squeezed her eyes shut until she saw stars.

Alfie Colton had been so proud of what she'd made here, the changes she'd helped to bring to this community. Both her parents had always instilled the importance of giving back, of making a difference, and of building something lasting in her life. Not only for Tatum, but for her sisters, as well. January and Simone had taken different tracks to get there—January as a social worker and Simone as a psychologist—but they'd accomplished the one thing all the Colton sisters had as a goal in common: making their parents proud while living completely independent lives.

The air in her lungs seemed to vanish. For the first time since her father's murder, as much as she missed him, as much as she could have used Alfie Colton's advice, she was grateful he wouldn't witness whatever fallout there was from what had started tonight.

Anger and bitterness cut through her like a honed porcelain knife. How could she think such a thing? Shoving her laptop away, she sank back in her chair, drew her knees up and stared at the too-bright screen.

Tears trailed down her cheeks as she wondered for what felt like the millionth time what, if any, progress the police were making in finding whoever was responsible for her father's and uncle's deaths. It had felt as if their family had been swarmed with detectives and officers early on, but in the last few weeks since the funerals? She'd been questioned not once but twice, and she resented the notion of having to give them her irrefutable alibi. She'd been here, at True, when her father had been killed, just as she was every night. That she—or any of her sisters or close-as-sibling cousins—was considered a suspect had bile rising in the back of her throat.

It seemed to have taken forever to convince those detectives that they were a family that loved each other without reservation or hesitation. Not that there weren't issues. Of course there were. But for those issues to lead to murder?

It had been the most preposterous accusation she'd ever heard. Until tonight.

Now the detectives were going longer and longer between phone calls and new information. Her mother and aunt, both beyond heartbroken at having lost their husbands in the same violent way, were standing strong. They were, after all, Coltons, even if only by marriage. A Colton was a Colton, and if there was one thing her family was, it was strong. They might bend, but they never, ever broke.

Tatum as well as her sisters and her three cousins were all adrift with grief and anger, but also more cognizant than ever of how important family truly was.

She was not, Tatum decided as she swept her fingers under her eyes and stopped the flow of tears by sheer will, going to let one hint of scandal hit True or the Colton family. She couldn't. Not only because the restaurant was her livelihood and her life, but because she would not taint the Colton name.

"Let him investigate on his own," she said to the empty room. "He won't find anything."

Chapter Three

Cruz stopped at his parents' house on his way home. Because he saw the kitchen light on, he told himself. Not because he was feeling slightly uneasy about having lied to Tatum Colton about taking the damage potentially done to her restaurant into consideration. He couldn't afford concerns.

"Stop worrying about that," he muttered as he pulled into the driveway and climbed out. "You're doing your job." He couldn't take collateral damage into consideration. Not if he was going to make a dent in the drugs streaming into his city. Streaming? Ha. In recent months the trickle had turned into a flood and people were dying. Long-time addicts and the newly curious. And kids. So many, too many kids.

The crisp March air had him shivering despite his lifelong acclimation to the Windy City. Growing up in a working-class neighborhood had been a paradise of bike riding, baseball games and trick-or-treating for him and his younger siblings. Lawn mowers rumbled on the weekends and cars moved in and out of garages and driveways with consistency. Being raised in an area where his neighbors were friends, where he had been exposed to multiple cultures and family types had been the best preparation for becoming a cop. He liked people. He understood people. And he loved his neighborhood.

He would do whatever he had to in order to protect it.

When he ran up onto the porch, he found himself wishing he'd worn his jacket, but that thought vanished the instant he stepped inside. The two-story brick structure had been his parents' home for the past thirty-two years, and he found himself encased in the instant, familiar warmth.

He didn't, as he had all those years growing up, call out to them. Instead he closed the door, wiped his feet and ducked into the kitchen, where he found his mother precisely where he expected to find her on a Sunday night—sitting with his father at the polished round table, going over the family budget.

"Cruz." Patricia Medina's all-seeing, all-knowing brown eyes narrowed in suspicion as she pulled off her reading glasses. "It's after midnight. What are you doing here?"

"Just thought I'd stop on my way home."

"You working a case?" Saul Medina picked up his coffee mug and headed to the ancient, sputtering pot as Cruz pulled open the fridge. "Or just raiding our fridge?"

"Yes and yes." Cruz grinned at his parents. "Unless Frankie and Inez polished off tonight's leftovers already?" The twins, his college-age brother and sister, ten years his junior, were notorious for their all-night study sessions that usually left the refrigerator and cupboards bare and the kitchen sink overflowing.

"Midterms are over. Our food supply is safe for a while." His mother moved in behind him, waving him away even as she brushed a gentle hand over his hair. "I'll fix you a plate."

"Let the man-child feed himself," Saul told his wife as he reclaimed his seat. "He's capable."

"Feeding him lets me pretend he still lives here."

"He hasn't lived here in over a decade, Patty." Saul rolled his eyes as Cruz took a seat beside his father. "Sometimes I think she's living in a time warp."

"School going okay?" Cruz asked his college professor dad.

"I admit the older I get, the more I look forward to the summers," Saul said. "But I have a good group of students this semester. Most of whom even seem to want to be there."

"Always a good sign," Cruz agreed. "Ma?"

"Your mother and I were just discussing her job, actually," Saul said and barely grimaced when Patty shushed him. "What? He's going to find out eventually. Your mother's school is implementing cutbacks. They've offered her early retirement, but if she goes, so does the library."

"What?" Cruz almost choked on his coffee. "But they can't do that. How can you have a high school without a library?"

"Spoken like my favorite child," Patty said with what to Cruz looked like a soul-sad smile. "Funds are stretched thin in this district. They are in every district."

"But you've been there twenty-seven years."

"They see numbers, Cruz," his father said. "Not people. There's talk of a fundraiser, both to save the library and your mother's job."

"Along with the assistants," Patty said, setting a reheated plate of her unique albeit delicious, spicy spin on shepherd's pie, along with a fork, in front of Cruz. "I'm not staying without them."

"And so the conversation continues," Saul said. "We'll be fine," he told Cruz, who was already trying to figure out how much his parents owed on their mortgage. "Are you still working that narcotics case you can't talk about? The one you and Johnny were on?"

"I am." Guilt swam through his stomach, trying to stifle his appetite, at the mention of his partner. Cruz spooned in the comforting tastes and textures of his childhood and felt instantly better. "Have a new lead I'm following and it'll probably mean I won't be coming around very much for a few weeks."

"You're not going undercover, are you?" Patty's voice took on that edge of fear Cruz hated to hear.

"Not really. Not dangerous undercover," he added at his mother's narrowed gaze. "I promised you and Dad I wouldn't do that again." Especially after what had happened to Johnny. During his two years in deep cover, Cruz had earned enough scars, not all of them visible, to last him a lifetime. He wasn't looking to add to them. "I'll be working at a restaurant, actually. Which no doubt means free food." If Tatum Colton agreed to his request. As of now, he was guessing that was a big if.

"Well, that'll save us money on groceries at least," Saul teased, then sobered. "I saw Jackie and Carlo Ruiz this afternoon. They're still having a hard time adjusting."

"Do any parents ever adjust to losing a child?" Patty

asked and added a slice of homemade cheesecake to the table.

Cruz winced and kept eating. Benji Ruiz had been only the latest in a list of overdose victims they knew from the neighborhood. This one had struck closer and harder than most, as Cruz's sister, Inez, had babysat Benji for most of his elementary school years. Kids like Benji—the ones they'd lost and the ones he could still save—were what kept him going. He worked every single day to ensure his parents, his siblings and friends would never have to attend another drug-induced, be-fore-their-time funeral.

"So this new avenue of investigation," Patty said as she slid back into her chair. "Will it leave you much time for a social life?"

"Dad, I thought you were going to get her to back off." Cruz sent his father a warning look, but Saul just shrugged. "No, Mom, I don't think it will." Even as he said it, he could hear Tatum Colton's rich, sultry voice ringing through his head. He wondered what her laugh sounded like.

"Once, just once I'd like to meet someone you care about, Cruz." Patty shook her head in that disapproving way she had that made Cruz feel like a misbehaving teenager again. "Such a shame. You should be going home for a hot meal and not stopping off here. You need someone in your home, Cruz. You need someone in your bed."

"Jeez, Mom!" Inez Medina came skidding to a halt in the kitchen doorway, her anime-inspired pajama pants and matching pink tank glowing like a beacon. "Lala-lalala." She covered her ears and ducked around them to grab a bottle of water. "Can we please not discuss Cruz's sex life? Ick."

"Ick is right," Cruz agreed and gave his sister a grateful wink. "Find a way to conquer our ever-expanding environmental issues yet, kid?"

Inez, who took after their mother with her short stature and thick, dark hair, came over to stand between her parents. "I'm working on it. Speaking of which, we're organizing a protest march for next week. A new pharmaceutical company is opening up offices downtown. They've been fined multiple times for illegal disposal of their waste and inhuman animal testing. I'm in charge of the permits for the protest."

Food had never held so much interest for him before. He didn't need to look up to know both his parents had pinned their eyes on him. "Contact Sheryl Cunningham at the city offices. Tell her who you are and what's been planned and where. She'll get you set up."

"Oooh, I get to name-drop? Cool! Thanks, Cruz." She kissed both her parents on the cheek and hurried back upstairs.

"Cruz." His mother's warning was loud and clear, but this was one instance where Cruz felt secure.

"She's asking about permits, Ma. She's thinking ahead because she's smart and she's planning for every contingency." Of course she was. She was prelaw and already clerking at a local ACLU office. "It's not like you and Dad didn't do the same at her age. Isn't that about when I was conceived? At a pro-immigration rights rally?" He heard his father guffaw and took it as a win.

"It was after the rally," his mother said without missing a beat. "And if Inez protesting endangers her scholarship? What will we do then?"

"Knowing Inez, she'd vlog about it on YouTube and end up with a GoFundMe campaign that would get her through graduate school." This from Saul before Cruz could put the words together. "We've raised activists, dear. Nothing we can do about it now."

"At least Frankie keeps his nose in his books and off social media," Patty said. "I bet he'll be the first one to give me grandchildren."

Cruz snorted but quickly covered by finishing off his late-night dinner. Science-minded Frankie hadn't taken his nose out of a book long enough to even recognize that girls flocked after him like he was a one-man K-pop band. He would, eventually, though. Then they'd all be in trouble.

"Only you have the power to make her stop talking about grandbabies," Saul told Cruz in the same tone he remembered when he'd been warned about preventing forest fires. "Maybe give that some thought, would you?"

Cruz rolled his eyes. He wasn't about to admit that seeing his parents this way, coming home the way he had—the way he did most weeks—was something he longed to create for himself. But this kind of life—quiet nights worrying over household budgets, raising children and eating leftover shepherd's pie and cheesecake, that wasn't possible for him. And it wasn't fair to expect someone to be able to live it with him.

It was an argument he'd had with himself and his parents so many times he'd lost track. But as he trudged back to his car, filled with the warmth and love only his

parents could provide, instead of lamenting the impossi-
bility of a family of his own, he found himself thinking
of a honey-blonde, spitfire chef with bright blue eyes
and a taste for tequila.

And wondered if maybe there was hope after all.

WHATEVER DREAMS TATUM had of losing herself to oblivion and sleep vanished when she pried her eyes open
after only five hours. She groaned, squeezed her eyes
shut and tried to ignore the digital evidence that 8:00
a.m. was creeping close. "So much for sleeping in on
my day off," she grumbled into her pillow and burrowed deeper.

Instead of the blissful unconsciousness she'd hoped
to drop into, dreams of an intensely erotic and squirm-
inducing nature had descended, with one central, irritating law enforcement character on center stage. It wasn't
fair. Mondays were normally her catch-up-and-rejuve-
nate day. Her reset day. Her create-new-recipes-and-be-
inspired day. Instead she was going to spend some of it
telling an estrogen-spiking detective he could get bent.

She groaned, felt the faint hitch in her stomach and
pounding in her head. The tequila was not going to
leave her system without a very painful goodbye, it
seemed. Rolling over, she stared up at the ceiling and
tried to shove all thoughts, images and feelings about
Detective Cruz Medina out of her cluttered, sleep-and-
man-deprived mind.

She smashed a pillow over her face and wished time
to rewind. Just a day or two or... Tears burned behind
her shut eyes. Five weeks ago. What she wouldn't give

to take everyone back five weeks and stop her dad and uncle from leaving the office when they had.

Voices echoed in her ears. Muffled, insistent and all too familiar. She yanked the pillow clear just as her bedroom door swung open. "Mom!" Tatum sat up in bed, clutching her sheet and duvet against her pajama-clad chest. "What are you doing here?"

"Tatum." Farrah Colton stood in the doorway, a book of fabric samples dangling from one hand. "What are *you* doing here?"

"I live here," Tatum reminded her, and for a moment, the last month faded away. "Or so it says on the lease."

"But it's Monday. You stay at the ranch house Sunday night." Farrah glanced over her shoulder, her stylish, shoulder-length curly brown hair brushing against the yellow fabric of her shirt. "Oh, um." She cringed and looked more than a bit guilty. "Darn it, this was going to be a surprise."

"Trust me, it is," Tatum muttered as she slung back the covers. As her feet hit the floor, an identical albeit thinner face popped up behind her mother. "Aunt Fallon, not you, too."

"Always me, too." Fallon Colton offered a somewhat dimmer smile than her twin sister. "Why aren't you at the ranch house?"

"I didn't feel like driving out there last night after we closed." Mainly because she knew she shouldn't be driving. She dragged herself out of bed and stood there, feeling oddly like a teenager caught after curfew. "Do one of you want to tell me what's going on? What are you doing here?"

"Oh, well, it's meant to be a—"

"Surprise, yeah, got that. I need coffee." And about ten aspirin. Then she might be able to function with the flood of information streaming into her head.

"Put on a pot, would you, sweetheart?" her mother called. "We'll be quick in here so you can take a shower."

Tatum stopped halfway down the hall, mouth open, question poised, but she shook her head, left them to whatever they were going to do in her bedroom, and headed into the kitchen.

It was the kitchen that had sold her on the space, even before she'd fully decided she needed a place in town while she worked. The loft-like setting, the hardwood floors, the beautiful picture windows overlooking the neighborhood, that was all nice.

But it was the six-burner gas range, the smooth gold-and-black marble countertops, the bay window filled with pots of fresh herbs, and the dual wall ovens with warming and proving drawers that made the place irresistible.

Contrary to how most women thought, the way to her heart was definitely through an electrical appliance. She loved her ranch house out in Livingston, had from the moment she'd first seen the house on sprawling land that acted as a retreat as well as a home. But it was too easy to bring the pressures of work there. This one-bedroom condo, only a ten-minute drive from True, was the perfect solution. Although at the moment she was seriously regretting handing out keys to her family.

As her mother suggested, she set an entire pot to brew rather than her cup-at-a-time pod and began rummaging through the refrigerator for the makings of an omelet.

"I've never understood how you do that," her mother said a few minutes later when she joined her in the kitchen.

"What? Cook?"

"Ha ha."

Tatum couldn't help teasing her mom. Farrah Colton was many things: a warm, caring and sometimes over-attentive mother, a brilliant woman with a successful and expanding interior design business. And she'd been a happy, devoted, if not challenging wife. But Farrah had never mastered the kitchen. Or what came out of it.

Tatum set aside chopped onion, peppers and mushroom, and popped open the carton of eggs. "Are you two hungry?"

Her mother shrugged, and then, after glancing over her shoulder, nodded. "If you cook for her she'll eat. And I meant I never understand how you can cook all night, every night, and still want to do it on your day off."

"Because it makes me happy." And that, Tatum thought when she glanced up at her mother, was all the answer Farrah needed. She set a pan on the stove, dropped in a mother-gasping amount of butter and set the burner to low. "So when are you going to spring it on me? This surprise you two have cooked up," she added when Farrah looked purposely confused.

"We are redecorating your condo." It was her aunt who answered as she joined them, setting down her own pile of fabric swatches and wallpaper books. "We need a project to get us back into a creative space, and this was on the top of our list."

"Oh." Tatum frowned. "Is it really that bad?" To be

honest, she hadn't paid much attention. It had what she needed: a bed, a bathroom and a kitchen. The beige walls and brown curtains had been in place when she moved in a little over two years ago. Sure, the muted colors were a bit boring, but... "Never mind," she said when her aunt gaped at her. "I see it now. It is."

"You don't mind, then?" her mother asked.

Even if she did, she wasn't going to turn them away. For the past few weeks she'd watched her mother and aunt struggle daily with getting through the endless hours of grief as they were thrust into widowhood. Tatum's grandmother had been instrumental in helping her daughters put one foot in front of the other. Even after her stroke last year, Abigail Jones was a commanding enough presence the family looked to in times of turmoil.

Losing both her sons-in-law had taken its toll on her as well, but she led by example, and it seemed, considering her mother and aunt were currently standing in Tatum's condo looking as clear-eyed and determined as she'd seen in weeks, that example was to persevere. Just as every Colton would.

"As long as you leave my kitchen alone, the rest of the place is yours," Tatum told them. "Have at it. But you know the rules."

"Don't worry, we learned our lesson when you were sixteen," Aunt Fallon said. "No orange—"

"No flowery froufrou—" Tatum's mother chimed in.

"And no frogs," Aunt Fallon finished for her twin. "Although I still don't get the no-frogs thing."

"Blame your son for that one." Tatum shuddered, remembering when Fallon's youngest boy, Jones, had left a rather slimy toad in Tatum's sleeping bag during one notorious backyard campout. "Not that any of you particularly cared," she chided good-naturedly. "The fact that Daddy fell into the pool because he was laughing…" She stopped, a wave of grief so large, so suffocating, overwhelming her she felt sick. "I'm sorry." She shook her head and turned away, having to press a hand against her chest to remind herself to breathe.

"Tatum." Her mother's hand came to rest on her shoulder, turned her around so she could cup her face in her palms. "I know it's hard. I know you miss him. Miss them. I do, too." The grief was there, reflected in her mother's deep green eyes. And it broke Tatum's heart. "Some days it's almost impossible. But we have to go on, don't we? It's what he would have wanted."

"I miss him so much." Tatum's voice broke as she stared down at the sizzling butter. "He should be here. Teasing me about what color you're going to paint my walls."

"Or leaving a stuffed frog on your bed," Farrah said with a laugh.

Tatum choked on her own chuckle, wiped the tears from her cheek. "What a housewarming present that was. Oh, Mom." She glanced to Aunt Fallon, who was dealing with tears of her own.

"There's to be no more of this, Tatum Colton." Her mother's hold on her tightened. "We remember with joy and gratitude and leave the sorrow and grief for the night. And in the morning, we start again. You know what he always said. We do what's right, and we do what's good. Even when it feels impossible."

An image of Cruz Medina floated into her mind: an

image of a determined, sure-footed detective who had asked for her cooperation. Cooperation she now realized she would have to give him. On one condition.

She'd do what was right.

But she would also protect what was hers.

It was, after all, the Colton way.

Chapter Four

There were few places that brought Cruz Medina any sense of peace, especially on a Monday. And by peace he meant someplace that provided enough noise and distraction he could stick his earphones in, kick back and attempt to sort through the mess that was his investigation into the Nacio drug cartel.

Feet up on his desk, the mind-numbing tones of classic rock blasting in his ears, he leaned back and closed his eyes, mentally programming his respite to end in ten, nine, eight…

His chair tipped back and Cruz kicked out, flailing as he struggled to right himself. When he pitched forward and braced himself on his desk, he spun his chair and glared up at the interloper. "What the what, Cunningham?" He ignored the ego-checking chuckles coming from his fellow detectives.

Sheryl Cunningham, all five feet eight inches of her, stood, arms crossed over her chest, obsidian eyes glinting. She was not only stunning in her designer fuchsia suit that complemented her black skin, she was also glowing for two as she neared her delivery date. "You sicced your little sister on me, Medina."

"Ah." Cruz choked back a laugh. Mostly because he didn't feel like dying today. Sheryl arched a brow, clearly waiting for a response. "Problem with Inez?"

"The only problem is now I know there's two of you." Sheryl grabbed an empty office chair and wheeled it over, sat down and let out what Cruz could only imagine was a sigh of relief. "Someone should have warned me you had a Mini-Me. Why send her to me? What did I ever do to you?"

"Well, I didn't do that." He pointed at her very pregnant belly and earned a hearty snort. "I wanted to make sure she had what she needed for the protest. You don't let anything slip through the cracks. I trusted you with her."

"Well, hell." Sheryl sagged a bit. "That's all right then, I guess. And I have to admit, the idea of a protest march against that creepy drug company will make my day brighter. I'm on her list now, aren't I?"

"I want her to know who she can trust," Cruz told his former flame. A flame that had flared quick and bright and left them as friends. "She's prelaw and looking to save the world."

"It's the Medina family motto, isn't it?" Sheryl's face softened. "How's your mom?"

"Lamenting the fact I'm not settled down and giving her grandchildren."

"We're all lamenting that," Sheryl teased.

"What brings you down here?" Cruz popped out his earphones and tossed them onto his desk. "You could have reamed me over the phone about Inez."

"I needed an excuse to take a walk. Kid's coming up on overdue and I want her out. Doctor said physical activity would help, and seeing as I'm not feeling particularly sexy these days—"

"Understood." He held up his hands in the universal male TMI surrender gesture.

"Yeah, well, I also have that information you requested." She handed him the manila envelope she had in her hand. "Permit checks on that restaurant, True. Ran you off copies of everything on file. Most recent one was from a little over a month ago."

"Oh? What for?" He slipped the papers out, skimmed them.

"Restaurant's expansion into catering. Wouldn't be surprised if a food truck's next. That place sounds mighty tasty. You been?"

"I was there last night, actually," Cruz admitted. The name on the permits, building, liquor license, catering, everything had Tatum's signature. "Good calamari."

"Huh." Sheryl looked impressed. "Guess you got some taste after all."

"Thanks. Sorry if Inez gave you a bad time."

"Nah." Sheryl waved off his concern. "Gave me something to rag you about, though. Seems like a good kid. Definitely a cross-her-t's-and-dot-her-i's kinda girl. You find yourself needing someone to have dinner with at True, you let me know. It's on my and Luce's list of must tries."

"Before or after the baby?"

"I wouldn't say no to before." A wistful expression crossed her face. "Do they take waddlers?"

"Save it for after." Cruz tried to sound nonchalant. He didn't want people he cared about anywhere near that place until he knew it was safe. "It'll be worth it, I promise."

"Uh-huh." Sheryl's brow went back up. "Don't worry. I won't tell anyone it's under investigation."

"I'd appreciate that."

"Sheryl, you're early." Lieutenant Lucille Graves came out of her office, joined them, gave her wife a quick kiss and Sheryl's belly a quick rub. "I thought we said noon."

Cruz looked at his watch, then back at his boss. "It is noon, LT."

"Smart answer for everything," Graves said with a smirk. His commanding officer had a constant if not bewildering sense of humor. She also had ten years, a good twenty pounds and about fifty IQ points on him. "You get what you wanted from Tatum Colton?"

"Waiting to hear." Cruz had been avoiding his LT most of the morning. He liked to think he'd been persuasive, but he wouldn't put it past Tatum to tell him to get lost just to see where it got her. He wasn't sure himself, considering he didn't have many other ideas at the moment. His cell phone rang, and after a glance at the screen, Cruz had to wonder if his luck had just changed. "Hang on, LT." He held up a finger, took the call. "Ms. Colton."

"I think—" Tatum's voice floated over the phone and had him sitting up straighter in his chair "—given the fact we'll be working together, you'd best call me Tatum."

"All right, Tatum." He grinned, glancing back at his boss and her wife. Luce and Sheryl both rolled their eyes, as if lamenting the fact another female had fallen under his spell. "I take that to mean we should get together and discuss some things?"

"You take it correctly. Since the restaurant's closed today, why don't you come by my place and we can work out the details here." She rattled off an address. "Anytime after... Mom! Get off that chair! It's not... Darn it."

"You live with your mother?"

"Heaven forbid," Tatum said in a tone Cruz completely understood. "She and my aunt are doing some redecorating for me. It's keeping them busy."

Cruz winced. He'd almost forgotten about her father and uncle.

"Anyway, how about you come by after three. They should be gone by then. I hope. Please let them be gone…"

"Three it is."

"Oh, and you'll need to do some shopping beforehand. You have a pen handy?"

By the time he hung up, he found Sheryl and his LT peering over his shoulder at the most unusual shopping list he'd ever written.

"Wonder what you two will do with all that olive oil," Sheryl teased.

"Let's go. Where do you want to go for lunch?" Luce Graves asked Sheryl as they left the squad room. "I'm thinking pizza."

"Really?" Sheryl winked back at Cruz before they turned the corner. "I have a craving for squid."

It took twenty minutes, a care package of fresh-baked sourdough bread for both her mother and her aunt, along with a promise to be out of the condo as of ten tomorrow morning, to get them out the door.

She was cutting it close. It was quarter to three, and she did not want to become family gossip by allowing her mother to see her with a man in her condo. That was one distraction Tatum most definitely did not want to use on her mom.

If her instinct was right—and it usually was, thank goodness—her sister January was on the verge of being engaged. The second her mother and aunt had a wedding to plan, the pressure to entertain, distract and worry would ease, and Tatum might, *might* start to feel her life slip back on track.

"I bet you're getting a real laugh out of this, aren't you, Daddy?" Tatum brushed a finger over her father's photographed face. The picture had been taken at Tatum's culinary academy graduation. Where her sisters had caps and gowns, Tatum had donned a chef's jacket and worn it and her honor ribbons as proudly as a princess wore a tiara. Her father had worn his pride and love not only on his sleeve, but on his face.

The downstairs buzzer blared into the condo, making her jump. She hurried to the front door, clicked on the intercom. "Yes?"

"Medina delivery service," came the sardonic response. He was irritated. Tatum grinned. Perfect. "Second floor. Two-oh-four." She buzzed him in.

Something tingled inside her. Unease? Nerves? Anticipation, maybe? "Get a grip, girl," she told herself as she tightened her ponytail and tugged down her blue T-shirt. "He's investigating you for a crime, not taking you out on a date." She heard the footsteps outside and opened the door before he could knock. "Hi. Come on in."

"Thanks." He carried two fabric totes, one in each hand. "Can I put these over there?"

"Yeah, sure. On the counter's fine." She twisted her hands together. She'd thought maybe her attraction to him last night had been the result of the tequila, yet here she was, stone-cold sober, and admiring every single fit inch of him. Dark slacks and T-shirt again, and the blazer he wore today looked slightly more worn than last night's attire. She couldn't help wondering how he looked out of those clothes. "Did you get everything on the list?"

"Enough to make my credit card whine," he confirmed. "I'll unload and you store."

"Yeah, sure. That works." She hurried forward. "I kind of took advantage. There were some things I needed to restock, so—"

"I figured. Let me guess? My penance for last night?"

"Maybe a little." She couldn't stop her lips twitching. "You are familiar with the concept of penance, then?"

"With twelve years of Catholic school, I ought to be."

"Catholic school?" She wasn't sure why she was surprised. "Did you go to Sacred Heart?"

"Saint Ignatius," he corrected. "All-boys. My sister went to SH, though. You?"

"Saint Mary's. Me, my sisters and my cousins. There were a lot of Coltons on the roster for a while." She was babbling. And talking about silly, meaningless stuff. She hadn't been nervous around a man since…who was she kidding? Men didn't make her nervous.

But she'd never met Cruz Medina before.

She stashed the gallon of olive oil in the cabinet near the sink, dumped all the produce into the basin where she'd wash it later for storage. The eggs, butter and various proteins she'd had him grab went into the fridge.

"So I've been thinking about my job," Cruz said.

"As a cop?"

"No. My job at the restaurant." He looked at her as if he was surprised she didn't understand.

"Right. That job." She considered pouring herself a glass of wine, then realized what trouble that might get her into. "I've already taken care of it. You want a beer?"

"Yeah, sure. Thanks. You have?" Surprise filled his eyes. Along with something else she couldn't quite define. He accepted the imported beer with ease, knocked off the cap.

"Yeah, well, it isn't like we've got a lot of openings at True right now. I have low turnover. People like working for me." She meant for it to sound like a warning of sorts. For him to remember that his investigation would affect more than his case; it would affect her business and her employees. "The only job we have right now is for a sous-chef."

"That sounds…complicated. I was thinking more of bartending."

"Like I said, we're pretty full with employees and we don't need another bartender." She didn't really need another sous-chef, but it was the one position Richard had recommended adding another of. "How are you with a knife?" She grabbed a bottle of water for herself, then led him into the loosely serviceable living room. "Ignore the paint swatches on the wall. My mom and aunt were testing colors."

"I like the blue," he said, gesturing to the dark peacock-inspired color. "Cozy."

"I will definitely consider telling them I like it, then."

Cruz smiled and settled into the corner of her sofa. "Before we talk more about the job, I wanted to say, and I should have said before, how sorry I am about your father and uncle."

She ducked her head, longing for the day when the mention of her father wouldn't feel like a gut punch. "Thank you. It's been…" she shrugged "…difficult. I'm sure you know. You deal with cases like this enough, I suppose."

"I deal with a lot of death," he said. "But I don't think anything can ever prepare you for losing someone, or in your case, two someones the way you did. Do you know who's running the case?"

"Ah, yeah." She rubbed her fingers across her forehead. "A Detective Joe Parker. He seems very competent."

"He is. He's good people. He'll take care of them."

"I suppose family members are always the first suspects in a case like this." It was impossible to keep the disgust out of her voice. She'd witnessed firsthand how the accusation against her cousin Heath, president of Colton Connections, had been handled, the effect it had on him.

"I did a little investigating of my own," Cruz said. "Just asked around a bit to get a feel for the case and how the investigation's going. They've cleared the entire family as suspects."

"I'd say that's a relief, but it's not." Tatum faced him, stretching out her arm along the back of the sofa. "They still aren't anywhere close to finding out who did kill them. Or why. They never hurt anyone. It doesn't make any sense."

"It rarely does," Cruz told her. "Even when we find a motive or explanation, it still won't make sense. I'm sorry you're all going through this."

"Not sorry enough to stop you from investigating my restaurant."

"No." He didn't seem ashamed by it, or even contrite. "I won't apologize for doing my job."

It was admirable, she supposed, despite his determination putting her smack-dab in the middle of one of his cases. "I won't apologize for doing mine, either. Which brings us back to you being a sous-chef."

"Yeah, about that. I really think—"

"It's a done deal." Tatum had been waiting for the right moment to reveal her morning and early-afternoon activities. "I called my manager a while ago and told him I'd hired you. I said you came highly recommended by a fellow chef friend in New York. While you'll be a sous in title, you'll do various jobs…prep chef, line chef. We'll get your résumé together, get you acclimated as to how a restaurant kitchen works. How are you in the kitchen, by the way?"

"Passable." His grin was slow, almost flirtatious, as if he was conjuring images he shouldn't be. Then he shook his head. "I don't like to cook but I'll do it. I used to help my mom when I was growing up. Doing all the chopping and stuff for her."

"Perfect." Covering her surprise with a long drink

of water, she continued. "Then you're already on your way. Being a sous is mostly about prepping. For you, anyway. For others it's a rung on the ladder to head chef. You're backup to me, but you also move in and out of the kitchen doing whatever needs doing, especially when people take their breaks. I did think this through," she said when he looked mildly impressed. "Being a sous gives you access to almost every area of the kitchen and also the restaurant at large. You want access, you'll have it. You can get to know your fellow employees, wheedle out which one of them might be running drugs out of our freezer."

"You still don't believe I'm right, do you?"

"No." Tatum didn't leave any room for doubt. "I don't. I can't. These people are my family, Cruz. Believing you're right, that one or more of them are working against me, committing crimes using my restaurant? I honestly don't think my heart can take that right now."

"Fair enough." He took a long pull of his beer. "So when do we start my sous lessons?"

"You hungry?"

"Always."

"Perfect. Then we'll start now."

Chapter Five

"Don't take this the wrong way," Tatum said as Cruz
effortlessly used the back of his chef's knife to scrape
chopped peppers into a waiting bowl. "But I assumed
your definition of passable meant you knew which side
of the knife was sharp. You're actually pretty good at
this."

"Not sure there's any other way to take it." His smile,
even as he kept his eyes on his prep work, made her insides do that inconvenient albeit insistent dance. "When
I was ten my mom and dad had a surprise pregnancy."

Tatum frowned, set her bowl of hand-crushed tomatoes aside. What did that have to do with—

"I like to say the surprise was that it was twins," he
continued. "But in truth, it was *Surprise! You're old
enough to help more around the house!* My parents
gave me the choice between cleaning and cooking. As
the vacuum cleaner and I had multiple disagreements
over the years, I went with the kitchen." He shrugged,
as if that said it all. "They timed things perfectly with
the advent of all those cooking shows, even though my
mom loved watching old Julia Child reruns."

"I love Julia Child." Tatum couldn't help but be entranced. Not just by his voice and the obvious affection he had for his mother, but with the elegant way he moved around her kitchen, as if he'd been working in it all her life. How did a big-city detective fit so effortlessly into whatever setting he stepped into? "So you have twin siblings?"

"Frankie, well, Francisco, and Inez. They're nineteen. Just started college last fall. But when they were ten they got the same lecture I did, and both ended up in the kitchen. The Medina family will never starve, that's for sure."

"Well, I have to say you're easing my mind about how well you'll fit in at True. You follow instructions well, at least for the prep work."

"Speaking of prep, you're using me again, aren't you? Getting your *mise en place* done for the week?"

"Listen to you with the jargon. Yes, and no. Not for the whole week. Just the next few days." She chuckled at his *uh-huh*. "One thing you'll need to know how to do is pasta."

"I take it you mean I won't just be opening a box."

"No." She shook her head, retrieved the eggs she'd left out earlier. "All our pasta is made fresh. Not to order, but fresh every day. And we make a lot of it." She pulled over the organic flour, salt and imported olive oil. "When you're done with those." Tatum gestured to the last of the vegetables she'd set out for him, then returned to her laptop to finish typing up a list of things he'd need to know coming in. "What first put True on your radar?"

"GPS mapping." he answered, unfazed, then took his knife and cutting board over to the sink. "In part. The cartel I'm investigating has a number of connections and dealers in and around this neighborhood. True is right in the middle of it all."

"You're ready to blow up my entire life over the GPS readings of drug dealers?" How did the crazy continue to spiral into surreal?

He dried his hands, leaned back against the sink and looked at her. "You're acting as if this is somehow personal, and it isn't, Tatum. It just is what it is. I go where the evidence—"

"You said you didn't have any evidence yet."

"I go where the trail leads me," he finished as if she hadn't interrupted. "None of this makes me happy, Tatum. I don't want to tarnish your business or your reputation. But I'm not going to give up seeing something through because it inconveniences you."

Inconveniences her? "You really don't get it, do you? All you see is your case. Black-and-white. Right or wrong."

"Actually, no, I don't. I'm more than familiar with all the varieties of gray. But I have a job to do."

"Right. And your job is more important than my livelihood. Just because True pops up on your GPS analysis it doesn't mean it's involved!"

"It doesn't mean it's not, either." If he understood she was spoiling for a fight, he didn't rise to the bait. If anything, her arguing with him seemed to steel his argument. "We can go around and around with this forever, Tatum. We aren't going to change the other's mind. The investigation is moving forward with or without your help. Isn't it easier, wouldn't it be better if we agreed to disagree while working toward a common goal?"

"Forget police work. You should run for office."
She'd rarely heard such a rational, almost practiced argument that both irritated her and made complete sense.

"Something tells me that'll be what my sister does at some point. Look." He tossed the towel down and walked over to her, the warmth of his closeness tempting her to lean closer, to lose herself in it. To surround herself with it. "I understand what's at stake for you, Tatum. But I need to stop this group of traffickers before more innocent people get hurt or killed. If we're lucky, by the time we're on the other side of this, True will be free and clear and so will you and your employees. It'll be a blip on your professional history that no one will even remember a few months from now."

"It'll only be a blip if no one hears about it," she tried again.

"How about this." He covered her hand with his, moved closer yet again and lowered his voice. "How about I promise to do my best to protect your business? Within the confines of my job, of course. I can't promise anything beyond that."

She looked down to where he touched her, the feel, the heat of his touch racing up her arm and sliding through her entire body like she was sinking into a warm, sensuous bath. "I suppose it's something."

Tatum could almost feel his smile even before she glanced up. That mouth of his, those lips that widened to expose a perfect, white-toothed smile that very nearly reached all the way to his somewhat jaded dark eyes. "How magnanimous of you." He lifted his free hand, brushed a solitary finger down the side of her face.

She shivered and resisted the urge to turn into his

touch. "Just so you know." She shifted, stood before him with a breath between them. "While I don't forbid workplace involvement, I don't encourage it, either."

"And just so you know." He dipped his head, just a bit, enough she could feel his warm breath caress her skin. "It's been my policy not to get involved with someone connected to an investigation. It's frowned upon, in fact."

"Is it?" She arched a brow. "That sounds suspiciously like a challenge." It took every bit of effort she possessed to hold his gaze, a gaze that made her feel as if the world around them had melted into oblivion. "I enjoy challenges. I find them exhilarating." Her hand came up, fingers trailing up his bare arm until it brushed against the short sleeve of his dark shirt. "Do you like challenges, Detective Medina?"

"Almost as much as I like complications." His mouth brushed across hers, featherlight, as if testing the waters of a particularly tempestuous river.

"I strike you as complicated?" She breathed out the question, surprised she could find the voice to speak. His beard scraped against the softness of her skin, making her shiver. The energy surging through her system, the absolute desire she felt at this moment, as if she would literally burst into flames if he didn't shut up and kiss her, had her struggling against reason. This was a bad idea.

A really bad, horrible, messy...

"You strike me as a lot of things." He pulled his hand free of hers, and for a moment she thought he was moving away. Instead, he took that last, final, cavern-sized step closer and took her face in his hands. "Something tells me this is going to open up a whole new area of complicated," he murmured an inch from her mouth. "That okay with you?"

"Uh-huh." She wet her lips, the anticipation suffocating whatever rational thought she might still have. "It would just be a kiss," she reasoned and saw the humor flash in his eyes. "It doesn't have to change anything. Or mean anything. We'd still be partners."

"No," he said with a sharpness in his eyes. "We aren't partners. But on the other thing? Let's test that theory." But he didn't kiss her. Not right away. For what felt like an eternity, he did nothing more than stand there, holding her face gently between his hands, his thumbs caressing her cheeks as if they were made of precious spun gold.

Tatum was not a patient woman. Not when it came to what she wanted, and right now all she wanted was Cruz Medina's mouth on hers. Hot. Hungry. Commanding. And when he made no move to give her what she wanted, she slid her hands around to his chest, fisted her fingers in his shirt and dragged him in.

It was as if his kiss ignited a lifelong dormant pilot light inside of her. Instant heat. Instant combustion. Instant desire. All three mingled into a dance that had her moaning against his mouth. He wasn't coy about it. Didn't take his time to investigate or coddle. He simply dived in and took, demanded, and pulled her solidly into arms that folded around her.

She met him moment for moment, touch for touch. She'd kissed her fair share of men over her twenty-nine years. She liked men. She liked sex and had no trouble finding it when she needed or just wanted it. But this encounter, this experience, this *man* was different. Everything she thought of doing to him he was a step, a stroke, a thrust ahead of her as he kissed her deeply. Completely.

When he lifted his mouth, she could see her own surprise, her own desire, reflected in his uncertain if not shocked gaze. "Well." He stroked his thumb over her lips before he stepped back. "I guess that answers that question."

"And raises a few others," she managed and held up a hand when he appeared to want to step forward again. "I think it would be safe to say we have a healthy attraction toward one another."

"I don't think we can call any of what we just started safe."

"No," she agreed. "I don't think we could. Intense sexual attraction can't override the need for rational behavior. As you said, getting involved would be ill-advised on your part."

"And on yours?"

Oh, how she wanted to leap at him and kiss that cocky grin off his face. "On my part it would be self-destructive. For a number of reasons, but mainly because I know you don't have my best professional interests at heart." Hearing her own words echo in her ear doused the still raging flames of desire she felt for him. "Despite your promise, I have the feeling that given the choice, you're going to do what you have to in order to solve your case. Even if it means hurting me."

"It's your business that's in trouble, Tatum. Not you."

"That's what you don't seem to understand, Cruz." She planted a hand on his chest and pushed him away.

"They're one and the same. So." She pulled herself together, shoved what might have been down to where she couldn't access it, and refocused on the only thing that mattered. "Let's call that a completed experiment, accept the results and get back to the job at hand as partners." The sooner he was out of her business, out of her life, the better. She reached for the canister of flour and a measuring cup, handed the latter over to him with a barely trembling hand. "Measure out two cups."

CRUZ KICKED THE door to his two-bedroom bungalow closed behind him and carried an oversize tote into his own meager, completely uninspired kitchen. For a man who prided himself on following plans, he'd sure taken a serious detour today.

He returned to the living room, turned on a few lights and tapped a finger against the glass of the oversize aquarium that housed Norbert, his pet tortoise. The creature lifted his wrinkly head, blinked his teeny eyes, then seemed to let out a silent sigh of irritation that his nap had been interrupted before he tucked back into his shell. "Serves me right for not getting a dog."

He clicked on the TV, grateful for the background noise, then returned to the kitchen to unpack.

Not only had Tatum sent him home with enough pasta to feed him for a few nights, she'd also given him homework in the guise of an advanced, illustrated techniques cookbook and a number of books on the restaurant business.

"I want you to walk in the door to True on Wednesday as if you can jump into the job immediately," she'd told him as she'd pulled books from her dedicated case against the wall between her kitchen and living room. "I'll have your résumé tweaked and done by tomorrow morning and will email it to you. I suggest you memorize it to be safe."

The detached professionalism didn't sit well with him. Clearly, they could now divide their history as BK and AK. Before kiss and after kiss. He much preferred the BK Tatum Colton.

Before he realized exactly how much heat there was between them.

He should have known touching the flame would get him burned, and Tatum Colton had most definitely scorched him. Cruz set the leftover containers in the fridge, grabbed a beer and lugged the books into the living room, where he flipped around until he landed on an exhibition game between the Cubs and Cardinals. Before he'd been summoned to Tatum's condo, he'd had plans to watch the game down at Santino's, the sports pub two blocks away, but as he was fond of reminding Tatum, he had a job to do. And work had to come first.

"Even before kissing beautiful chefs," he told himself. He wished he knew what he'd been thinking, giving in to that impulse. An impulse that clearly she'd shared. It was, after all, she who'd hauled him closer to get the deed done. And in that one instant he understood just how powerful attraction could be.

The revelation could not have come at a more inconvenient time.

He took a pull of his beer, set the bottle down, then settled in on his sofa to read. He was a skimmer by nature, a fast skimmer who could absorb information like a sponge. Speed-reading was a natural ability for him and had served him well in the various undercover operations he'd been a part of since becoming a cop. He also had a memory like a steel trap. Not eidetic exactly, but pretty close. One of the reasons all his partners had been thrilled to work with him. No one did paperwork as efficiently or with as much detail as Cruz Medina.

Johnny had been pretty darn good at it, too. He'd even enjoyed doing it. For once Cruz had been happy to turn that part of the job over to his partner.

Cruz winced, tried to focus for a few moments on the game. It had been two months. Two months since he'd last sat with his partner, his friend, and laughed as they tried to navigate this crazy profession they'd both chosen. Two months since Cruz had been able to tease his fresh-off-the-farm partner about his tooth-achingly sweet plans to propose to his long-time girlfriend. Two months since Johnny had dragged Cruz with him to pick out the ring he planned to surprise his Jade with.

Johnny wasn't laughing anymore. He wasn't spouting proposal plans or even planning a wedding. And chances were pretty damn good he never would.

Cruz finished his beer, resisted the urge to get another. One thing he'd learned early on in this job was to limit his chosen coping mechanisms. Whether it was women, alcohol or hours at the firing range, they were all to be enjoyed in steady, limited amounts.

But he hadn't gotten close to his limit of Tatum Colton. He knew it as soon as his mouth had brushed hers. There was something different about her, about them. Something he had never expected to find for himself. Something he didn't want to find.

"Focus on the books, Medina." He returned to read-

ing, to skimming, pushing all other thoughts firmly
out of reach.

The sooner he got this case solved and behind him,
the better. More important, the sooner he could distance himself from Tatum, the better off both of them
would be.

Chapter Six

"Tatum, you got a minute?"

"Sure." Tatum glanced up from her menu notes when Richard knocked on her door midmorning on Wednesday. Her manager was tall, a little on the bulky side, and possessed a mind born for the business world. He waited for her to wave him in, and then entered. "What's up?"

"About this sous-chef you hired." Richard reminded her of a Ken doll, very well put together, perfectly presentable, and happy to reside in the shadows of a successful woman. They only rarely butted heads, which usually told her she needed to consider things from another perspective. Most important, he knew when to pick his battles.

She let out a long breath. Clearly, this was going to be one of those times.

"Cruz Mendoza?" Her stomach clenched as the moment she'd been dreading arrived. Richard had been in and out of the restaurant most of the day overseeing the catering deliveries. He looked slightly haggard and stressed beneath the pressed dark suit and blue tie he wore. She motioned for him to sit and reminded herself yet again she was doing what had to be done. For now at least. "What about him?"

"I was just wondering how or where you found him." He waved a printout of the résumé she'd fabricated for Cruz. "I had a list of potentials lined up."

"Yeah, sorry about that." She kept her voice even, scribbled meaningless notes to appear somewhat normal. "Kelly Spangler recommended him." Her colleague was currently on maternity leave and had gone incommunicado. "They worked together a couple of years ago when he was just out of culinary school." She'd committed Cruz's false history to memory while she and the detective had worked out the details. "He moved here to be near family, so I reached out. Why?" She glanced up and frowned. "Is there a problem?"

"No. Not really." But she could tell by the strained expression on his face there was. "I guess I've gotten used to taking care of the employment aspects of the job. Plus, I got the feeling I hadn't quite convinced you we needed someone else."

"It felt right." She added a shrug. "Right time. Right person. He's coming in this morning. You good to show him around?"

"Ah, what time?" Richard glanced at his watch. "I have a meeting at eleven thirty with a potential new catering customer."

"Don't worry about it." She waved him off. "I went ahead and set him up in the payroll system. I got back early from the farmers and fish market so jumped at it. Deliveries should be here in a little over an hour." They opened for dinner at five, but there was always prep work and planning that needed doing. And of course staff dinner, which all the employees ate together a few hours before they opened. First thing she'd done when she'd come in today was put on a huge pot of her employees-only minestrone. It would simmer the next few hours and soon the aroma of fresh-baked bread would begin wafting through True. "Since I'm ahead of things I can take care of getting him acquainted with the restaurant."

"I can call Susan," Richard offered. "Have her come in early?"

"It's fine." She didn't want to hand Cruz off to anyone else. "I'll introduce you when you get back. Anything else?" Her cheeks strained with the effort it took to smile.

"We've locked down the Wilmington wedding in July and the Eppes' Bar Mitzvah next month for catering jobs. I'd like to set up some tastings for them in the next week or so."

"Shouldn't be an issue." She scribbled a note to herself to do a little research on both families. She liked, if possible, to add special, personal touches to events like this, incorporating familiar or comforting menu items that would be that added attention to detail. "How's Jeremy working out as driver? I bet he's glad to get out of washing dishes once in a while."

"Pike?" Richard glanced down at his notepad. "Yeah, doing okay. We get along okay and he likes the change." He shrugged. "Can't ask for more than that, can you?"

Of course she could; she always asked a lot of her employees and she expected the best. Given the catering program had been in Richard's hands, navigating her interest could be...tricky. She didn't want to come across as taking over when it was a job he was more than qualified and eager to do. But if Cruz's appearance in her life didn't teach her anything else, it taught her that she needed to keep a closer eye on what was going on in all aspects of her business. Although the kitchen would always be her main priority, and Tatum would never relinquish control over the food she and her staff produced.

"Over the next few weeks I'd like to work on getting some consistent summer events booked," she said. "I know a lot of people think of us as high-end, but we need to appeal to smaller businesses and activities as well, to ensure long-term success." If all went well, she could look into expanding next door with a dedicated and separate catering operation. She already had some ideas as to who she'd like running it, once they were solidly in the black.

"I can go through the list of city festivals and events, see if anything pops there." Richard tapped away on his phone. "There's always Eataly, and it is one of Chicago's premier food festivals, but that's this month and they're probably booked out for booths. Maybe someone's canceled."

"Can't hurt to check. What about those business lunches we've been catering for the past few weeks?"

"Belma Trade? They want to sign a long-term agreement. Gourmet lunches for their employees and board of directors. About a hundred and fifty meals every Thursday. Nothing fancy so far, but enough to keep things moving and word of mouth rolling. Sam's doing good overseeing the preparation. He and Colby seem to have it running well."

What would she do without Sam? "What's that costing us?"

Richard glanced up. "We're not quite in the black yet. Why? You want to see numbers?"

"I've looked at the sheets, but I'd like specifics and an accounting report. Is that a problem?"

"No." But Richard's brow furrowed. "Of course not. I'll put one together for you this week."

"Great, thanks." Her gaze shifted over Richard's shoulder when a familiar and distracting face strode into view. "Cruz. You're early." She got to her feet, ignoring the surge of excitement that shot through her at seeing him again, which didn't make sense because she did not want him here.

He'd taken her advice and come dressed to work, from his loose-fitting slacks to the cushioned shoes on his feet. His shirt was a shade of blue that reminded her of lazy sails on the ocean and long, languid dives into the deep. Heaven help her, this was going to be more difficult than she thought.

He carried a backpack like most of her employees, and his hair was tied back in a short ponytail at the base of his neck. She didn't see any hint of the intense, intractable detective she'd been dealing with. "Cruz Mendoza, this is Richard Kirkman, my manager and all-around right hand."

"Pleasure." Cruz stepped in and held out his hand. "Thank you again for this opportunity, Ms. Colton. I can't tell you how relieved I am to have a job again."

"We're looking forward to working with you," Richard responded for her. "So how's Kelly Spangler doing these days? I had lunch with her a few months ago.

She'd just been promoted to executive chef at Ladle and Spoon."

Tatum's eyes went wide for an instant before her gaze flew to Cruz. Darn it! She'd thought she'd chosen someone completely off Richard's radar.

"Sounds like you're spending too much time in a Tardis," Cruz said easily and with a chuckle. "Kelly left Spoon just before she had her first baby. She's at Bread and Butter now. Or she will be once she's back from her second maternity leave."

Richard snapped his fingers. "That's right. I forgot. She's running their bakery, isn't she?"

"Once they open it, yes. This sounds like some kind of test." Cruz played the concerned applicant with deference, but the ease with which he lied had Tatum's stomach looping into uneasy knots. "Have you changed your mind about hiring me?"

"No, we haven't." Tatum found her voice again, came around her desk and put an end to the inquisition. "I don't think Richard appreciated me going around him to hire you. But seeing as it is my restaurant, it is my prerogative." It was perfectly okay for Richard to do his job and make recommendations, but when push came to shove, decisions like this were hers. It must have been a while since she'd reminded her manager of that. "Isn't that right, Richard?"

"Of course. No offense meant." Richard nodded, stuffed his hands in his pockets. "Normally I'd be the one to get you all set here, but I'm afraid I have an appointment. I believe Tatum will be taking care of you from here on. I'll let you know how things turn out with the new client, Tatum," he said on his way out.

Tatum stood where she was until she was certain he was out of earshot, then turned her still wide eyes on Cruz.

"Would it be out of line for me to just call him Dick?" Cruz muttered under his breath as he closed the door.

"He means well." Tatum bit back a grin. "And you are early. Why? Is there something wrong?" Had he realized he'd made a mistake? Did they not have to go through with this charade after all?

"No. Just anxious to get started." He glanced around her office, gave what she took as a nod of approval. "I didn't have anything else to do, so I figured I'd best jump in. What's first, boss lady?"

He spoke so casually, as if what he was doing here wasn't spying on her business. How was this so easy for him? And how had he brushed aside what had happened between them yesterday? Okay, so she'd been the one to insist they keep things professional. Still, it would be nice to know she wasn't the only person who'd had her circuits fried.

"That's Chef while we're working. Tatum is fine the rest of the time. How'd you know all that about Kelly?"

"It's my job to know my legend inside and out." Cruz shifted his pack higher on his shoulder. "The internet is a detective's best friend. I did a search on everyone you mentioned in my résumé. He was testing me, wasn't he?"

"Probably." She pulled open the door again. "He's been very meticulous about who we've hired. It's a point of pride with him."

"Meaning I wouldn't have passed muster if you'd left it up to him?"

"Meaning there was no guarantee, and as you said, we don't have a lot of time to play with. Drug trafficking being what it is and all."

Given his arched brow and his pursed lips, she must have sounded snarkier than intended. "How about I show you around," she said. "We'll get you a locker, and you can meet some of your fellow employees."

WHATEVER CRUZ HAD been expecting as an employee of True, his downtime, whatever there was of it, would definitely be a plus. The employee locker room, as it was loosely called, was, well, something he would have expected to see in an upscale gym or private club. The walls were painted the same green as the restaurant ceiling and accentuated with swirls of gold. The requisite bank of polished wooden lockers sat against one long wall, and on either end were doors leading to both men's and women's rooms.

Behind those doors were areas that included changing rooms as well as well-stocked showers. That he didn't find a monogrammed robe behind his narrow, numbered locker door came as something of a surprise.

The break area consisted of a couple of tables with multiple cushioned chairs as well as a flat-screen TV, something he couldn't quite wrap his brain around. And was that an…an old-fashioned movie-style popcorn machine?

"We've got a staff of baseball fans," Tatum told him at his befuddled expression. "They watch games on their breaks."

"And throw popcorn at the screen when we lose," someone chimed in.

"We also get the best leftovers in town. I'm Sam Price." One of Tatum's staff members introduced himself as he slipped on his white chef's jacket. He was Black, slightly shorter than Cruz, and had what Cruz could only describe as a mischievous twinkle in his eyes. "Still time to get in on this year's pool, Chef."

"You know I can't tell a shortstop from a midfielder," Tatum said.

"Yeah." Sam grinned. "That was kinda the point."

"How about you, new guy?" The woman who sidled over was compact, reached almost to Cruz's bicep, and wore her stark pink hair in a face-tightening bun on the top of her head. Tiny, tattooed stars dotted the side of her neck. "You a baseball fan, Mendoza?"

"Since I could hold a bat," Cruz confirmed. "Cubs fan to the marrow."

"Cool." As if he'd passed another test, she offered her hand. "I'm Colby Quinn."

"Nice to meet you, Colby."

"My man." Bobby Quallis, all of six feet four inches, towered over Cruz and gave him a hearty slap on the back. "You being a Cubs fan earns you bonus points. You see that exhibition game last night? Vicious."

"I might have caught an inning or two." Cruz did his best not to wince in pain. He could already feel a bruise forming between his shoulder blades even as his mind circled through the larger man's history.

Quallis had played football once upon a time, before serving two years for auto theft. The fact he was caught because he'd pulled over to help an elderly woman cross through a nasty intersection of traffic had earned the two-time offender a sentencing break along with the hearty reputation as a behemoth with a heart of tarnished gold.

Tatum introduced him to the others, the bartenders and wait staff, the dish room crew and busboys, most of whom were young women working their way through college or culinary school. He quickly put faces to names but couldn't get much more without looking at their employee files. Cruz was waiting for the right moment to ask for those.

"Cruz is going to be working with you tonight, Sam," Tatum said. "I want him acclimated to how we work before we throw him in the deep end as my sous. That work for you?"

"Pizza duty's the best in the kitchen." Sam raised his fist in a mock bump. "You good with your hands?"

"I do okay." Cruz swore he could feel Tatum's face heating up from here. "Do you throw or stretch?"

"Combo, my friend," Sam said with a wide smile. "I'll teach you what you don't know."

"I'm up for anything."

Tatum cleared her throat and, as Cruz suspected, when he glanced at her he found her cheeks had turned an amusing shade of pink. "On that note, I will leave you in their capable hands. Thanks, guys. See you in a few."

Cruz turned to stash his bag in his locker once she'd left, not surprised to find the locker room had gone oddly quiet. "Something I can help you all with?" He glanced behind him in the mirror on the interior of his locker door.

"So, you, um, known Tatum for long?" Colby asked, then yelped when a tall, thin, almost anemic-looking young redheaded man elbowed her in the ribs. "Ow! Geez, Chester. I was just asking."

"Snooping for gossip, you mean. Ty Collins." The third of Tatum's former parolees stepped forward. The almost-fifty-year-old looked as if he'd seen a lot more life than most, with his haunted gray eyes and sad smile. A look at his file had told Cruz the man hadn't caught many breaks over the years. "I work mainly pastries and desserts. And I think what Colby meant to say was however you got this job, welcome aboard. Looking forward to working with you."

However he got the… Cruz covered before he blinked in shock. They seemed to be under the impression he and Tatum were…involved. "Ah, thanks. I guess." He cleared his throat and earned a knowing laugh from his new coworkers. It took him a few seconds to realize he'd made the exact same sound Tatum had before she'd left the room. "Look, it's nothing like—I mean, Tatum and me—"

"Don't sweat it." Quallis loomed over him, slapped a hand on Cruz's shoulder and nearly made his knees buckle. "Just know if you hurt her we know how to get rid of your body." His smile was quick, surprisingly friendly, and came with a warning glare that, as a protective big brother himself, Cruz completely understood. "But keep it out of the kitchen," Quallis added with a wink. "In there, it's all about the food. No drama. No personal crap. It stays outside."

"Truer words were never spoken." Sam stood and straightened his jacket, finished the last of his coffee. "The kitchen gets hot enough. Leave whatever it is you've got simmering with her outside."

"But there's nothing…" Cruz trailed off, gaping at the knowing, amused expressions on the faces that trailed out and headed to work. It wasn't until he was alone that he realized that by hiring him the way she had, by being as bad a liar as she was, Tatum had inadvertently given him an added layer of protection. If her employees were focused on his supposed relationship with Tatum, they'd never even consider he was anything more than that.

He shrugged out of his zip-front hoodie, hung it in the locker and pulled out the white chef's jacket Tatum had instructed him to pick up at a local uniform store. He'd also grabbed a few pairs of the relaxed pants and a good pair of solid work shoes. His backup cell and wallet—filled with new IDs that matched his current working identity at True—were in his pack, along with a few innocuous items a man might keep with him on a long workday that included a loaded-to-the-gill sereader and a fresh pair of clothes.

His detective badge and real ID were locked away in the safe back home in his bedroom, but he had his gun secured in the bottom of his bag. From the time he stepped foot outside his house, for the foreseeable future, he was Cruz Mendoza, sous-chef and devoted son of two elderly, ill parents.

The back of his neck prickled. Now that the break room was empty except for him, he had the strangest feeling he was being watched. He glanced around the ceiling edge. He didn't see any cameras, nor had Tatum mentioned any, and she would have, wouldn't she? Until he was sure, he'd postpone his search of his fellow employee's lockers. Maybe convince Tatum to let him come in after hours so he could take a more thorough look around.

The warrant he'd got was already burning a hole in his pocket. It covered the restaurant and everything inside it for the next seven days. That was the judge's call, having severely narrowed Cruz's requested three-month window. He had a short time to find the evidence he needed to expand the warrant and that time was already running out.

Buttoning up and tugging his jacket into place, he rotated his shoulders, trying to get used to the added fabric. He'd be sweating in no time, and he could only imagine how restricted his movements were going to be. How did she—how did any of them—wear this day in and day out, night after night? He slid a finger under the collar, rotated his neck. One thing was for sure.

He had the distinct feeling this was going to be a very, very long day.

TATUM TOOK AN extra half hour over the night's special menu, going over it more times than usual. She told herself she was being cautious. That she just wanted the perfect choices possible from her trip to the farmers and fish market earlier that day.

But that wasn't it.

Being down in that locker room with her staff, she'd felt almost sick at the idea of what was really going on. Cruz was here because he believed someone was running drugs out of her restaurant. And there she'd stood, talking about baseball and blushing to high heaven because of a throwaway comment by someone she considered a friend.

For the first time since she'd opened her restaurant, True didn't feel like a haven or an escape. It felt like a trap where every single one of them had been caught.

The only way, the absolute only way to get through this with her business still intact, was to make sure the case was never brought to anyone's attention. She'd prove Cruz wrong. Easy as that.

And if he's right? That irritating little subconscious of hers would not stop pestering her with that question. "If he's right, I'll find a way through it." But he wasn't right. There were no drugs in True.

She'd bet her life on it.

Who was she kidding? She *was* betting her life on it.

Forget butterflies, she had a swarm of murder hornets buzzing around in her stomach. And that buzzing grew more intense as she headed down to the kitchen to begin preservice prep.

She stopped outside the swinging door, pressed a hand to her stomach. She hadn't been this nervous in the kitchen since she'd landed her first *sous* job. Nerves. Jitters. Uncertainty. And it was all because of Detective Cruz Medina.

"Mendoza," she muttered. "Mendoza, not Medina."

"You all right there, Chef?" Quallis came up behind her.

"Fine, thanks." She turned around and pushed her butt into the door to open it. Clipboard in hand, she called her team of chefs and servers together to run through the night's menu. She watched them gather, felt a swelling of pride lift her confidence even as she caught Cruz's gaze. She could do this. Tatum took a deep breath. She could do it.

"Okay, so tonight we're going Mediterranean. Italian and Greek. We're doing branzino with early spring vegetables and a lemon rice pilaf as our main special. Colby, that'll be you on fish with Chester on backup. We've been slow on vegan lately, so I don't want you getting overwhelmed, Colby, and you two work well together," she added when she saw the young woman's brows pinch together. "Sam, you and Cruz are handling the pizza. I added the pear and gorgonzola back to the menu for tonight as an appetizer. Let's see how it does now that we've got the reduced balsamic glaze."

"We've got it," Sam called.

"Great." She recited the rest of the menu items, made note of the few changes she'd made to some of their mainstays. "We're going with chocolate lava cakes with a caramel ice cream as our recommended dessert. Ty, you've already gotten started on the baklava, right?"

"On it," Ty confirmed. "I was also going to recommend a honey gelato as an option for the future. We got a bottle of lavender honey with our market delivery today."

"Oh, that sounds good." She made a note. "Yeah, we'll work that in this week. As usual, I'm open to menu suggestions. I want to keep things fresh. For tonight, let's just focus on being fast and being good. I want every plate that leaves this kitchen to be pristine." She glanced at her watch. "We open in three hours. Soup's on for us in ninety minutes. Any questions?"

The nerves had mostly vanished by the time everyone went back to their stations. Soon the familiar, comforting sounds of True began ringing through her ears. It was going to be okay, she told herself even as she shifted her gaze through the kitchen and found Cruz in the back corner by the imported stone pizza oven. She watched as Sam showed him how to load the wood, shoving it through the flames into the back to maintain the constant fifteen-hundred-degree heat. It made for quick pizzas, especially given how thin their crusts were.

She took a step back, her lips curving as Cruz and Sam worked as a team; it was a good match. One she'd purposely made. Sam knew everything that went on at True whether people wanted him to or not. It was a good connection for Cruz to make. A good friend. She needed the detective to see that the people who worked for her were more than employees, more than names in a file or people with records. They were real people with real lives and she didn't doubt for one minute that they were loyal to her.

Still. She cringed. She really hoped this wouldn't blow back in her face.

Cruz took a step back, planted his hands on his narrow hips and turned his head. His gaze found hers, and for a moment, just like the other night in the bar, the world seemed to move into silence. His smile, when he offered it, scraped against her heart. As beautiful as he was, as effortlessly as he seemed to fit, he didn't belong here. Her own smile faded.

He didn't love this place like she did. To him, it was just another element to his case. Another circumstance he could brush off and move beyond, while to her it was the air she needed to breathe.

"Chef?" Colby waved at her. "I think we might have a problem with the branzino."

Just like that her trance was broken. "Coming," she called, and got to work.

Chapter Seven

It took less than the full shift for Cruz to gain a new respect not only for chefs, but for restaurant staff in general. Sure, he'd seen his share of TV docuseries spotlighting the "real world" behind the swinging doors, but that was nothing compared to being in on the action. The nonstop, hot, sweaty, ear-splittingly frenetic activity. The rolling with the punches that could be anything from a food allergy to a food critic.

Despite his crash course at Tatum's condo, there had been no way to properly prepare for this new job. Words and videos, warnings and advice might have helped, but this was being in the trenches, and he felt like a gangly cadet pushing through his first radio car shift.

If he'd expected to have a "getting to know you" conversation with Sam, that idea flew out the pizza door oven from almost the moment service started. There wasn't time to talk. And if he thought he'd slip into this without any difficulty, the overcooked pizzas that had piled up before he finally got the timing right was a definite ego check. They'd made good snacks for one of his breaks, though. On his other break he'd taken what he hoped was a new guy exploratory walk around the storage area, loading bay and alley behind the restaurant. He'd spotted the cameras he expected, but not in the most convenient of places, and not all of them seemed to be working. Interesting.

"Good job, everyone!" Susan Ford, True's hostess, gave them a quick round of applause as they ended the evening at just after eleven. "We had a full house that sent many kudos back to all of you."

Cruz watched Susan walk over to Tatum and speak to her for a while before they both headed out. Before Sam could comment on Cruz's distraction, Cruz refocused his attention and followed the cleanup routine Sam had down to military precision. Once the pizza station was sparkling, they shifted their way down the line, helping the various sous-chefs with their own cleanup, loading the dishes, pots, pans and everything else that had touched a morsel of food into the far back.

"You guys are the definition of a well-oiled machine," Cruz said and earned appreciative smiles from the two dedicated dishwashers currently elbow-deep in suds. "We didn't get introduced earlier. I'm Cruz Mendoza."

"Bernadette Chavez." Dark, frizzy curls sprang up around her sweat-dotted, freckled face. "It's nice to meet you."

"Jeremy Pike." The other dishwasher jerked his chin up in greeting. "Welcome to True." He continued loading one of the three industrial-strength rapid dishwashers while the dirty plates piled up.

"Thanks, Jeremy."

"Just Pike is fine. Only my mother calls me Jeremy." He was tall, only an inch shorter than Cruz, and leaned toward the lanky side. Beneath the collar of his T-shirt Cruz could see the edges of tattoo work, including a distinct symbol from the armed forces.

"You serve?" Cruz asked.

"Nah." Pike shrugged. "My dad. Marines. He was KIA when I was a kid."

"Sorry to hear it."

"Yeah. That's how life goes." Pike turned his attention back to the dishes while others filed in and out, re-supplying the kitchen with the just washed and warm plates.

"It usually takes us about an hour after closing to get everything ready for the next night." Ty took a stack of plates from Cruz and set them in their open metal cabinet. "You did real well for your first night here. You ready to do it all again tomorrow?"

"I am, actually." Although he winced as he said it and earned a laugh of sympathy not only from Sam but from some of his other coworkers. Given that he was supposed to be used to working in a restaurant, he couldn't exactly complain, but man. The gym had nothing on this place when it came to physical exertion.

"Most of us are heading over to O'Shannahan's across the street for an afterwork beer," Sam told him as they returned to the washing room for another load. "You're welcome to join us."

"Unless you're ready to go home and collapse," Quallis teased.

He was, but that would be admitting defeat. Besides, a beer with the crew was the perfect way to open up new avenues of information for him. "I'm more than ready for a beer." He was also hungry. How was that even possible after he'd scarfed down that amazing minestrone, fresh-baked bread and more than a fair share of scorched pizza?

"Great. We'll see you there." Sam, Quallis, Chester and Colby all grinned far too widely before they filed out, leaving Cruz surrounded by the remaining mountain of dishes. He groaned. He'd be lucky to be out of here by dawn.

"Let me guess," he said to Ty Collins, who appeared to have taken pity on him and was grabbing an armful of serving utensils. "Dishes are True's version of hazing?"

"You survived trial by fire," Ty told him, looking far more energetic than Cruz despite his added twenty years. "Better than Sam did his first night. He set off the fire alarm twice and ruined so many pies Tatum had to make a fresh batch of dough. Come on. I'll help you finish up."

By the time the kitchen was clean and the last of the kitchen staff was on their way home, Cruz completely understood why the locker room included shower facilities. And also why Tatum had suggested bringing a change of clothes with him. He gave brief thought to drowning himself under the hot water as it melted some of the soreness away, and felt some regret that the night was not over. One job was done. Now his real work began.

"You coming for a beer?" Cruz asked Ty back in the locker room as the older man tugged on a jacket over a fresh T-shirt and jeans.

"Not tonight." Ty offered an apologetic smile. "Not

that I don't want to celebrate your inauguration into the trenches, but I have somewhere I need to be."

Cruz moved his cell onto the top shelf of his locker before he closed the door and spun the combination lock. "No worries. Have a good night."

"Yeah," Ty said with a nod. "You, too."

AFTER-CLOSING WAS TATUM'S favorite part of the day. Not because it boosted her pride to see the receipts for the night, although that did give her a shot of satisfaction. And not because she could retire to her office after delegating the busy work she'd spent years doing in other people's restaurants. Tatum loved this part of her day because there was something special about retreating to her office and looking down at the empty, silent, dimly lit creation she'd brought to life.

True slept now, exhaling in relief as the last of her staff trickled out the front door. She watched them leave every night, enjoying the banter and camaraderie that had built up over the past few years. They'd spend an hour or so at O'Shannahan's, venting whatever they needed to get out of their systems in a safe place she didn't dare intrude into. As much as she would have enjoyed joining them for a beer, having the boss show up like some kind of after-hours overseer just felt... well, it felt rude.

Cruz wasn't in the first flood out. She chuckled to herself as she wandered over to her desk, unbuttoned and shrugged out of her chef's jacket. She stretched her arms over her head, untied her hair and shook her hands through it.

He'd have been given the brunt of the grunt work tonight. Sam would have seen to that. The ritual breaking-in of the new guy—and by guy she meant man or woman—had become a right of passage for her crew, one she fully embraced while staying completely, well, mostly, hands off. And it gave Cruz one more way to see who these people really were.

So it might be a bit passive-aggressive on her part. It wasn't as if he was unfamiliar with the practice. Tatum sorted through the various paperwork and receipts Susan had given her from the registers, the computer printouts. While it was part of Richard's job to maintain the books and accounts, this was one aspect of her business she hadn't quite been able to let go of completely. She liked seeing the numbers add up, and could still remember the thrill of seeing her profit margin move out of the red and solidly into black.

If Cruz was right and True was being used in some way, it had to show up somewhere in the books, didn't it? Her second skimming of the records didn't provide any new answers or suspicions. His investigation was, she decided, going to be quick, cursory, and a complete waste of time. She heard the faint echo of voices as the final group of employees, Cruz included this time no doubt, headed out for the night.

Casually, she knocked her hand against her laptop to wake it up, sorted through the papers and notes, and jotted down totals to keep track of the meals that had been preferred for the evening. When she was ready to put the information into her personal spreadsheet, she pulled her computer closer.

A loud bang followed by a door slamming had Tatum jumping in her chair. She took a deep breath, silently cursed Cruz for making her so darned jumpy, and tried to refocus. She'd had to pull the branzino off the menu special due to its suspicious quality, something she planned to discuss with her supplier first thing in the morning. It wasn't the first time this particular business had tried to slip something past her, but it would definitely be the last.

There it was again. Not a bang this time, but a crash, as if someone had run into something in the kitchen.

Tatum got up, pulled open the door and stood on the top of the landing, leaned over and yelled, "Richard? Are you still here?" She could have sworn she'd seen him leave with the others, but he wasn't exactly a joiner. He also wasn't the workaholic she was and had a tendency to take care of most of the business early in the morning.

Their styles might not be exact, and he did have the tendency to walk around with his nose in the air, something that came in handy with her snootier clientele. He was, above all else, an excellent schmoozer and marketer, and in just the last few months he'd helped her and True make their mark in Chicago's food world. One place he did not excel, however, was in the kitchen. Which was exactly how she wanted it. "Richard?"

Restaurants weren't the safest place in the world for non-chefs, and it was that thought that had her moving quietly down the stairs through the silent confines of True.

After successful nights like this she could almost hear the restaurant's heartbeat; her business was alive, had been from the moment she'd swiped her first paint sample on the wall. The bar and main dining room were bathed in dim light. The kitchen was dark, but she could move through True blindfolded. She wound her way around the counters and appliances toward the back office near the back alley and loading bay, past the walk-in refrigerator. "Richard?" she called again. "Are you all right?"

Something scampered behind her. An odd shuffling of feet and fabric. Tatum spun around, wishing she'd clicked on the light. "Darn it," she told herself in a harsh whisper. "Stop letting him spook you." Cruz. Her eyes narrowed. Was he behind this? Snooping around? Or was he deliberately trying to scare her into believing she had drug dealers in her midst? "You're being ridiculous." Then again, after having seen that cool determination in his eyes earlier this evening, would she put it past him? "Ha, ha, very funny, Cruz." She backtracked, stopped at the edge of the stainless steel work counter, and clicked on the lights. Electricity buzzed overhead as they flickered on. Rather than ease her nerves, the hair on the back of her neck prickled as she caught sight of the walk-in refrigerator's door standing open.

"What on earth?" She stalked toward it, ignoring the warning bells going off in her head. She poked her head inside the walk-in, reached for the light switch. She heard a shuffling behind her, more than a scamper this time, but before she could turn around, she was shoved forward into the icy room. She flailed, struggled to catch her balance, and smashed headfirst into one of the metal shelving units.

Before she could catch her breath, the door slammed shut.

CRUZ HAD SITUATED himself by the front window of O'Shannahan's to nurse his one-beer limit. The True crowd apparently had attained their own dedicated table in the seventy-five-year-old establishment. The throw-back-style pub had a history as rich and diverse as Chicago itself, from the scarred yet polished bar that had been salvaged and shipped from a now defunct hotel in Dublin, to the framed news clippings featuring Irish-influenced accomplishments and successes lining the faux brick walls.

According to the stories he'd heard over the last forty minutes, O'Shannahan's had nearly gone under a few years ago. Then True had opened. The rejuvenation of the neighborhood gave the beleaguered owners new hope. Rather than closing up and giving up, they'd taken the chance on a bit of rebranding and marketing, and now enjoyed a new lease—literally and figuratively—along with a steady clientele. A clientele that included True employees who, as a continuous thank-you from the pub, were all given half-off drinks their first hour each night.

"It's not like Ty not to join us after work," Colby said with something akin to motherly concern shining in her eyes. "Is everything okay with him?"

"Who knows." Sam shrugged and took a pull of his beer. "He's not exactly the chattiest in our bunch." He grinned at Colby, who rolled her eyes. "If he wants us to know, he'll tell us." When Cruz continued to watch the restaurant, Sam gave him a friendly nudge on the arm. "Can't leave it alone, can you?"

Cruz shifted his attention to the table, but only for a moment. The lights in True were low; he couldn't see a thing other than the steady glow in the back right corner, precisely where Tatum's second-floor office was located. Given the frenzied activity that took place most of the day, after-closing was the ideal time for anything illegal to go down. "Can't leave what alone?"

"Work," Sam said. "Feels good to find where you fit. Where you belong."

Hearing the sentimentality in the younger man's voice, Cruz stepped through the verbal door that just opened. "Is that what happened to you? To all of you?" he added so as not to single Sam out. "You found where you fit?"

"You know it." Sam toasted him with his bottle. "That woman over there? Tatum? She gave me the chance I needed in this business."

"She's saved a lot of our lives," Quallis chimed in. "Not many folks with her stellar reputation would hire ex-cons like us."

"Ex-cons? You've served time?" Cruz leaned forward. He feigned his surprise, but not his interest. There was always a lot more to people than what their criminal records said. "Both of you?"

"Three of us," Sam corrected. "Ty, too."

"You mind me asking what you were sentenced for?" Cruz knew of course, but reading a file and hearing about it firsthand were two entirely different things.

"Accessory after the fact. Armed robbery," Sam said with a familiar flinch of remorse.

"You didn't accessorize anything," Quallis told him, then looked to Cruz, who forced a smile at the intentional joke.

"Quall, drop it," Sam said with more than a hint of irritation. "I got seven years."

"Kid didn't know what his buddies had just pulled

off. He just gave them a ride," Quallis qualified. "Turns out they'd knocked over a convenience store earlier that night, then hoofed it over to where Sam was working and begged a ride."

Sam glared at Quallis. "You going to let me tell it my way or not?"

"They gave you seven years for that?" Why was he surprised? The sentencing of Black defendants typically skewed into the unjust realm. Cruz wasn't immune to the societal inequities; he had a close-up view every single day. As a Hispanic cop, he'd dealt with more than his share of racism and prejudice on both sides of the system. He liked to think he was making a small difference at least. He sure hoped so.

"They gave him seven years because he wouldn't rat out his friends," Quallis continued on his rant as if Sam hadn't spoken.

"I was out in three." Sam's voice quieted, as if he'd changed his mind and wanted to be discussing anything else.

"That sucks," Cruz said. Things had gotten better in the last…he took another drink of beer and longed for another. Who was he kidding? It was going to take a long time for things to get significantly better where the judicial system was concerned. It was a shame Sam had lost even that much of his life for a first-time offence. That said, there was something noble, if not misguided, about the young man not having ratted out his friends. "I'm sorry."

"I found a way through it," Sam said and shrugged. "Kept my head down. Didn't make trouble. Got a job in the prison kitchen. Took classes online and then finished my degree at a community college when I got out. I worked my butt off in a pizza place near my mom's house to pay for it. Now look at me." He toasted to True. "I'm a top sous-chef for Tatum-freaking-Colton. One day I'm gonna have my own place, serve my own food my way. But for now? I'm where I'm meant to be and learning everything I can."

"We're all where we're meant to be. Speaking of—" Quallis glanced over his shoulder "—Tatum's running late." He checked his watch, frowned. "She's usually heading out about now."

Cruz looked back at the light, saw shadows moving in and out. "You know what time Tatum leaves?"

"Why do you think we chose a table by the window?" Colby chimed in. "None of us go home until she does."

It took a lot to surprise Cruz. They'd managed to do so multiple times in just one night. "She doesn't know, does she?"

"Nope. We've worked hard to keep it that way." Quallis's crystal blue eyes narrowed. "So if she suddenly finds out we'll know who squealed." That grin of his spread slowly and reminded Cruz of a certain maniacal comic book villain.

Cruz chuckled, recognizing a challenge when he heard it. He leaned forward, reached into his back pocket for his phone. He swore, checked his other pocket, patted the front of his jeans. He swore again. "I must have left my phone in my locker."

"Uh-huh." Sam finished his beer. "That's believable."

"Agreed," Quallis teased. "A likely story."

"Work on your creativity, Cruz," Colby suggested. "You'd best get over there before she locks you out for the night."

"Right." He got to his feet, grabbed his bag, pulled a ten out of his wallet and tossed it on the table. "I'll see you all tomorrow."

TATUM HAD ONLY been truly terrified three times in her life.

Once when she was seven and had gotten separated from her parents and sisters at a Halloween fair, and found herself lost in a haunted corn maze. The second time had been shortly after she'd gotten her driver's license and had white-knuckled it through a thirty-minute downpour on the highway. Number three hit just a few weeks ago when the police had notified the family of her father and uncle's murder. The feeling of her heart lurching inside her body, as if it had forgotten how to beat, was something she'd never wanted to feel again. Something she'd never forget.

But she felt it again now. Surrounded by pulsating silence trapped in the one place she had always been, always felt safe. Tatum dived toward the beam of light streaming in through the small, square window. She grabbed the metal lever handle, but pushing or pulling proved futile. The handle wouldn't budge.

The door remained closed.

In those other instances, tears had broken through the fear, released her from the paralytic inability to think clearly. Even if she had the inclination to cry now, any attempt would have evaporated beneath the steam of anger building inside of her.

Tatum turned her back on the door, slammed her fist against it as her head throbbed. She touched cold fingers to her scalp, fingers that came away bloodied. She swallowed the panic climbing into her throat. Control and calm would get her through. She had to blink constantly to stop her eyes from burning against the cold. She found the light switch, flicked it on and breathed a sigh of relief when the bare bulb overhead fizzled to life.

"Cell phone." She found it in her back pocket, the one place she tried not to keep it because of her tendency to sit on and crack screens. Thank goodness for bad habits. Tatum almost kissed it as she tapped the screen. Until she saw she had no bars. No signal. No way out. Cursing, and as the cold began seeping into her bones, she started to pace. This wasn't supposed to be able to happen. She'd purposely chosen a walk-in refrigeration model that prevented someone being trapped. Which meant one thing.

Someone had locked her inside.

Chapter Eight

The cold air snapped through Cruz like a whip as he jogged across the street. True's dimmed interior displayed its elegant facade in the darkness of the night. Streetlights hummed and buzzed, and his footfalls echoed into the darkness. He tried the front door first, not surprised to find it locked. He rapped on the glass, but seconds ticked by without any response.

Cruz took a step back, then walked around to the front of the building where he could get a better vantage into the second-floor office, but as he found the right line of sight he spotted Tatum descending the stairs and circling into the kitchen.

He almost knocked again, then decided to wait until she came back out. He didn't like the idea of her being alone like this. Not at this hour. The neighborhood might have become safer in recent years, but as he well knew, no place was 100 percent safe.

Cruz stood there, staring at the outline of the swinging kitchen doors, mentally willing her to come back out so he could get her attention. When the seconds continued to tick by, he'd had enough. He raised a hand to knock on the glass.

Just as a figure in black streaked out of the kitchen and up the stairs to her office.

Cruz immediately dropped into cop mode. Whoever that was, was too big. Too frantic.

Too male.

Cruz swore, and as he ran around the corner of the building to the back alley, he dragged his backpack in front of him, rummaging inside for his gun. He tossed the bag aside and, pistol in hand, came to a skidding halt when he spotted the taillights of a dark SUV parked directly in front of the metal door of the loading bay. Cruz ducked behind a dumpster, staying out of sight of the idling car as he considered his options. He could call for backup, but that would risk blowing his cover. Once the cops set foot in True, he'd be out, and he had too much at stake to give up so fast. Besides, by the time anyone got here, they'd be long gone. The streetlamps were still blazing, but the nearby ones weren't close or bright enough to give him a good look at the license plate.

He needed to get inside. Tatum was in there. For a moment, impulse overruled reason and he nearly revealed himself. Tatum. His heart jackhammered in his chest. Exciting, entrancing, trusting Tatum who had been so certain no one on her staff could be involved in criminal activity. Anger and frustration boiled their way through his blood. She could be hurt or…worse. Cruz gritted his teeth, gripped his free hand around the edge of the dumpster, poked his head up as someone inside the car pushed open the passenger door.

Voices exploded in the night. Muffled, indistinct, unrecognizable. The shadowy figure he'd seen moments before ducked out the half-raised loading accordion door and into the vehicle. Cruz began moving when the car did, sticking close to the wall, focusing his attention on the grime-covered plate. He caught two numbers and a letter, but the popular make and model of the car would make it nearly impossible to trace.

He ducked into the loading bay, tucked his gun into the back waistband of his pants and hurried through the darkness as quickly as he could. Passing by the bright white catering van with True's logo painted on the outside, he collided with crates along with some boxes in his rush to get to the kitchen, but the gossamer quality of the plastic tarp draped between the main kitchen door and the loading bay acted as a beacon.

He stepped inside the creepy silence of True. "Tatum?" His voice echoed back at him as he made his way through the dish room, into the kitchen and around to the other side. "Tatum?"

He forced himself to stay in one spot, to listen and look. He turned in a slow, deliberate circle. There! A bang. Dull. Heavy. Weak. He inclined his head, and when it came again, he shifted his attention to the walk-in refrigerator.

Son of a…

The metal lever handle of the walk-in had been wedged closed with an oversize metal ladle. She was inside.

The bang sounded again, and this time the light inside flickered. "Tatum!" he yelled as he grabbed a towel and grabbed hold of the utensil to pull it free. He dropped it to the ground with a clang, but before he could open the door, it sprung open and Tatum, hands and arms filled with something he couldn't identify, flew out.

He caught her around the waist before she slammed face-first into the stainless steel counter. Her scream when he lifted her right off the ground had his ears ringing. She kicked and twisted, trying to hit him with whatever reddish brown rock-solid block she carried. He turned his head to the side to avoid being knocked out. "Tatum, stop! It's me. It's Cruz!" He set her down before he dropped her.

"Cruz." She went limp in his arms. Her knees folded and he kept hold of her, kept her on her feet as she caught her breath. "Okay. It's okay." She inhaled deeply, still clutching her battering ram of choice in her arms. "I'm okay."

"What on earth is that?" Cruz asked.

"This?" She hefted it up and nearly hit him in the chin with it. "It's an imported ham. It's the heaviest thing I could find in there," she added at his look of disbelief.

"Let's put the pig down, shall we?" He plucked the ham out of her hands and set it on the counter. When he faced her again, his gaze fell to the trickle of blood trailing down the side of her face. "You're hurt." He reached out, but she flinched before he even touched her. Cruz swore, grabbed a stool and pushed her onto it. "Stay here. I'll get the first aid kit."

"I'm fine." But the fact she sank onto the stool told him otherwise.

"It's either me or the ER. Take your pick." He didn't stop moving until he'd retrieved the red plastic box from the unisex bathroom off the dish room. When he returned to her side by the refrigerator, he found her staring into its chilly depths, her eyes slightly unfocused. She was shivering. Whether from the cold or the aftereffects, he couldn't be sure. "Maybe the ER is the right move."

"No." She shook her head, flinched a bit, but when she looked at him he saw her eyes were clear again. "No emergency room." She brushed her fingers against her scalp. "Head wounds always bleed like crazy." She pulled the medical box over and rummaged around, set out what he himself would have. "No one else is with you, are they?"

"No." He uncapped the antibacterial spray and got to work dabbing and trying not to make the cut on her head hurt worse. Cruz moved her hair behind her shoulders, took an extra moment to tuck it behind her ear. He looked down at her pale face, at what he could only assume was anger and hurt spinning in those endless eyes of hers. He cupped the back of her head, tilted her head back. "Are you sure he didn't hurt you?"

"Are you sure it was a he? Never mind." She sighed. "Of course it was a man. He just gave me a shove and then slammed the door. Momentum's a bi—" She pinched her lips together. "Took me a second too long to catch my balance. I hit one of the metal racks face-first." She lifted her hand, but he stopped her, caught it in his and curled his fingers around hers. "You know what really makes me mad?"

He couldn't resist, not when she looked so uncertain, so unsure of what to do or think next. He lifted her hand and pressed his lips to the back of her knuckles. "Tell me."

He wasn't sure whether to be impressed or insulted that his attempt at comfort and affection didn't distract her.

"He did this to me in my home, Cruz. He made me feel scared and afraid in my home." Her jaw tensed. "Did you see him? Do you know who it was?"

"No." He released her hand, refocused his attention on her head. "I was standing outside when you came down from your office. I knocked earlier but you didn't hear. Whoever it was moved too fast for me to get a good look"

"I heard someone down here." She was reciting it as if dazed. "I guess I thought maybe it was Richard or one of the employees. Or you."

"Me?"

Her smirk seemed almost normal. "I thought maybe it was you trying to teach me a lesson about being too trusting. You know, freak me out so I'd be more agreeable to your *investigation*."

As insulting as the prospect was, it wasn't a bad lesson for her to have learned. "I wouldn't have done that, Tatum."

"I know. But that's what I was telling myself when I came down here." She scrubbed a hand over the uninjured side of her face. "And before you say anything, I know it was stupid. Just like those idiotic dimwits in horror movies who go up to the attic in the middle of the night because they heard a noise."

"Or the basement," Cruz attempted some levity. He grinned at her irritated glare. "They make for good entertainment."

"The girls or the movies?"

He chuckled and stretched a small butterfly bandage over the cut in her hairline. "Both."

"Typical," she snorted. "Yeah, well, this wasn't scripted and I should have stayed in my..." She stopped. "What else did you see?"

Now it was his turn to wince. "Whoever was here went up to your office." She slid off the stool and shoved past him so fast it was as if he'd flipped a switch. "Wait, Tatum. Hold on." Darn it! He left the medical box open on the counter and hurried after her. She was already halfway up the steps before he caught up. "Let me go in first, okay?"

"It's my office, Cruz." She jerked her arm free of his grasp.

"And someone just broke in here to find something. Just..." He moved around her, backed up the last few steps to the landing. "Let me go first."

"Whatever, Mr. I-Have-a-Penis-and-You-Don't."

Hand braced on the door, he inclined his head. "That's not what this is about."

"Sure it is." She pointed to his back. "Gun, penis. Same diff as far as I'm concerned. There's no one in there, Cruz. They're gone, remember? You saw them leave yourself."

He pushed open the door and stepped into the dimly lit room. He stepped just inside, a bit stunned by what he saw.

"Well?" Tatum moved in behind him.

"Well nothing." He planted his hands on his hips. "The place is immaculate." Just as he remembered it. He'd expected it to be tossed. Whoever had been here had been in a rush. It shouldn't be this neat. Unless they knew exactly what they were looking for and where to find it.

"Well, then." She moved around him this time and headed to her desk.

"Do you see anything that's been disturbed? That's out of place?"

She sat in her chair and did a slow rotation to check the room. "Not really, no." She tapped on the keyboard of her laptop. "This is what I was working on when I heard the noise, and nothing new has been opened." Her gaze hesitated on the tall wooden filing cabinet. "Hang on." She got up and pulled the top drawer open.

"What?"

"This is supposed to be locked," she said and began sifting through the files. "I keep the key in the frame of that picture." She pointed to one of her and her sisters. "Everything seems in place, though. They're a bit more messy than I like, but that could have been me. Huh." She pulled out one file from the middle of the drawer. "This is in the wrong order. I'll give you one guess whose employment file this is."

"Given the look on your face, I only need one." He plucked it out of her hands and flipped open the now empty file. "It's mine."

TATUM STAYED IN Cruz's SUV while he ran the towel-wrapped ladle that had nearly sealed her doom into the precinct lab. She hadn't been up for another argument, which was why she agreed to let him drive her home. Although why he hadn't done that first before coming here was beyond her.

It was closing in on 1:00 a.m. and her body was

screaming for relief in the form of a shower, a handful of aspirin and sleep. Not necessarily in that order.

Resting her arm on the door, she pressed gentle fingers to the sore spot, which would no doubt transform into a lovely shade of eggplant by morning. She supposed that years from now, when she'd rediscovered her sense of humor, she'd find this entire situation borderline hysterical, but for now? For now she was definitely going to have to take things one minute at a time.

She closed her eyes, felt her head loll forward, but before her eyes drifted shut, she saw a shadow heading her way. Tatum jumped, suddenly wide-awake, and instantly realized it was Cruz. She glanced at her watch. It had been almost an hour since he'd parked.

Tatum shifted in her seat as he opened the door and dropped in behind the wheel. "Sorry. Paperwork's always a pain. You all right?"

"I'm fine." Given it was the tenth time he'd asked her that question since they'd left True, she managed this one through gritted teeth. "Will you take me home now?"

He grinned, starting the engine. "Sure."

She rolled her eyes, which added to the pain in her head. "Just drop me off at my front door, Valentino. I'll walk in tomorrow."

"Valentino, huh?" he echoed with that side-eyed smile of his. "Charming, romantic, the epitome of male virility—"

"In the *silent* movie age," she cut him off.

"Not to mention the fact Rudolph Valentino was Italian and I am—"

"Not." She smirked, ducked her chin before he saw

the conversation was actually entertaining and thus distracting her. "Do you like silent movies?"

"I do, actually. Buster Keaton is one of my favorite silent stars. Who's your favorite?"

"Clara Bow." She'd always thought the women of that era had gotten the shaft when it came to the history of film. "They're having a silent movie retrospective in Edgerton Park next week. Before tonight I was thinking about taking Thursday off and going."

"How does tonight change that?" He made a U-turn at the light and headed toward her condo.

"Call me overly cautious, but I'm not feeling particularly secure in leaving my restaurant in someone else's hands right now." She knew once the fog lifted from her brain she was going to have to deal with the fact that someone—someone she trusted and considered family—was probably responsible for her getting shoved into the Deepfreeze.

"When was the last time you took a day off?"

"Monday, remember?" She could feel her eyes beginning to droop again and stifled a yawn.

"I mean a day that wasn't already designated. You're the boss. You should take a day every once in a while."

She rolled her head against the back of the seat to look at him. "When's the last time you took a day off?"

"February 17," he said without hesitation. "My brother, Frankie, was participating in a debate competition."

Tatum's mouth twisted. Sometimes Cruz Medina seemed entirely too good to be true. "I think my staff would fall over in shock if I took a day off."

"All the more reason to do it." Cruz shrugged. "Put

them off guard. Maybe see what happens as a result."
He glanced at her. "You might be surprised."

"Speaking of putting them off guard," she said
slowly. "Thank you for letting it look like we were leaving separately tonight."

His lips twitched. "Not a problem."

"They watch out for me," she explained. "They're
protective. They actually wait at O'Shannahan's until I
leave True for the night." One of the reasons she didn't
like to leave too late. "Isn't that sweet? What?" Tatum
asked when Cruz glanced out his window.

"They think you don't know." That grin of his needed
a dimmer. "Don't let on you know. I'm under strict orders not to tell you."

"I'll keep your secret if you keep mine. I'm just glad
they didn't see us leaving together." She sank back farther in the seat as she felt her body begin to loosen. The
adrenaline and nerves were fading. "The last thing either of us need is for them—"

"To think we're involved?" He took a left and slowed
down as they came up on her street. "Hate to tell you,
but I think that ship hasn't only sailed, it's beyond the
horizon."

"What's that mean?" All thoughts of sleep and re-
laxation faded.

"They think we're sleeping together."

"What?" She shot forward in her seat only to have
the seat belt snap her back. "Why would they think
that?"

"You said yourself the way you're hiring me was a
little out of the norm. Plus, you aren't great at deception. You can't lie worth a da—"

"Some people would consider that an admirable quality," she grumbled.

"It didn't help that you blushed to high heaven when you introduced me today."

"I...did not." Her hands flew to her cheeks that were warming even now. "Did I?"

"We could have roasted marshmallows on your face. Don't worry. It actually works to my benefit if they think we've got something going on."

"Well, it doesn't work to mine," she snapped, and then, curious, shifted to face him. "Sleeping with one of my employees. How...cliché. How exactly does it work to your benefit?"

"Us being involved is a good distraction. Not to mention it is a stellar explanation as to why I'm suddenly around. Getting the prime jobs. Having private meetings with the boss." As his humor increased, her irritation grew. "If they're thinking I was hired because we're involved, they won't even consider the real reason I'm there."

"But..." She shook her head. "Us sleeping together would be unprofessional." Not to mention completely out of character for her. Doesn't mean she hadn't thought about it. More than she should have. "And it's a lie."

"Yet not wholly untrue." He pulled into the driveway of her underground parking lot, hit the universal emergency code into her security gate and waited for the metal gate to rise. "We did share a pretty steamy moment in your kitchen the other day. That could qualify as involved."

It qualified as Tatum trying to get Cruz Medina out of her system, she thought sourly. Unfortunately, it hadn't worked, and had, instead, only increased her curiosity, not to mention her desire for the man who could literally destroy her life. "The deal was," Tatum said with exaggerated patience, "I let you work for me so you can prove your theory about drugs being run through my restaurant." As he pulled into her parking spot, left vacant since her car was still at True, she felt compelled to remind him, "It didn't include deceiving my employees into thinking I'm hot for one of my chefs."

"Yeah, well, deals change. Speaking of changing things." He got out and came around to open her door. The next thing she knew he went into his trunk and pulled out not only the pack he'd carried into the restaurant, but also a small duffel bag.

"What's that?" she demanded, but she already knew, by that sly expression on his face. "No. Absolutely not." Her insides sprung into this odd, unfamiliar dance that had her palms sweating. "You are not moving in with me."

"Just for tonight." He took her arm and steered her toward the elevator.

"I said no." She pulled her arm free and took a step back. "You've already invaded my restaurant, turned me into a nervous wreck around my employees and worried someone enough to shove me into a freezer. You are not staying here tonight."

"Let me break this down for you." He took a long breath, let it out. But this time when he smiled, there was no humor behind it. No friendliness. It wasn't Cruz Mendoza, sous-chef and employee of True, looking back at her. This was Cruz Medina, the determined, almost detached cop. "Even if you didn't believe me about the drugs, someone broke into your restaurant tonight. They knew you were there and they came in anyway. They had a plan, Tatum. And it's only blind luck you don't have anything worse than a bump on the head and a case of the chills."

"It was your information they took, not mine," she argued.

"We don't know that for sure. For all we know, taking my file may have been a cover for what they were really after." He pressed the elevator button and stepped back when the doors slid open. "What we do know is they were confident enough in your routine that you'd be alone." He held open the door and waited for her to step inside. "And while the case is my top priority, I'm certainly not going to take a chance with your safety. Not tonight." He hit the button for the second floor. "So whether you like it or not, for tonight at least, I'm your roomie."

THERE WAS SOMETHING immensely satisfying about Tatum Colton in a simmering temper. For years Cruz remembered hearing what a turn-on an angry woman could be, but he'd never gotten the appeal. Clearly, it all depended on the woman.

He wandered around the semi-chaotic living room, where the sparse furniture she did have was out of place and covered in paint tarps left behind by her interior decorator mother and aunt. Cruz had already whipped the coverings off the sofa and coffee table, onto which he set the gun and badge he'd retrieved from his place, along with his phone so all would remain in reach.

It was funny. She'd made it abundantly clear she didn't appreciate his intrusion, and when it came to stubbornness he could think of few rivals. He'd always said he could never be with anyone who wouldn't stand up to him and push back, at least not without irritating him. It had acted as a kind of emotional safety barrier no woman had been able to cross. Enter Tatum Colton.

The more time he spent with her, the more he admired her. Not just admired, but liked. For once, he might be willing to put up with the complications that came with getting involved. Except this would be taking one whopping chance given everything that hung in the balance. The case, the job always would have to come first, always did. Getting distracted by one seriously hot chef was only going to blow up both their lives. And not in any way that was good.

From his spot on the couch—a couch significantly more comfortable than his own bed—he listened to the sound of the shower running. She'd given him the tour beyond the kitchen, the only room he'd inhabited on his previous visit. The kitchen turned out to be the largest, most organized and well-stocked room. It made sense, he supposed. Her love of cooking didn't stop at the doors of True, as evidenced by the spills of herbs lining the small garden window over the sink and the meticulously arranged appliances, utensils and collection of antique rolling pins that made up an odd kind of wall sculpture.

He changed into sweats and a T-shirt, and gave the space outside her bedroom a thorough once-over by checking the windows and the sliding patio door. He double-checked the front door and added suggesting she put a second dead bolt on for added security to his mental list. A single woman couldn't be too careful. Especially if said single woman had drug dealers hovering around her business. But that could wait for when she'd burned off her mad.

He stashed his bags in the small half bath off the kitchen and had made up the couch with the sheets and blanket she'd delivered with her special brand of resentment. Those eyes of hers could scorch glass, and time after time he found himself smiling in the heat of them. It was no doubt obnoxious of him, to take personal delight in what he knew was a difficult situation, but he had a job to do. Tatum's wounded pride and feelings couldn't enter into it.

Lights dimmed, he sat on the couch and checked his voice mail and email. Nothing new to report except… his heart clenched at the text message he'd missed from Jade. He glanced at the time. Too late to message her back now, except…

He typed quickly, his pulse racing as he promised to stop by the Stanhope Rehabilitation Facility tomorrow morning. Hitting Send, he wanted his former partner's almost fiancée to know he'd responded when he could. It wasn't a minute before his notification banner glowed with a simple TY.

Cruz clicked off the light, lay down on the couch and squeezed his eyes shut, trying to block out the rush of memories, the torrent of guilt that flooded through him. He could replay that night in his mind a million times and he'd never see any other way out. But he should have done better, should have done more to protect Johnny. Johnny, who had so much more of a life to live for than he did. Johnny, who had put his life in Cruz's hands only to have things go horribly, horribly wrong.

He needed noise, he needed a distraction. He needed this condo not to smell like jasmine and fresh-baked bread, scents that only evoked endless images of Tatum Colton and her wild, sexy, untamed mane of golden hair. The only image, it seemed, capable of pushing the guilt and anger into the back corners of his mind.

Even now, as he tried to block everything but the thought of sleep, he could feel her, smell her. Hear her bare feet padding across the hardwood floors...

"Cruz?"

He opened his eyes, tried not to inhale too deeply, but he caught the scent of flower-rich soap on her freshly scrubbed skin. Her damp hair was tied up in a knot. She wore a tank top that clung to every curve of her tight, tempting body, along with boxer shorts that confirmed those legs of hers really did go up as far as he'd imagined. He'd dreamed what those legs would feel like wrapped around him, drawing him near her, closer into her. "Yeah?" He didn't move for fear he might shatter.

"This is a one-off."

He turned his head, arched a brow. Seeing her there, standing in the barely-there light of her kitchen, suspecting what temptations lay beneath the fabric concealing her form from him, had him clearing his throat. "Oh, yeah?"

He couldn't help it. He loved watching her eyes narrow like slit arrows of anger.

"I don't need you here," she said. "More to the point, I don't want you here."

"I know." He sighed as if the argument had become tiresome. "Deal with it." When she didn't move away, he continued. "How's your head?"

"Fine."

But he could see it wasn't. She was scared. Despite trying not to be. It was in the sudden shift of her eyes, the way she hugged her arms around her waist. It was all he could do not to wrap his own around her and draw her down beside him.

"I won't change my schedule for you. I won't change my life any more than I already have."

"Change it for yourself, then," he said. "And get some sleep."

"We need to be out of here by eight," she said. "I mean it. Eight a.m."

"Right. Eight. Got it." He looked away, snuggled deeper into the sofa and threw his arm over his eyes. "Go to bed, Tatum."

Still, she didn't move. He could hear, could feel her breathing.

"I mean it, Tatum." He'd never growled a statement before in his life. But he did so now. It was the only way to push the words free. "Go to bed before we both do something you'll regret."

It took longer than he expected, and she didn't scamper. She moved away without another word, but the hesitation in her steps, the slight sound of her increased breathing, had him realizing it was only a matter of time before he was in her bed.

Bap! Bap bap bap!

Cruz shot awake, reaching for his gun, and was on

his feet in the blink of a sleepy eye. When he looked to the source of the sleep-shattering noise, he lowered his sidearm and glared across the room and into the kitchen.

The sun was peeking in through the kitchen window, announcing the start to a new day. And instead of an in-house rooster, Tatum Colton's alarm consisted, it seemed, of her bashing a significant round of dough against her floured counter. Plumes of white puffed up and around her, coated her skin and set his pulse to jackhammering.

"Sorry." She sounded anything but as she grabbed the dough, whipped it up and over and slapped it back down. "It's almost five."

He pressed his thumb and forefinger into his eyes. "You say that as if it means something."

"I didn't want us to be late. We need to be out of here by—"

"Eight a.m. Yeah, I got the memo." She'd all but carved it into his brain last night. "What are you doing?"

"Making bread." And she seemed scarily focused on it. "Baking is one of my coping mechanisms." She winced, shifted the dough around and began to knead it with a ferocity that had Cruz wincing. "I couldn't sleep."

With sleep a forgotten desire, he made his way to the kitchen, poured himself a cup of coffee from the pot she'd already brewed, and took a seat at the bar. When he set his gun on the countertop, her eyes shifted briefly before she refocused on her task. "What's wrong?"

She snorted, a sound that had him torn between laughing and offering sympathy. Rather than provoking her, he simply sipped appreciatively and waited.

"True has been open for three years. Three." Slap. Bang. Slap bang. "Years. Never once in that time have I felt remotely unsafe in its walls. Among my people." Slap bang bang bang. "And now…" She folded the dough over, shoved at it with the heel of her hand and began kneading again. "And now…"

"And now you aren't sure who you can trust." He heard the tears in her voice. Not the feel-sorry-for-me tears of a woman whose business might be in serious jeopardy, but the hot, angry, frustrated tears of not being able to do anything about it. "I'm sorry, Tatum."

"Are you?" She slapped the dough hard enough to make him jump, grabbed it to whip it around again only to have it fly out of her hand. He caught it one-handed as it arced over his head, as if he'd caught a home run at Wrigley Field.

The horror in her eyes kept the humor off his face. He reshaped the ball of dough before handing it back to her as a peace offering. "Yes. None of this is your fault. Someone's taking advantage of you." And the generous nature that was bound to get her into trouble.

"Don't say that," she snapped, and after poking the dough, seemed to decide it and she had had enough. She retrieved a prepared and parchment-lined loaf pan from behind her. "That makes me sound like some dim-witted dolt who can't see what's happening in front of her face."

"No," he argued, wishing he was feeling a bit more coherent for this conversation. "It means whoever is doing this knows what buttons to push. I'll figure this out, Tatum. I promise."

"*We'll* figure it out, you mean." She pressed the bread

dough into a rectangle, folded over the ends and pinched it together. Within seconds she had it settled in a loaf pan and set to the side for a rise beneath a towel. "We're partners, remember?"

"No," he said and purposely looked into the dark liquid of his cup. "We are not. I'm the cop. You're a chef. You keep your nose in your area and I'll do my job. That's the deal."

"See, I don't like that deal. You have nothing to lose if this all goes heels up. Whereas I lose—"

"Everything. Yes, again, I know." His cell phone vibrated, the sound reaching him from the coffee table. As it gave him the perfect excuse, he walked away from the counter to get it. The text message was another reminder from Jade. Just three words: Please don't forget.

I'll be there by nine, he replied, and before Jade could respond, he set the phone back down.

"Bad news?" Tatum had come around the counter, had her own mug of coffee in her hand and looked over the rim at him as she sipped.

"Just an appointment I have to keep this morning."

"Oh. It looked like it was bad news."

She wasn't wrong. But the bad wasn't new. It was old enough to have sunk into his bones so deep that it made him ache. "A friend of mine's in the hospital. A recovery facility." He shrugged as if it wasn't a big deal.

"I'm sorry. Look, Cruz—"

He held up his hands, not in surrender, but in emphasis for her to listen to him. "I need you to hear me on this, Tatum. And I need you to understand. We are not now, nor will we ever be partners. You watch out for your business. I'll watch out for the bad guys. You've gotten me in to where I need to be and I will take it from here, all right? All you need to do is just keep cooking, keep acting as if everything is as it should be, and if perchance you come across anything that's amiss or doesn't sit right with you, you tell me. Got it?"

"I don't know." Her frown disappeared behind her mug. "Could you maybe tell me all that again in a less condescending tone? I don't want to miss any of my agreed-upon obligations."

He swore, vehemently enough that his mother would have smacked him on the back of the head, but instead of looking surprised or even offended, Tatum rolled her eyes and returned to the other side of the counter. "You're going to have to do better than that to offend me. I got in trouble more times than I can count in school for swearing. And far more creatively than that."

"You did not," he accused.

"Oh, I sure did. Sister Damien sent me to the principal's office so often you could have called me ricochet. I ended up in detention for a month the first time. After that I just planned it into my schedule. I even got points for creativity. Off the record, of course."

"Sister... Damien?"

"Ironic, right?" Tatum's lips twitched. "Look, I get it. You have a job to do. But the sooner you realize you aren't in this alone, the better off we'll both be."

"You think so?" He strode toward her, partly because he knew she wasn't paying attention as she turned on her oven.

"I do think...oh!" She almost bashed into him when she stood up. "Well. Good morning." She pressed a hand against his chest, just over his heart. He could feel the warmth of her skin through his shirt, as if she was slowly branding him with her touch. "What's this, then?"

"I'm just wondering if there's any way to get you to stop talking." He said it while purposely looking at her mouth, a mistake, he realized too late, as he could only imagine what those lips of hers were capable of.

"And I'm wondering if maybe I should ban you from my kitchen." Instead of backing away, like he thought she would, like he hoped she would, she straightened her spine and inched up her chin. "We got in trouble like this before, Cruz. Are you sure you want to give it another try?"

"I shouldn't." It was like being tempted by a decadent dessert and knowing he was allergic to the ingredients. It didn't dim the want, the desire, even as he knew the aftereffects could be dangerous. "You've got an escape route," he told her even as her smile widened. He knew that look by now, that challenge only she could offer. There was something about this woman, something he couldn't define if he tried to, that pushed all thoughts of rationality and reason away and left him only with want.

"I'm not the kind of woman who runs," she told him as she traced her index finger down the center of his lips. "You're a big part of the reason I couldn't sleep, you know."

"Oh?" He leaned in, brushed his mouth, ever so lightly, across hers.

"Uh-huh." She returned the favor, upping the ante by nipping at his bottom lip, catching it between her teeth with the barest hint of pressure. "Maybe we just need to get this out of the way. You know. Scratch the itch."

He caught her hand as it slipped up his chest, almost curved around his shoulder before he threaded his fingers through hers. "You really think one time would do it?"

She kissed him, with only her mouth and hands touching him, and set him on fire from head to toe. When Tatum pulled away, she left only a breath between them as she bit her own lip, lifted her gaze to his. "I'd be willing to find out. Let's see." When her lips opened in silent invitation, he slipped his free hand around her waist and, pressing his palm flat against the base of her spine, pulled her against him. He wanted, he thought as he claimed her mouth, for her to feel what she did to him. From the fire raging through his blood to how ready he was to take her right now, right here, in her personal fortress.

He was used to being in control, in every aspect of his life. But as he felt her grab hold and hook her bare foot around the back of his calf, when she opened her mouth wider so that he could slip deeper into her, he relinquished it eagerly. She matched him move for move, touch for touch, breath for breath until he could feel her heart beating to the same erratic rhythm as his own.

Her hands released him and he felt himself slipping away, until those nimble, strong fingers of hers trailed down his sides and beneath the hem of his shirt. The second he felt her hands on his bare flesh he grabbed hold of her hips and turned her against the counter, pressing his hardened arousal against her.

Her gasp was like a bullet to his system, sharp, intrusive and strangely exhilarating. As her hands roamed over his back and her mouth and tongue continued to enrapture him in blind capitulation, he knew there was only one place for this to end. There was only one place he wanted to be. In Tatum Colton's bed, with her wrapped around him.

"Tatum." He murmured her name against her lips, felt the ever so faint acknowledgment of understanding as her mouth pulled away. "Just how important is eight a.m. to you?"

"What?" The dazed, foggy look in her eyes nearly had him throwing reason and caution out the window and hauling her back into his arms. "Eight oh…oh!" Reality seemed to hit her like a bucket of ice water. "Jeez. Okay, you're right. Stop." She planted her hands on his shoulders, but instead of pushing him away, she simply looked at him.

Was that regret he saw? Or did he just imagine that because he felt it, too?

"If you don't believe anything else I say to you, Cruz, believe this." Tatum seemed to have a hard time catching her breath. He couldn't wait to make that happen again. "If we aren't out of here by eight, both of us are going to regret it in ways you cannot even imagine."

"So…" He nipped at the side of her neck, felt her shudder, and suspected it wouldn't take much to put that warning out of her mind. "Is it okay to use your shower?"

"Yes." She drew in a shaky breath. "Yes, good idea. Go." She shoved him playfully, and hard enough for him to understand it was just as difficult for her as it was for him to stop. "I'll have breakfast waiting for you when you're done."

SHE'D MAKE WAFFLES, Tatum decided. Fluffy, butter-milk waffles stuffed with bacon, cheese, and topped with thick, sugary maple syrup that would send even the most recovered carb addict into a blissful coma.

"Yeah, that should make me stop thinking about whatever that kiss was." She had her virtual media player turn on the music, not so loud as to disturb the neighbors at this hour, but definitely so she could lose herself in the frenetic beat. All the better to drown out the sound of the shower running in her bathroom.

She would not think about Cruz Medina being naked in her shower. Or how his firm, toned torso had felt beneath her far too curious fingers. Nor would she en-tertain the all too easy notion of joining him to finish what both of them had clearly been far too eager to start.

"Think food," she sang in time to the melody. "Food is your safe place."

Pulling out the waffle maker had always been a sig-nal to her family she was stressed or uncertain about something. Come finals time the freezer would be set to overflowing with the varying recipes she tried, bulking up the basic recipe she'd memorized before she'd gotten through grammar school. One of the largest cabinets in the kitchen was filled with the selection of waffle irons she'd gotten for Christmas from someone she'd grown up with. It had become something of a Colton holi-day tradition, and while it was something they laughed about every year, it was also one of her favorite col-lections. There was always one to suit whatever mood she was in.

"Don't think anyone's gotten me one for sexual frustration yet," Tatum mumbled to herself as she dug through the cabinet. She bypassed the small, heart-shaped novelty waffle maker and went for the traditional, oversize, chunky square machine that couldn't be interpreted—or misinterpreted—in any way.

Batter made and resting, she slid a cookie sheet of thick-slab bacon painted with maple syrup and topped with a sprinkling of brown sugar into the oven. Within minutes the air was filled with what she considered the most wonderful aroma in the known universe.

Out of habit, she started toward her bedroom to get dressed, only to stop short when she heard the water turn off.

"Bad idea, bad bad bad idea." She pivoted so fast she almost tripped, then let out a panicked gasp as she heard a key snap open the lock on her front door. Tatum whimpered, cast a frantic look at her closed bedroom door and dived forward as her front door swung open. Her mother and aunt, deep in conversation, weren't even looking as they walked in. "Mom!" She tried, but there was no stopping them. "You're supposed to come after I've left for the day."

"Pfffth." Farrah Colton waved her off as if she was a pesky fly at a picnic. "We needed your input on the drapery fabric."

"No," Tatum said. "You really don't. I don't care what fabric—"

Farrah sniffed the air, elbowed her twin sister and earned a smile in return. "I told you if we were early enough we'd get breakfast. Oh, honey, you've made waffles. What's wrong?" She dumped her armload of fabric samples onto one of the tarp-covered chairs and strode into the kitchen. "Did something happen at work?"

If they only knew. "I just wanted waffles," Tatum protested to no one who would believe her. "Can't a girl just have waffles for breakfast when she wants them?" She couldn't stop herself from glancing back at the bedroom door. Her heart hadn't beat this fast since... her cheeks warmed. Well, since just a few minutes ago when Cruz had his hands on her. "I'm sorry. I had a difficult night."

"I can see that." Aunt Fallon walked over and touched a gentle hand to Tatum's scalp. "That looks like a nasty cut. What happened?"

"Tatum?" Farrah's concern shifted. "You hurt yourself?"

"It's nothing," Tatum said in such a rush her tongue nearly knotted itself. "I bashed into one of the racks in the freezer. I got distracted. Really, Mom, it's nothing." She held up her hands and backed up as her mother approached. "Can we do this another time? I've got—"

"Oh."

Tatum froze and closed her eyes. Never before had one male-uttered syllable threatened her sanity more.

"Sorry." Cruz's amused voice floated through the room. "I, uh, forgot my bag in the other bathroom."

When Tatum opened her eyes, she found both her mother and aunt exchanging unreadable looks before they turned their mutual attention first on Cruz, then on her. "I can explain," Tatum managed in a whisper.

Then she turned around and found Cruz standing just outside her bedroom door, skin and hair still dripping, one hand gripping the edges of the towel draped low across his hips. She swallowed hard, unable to stop herself from taking pulse-pounding inventory. Her imagination hadn't come close to the reality of him. Nor, it seemed, had her subconscious.

Detective Cruz Medina had been beautifully made by nature, and clearly enhanced by meticulous attention paid at the gym. There wasn't a part of him that wasn't sculpted, from his distinct abs right down to those hip muscles that drove women like her over the edge of reason. The way his dark hair lay damp against his shoulders and tiny beads of water dotted his neatly trimmed beard had her internal thermometer spiking into the danger zone.

"Then again." Tatum covered her mouth. "Maybe I can't. Ah, Cruz, this is my mother, Farrah Colton, and her twin sister Fallon. My aunt. Mom, Aunt Fallon, this is Cruz—" she hesitated at the flash of warning in his gold-flecked brown eyes "—Mendoza."

Tatum caught his gaze when it flew to hers, and prayed he could somehow read her mind. *Don't make this worse*, she silently pleaded. *Please don't make this...*

"Ladies. Pleasure to meet you." As if he was wearing an imported suit and welcoming them to a night at the opera, he strode forward and offered his free hand to each of them. "Apologies for my current appearance."

"No apology necessary," Tatum's mother said. "Except from us, of course. We had no idea we'd be interrupting anything by coming over early. Tatum, why didn't you say you had company?"

"Ah, I...um." Despite rarely being at a loss for words, she couldn't seem to find any at the moment. "Cruz, don't you think you should go get dressed?"

"Right," Cruz said and darted into the guest bathroom for his things. "I'll just…" He backed his way toward her bedroom. "Carry on, ladies."

"Uh-huh." Fallon nodded. "He didn't have to leave on our account," she said and earned a snicker from her sister.

"Or get dressed," Tatum's mother added.

"I guess I should be glad you didn't have your work crew with you." Desperate for escape, she hurried into her personal safety zone of the kitchen.

"He seems nice." Farrah took a seat on one of the stools, leaned her chin in her hands. "Known him long?"

The fact her aunt joined her mother at the counter was a sure sign this conversation was happening whether she wanted it to or not. "A while," she lied. "He's, ah, working at the restaurant."

"Really?" It was her Aunt Fallon who spoke. "I didn't think you approved of workplace romances."

Tatum set a stack of plates on the counter with a bang. "That's not what this is. Exactly," she added at their skeptical looks. "It's complicated, okay?" No way was she going to tell them the truth, that her restaurant was being used as a possible front to distribute drugs. Or that an undercover detective was investigating the claim. "Trust me, it isn't going to last."

"Just getting him out of your system?" her mother asked far too innocently.

"Really, Mom?" If Tatum's face was any hotter she could cook breakfast on it.

"There's nothing wrong with a healthy physical and sexual relationship," Farrah continued in a way that had Tatum wanting to cover her ears. "Although he looks more than capable of dealing with you on a more permanent basis."

"Definite son-in-law material, for sure," Fallon agreed.

"Son-in...okay, stop right there." Tatum pushed out the words over her reaccelerated pulse rate. "You run a design business, not a wedding planning one. And don't you dare start shifting attention away from the job you've started here. Keep on track, you hear me?" Tatum glanced over their heads as her bedroom door opened again and Cruz emerged. "No interrogations. And no teasing. He's a nice guy, Mom," Tatum said when her mother got that gleam in her eye. "He really is."

Farrah's amusement faded, replaced by understanding that still contained more than a hint of interest. "All right. We'll behave."

"Speak for yourself," Fallon teased, then sobered at Tatum's huff. "Oh, let us have some fun, Tatum. You haven't been this smitten about anyone since—"

"Smitten?" Tatum gaped. "I'm sorry, did we just join the road cast of *Oklahoma!*?"

Apparently a glutton for punishment, Cruz emerged from her bedroom, fully dressed and completely appealing.

Her mother began humming an all too familiar show tune as she spun around on her stool. "So, Cruz. How about while Tatum finishes breakfast, we get to know each other?"

Chapter Nine

"I am so sorry."

"Don't be." Cruz wasn't sure what entertained him more. Her mother and aunt's completely unsubtle interrogation over the best waffles he'd ever eaten, or the fact that Tatum continued to provide him with more layers of cover. Both lost out to Tatum's mortified reaction. He hadn't had this much fun in a long time. "I thought it was funny."

They took the stairs down to the parking garage in her building, leaving well after the previously designated eight o'clock escape hour. He now completely understood why she was determined to get out before Fallon and Farrah arrived. That said, he wouldn't have changed anything—and he meant *anything*—that had happened this morning for the world.

"Of course it was funny for you. It wasn't your mother who walked in and found us…well." She made a motion with her hand that went up and down his body.

"True enough. If it had been, we'd have been looking for a justice of the peace by lunch."

Tatum snorted and laughed until she saw his face. "Oh, my…you're serious, aren't you?"

Cruz shrugged. "Not really. But she hasn't met any of the women I've dated since I moved out of the house. Something she's mentioned on more than one occasion. Along with her growing desire for grandchildren." They reached the bottom floor, and he pulled open the door for her. "Until I hand one over to her I'm pretty much considered a disappointment."

"Do you want kids?" Her own question seemed to catch her off guard. "Sorry. That's none of my business."

"That's all right." He dug out his keys, clicked the alarm off his car. The beep echoed around them. "When I was about six months out of the academy I was first on scene to a domestic call. It was Christmas Eve, the first one I wasn't spending at home. I walked into this house behind two other senior patrol officers." He opened the passenger door, let her in, then stood there with his hand braced on the door as she looked up at him. "They'd been there before. To this house. Abusive situation, the husband with the wife, the wife with the kids. It just…" He shook his head, flinched against the all too familiar imagery that still haunted him. "As bad as you can imagine, it was worse. I remember thinking, why would anyone bring children into the world if you aren't going to love them. Three beautiful, traumatized kids whose last moments on earth were filled with nothing but violence and rage."

For an instant he was transported back, to another day that haunted him, another that had defined him.

"Cruz." Tatum reached up and covered his hand with hers. In that moment, her touch felt like a balm on his heart. "I'm so sorry."

"Yeah, me, too." He tried to cover, but there were times he was reminded of how truly hopeless his job seemed sometimes. "In answer to your question, it was a while before I could even let myself think about maybe having a family. Kids deserve the world, you know? They deserve attention and love and the promise of everything good. Like my parents gave to us. Like your parents did for you."

Her smile was sad, and he knew she was thinking of the father she'd lost only a short time ago. "So, do you now? Want kids?"

If anyone had asked him a year ago, a month ago, heck, even a week ago, his answer might have been different. Now he found himself saying, "With the right woman, yeah." He squeezed her hand. "I think I do."

Before the conversation went too far off the deep end, he motioned for her to pull her hand inside and closed the door. By the time he got behind the wheel and backed out, the topic was closed. "I'm scheduled to start work around one. I'll do my best to be on time," he told her in a way that reminded both of them that he still had a job to do. "Lab results came back on the ladle. No prints."

"No prints at all?" Tatum frowned. "That means whoever it was wiped them off, right?"

"That's what I'm guessing. I actually came back to the restaurant last night to try to get a look at people's lockers. Since I didn't get to, I need to do that today."

"Right." She was back to being tense, to folding in on herself and tucking into the corner of her seat. "Back to business. Are you going to tell me if you find anything?"

"I'll tell you what you need to know," he said and

hoped that was a good enough answer. "The further you stay out of this—"

"I'm already in it, remember? If they're breaking into the restaurant after hours—"

"They didn't break in, Tatum."

"What?"

"They knew how to get in, through the loading bay door. It was partially open. That's how I got in so quick." He waited a beat. "Who all has access to that door?"

"Well, I do obviously." She tucked a strand of hair behind her ear, looked out her window. "Richard and Susan. Sam and Ty, too. And the cleaning crew who comes in on Sunday morning."

"All right." He made a mental note. "I'll see about tracking down their alibis for last night." At this point the only one he knew wasn't involved was Sam, since the young man had been sitting next to him at the bar the entire time since closing. The idea that Ty could be involved didn't sit well; Cruz didn't usually misjudge someone so completely. "Can you give me a list of all your vendors along with copies of your employee files? Anyone who's had anything to do with True since you first opened?"

"Of course." The cool detachment wasn't wholly unexpected. Being with her in her condo had felt almost like a fantasy world where they could leave reality behind. But they were back in the real world now. One that wasn't particularly welcoming for them at the moment. "Let me out here, will you?" She pointed to the bus stop a few blocks from True. "I need to clear my head."

He hesitated. Cruz didn't like the idea of her being out of his sight right now, but he couldn't be sure if that had to do with the case or his growing attraction for her. He needed to keep things separate, even while giving the appearance of the complete opposite. Besides, he had somewhere to be.

Cruz steered the car into the empty space. "I know this is difficult for you," he said when she pushed open the door. "I do see that, Tatum."

"Even if you do." She didn't smile at him. She only stared straight ahead as if she couldn't bear to look at him. "You've made it pretty clear it doesn't matter. I'll see you this afternoon." She got out and closed the door, hitched her bag over her shoulder, and went around the back of the car to cross the street and vanish around the corner.

"COLBY SAID YOU'RE HURT." Tatum's assistant manager hurried into the kitchen just before noon. Susan, undeterred by Tatum's stern expression, scooted around Sam and Quallis, who were both wrist-deep in the endless pile of shrimp delivered fresh that morning. "Tatum, what happened?"

"I should have pinned an announcement on the bulletin board," Tatum said, turning down the heat on the béchamel sauce she was making for the employees' early dinner. "I was taking a look around the restaurant last night and tripped going into the refrigerator. I just banged my head is all." Even now the bruise throbbed as if protesting her story. "It's nothing, you guys, okay?"

"That's horrible! We should check the threshold," Susan announced. "You could have been seriously injured."

"Or next time I could turn on a light." She hated having to explain something she'd thought for sure she'd managed to conceal with makeup. But of course all the makeup she possessed sweated off in the kitchen in a matter of seconds. "Just let it go, okay?"

Sam didn't look convinced. The high-intensity expression on his face had Tatum glancing away quickly. It had only been a day since Cruz had been working at True and already she could feel a change. At this rate, by the time he was done with his investigation, her tight ship was going to unravel at the sails.

Her tone must have been enough to get her message across, because Susan withdrew back to the front of the house and the rest of the kitchen fell into an uneasy silence. While Tatum focused on making a revamped recipe of lasagna primavera, something she was testing as a possible late spring menu item, the rest of her crew and staff trickled in. Chester arrived with oversize coffee drinks in his hands while Ty quietly snuck in with a quick nod of acknowledgment before disappearing into the break room. She was sprinkling the final layer of fresh grated parmesan cheese on the top of the pasta when Cruz strolled in.

"Afternoon." His friendly greeting, Tatum noticed when she glanced up, didn't quite reach his eyes. "Cutting it close, I know." He gestured to the clock. Only ten minutes to spare before his shift started.

"Not a problem," Tatum said in what she could tell was an overly happy tone. She saw Sam elbow Quallis, who gave a reluctant nod. Sam washed his hands then, and followed Cruz down the hall. Tatum frowned, her stomach knotting.

"What's that about?" she asked Quallis, who deadpanned his face and just shrugged. "If there's a problem you need to tell me."

Quallis, who she knew came across as a cross between a grizzly bear and a linebacker, merely shrugged. "That goes both ways, Chef."

"Right." Tatum blew out a breath. "I guess I'll just wait and find out, won't I?"

At the sound of raised voices and a distinct crash, Tatum jumped, her eyes widening in alarm as Quallis actually offered an approving nod. "That's probably your cue."

Tatum didn't have to be told twice. Gesturing for Quallis to stay where he was—not that he looked remotely interested in whatever was happening—Tatum hurried into the break room.

IT HAD, CRUZ thought as he stashed his backpack and sweatshirt in his locker, been one seriously crap morning. His only saving grace had been the idea he could come here and lose himself in the physical work, and get the last few hours out of his head.

He sank onto the narrow bench in front of the bank of lockers, dropped his head into his hands and squeezed his eyes shut.

The bubble of pressure that had lodged itself in his chest two months ago was expanding, threatening to block the air from his lungs. He'd kept his promise and met Jade at the rehabilitation facility, along with two of Johnny's doctors. As bad as he thought the news was going to be about his former partner, it was worse. Horrifically, heartbreakingly, predictably worse.

"Mendoza." Sam's voice shot into the locker room like a bullet.

Cruz's head snapped up, recognizing the tone and the angry energy catapulting at him. He rose to his feet. "Sam?"

The friendly, easygoing, teasing Sam Price he'd met yesterday was nowhere to be seen. Cruz had to bank his instinct to block the young man from grabbing the front of his shirt and slamming him back into the lockers with a lock-rattling bang.

The nearby water station table shook, sending half a dozen glasses shattering on the floor.

"What the—" Cruz managed to land a solid self-defense punch into Sam's jaw and break loose, but Sam recovered quickly, grabbing for his throat.

"You put hands on her."

"What?" Cruz couldn't for the life of him make sense of the accusation. Not until he saw Tatum running into the room. He saw the bruise on her forehead, looked back to Sam and the rage in his eyes. Obviously the lie they'd come up with to explain her injury hadn't gone over well. "No, Sam, I didn't. I swear—" He raised his foot and brought it down hard on the side of Sam's knee, sending the younger man collapsing down and back.

"That's enough!" Tatum yelled. She hurried over not to help him, but to check on Sam. "Sam, are you all right?" She grabbed the younger man's arm, helped him to stand.

"Is *he* all right?" Cruz heard the cop in his own tone and pulled himself back. He swore, took a few steps away, then placed his hands on his hips and watched

Tatum guide Sam back to the bench. "I barely touched him, Tatum."

"I won't tolerate violence here. Not in any way." She stepped back and glared at both of them. "Not for any reason. Do you hear me?"

"Hard not to," Cruz tried to joke. Sam lifted his chin and glared at him. "Sam." He took a deep breath, forced himself to calm down and not think like a cop. "I didn't hurt her."

"You didn't…what?" Tatum's eyes went wide as she absorbed the information. "Oh, no. Oh, Sam, no." She touched fingers to her face. "This wasn't Cruz." In an instant she transformed from boss to friend. Tatum crouched in front of him, caught his face in her hands. "You lovely, stupid man. While I appreciate the sentiment, I promise you, Cruz didn't hurt me."

"How do I know you aren't saying that because he's standing right there?" Sam demanded.

"Oh, for cripes' sake." Tatum pushed to her feet. "You know me, Sam. Do you honestly believe that if Cruz had lifted a hand against me I'd have let him walk back into True the next day?"

Sam blinked. "I guess maybe not."

"You guess?"

Cruz could feel her temper snap from across the room. Out of the corner of his eye, he spotted Colby, Ty and Chester standing in the doorway. "Is that what all of you thought?" Tatum demanded. "That Cruz hit me?"

"You said it happened last night after we all left," Sam defended himself. "And we all knew he was coming back here."

"Yeah, for his—" Colby air-quoted "—*phone*."

"Next thing you show up with a bruise on your face," Sam finished. "It didn't take much to put it all together."

"Well, your math is wrong," Tatum snapped. "One more time, and for the record, I was stupid last night and tripped and locked myself in the refrigerator. It was Cruz who found me and fixed me up, so forgive me for not telling you the entire humiliating truth."

Realization drifted across Sam's face. "I guess maybe I may have misconstrued the situation." His black eyes shone with regret. "I'm sorry, man. I just saw that bruise and…"

"You were protecting one of your own," Cruz said, admiring Sam's ability to admit he was wrong. "I get it. It hurt, but I get it."

Sam let out a light chuckle and just like that, they were back on even ground.

"Men," Tatum muttered and gave Sam a gentle shove on the shoulder. "I can take care of myself, Sam Price. But I thank you for the assist. Something tells me your knee's going to be killing you later, so take some aspirin now. As for the rest of you—" she snapped her fingers when they began to back out of the room "—one of you clean up this glass, then let's get back to work. We've got a book full of reservations and food to cook."

Cruz headed toward the changing room, only to come up short when Tatum stepped in front of him and put a hand on his chest. She kept her voice low, so only he could hear. The intensity in her voice, the ferocity in her eyes had nothing to do with any attraction between them but everything to do with her anger. "Whatever you have to do to close your investigation and get out of my restaurant, you do it, you hear me, Cruz?" The flour-coated woman he'd kissed this morning was no-where to be found. "You do it and get out."

BY THE TIME True closed, it was a miracle Tatum hadn't downed the entire bottle of tequila in her office. As tempting as it was, Tatum opted instead for two pain-killers and an ice water chaser, following it immediately by locking her office door and retreating to her desk. She abandoned her nightly ritual of watching her crew file out and across the street to the bar, wanting, need-ing the absolute solitude the space provided.

It had, she admitted sadly as she lowered herself into her chair and leaned back to close her eyes, been one of the worst days she'd ever had in the kitchen.

Her normally streamlined, fluid employees had spent the entire night being overly cautious and solicitous or frantic and uncertain. Sam and Cruz were both out of sync, and their negative energy trickled down to the rest of her people. She'd eventually sent Cruz to work with Ty in food prep, but that just shifted things. It didn't help she was just as off her game, worrying about her business and her friends and her future. All of it—all of it—came out in the food. The result had been mul-tiple returned dishes, displeased customers and a very, very irritated Tatum.

It was her fault. She couldn't put the blame on any-one else. Leadership began at the top. She'd always led by example, always stayed focused on what was impor-tant: giving their patrons the best experience possible. Instead, tonight she'd let her annoyance with Cruz and his "investigation" get the better of her. She needed to come in with a more positive attitude tomorrow, give them all a pep talk, or sit them all down and let them vent whatever they needed in order to get themselves back on track.

The knock on her door didn't surprise her. She'd expected it, especially after last night's break-in. But she remained where she was, staring at the door as if she could laser-beam the man on the other side out of her existence.

"Tatum." Cruz knocked again. "I know you're in there. Open the door, please."

She pressed her lips together until they went numb. Childish, she knew, to leave him out there like that, especially when she had agreed to be at least partially cooperative.

"I'm not leaving." The silence stretched. Just as she was about to get up and let him in, he added, "I still need that list of employees and vendors I asked you for."

Tatum's self-pity party ended in an instant. She grabbed the file folder containing her list of vendors along with copies of her employee files, stalked to the door, flung it open and shoved it into his chest. "Here. Take it and go."

"Tatum." He caught the door with his hand before she could slam it in his face. "I'm sorry about what happened today. I had no idea Sam was going to think I'd hurt you."

He should have, she seethed. If he'd truly done his homework on Sam Price he should have known exactly what the young man's reaction would be to seeing her with a bruised face. He'd grown up in a violent home, one he and his mother had finally escaped from. But it wasn't only Cruz who should have anticipated such a reaction. She should have, as well.

It seemed she should have known a lot of things.

She released her hold on the door, headed back to her desk to collect her things. "I just want to go home, go to sleep and forget today ever happened."

"Right there with you."

It was the way he said it that had Tatum freezing. She stood there, her back to him, half steaming, half curious. When she turned she found him at her window, looking down at the heart of True. His shoulders were slumped, his posture giving every indication of him being dejected, lost even.

"You've learned something, haven't you? About the case," she added when he glanced over and his brow furrowed. "Something you've been wrong about?"

He shook his head, turned and leaned against the sill. "More like I'm reevaluating my approach. I should have handled things with Sam differently. You were right. The way this place operates, my presence is disrupting everything."

"Maybe not everything." Tatum hesitated. It was such a small thing, but that voice in her head, the one that sounded an awful lot like Cruz, wouldn't shut up. "I found your missing employment information when I was getting everyone else's together."

"Oh?"

"It was back in the folder this afternoon and filed under *C* rather than *M*." A feeling she could only define as reluctant grief washed over her. "Someone took your file then put it back, probably assuming I wouldn't notice it was gone. I don't misfile things, Cruz."

"No. I wouldn't think so." His statement was slow, thoughtful, and did little to ease her anxiety. "I don't suppose you lock your office?"

"I never have." There'd been no reason to. The idea she'd have to start doing so triggered that dormant anger she'd pushed aside. "But that doesn't mean it's someone who works for me. I mean, someone could have come in as a patron and snuck up here."

"You really think a customer could come up here without being noticed by someone? Your wait staff? The people in the bar?" Cruz shook his head, dismissing the idea as quickly as she had. "Someone's trying to cover their tracks."

"It also means they're suspicious of you." She knew it was his job, but if these people were as dangerous as he claimed, she wasn't the only one in danger.

"Don't worry. I can take care of myself." He made an attempt at that cheeky, borderline-defiant smile of his but failed miserably. "I am sorry about earlier with Sam. And for messing up in the kitchen tonight. I've been distracted."

"So I noticed."

"This morning threw me off. After I dropped you off today." He lifted the file containing her employee records in a helpless gesture. "It's just been one crap day."

She took a deep breath and let it out slowly, along with her frustration. Darn it. How was she supposed to stay mad at him when he was admitting fault? But it wasn't just that, she thought as shadows crossed over his handsome, bearded face. There was something more going on.

Let it go, she told herself. Let him be and deal with

whatever difficulties he was having on his own. But that wasn't who she was. Even with her own future at stake, as easy as it would be to walk away and let his investigation go wherever it needed to, it was clear that in this moment, the man standing in front of her was in pain.

"What happened?"

He shook his head. "It's not important."

Tatum gnashed her back teeth to the point her jaw ached. What was it with men and not talking about what was bothering them? Her cousins were the exact same way, especially Heath. It took a crowbar to get the man, the successful president of Colton Connections, to open up even to those he cared about the most. It seemed as if far more men were cut from that stubborn piece of cloth than she realized.

She dropped her bag and jacket on the table by the door and walked over to him. She sat beside him, close enough to feel the tension rolling off him in thick, heavy waves. "What happened?"

He stared straight ahead while she looked at him. His Adam's apple moved as if he were pushing down whatever he was feeling. The anger that had been her companion for the past few hours faded in the silence. Tatum reached out, slid her fingers through his and took hold of his hand, squeezing in what she hoped was comfort. She rested her head on his shoulder, settling in for him to finish fighting whatever battle raged within.

His hand tightened around hers, pulsed in what she suspected was the same rhythm as his heartbeat.

"My friend is dying." The quiet statement cracked her heart. "That's where I went this morning. To meet with his doctors. Whatever brain activity there was…"

He shook his head as if he couldn't quite believe it. "He's dying and there's nothing I can do to stop it."

She closed her eyes, let the grief he felt wash over her. It had been easy to forget Cruz was more than a cop who had her business in his sights. Easy to forget that there was anything beyond her own situation and circumstance. There was more, so much more to the man with the dark-eyed gaze, gentle, firm touch, and generous, pulse-kicking smile. He had a life, one that was just as fraught and complicated as her own. She didn't have a monopoly on pain. How arrogant of her to think otherwise. "I'm sorry." The most useless words, she knew, but still she uttered them. They were all she had at the moment.

"Yeah, me, too." He pinched his thumb and index finger against the bridge of his nose, squeezed his eyes shut and released a sigh of complete defeat. "He had so much going on before this happened. He was looking at houses, was going to propose to his girlfriend. I even helped him pick out a ring." His suppressed laugh had her lips twitching. "Like I know anything about engagement rings." She reached up, locked her hand around his arm and squeezed. "He never had a chance to give it to her."

"Life turns in the blink of an eye." She'd learned that herself only last month when her father and uncle had been murdered. "And it's not particularly kind to those left in its wake."

"No, it's not, is it?" He looked at her and in that moment, the case, the threat he posed to her future, melted away. "I screwed up, Tatum. I should have had a plan to explain this." Cruz tilted her chin up, his gaze skimming over the still sore bruise on her forehead. "Especially knowing how bad a liar you are. I saw how hurt you were today, after my fight with Sam." He cupped her cheek in his hand, stroked his thumb over her skin. "The last thing I want is to hurt you."

She wanted, more than anything, to believe him, but no matter how many times he said it, she couldn't escape the truth. Cruz's very presence did just that. His investigation threatened her career, her reputation, her livelihood, and now it was threatening her employees' future. And yet. She lifted a hand to his face, stroked the backs of her fingers down the beard. The sensations exploding against her skin had her silently gasping. Maybe for tonight they could set everything else aside and just be...friends. "How about we end tonight on a good note." Her smile widened at the sudden spark of interest in his eyes. "Not that good a note, Valentino," she teased, happy to see him grin. She pulled free of his hold and got to her feet. "I've got a cure-all guaranteed to help you feel better. You game?"

"I've got these files to go through and reports to fill out, but..." He let out a soft laugh, amusement and maybe a bit of gratitude shining in his eyes. "Sure. Why not?"

"Great. I'll drive. And when we get there you can tell me all about..." She hesitated. "What's your friend's name?"

"Johnny," Cruz said. "Detective Johnny Benton."

Her heart twisted at the professional add-on. "Okay, then." She held out her hand. "Let's go. And you can tell me all about Johnny."

THE TIME WOULD COME, Cruz thought a little later, when Tatum Colton would stop surprising him. He wasn't in any rush for that day. There was something to be said for the unpredictability and mood-lifting endorphins that came with the unexpected. But he had to admit, midnight hot dogs near the lake was something he wouldn't have expected at any time from a four-star, award-winning chef.

The air was warmer than a typical March night in Chicago, as if Mother Nature couldn't quite make up her mind which season they were in. He could still see their breath puffing into the night sky, along with the fragrant steam billowing out of the food truck cranking out after-movie snacks and late-night dinners. He inhaled the aroma of grilled onions, spicy peppers and oil-coated fries as he kicked one leg over the bench of the worn picnic table near the edge of the lake. He set the bottles of water down, along with a collection of napkins and utensils.

He'd barely glanced at the menu before Tatum was chatting with the cooks. Obviously they were old friends and he was unnecessary to the conversation. Leaving them to their discussion, he'd stepped back and instead embraced the silence of the night.

"You really don't strike me as the hot dog type of girl," he teased when Tatum joined him a few minutes later and lowered two stacked cardboard trays onto the table.

"Ricky's is one of the not-so-well-kept secrets in the neighborhood. Oh, shoot." She snapped her fingers. "Forgot the fries. Back in a sec." She hurried off, leaving Cruz on his own to enjoy the view. Not the lake.

Not the surrounding area. But her. He wondered if she had any idea how stunning she was. How breathtaking. Not in how she looked, necessarily, but in how she presented herself, how she moved and acted. How she cared about people.

No wonder Sam had come to her defense. She inspired loyalty in people, even in people who had every reason not to trust. But they trusted her. Even tonight, when it had been clear she was angry with him, she'd pivoted and ended up giving Cruz comfort, despite his intention to bring her some peace of mind.

She was also, as evidenced by the loaded and unusual-looking hot dogs she'd ordered, a bottomless pit when it came to food.

"You can't have these dogs without their double-fried garlic taters with lemon aioli." The third box was just as large as the other two. "So." She sat down and cracked open her bottle of water. "We've got my favorite, the Asian-inspired teriyaki, mango and sriracha dog. This is the homemade lobster sausage, and then the beef and blue cheese. But this one..." She lifted an old-fashioned, did-his-heart-good, Chicago-style replete with the requisite neon green relish and chunky tomatoes. "This one was my Dad's go-to."

"Your dad ate here?" Yeah, Cruz ordered himself as she cut each hot dog in half, he really needed to stop being surprised by her.

"Mmm-hmm." She lifted half of the teriyaki and bit in, held up her hand until she swallowed. "First time he brought me here was my first trip home after starting culinary school. I'd been so excited about going. I was nineteen, on my own for the first time, and so sure I knew everything." She lifted a fry, seemed to admire it a moment before she popped it into her mouth. "I nearly burned down the school kitchen on my first day. And it got worse from there."

Following her lead, Cruz chose the teriyaki and bit in. He nearly swooned at that ear-pleasing snap of the casing and the explosions of flavors on his tongue. "Worse how?" She had to be exaggerating. He'd seen her in the kitchen. She moved like a fish in water, as if it was where she belonged. Nothing frustrated or frazzled her, not even tonight, when things were off from the start.

"Let's just say I set off enough fire alarms to make my teachers cringe when I walked in the door. For that semester anyway. I felt defeated when I came home for that first break. Like I couldn't do anything right. I was ready to quit. Cooking was all I'd thought about for years. There was nothing else I wanted except to own my own restaurant, and I felt it slipping away. I don't think I got out of bed that whole first day. My mother told me to stop wallowing, but my dad..." She slowed down, wiped her hands and looked out over the moonlight-kissed lake. "He knocked on my door that second night I was home, said he had somewhere he wanted to go and for me to get dressed and come with him. I was not happy at the prospect. I am a first-class sulker," she added.

"Noted." Cruz toasted her with his dog.

"He brought me here." Cruz could see the tears in her eyes, but they didn't fall. And her voice didn't break. It was as if she'd found a memory she could share without breaking her own heart. "Ricky Sr. owned it then. He and my dad were friends back in the day. We ordered four dogs, just like I did tonight, along with fries and sodas my mother never would have approved of," she added with a laugh. "We sat right here. At this table. And he told me to eat. I was still in my food snob phase, turning my nose up at what I of course saw as utter pedestrian fare. I had plans to be a Michelin-rated chef. Hot dogs? As if I'd deign to eat these." She took another bite. "But these were, are anything but pedestrian. They were flavor explosions, made with love and affection and attention to detail. Because the people who work in that truck over there, they're doing it because they want to. Because they have to. Feeding people fulfills them. That's what my dad wanted me to understand. That cooking was about more than degrees and plans and techniques and star ratings. It's about people, and feeding not only them, but their souls. Food creates memories and memories create lives. Full lives. From that night on, things smoothed out. I found my way." She plucked up another fry. "And whenever I came home, Dad and I would make it a point to come here and have midnight hot dogs together." One of the tears slipped out of her control and slid down her cheek. "I haven't been here since he died. But tonight it felt right. He'd approve, I think," she added and gently wiped the tear away. "So." She took another bite of hot dog. "You and Johnny were partners? For how long?"

"Three years," Cruz answered automatically, as if talking about Johnny didn't feel like a knife to the gut. "I'd just finished a case that showed me I wasn't cut out for undercover. Well," he added at her raised brow. "Not deep undercover. The kind that kept me cut off from my family for months at a time. Being your sous-chef is a little bit different than building up a reputation as a drug dealer's best friend. True is a much more hospitable environment than drug dens and flophouses."

"Good to know." Her mouth twisted as she pondered her choices, eating more fries as she debated her next hot dog. "What happened with Johnny?"

"One of those fluke things." Despite his stomach twisting in knots, he continued to eat. Partially to honor her tradition with her father. In part because it gave him something to do. "He made arrangements to meet with a CI, confidential informant. I was supposed to meet up with him later that night, compare notes. When I got there, he was already down, barely breathing." He winced. "The bullet caught him in the neck. I remember kneeling there, hearing that death rattle breath we're all taught about but never want to hear, knowing the man who had shot him was getting away. I couldn't stop the blood." Some nights he woke up expecting to find his hands covered in it.

"Cruz." Tatum reached across the table, took his hand. "I'm sure you did everything you could. Like you said, it was just one of those fluke things."

He set his food down, reached for his water. "Flukes like that shouldn't happen. If I'd just gotten there sooner, or if I'd just gone with him." How many times had he replayed that night in his head? IA had cleared him without much fanfare, despite the fact their original suspect had gotten away. "Jade, that's his girlfriend, and I both had hope he'd recover, but the doctors made it clear this morning it's time. We have to decide when we'll let him go." It was not a decision he ever thought he'd have to make. He didn't want to make it, but Jade couldn't do it alone. He owed her, he owed Johnny, at least that much.

"I can't imagine what it must be like, worrying about someone you love, being in a job like you have." Tatum's observation sounded almost wistful. "My sister January is dating a cop. Sean Stafford."

"I know Sean." Cruz found his appetite returning. Or maybe the hot dogs were just that good. "He works Homicide. My partner before Johnny was Harry Cartwright, who's worked with Sean recently."

"The Chicago Police Department is one big happy family, then?"

"Well, we're a family, I guess," Cruz agreed. "Not sure happy applies. Dating a cop isn't easy." It felt odd, making that statement sitting across from a woman he would definitely like to shift from the professional side of his life to personal. "I'm sure she worries about him a lot. Like Jade worried about Johnny."

"That must have been the call she was dreading," Tatum said.

"It's the call all family members of cops dread," Cruz said. "Just ask my mother," he added at her nod. "When I was done with deep cover work she made me promise never to do something like that again. She said it felt like she was dying a little each day, just waiting to hear I'd been hurt or worse. I guess now I understand a fraction of what she felt."

"Because your mother loves you." Tatum squeezed his wrist. "Just like you love Johnny. You'll do right by him, Cruz. From what I can see, you already have."

He nodded, finished off one of his dogs, but barely

tasted it. "The kid who got away, whoever shot Johnny, they're connected to the investigation I'm running now." He watched as her eyes glazed over and she pulled away. "I can't walk away from the case that cost Johnny his life. I can't. I'm sorry, Tatum, but that's the truth. And I need to work it the way it needs to be worked."

She nodded but didn't make a sound.

"I need you to understand why this is so important to me. I don't want to destroy your business, Tatum. I don't want to hurt you or Sam or anyone working for you who's innocent, but shutting this down, exposing them once and for all gets me that much closer to finding whoever shot my partner. I can't let that go." No matter how much he might want to.

Watching the disappointment and hurt flash across her face had him wishing he could do just that. If it was anyone else, would he feel the same? Would he feel so torn and conflicted about doing his job? He didn't want to know the answer.

The answer couldn't matter.

"Just promise me you'll do your best to minimize the damage." Her tone sounded almost teasing, but she wasn't laughing. "And that you'll keep me informed. Promise me you'll let me protect True in every way I can."

"I promise to try." It was the best he could offer, and it seemed his best was enough. At least for tonight. "Now, tell me—" he cleared his throat and pointed to one of the uneaten hot dogs "—which was that one again?"

"You didn't have to walk me upstairs," Tatum told Cruz at two in the morning, as they climbed the last of the stairs. "I'm fine once I'm in the door."

"I needed the stairs to walk off those dogs. Honestly, woman, where do you put it?"

"Onto my treadmill," she laughed. "It's currently under a painting tarp, but it'll definitely get a workout in the morning." Nerves sparked through her blood. It had been a nice night, under the cold spring stars, sharing gourmet hot dogs by the lake. Heart-wrenching at times, for both of them, but lovely nonetheless. When they reached her door, she stuck her key in the lock and faced him. "I guess this is where I say see you at work tomorrow."

He nodded. "As much as I'd love to suggest otherwise, I don't think tonight's meant for anything else. Besides, I think polishing off those garlic fries canceled out any amorous activity for tonight."

She smiled. "Actually." She moved closer to him. "Since we both ate them, the garlic cancels out. They teach you that in culinary school."

"Do they?" His hands snaked around her waist, his fingers brushing up and under the edge of her shirt. Temptation to slide his hands, his palms, over her smooth, warm skin had him pulling her closer and dipping his head. "I think that's a theory I'd like to test."

When his lips claimed hers, she was ready, oh, so ready for this and more. She heard her own moan in the back of her throat as she slipped her arms around his neck, her fingers diving into the soft, silky length of his hair. The more she kissed him, the more she found his beard achingly arousing as his lips and tongue invaded and challenged her to rise up and meet him.

There wasn't an inch of her that wasn't overheating like a blast furnace. Reason drained out of her head while desperate thoughts of dragging him inside and into her bedroom threatened to override sense.

How was it that the absolute wrong man at the wrong time could feel so right?

"I should go." His protest whispered against her mouth. Was it a question? she wondered. "We're on the precipice of breeching protocol. For both of us." His gaze bored so deeply into hers she felt as if he'd dragged her into a trance. His fingers stroked the side of her face now, as if memorizing what she looked like. "Tell me to go, Tatum." He kissed her again, a mere pressing of lips. "Tell me."

"Go." The word emerged on a whimper, a desperate, regretful whimper she wanted to pull back, but instead she moved out of his hold and reached for the handle of her door. "I'll see you at work tomorrow."

"All right. Lock up when you're inside." He reached out, touched her face again. "Tatum?"

"Yes?"

"When this is all over? When the case is closed? We're going to finish what we've started." She'd never believed anyone more in her life.

Every cell in her body gave a joyous cry of release. "In that case." She cleared her throat and attempted to sound stern. "Might I suggest you work a bit faster, Detective?"

Before he said anything more, she walked inside and closed the door.

Chapter Ten

"What's going on with Tatum Colton?"

Cruz choked on his coffee as his lieutenant's question shot at him over the cubicle wall. He sputtered and got to his feet, reaching for a pile of old fast-food napkins shoved into the corner of his desk cubicle. "Going on?" he managed and gave himself points for not cowering beneath Lucille Graves's steely stare. "Ah…" Coherent words were nowhere to be found, even as he scanned his fellow detectives' empty desks. "Fine. Things are going fine, I guess."

"Uh-huh." Lieutenant Graves motioned for him to follow, which he did, and found himself in what he would now laughingly call the break room. As well-supplied, organized and decorated as True's break/locker room was, the precinct offerings left much to be desired. They might very well be cause to call in the biohazard disposal unit. Three other detectives sat around the room at mismatched tables and scarred, padded chairs, drinking their coffees and mulling over their phones or open files. The windowless room maintained the scent of scorched coffee, day-old pastry and stress. "Haven't heard much from you since you started working at True. Any progress?"

"Some," Cruz said and declined a refill on his coffee. He'd kept one eye watching his back as the job at True drove him into nightly exhaustion. He still needed to get to the restaurant by one, but he'd forgone his morning workout in favor of sleeping in before coming into the station to catch up on stuff. Even with the extra hours, he was dragging. How did Tatum do this night after night, week after week? But he was quickly falling into the routine of a powerhouse restaurant that met every expectation of perfection.

"I'm making my way through the employees." So far he'd kept the break-in and the theft of his employee file to himself. His lieutenant was already on shaky ground with the time this case was sucking up. He didn't want to give her any reason to shut him down. Besides, nothing beyond that had happened, so whatever they'd read in his file must have passed muster. Not surprising given Tatum's attention to detail. So far as he knew, his cover was still in place. "I have someone in my sights I hope to make progress with tonight." Ty Collins had yet again passed on the afterwork nightcaps with his fellow workers. While Cruz hadn't seen the ex-con hanging around True after-hours, near as Cruz could tell, he had no alibi for the night Tatum had been hurt.

The only difficulty he was having was finding time alone to get a deeper look at the restaurant itself. So far his plans were to continue observing the staff, tail a different employee home each night and look into their financial records. Of course he couldn't do the latter until his warrant was approved, and red tape being what it was, he was still waiting. That said, he'd pretty much cleared Colby, Chester and Bobby Quallis. Nothing they did raised any suspicions, and their loyalty to True and Tatum seemed genuine. She garnered loyalty, which meant either someone on the inside was an excellent liar, or he was off base with his suspicions.

"Hmm." Lucille Graves opened an overhead cabinet and, after digging into the back, came out with a tin of butter cookies. "Don't tell Sheryl about this," she said in much the same way she told her detectives to be careful on the streets. "My wife is trying to kick sugar before the baby gets here, so I've been relegated to work-hour binges only."

Cruz held up a hand and refused a cookie. Since having partaken in Tatum's homemade and back-of-house cooking, he found himself avoiding packaged and processed food. This morning he'd actually fixed himself an omelet instead of emptying out a box of cereal. All the while he could swear he heard Tatum laughing and urging him on.

"Is your gut still telling you True is at the heart of the distribution?"

"Yes." He was stubborn enough to cling to his belief, even though he didn't want to cost anyone at True anything, especially Tatum. But what choice did he have? He needed to see this through. He had a job to do. End of story. "Tatum's not a part of it."

"Because you've examined her financials?"

"I've gone through them right up to last year." He planned to finish tomorrow, on his day off from True. "The fact she's turned everything over and given me access is legit."

"Well." Lieutenant Graves polished off a cookie and slapped her crumb-coated hands together. "Let's keep things moving along, shall we? You've got three days to make some progress, otherwise I'm shutting you down."

"You can't be serious." His disbelief sent the break room into an uneasy silence. "Ma'am," he added at his lieutenant's arched silver brow.

"You and Benton had six months, Cruz. That means we're going on eight with you solo. There's only so much circling you can do before you have to pounce. Unless there's a reason you're dragging your feet?"

"I'm not—" His temper caught, but before he tanked his career, he pulled back. "I'm not dragging my feet. And even if I was, like you said, I'm single-handed now, aren't I?"

"That's by choice." His LT looked far from entertained. "It's also something I can fix easily if that's the problem. You want another partner, I can make that happen by the end of the day."

He didn't want another partner. He didn't want another one ever again, but he was also a realist. He was on borrowed time as a solo detective. And he had to make use of every minute. That said, he also wasn't going to admit, out loud anyway, to being overly cautious in order to prevent Tatum from paying a life-altering price. "Give me a week, LT. Three days won't do it."

She picked up her coffee and walked out of the break room, leaving Cruz no choice but to follow. "All right. One week from today. You want to close down this drug ring, you want to find whoever it was who put Benton into that coma, I suggest you focus, Cruz. We've got dozens of other cases that could use your attention.

While I appreciate your determination to finish what you and Johnny started, you don't have an open calendar. Bring me something substantial by then or I'm pulling the plug."

"Yes, ma'am." He resisted the impulse to salute, mainly because he didn't want to lose the week he'd been given. Instead he glanced at his watch, cringed, then cursed. Cruz hurried back to his desk and grabbed his jacket. He was going to be late.

Again.

It was a line Tatum resented walking: lying to her staff for the greater good while having to suspect one—or maybe more of them—were involved with drug distribution. She found herself distracted and at the same time hyperattentive to everyone around her as she watched for hiccups, inconsistencies, little things that would somehow prove Cruz right or wrong.

Midshift during one of True's busiest nights of the week was not the time to have this epiphany, but nonetheless, there it was, staring her right in the face. Why was she trusting Cruz, a man she'd never laid eyes on before last week, more than the people who had helped make her business the success it was?

It didn't help that her increasingly frequent calls to her sister Simone were going unanswered. Simone was her sounding board, her go-to when things got tough. And these last weeks since losing their father, there wasn't anything that had been easy. But Simone was dealing with things in her own way, according to her mother, who was growing increasingly worried for her firstborn. Psychologist Simone was determined to find an explanation behind the murders, something that would help them make sense.

But nothing ever would. Tatum had already suspected that before Cruz confirmed it. And if anyone should know about such things, it was a decorated detective.

She flipped the three filet mignons over in the stainless steel pan, spooned luscious, golden herb-kissed butter over the top to ensure that glistening crust. Behind her the line chefs had the plates ready for the table full of carnivores outside. Roasted baby carrots and radishes lay piled on one another and were treated to an extra sprinkling of flaked sea salt before Tatum pivoted and deposited the steaks between the fresh, farmers market vegetables she and Sam had picked up this morning. Her aim was always to present farm to table with as few stops on the way as possible, and the ever-expanding daily market was the perfect place to make that happen. Having Sam accompany her was unexpected, but Ty had called in sick for the second day in a row. The timing of that—coincidental though it might be, hopefully—had her stomach knotting every time she thought about it.

"Order up. Three filet specials." She pushed the plates across the table for pickup, glanced up when Richard waved to catch her eye. "What's up?"

"Got a minute?" Richard pointed toward his small office down the hall toward the loading bay.

Tatum glanced at the clock, then wiped her hands. "Sure. Sam? You and Colby have this?"

"On it," Sam said and moved effortlessly from the

pizza oven to the main burners. "Cruz, holler if you get behind."

Tatum watched Cruz slide the classic margherita pizza from peel into the oven with practiced ease. The way he moved in the kitchen shouldn't be possible, not with as little time as he'd spent there in the past. But inhabiting other people's lives was part of his job, wasn't it?

"Tatum?" Richard called again.

"Yeah." Tatum grabbed a bottle of water and followed him into his office, a bit guarded at the uncharacteristic glee spinning in her manager's eyes. "Slow night?"

"Full up," Richard said. "Susan's managing fine for right now. I finally heard back from Constance Swan. She's agreed to review True for her vlog."

The water halted halfway to Tatum's mouth. "You'd better not be kidding, because that would be the cruelest joke anyone has ever played on me."

"Not kidding." Richard's chest puffed out more than usual. "I wanted to get everything set before I told you. Next Friday. I could have made it sooner, but I figured you'd want more lead time with the menu."

"Oh, wow. Okay. Wow." Tatum's head spun. Less than a week. Not a lot of time, but she could do it. Constance Swan was to online food communities what Martha Stewart was to home perfection. She'd been the leading voice in the culinary world for almost a decade, and had a worldwide following of millions on every social media platform available. Tatum had been trying to snag a review ever since she'd first opened True. "How'd you do it? What magic wand did you use?"

"You can thank Nancy."

"Your wife?" Tatum chugged water, feeling exhilarated and anxious to get started on fresh and new menu offerings.

"Turns out they're in the same Pilates class." Richard sat on the edge of his desk and folded his arms over his chest, the barest hint of ego glowing on his fashion-doll handsome face. "Their last class got canceled, so they went out for coffee. Conversation ensued and Nancy turned on the charm, told her all about you and how amazing this place is."

Tatum actually squealed and grabbed his shoulders, kissed his cheek. "I am going to send your wife a case of her favorite wine first thing tomorrow." She needed to write that down. She needed to write a lot of things down. "Do you know what a positive review from her would mean? We wouldn't just be made here in Chicago, True could become a destination dining experience. Oh." She fanned her face. "Oh, man, I could even think about opening a second restaurant." A dream she'd only let herself have after the best of nights. "You are the best! I can't wait to start planning. Staff meeting first." She snapped her fingers, pushed him aside and grabbed a notepad off his desk. "Or maybe I'll tell everyone tomorrow before we open, after we're done eating. Yeah, that's what I'll do." She was babbling. She didn't care. Right now she felt as if she could walk on air. "Let's make sure we're booked for that night. I want every table filled. I bet I'm not going to sleep at all this week."

"It's all in your hands now," Richard said as she danced out the door and plowed straight into Cruz.

"Oh!" Cruz locked his hands around her upper arms before she bounced back against the wall. "Sorry."

"What's wrong?" She saw the cop light in his eye, brighter, steadier and more critical than she had seen in the man who had been cooking in her kitchen the past few days. "Something happen?"

"Something amazing!" Professionalism out the window, Tatum took his face between her palms and pressed her lips to his. The tingle of attraction that zoomed through her wasn't dulled by her happiness. "Constance Swan has agreed to review True."

"Congratulations?"

Tatum rolled her eyes at his confusion. "She's only the biggest and most influential food critic in the country right now. I so needed some good news. I'm not telling anyone else until tomorrow, so keep it to yourself. Hang on—" she frowned, craned her neck to try to see back into the kitchen "—what are you doing here? Who's manning the pizza oven?"

"I'm on a break and Chester is covering." He ran his hands down her arms. "Relax, Tatum."

"Easy for you to say." Right now she felt like she had a swarm of bees buzzing inside her. "We're already a man down tonight."

He drew her away from Richard's office, down the hall toward the exit into the storage area and loading bay. "I want you to leave with the rest of the crew tonight. Don't stick around after-hours."

"Why?" Just like that, the balloon of expanding excitement inside her popped.

"Because I have something I need to do, and I won't be here to escort you home."

She fluttered her lashes and pressed a hand to her chest. "But however will I take care of myself without a big strong man around to protect me?"

"Tatum."

She'd known him long enough to recognize that warning tone; not that it had any effect. "I don't need anyone looking after me, Cruz."

"Tell that to your head." He brushed gentle fingers against the bruise that was finally showing signs of fading. "If you aren't going to leave with the others, I'll just have to make sure one of them sticks around so you aren't alone."

"No." As much work as she had to do, she didn't want to put anyone else at risk. "I don't want you to do that. I don't want any of them knowing about this, remember?"

"Great. So you'll leave right after we close?"

"Where are you going?" Did he notice she didn't answer his question? "Is it to do with the case?"

"Everything has to do with the case."

Did the man have to be so infuriating? Nonanswer answers were not productive. "I need to know what's going on. If you're onto something, I need to know." She swallowed hard. "Even if I don't want to."

"All right, then." He lowered his voice. "I'm going to find out why Ty hasn't been coming in to work."

"Because he's sick." Even as she said it she could hear how naive she sounded. "You don't think he's sick at all." Her stomach rolled. Not Ty. Please, not Ty.

"I don't believe in coincidences. Someone breaks in and steals my employment file, and soon after, one of your employees stops showing up for work?"

Tatum pinched her lips tight. There had to be another

explanation. Ty was her stalwart sentry; she'd been able to rely on him from day one. Never once had she got any inkling of an ulterior motive from him. She couldn't have been wrong. She wasn't wrong. Not about him. But darn it if Cruz's suspicion had doubt creeping in. And a tiny part of her resented Cruz for that.

As if reading her mind, his tone shifted to what she could only describe as total cop. "I still have a job to do, Tatum. But I can't focus on that if I'm worried about you. I need to know you're somewhere safe. And right now, if I can't be with you, that means you need to be at home."

Even with the obvious frustration in his voice, the sentiment warmed her heart. She moved a step closer, felt that tingle of attraction shoot straight up her spine when he dropped his hands to her waist. "You worry about me?"

"Constantly." There was that twinkle again. Just a flash, but enough to convince her he was right. Until they knew for certain, until he'd cleared everyone in her employ, she wasn't safe here alone.

"You know what?" She linked her arms around his neck and inclined her head. "I think I like the idea of you worrying about me."

"What happened to professionalism in the workplace?" he asked when she lifted a finger to his lips. He kissed her fingertip. She bit her lip and wondered how or even if either of them was going to be able to hold out until the case was closed. There wasn't much more she wanted right now than to get Cruz Medina into her bed.

"I told you. I'm very happy tonight." And she wasn't

going to let anything, not even the so-called suspicions he had about True, ruin it. "And when I'm happy I—"

A box came skidding down the hall floor, stopped right at their feet. Tatum spun just as Quallis stepped into sight. "Might want to start putting up warning signs, boss," the big man said with a naughty glint in his eye. "Never know when someone might walk up on you two."

"Thanks for the warning." Cruz squeezed his hand on Tatum's hip to keep her quiet. "Not a lot of places for privacy around here."

"Then you aren't looking hard enough. Loading bay is full of them. Not that I'd know personally," he added at Tatum's sudden interest. "As you were." He moved past them and, pulling out a pack of cigarettes, headed out the loading bay door.

"I thought you quit smoking!" Tatum yelled after him, but Quallis only shrugged and flicked open his lighter. "Going to have to come up with an incentive for him," Tatum muttered.

"I've still got a few minutes left on my break," Cruz said when she faced him again. "It would probably be best if I didn't take them with my boss."

"I suppose not. Rain check?"

He hauled her to him and kissed her quick and hard. "Count on it."

She slipped away, fingertips to her mouth and smiling to herself.

It wasn't until Tatum was out of sight that Cruz realized she hadn't promised not to stay late at the restaurant. She'd distracted him. Effectively. When was

the last time a woman occupied his thoughts and overwhelmed his senses so completely he forgot to do his
job?

"Never," he muttered as he followed Quallis's path
into the loading bay. Being distracted was not going to
help him close this case. Or get him through the maze
of shelving and storage. "Guess there really is a first
time for everything." His break time could no longer be
used to recuperate from the hours he spent on his feet
and in front of a hell-fire-degree pizza oven. He had a
week to make significant progress on the case or else
he'd lose it forever. No way was he going to let Johnny
die for nothing. If his partner was leaving this world,
the least Cruz could do was to lock up whoever was responsible for killing him. That meant refocusing. Besides, the sooner he solved this case the sooner he and
Tatum could work out whatever it was raging through
both their systems.

Nice to know the sexual frustration went both ways,
sure, but man. He pushed through the slatted plastic curtain into the dim warehouse-type setting. His empty-
bedded nights were becoming excruciating.

Why True? What did someone see here that made
this place useful to them?

Stacks of boxes and aisles of the same metal racks
that filled the walk-in refrigerator stood in a type of
labyrinth, leading this way and that. The lack of tem-
perature control meant the air was chilly and would no
doubt be roasting in the summer humidity. Keeping
one eye on Quallis, who he could see was standing by
the open landing bay door, Cruz set his phone timer,
clicked on the flashlight app and took a look around.

Multiple skylights provided light during the day, and as far as he could tell, sporadic fluorescent bars illuminated the space when needed. The overstock of towels, aprons, tablecloths, napkins, plates and all the table fixings were neatly arranged. A clipboard hung off the side of each rack, a continuing inventory for catering and supplies for the restaurant. The number of glasses alone had him gaining even more appreciation for Bernadette and Pike, who made them all sparkle and shine.

Most everything else seemed to be transportation items, like insulated food carriers, multiple sizes of wheeled ice chests. Everything around the catering van was neatly arranged. He moved around the truck, smoothed a hand over the gold-and-black lettering of the True logo.

"You looking for something in particular?" Quallis's voice carried in along with the cold night air. "Or are you naturally nosy?"

Cruz shook his head. "Just getting a feel for the place. You know." He shrugged off his having been caught and continued his inspection in clear sight this time. "I like to know everything about a place I work in."

Quallis crushed out a cigarette under his foot, checked his watch, then lit another. "The other night we had a bit of a joke about you and Tatum."

"So I recall." Cruz trailed his fingers along the hood of the van. Ice-cold. Hadn't been driven in a while, or today at least.

"I didn't think it much of a joke, to be honest." Quallis waited until Cruz faced him. "Tatum's had a rough few months. You know about her father and uncle?"

Cruz nodded. "I do. We've talked about it."

Quallis's bushy eyebrows went up. "I guess that's good news, then. Now's not a good time to be messing with her, is all. I'd appreciate it if you kept that in mind going forward."

"I don't plan on hurting her." It was true. Didn't mean it wasn't a possibility. "Is someone going to warn me off every night like a ritual or something? You all taking turns?"

Quallis shook his head. "Sam had his say. Colby and the others, they think it's built-in job entertainment. Me?" His eyes narrowed. "There's something I can't quite figure out about you. I'll work it out at some point, though. I always do."

"Translation, you'll be watching me."

"You catch on quick." He tossed his cigarette down, crushed it out and slapped that now familiar hand on Cruz's back. "Good not to have to spell things out. See you back in there." He headed back inside, leaving Cruz out in the alley, the faint and familiar sounds of night traffic and meandering crowds echoing against his ears. There was something oddly comforting in being warned by Quallis. Comforting and affirming.

If the big guy was part of the drug running, Cruz doubted he'd have been so light-handed in his advice. More likely he'd have used his girth and strength to try to intimidate Cruz out of a job. Instead he'd come across as a big brother, something Cruz appreciated and, in a strange way, welcomed.

Alone now, Cruz finished his search of the warehouse-like area, finding nothing that raised his suspicion. If he hadn't witnessed the break-in the other night, he'd be seriously reevaluating his suspicions about True. He needed to find something, and fast.

Otherwise the case was going to be closed. And Johnny would have given his life for nothing.

TATUM RARELY APPRECIATED being told what to do. Especially in that assumptive, borderline-condescending tone Cruz tended to use. Was she special? Did he use that particular intonation just for her? Part of her hoped so. The other part wanted to stuff those words down his throat and make him swallow them.

She'd do as he suggested and leave with the rest of the employees, but beyond that...

"Early night tonight?" Colby swung her bag over her shoulder as she joined Tatum in the bar. The place had been cleaned and ready for tomorrow's shift; the bar was sparkling against the dim glow of the after-hours lights. The ever so faint echoes of conversation and banter made their way through the depths of the almost empty restaurant.

"Shaking things up," Tatum confirmed and earned a smile from Colby. "You doing okay?" The revelation that one or more of her employees might be using her business as a front for crime had Tatum realizing she hadn't taken as much personal interest in their lives as she probably should have. She considered them all her friends, but were they? Friendship worked both ways, didn't it?

"Yeah, I'm good." Colby's raised brows confirmed Tatum's suspicion. "You want to join us for drinks over at O'Shannahan's?"

"I'd love to," Tatum started. "But I've got plans for

tonight. But I will soon. And I'll buy the first round."
Right now she couldn't wait to get started on planning
the perfect meal to offer Constance Swan.

"Wicked good." Colby nodded in approval. "So you
and Cruz have plans tonight?"

"Remains to be seen." Tatum was really getting tired
of Cruz being right, but letting those at True believe she
and Cruz were involved really did make sense. That
said, he was also right that Tatum was a terrible liar.
"If not, I'll just have a quiet early night. Work on some
new recipes. Maybe drink some wine." A lot of wine.

"He seems nice." Colby tugged on her jacket.
"Wouldn't have thought he was your type, but what
can you do." She shrugged. "The heart wants what the
heart wants."

Tatum's lips twitched. Funny how she'd been thinking that herself these past few days. "What about you?
Are you seeing anyone special?"

Colby's cheeks went almost as pink as her hair.
"Maybe. It's too early to talk about yet." She looked
away when the kitchen doors swung open and the rest
of the crew appeared. Considering the group consisted
of everyone from Jeremy Pike to Quallis, there was no
telling who Colby's paramour might be. But he was
here. That much was evident. "Hopefully soon, though."

"Boss is cutting out early, huh?" Sam elbowed Chester in the ribs and earned some hearty chuckles from
Quallis, Pike, Bernadette, and even Cruz. "Check the
news reports, because hell might have frozen over."

"Ha ha." Tatum pushed open the door and waved
them all out, then locked up behind them. Colby, Sam
and Chester broke off and headed across the street to

O'Shannahan's while Bernadette, Pike and Quallis made their way to the parking lot on the far side of the building.

Tatum walked right past her own car and followed Cruz to his. "So where are we going?"

"You're going home." Cruz walked around and pried her fingers off the passenger door. "Remember?"

"I remember you telling me what to do. I don't recall agreeing."

He sighed, dropped his head back as if asking a higher power for patience. Why did she find it entertaining to irritate him? After a moment, he planted his hands on the car on either side of her, blocking her escape, and leaned in close. His breath was warm against her face, making her shiver in the cool, early spring air. "I cannot keep having this same argument with you, Tatum."

"Stop arguing and we don't have to." She patted the oversize bag on her hip. "I made stakeout snacks. There's enough for two."

"You made…" The fact he struggled not to laugh boosted her mood. And her optimism. "Okay, here's how it's going to be. You're going to go home and stay there until you leave for work tomorrow, or I'm going to get on the phone and tell your mother exactly who I am and what I'm doing working at your restaurant."

The warmth drained from her face, probably, Tatum assumed, with all her color. "You wouldn't."

"Try me." He slid his hands down her arms, slipped one hand around hers and gave her a gentle tug. Seconds later he waited while she climbed into her car. "Go home, Tatum. If I find something out you need to know, I will tell you. *That* was part of the deal."

She sat there, hands on the steering wheel, engine rumbling, and glared at him. "You're no fun."

"Glad to hear it. I'll see you tomorrow." He closed her door and backed away.

"Wait!" She scrambled for her bag, dug through it to find the pair of containers she'd packed from leftovers at the restaurant. Powering down the window, she held them out. "In case you get hungry."

He strode back, accepted the offering, then bent down, caught the back of her head in his hand and kissed her.

The time for lazy, curious, testing exploration was over. His mouth was hot, insistent, demanding, and tasted like heaven. She found herself whimpering and grabbing for him when he stepped away. "Go home."

"Right." She nodded, her head a bit fuzzy as she slid the car into gear. Being kissed by Detective Cruz Medina definitely had lasting effects. She bit her lip, caught between sighing and smiling. She could almost, almost forget her life's work was balancing on a very, very thin edge.

CRUZ FOUND TY Collins's house as easily as expected. He'd already searched it out on GPS, knew it was in a neighborhood not altogether different from the one Cruz had grown up in. He parked amid the cars across the street, near a park and out from the glare of streetlamps.

Ty's saltbox-style house, even close to midnight, was ablaze with lights. The yards on the street were neatly tended for the most part. Bikes and toys littered lawns and swing sets sat behind weathered wooden fences. Dogs barked. Windows flickered with the glow of televisions, and behind him thrummed the incessant beat of music turned up too high.

Cruz brought out the employee files Tatum had given him, and on the tablet he pulled out of his center console, he logged into the department database and pulled up Ty's arrest record. It wasn't long, but it was varied, starting back more than thirty years to the man's first arrest and adult charge for breaking and entering. The rest of his criminal résumé had everything from forging checks to criminal trespass, nothing particularly violent. The single assault charge, given Cruz's own experience with the man, seemed out of character, but this wouldn't be the first time a felon had surprised or disappointed him. Nowhere did he see any connection to narcotics. Not before or after he served his time. Logic and Ty's sudden disappearance told him he needed to look deeper; someone inside True was involved. But Cruz's gut told him this was the wrong direction.

Cruz glanced up as a car approached from behind and turned onto Ty's street. The aged, rusted sedan wheezed and knocked as the driver parked in front of Ty's house. Instincts spinning, Cruz tapped open his camera app, angled the phone and snapped a shot of the plate. Typing it into the police database, he pulled up the information on one Eddie Russo.

White. Thirty-one. Felon. Connections to various white power gangs operating within the prison system. Convictions included... Cruz's stomach took a bit of a dip as he scanned his screen. "Possession of narcotics with intent to sell." Was that the connection he'd been looking for? But as he read further, doubt crept in. Domestic assault. Possession of an unlicensed weapon. Those charges explained the restraining order currently out against him. As did his pleading guilty to endangering the welfare of a minor...

Cruz glanced up as the man exited the car and the front door to Ty's house opened. Dim light streamed out as Ty stepped outside, his girth and stance unmistakable. The curtain overlooking the front porch shifted. Cruz sat up straighter at the sight of a smaller person darting out of sight. Smaller person? That was a child.

Instinct and experience had the pieces dropping into place. He swore, and leaned over to retrieve his badge and weapon out of the glove box. He ejected the magazine, checked it, slammed it home and chambered a round.

Setting the gun on the center console and shoving his badge into his back pocket, he powered down the window and strained to hear, hand poised on the door. He didn't want to interfere; he wasn't looking to blow his cover where Ty was concerned, but he'd be damned if he'd let Ty get hurt because Cruz was too busy protecting his case.

The voices rose; rage and frustration wafted off the visitor in thick, pulse-kicking waves. Ty took a step down off his porch when Eddie kicked his way through the yard gate. The shouting split through the night.

Unlit porch lights suddenly blazed on. Doors were opened, heads poked out, curiosity getting the better of them until they assessed the situation and ducked back inside.

Cruz wasn't going to assume any of them were calling the police. He picked up his cell and dialed. "Yeah, Dispatch, Detective Medina. Badge seven-oh-seven- two-two. I need two squad cars rolling to..." he rattled off Ty's address. "Possible felonious assault in progress. Be advised undercover on scene. Situation is escalat- ing. I need backup."

Assured someone was on the way, Cruz clicked off, shoved his phone into his back pocket and, grabbing his gun, pushed open his door.

Ty took a step toward Eddie. Eddie didn't budge, but his hand did move toward his back. In the dark, Cruz couldn't be certain the man had a weapon, but he wasn't going to take the chance. Ty had a good four inches, twenty years and at least a fifty-pound advantage, but that didn't seem to matter. The closer Cruz crept, the better picture he got of Eddie Russo. Shaggy hair, un- shaven face, ragged, filthy, too-big clothes meant he was in a bad way, and probably, given his record, hyped up on something.

Eddie seemed to spring like a cat, but Ty's hands shot out and slammed solidly into Eddie's chest, knock- ing Eddie back a few steps. Cruz was closer now, close enough to see the sweat beading on Ty's forehead. Close enough to see, even at a glance, the face of the young boy standing at the window, eyes wide in terror and glistening with tears.

"You're trespassing." Ty's words echoed through the street and brought Cruz back to attention. "I'm not going to tell you again, Eddie. Get gone."

"You can't keep me from what's mine!" The younger man twisted and groaned, pulled something out of the back of his belt.

Gun raised, finger poised beside the trigger, Cruz stepped out of the shadows and into Ty's line of sight. "Don't do it, Eddie."

Eddie Russo seemed to trip over his own feet as he spun, the gun in his hand nearly slipping free of his grasp as he struggled to catch his balance.

"You're in violation of your parole, Eddie." Cruz kept his voice calm and even. The trembling hands, the wide, spinning eyes. He was strung out, panicked, and hopeless. The trifecta of horrible combinations.

Sirens sounded faint in the distance, not loud enough to convince Cruz his backup was close. He was going to have to handle this himself. He moved in, slowly, keeping his weapon aimed center mass, just as he'd been taught in the academy. He'd do everything he could to avoid shooting him, but he was ready to do what was necessary to keep Ty and whoever else was in that house safe.

"I just want what's mine, man." Eddie's pathetic whine might have had some effect had Cruz not seen the abject terror on what had to be Eddie's son inside Ty's house. "She's keeping me from my kids. They're my kids. Mine!"

He sounded like a spoiled toddler who hadn't gotten his nap. But he looked like a crazed, pushed-to-the-edge addict who might be willing to do the absolute worst before this was over.

"You aren't going to see your kids, Eddie." Cruz stepped in through the gate, flicked his gaze to Ty, who looked at him with both confusion and relief. "You think about that. You think about where you are at this minute. You hear that?" He inclined his head as the sirens approached. "I've already called for backup. You're going in, Eddie. Like Ty said, you're trespassing and you've violated a restraining order." He'd skimmed the document; he knew the threat he posed. "You've got maybe seconds to decide how this goes down. You put that gun down and surrender, and there's still a chance you'll see your kids someday. You don't?" Cruz shifted, made certain Eddie saw he had control of the situation. "This only ends one way."

Two squad cars screeched around the corner, came to a halt outside Ty's house.

Eddie's hand continued to shake. The barrel of the gun shifted from Ty to Cruz, who, in that moment, saw an image of Tatum flash in his mind. Of all people, at all times, he could see her. Hear her. Feel her.

"Eddie, you need to put the gun down." Cruz took one more step forward, shifted the gun to his right hand, held out his left to keep the patrol officers back. "Detective Cruz Medina," he yelled without pulling his gaze from Eddie. "I've got this, Officers."

One more step. He could see the rim of the barrel wavering, the terror take hold behind Eddie's frantic gaze.

"Cruz?" Ty's voice held its own ring of fear, fear he recognized as concern for the welfare of the children in his house.

"I've got this. We've got this, don't we, Eddie?" Cruz trusted his gut, listened to his instinct, and as he took one final step toward Eddie, he lowered his own weapon as he reached out to grab hold of Eddie's.

The gun fell free of his grasp and Cruz held it out for one of the officers to take as the uniformed officers flooded in through the gate. He set the safety on his gun and shoved it into the back of his waistband. "Okay, Eddie?" He lowered a hand onto the shaking man's shoulder. "You did real good. It's going to be rough for a while, and it'll take work, but you did the right thing. It's a good first step."

"I want to see my boy. And Katie. My little girl." Eddie's eyes filled with tears that took even Cruz's jaded heart by surprise. "I want to see my kids."

Cruz held off the officers for another moment. "You don't want them seeing you like this, Eddie. You aren't good for them this way. You aren't good for yourself."

For a moment, Cruz saw clarity in the older man's eyes.

"You do your time, Eddie." Cruz turned him away from Ty, reached out and wiggled his fingers at one of the officers, who handed over his cuffs. Cruz snapped them around Eddie's wrists. "You do your time, you get clean and sober, then maybe you'll stand a chance of being part of their lives. You keep going like you're going and you'll die. One way or the other." He passed him off to the officers. "You have a decision to make, Eddie. If you can't make the right one for yourself, you make it for your kids." Eddie was escorted to one of the patrol cars.

"Detective Cruz Medina working his usual junkie magic."

Relief surged through Cruz as he recognized the senior patrolman on scene. "Manny." He actually laughed, a release of adrenaline, he was sure. "Hey, man. How's it going?"

"Same old, same old." Manny Santiago, senior patrol officer with more than twenty years' experience and the gray hair to prove it, gave him a smack on the arm. "Cruz, what are you doing around here? I thought you were Narcotics these days. Now you're adding neighborhood watch to your résumé?"

"I was visiting a friend." The lie came easily. "Got here just as this guy turned up with that." He pointed to the gun one of the officers had now. "I'd charge him with trespassing and attempted aggravated assault." Personally he'd go with attempted murder, but Eddie hadn't gotten a shot off. "You need a witness, you've got one." Or maybe two. He glanced at Ty, who hadn't moved from his last position.

"Dude's seriously strung out," one of the patrolmen said. "We might want to run him by the ER on our way to booking."

"Never pass up a trip to the ER." Manny's smile actually widened. Cruz patted the older man on the back. Manny's wife of eighteen years was an ER nurse and frequently worked the night shift. "Get your statement tomorrow?"

"You got it. Thanks, Manny." Grateful the arriving officer had been a friend, Cruz stood on one side of Ty's fence while Eddie was hauled away, along with his shotgun.

He and Ty stood there in Ty's front yard as the neighbors got their curiosity quotient filled for the night.

"So." Ty cleared his throat, shoved his hands in his front pockets and rocked back on his heels. "You're not a chef."

Cruz shook his head. "No."

"If Tatum put you in her kitchen, she must have a

good reason." He hesitated, leery eyes considering. "She in trouble?"

"Yeah." Cruz wasn't going to sugarcoat it. And he wasn't going to lie to Ty. Not now. And not about this. "Yeah, she is."

"Well, I owe you for the assist, so you may as well come inside and fill me in. I'll get the coffee going." He turned as the door opened and the young boy Cruz saw in the window peeked out. "Julian, I told you to stay in the house." Ty moved lightning-fast to scoop up the little boy and tuck him securely in his arms.

"Is the bad man gone, Grandpa?" Cruz judged the boy to be about six, but he was burrowed into his grand-father so deep he couldn't really see him. Other than the construction vehicle pajamas he wore that were sag-ging around the butt.

"He's gone. And he's not coming back." Ty rubbed the boy's back. "Where's your sister?"

"Hiding in the bathtub." Something in the way he said it told Cruz that Julian had been there not too long ago, as well. "It's where Mama always tells us to go when there's trouble."

"Well, let's go get Katie and put you both back in bed, all right? Cruz?" He headed inside. "If you want to get the coffee going while I—"

"Take your time," Cruz assured him and felt his heart pinch at the relief on the older man's face. "I've got all night."

THERE WERE FEW truths in life, but for Tatum the very idea of a nationally renowned food critic coming to True was enough to give her a second wind. She practically floated into her condo and straight into the shower. Donning sweatpants and an old T-shirt from a rock concert she and Simone had gone to well before their youngest sister, January, was allowed, put her in the perfect creative mood. The ratty, faded fabric always brought a smile to her face, and that was definitely needed for creating a stellar menu selection for Constance Swan.

The wine she'd assured Colby she'd drink hit her glass in a healthy splash. The kitchen, her world, beckoned.

It wasn't enough to yank out every cookbook on her shelves, or to spread printouts from True's menus from the past three months. She did a quick survey of her pantry and refrigerator contents and found both sorely lacking. Obviously, she was in a severe creative slump. More than an hour passed with her scouring her favorite foodie websites for inspiration, the notes scribbled beside her almost unreadable thanks to her abundance of excitement.

"This isn't cutting it." She glanced at the clock. Just after 1:00 a.m. Tatum bit her lip, the idea forming before she could stop it. Five minutes later, she'd stuffed her feet into sneakers, grabbed her bag, notebook, jacket and cell phone, and headed back out to the twenty-four-hour gourmet market located a few blocks from her house. Not wanting to deal with the gate and parking, she walked. Being out in the cool air, with the streets and sidewalks pretty much empty, let her mind continue to flow through and over the ideas she couldn't get control of.

It had been over a month since she'd felt this level

of anticipation and excitement. She'd begun to wonder if her father's and uncle's deaths had robbed her of
the ability to do anything but maintain the status quo
at True, but tonight was proving to be the beginning
of—what would she call it?—a reckoning? A reawak-
ening, maybe.

She needed to get all her ideas out and organized as
soon as possible so she could start testing and tasting.
And maybe, if he was very, very lucky, Cruz would
benefit from both. The idea of cooking for Cruz, using
him as her guinea pig, sent an unexpected and unfamiliar thrill of exhilaration through her. The good detective was featuring more and more in her thoughts,
and she wondered where they'd end up, when all of
this was over.

"Other than bed, you mean." Yeah, Tatum grinned
as she stepped through the automatic sliding doors of
Barley & Bakes Market. They'd definitely end up there.
Instantly she was welcomed, both by the night staff as
well as the comforting aroma of briny olives, fresh fish
and meat, and the promise of oven-baked bread awaiting the first bake of the day.

Cart obtained, Tatum put all plans and preconceived
ideas out of her head and began meandering up and
down the aisles, beginning in the gourmet imported-
food section where she filled her cart with jams, chut-
neys and a selection of cheeses that would be lucky to
make it home. She was already veering away from the
typical fare she'd been serving of late. There was only
so much pasta she could make, only so many ways to
cook chicken and steak. She wanted new. Different.
"Unexpected." She needed to think beyond her nor-

mal borders, challenge herself. She found herself examining the fresh olive bar and the imported saffron
that was on sale. Spanish. She'd read most everything
Constance Swan had ever written, and Swan had mentioned Spain multiple times.

Images of freshly roasted seafood, tender chicken
and spice-kissed saffron rice had her thinking paella
and tapas. Something caught in her mind and began to
spin. How could she make those dishes her own?

Her cell phone went off, filling the empty aisles with
the melodic tunes of Julia Child's theme music. Who
would be calling her at this time? She dug inside her
purse, pulled it out and didn't recognize the number on
the screen. "Probably a midnight owl telemarketer." She
still answered. "Hello?"

"Is this Tatum Colton?"

The officious-sounding voice had her thinking instantly of Cruz. "Yes. Who is this?"

"Officer Pearson, ma'am. Your sister January asked
me to call. I'm afraid there's been an accident."

"Jany?" Shopping spree forgotten, Tatum yanked her
bag out of the cart and raced to the door. "Where is she?
Is she all right? What happened?" She looked up and
down the street, judging the quickest route to her condo.

"Car accident, I'm afraid. She's being taken to the
hospital. She'd like you to meet her there. Mercy General."

"Yes, of course." Heart racing, she was mentally cal-
culating how long it would take her to run home for
her car. "I'm on my way now. Please tell her I'm on my
way." Cell still clutched in her hand, she stepped out
into the parking lot.

The sound of squealing tires didn't register until she caught the flash of headlights out of the corner of her eye. She froze, almost an instant too long, as the car barreled right at her. In the dim light, she saw a flash of gold inside the car. A thick-banded ring. She leaped to the side and bounced off the trunk of a parked car. As she rolled off, the tail end of the speeding vehicle clipped her at the last second and sent her plummeting face-first to the ground. Her purse soared out of her grasp, but her fingers tightened around her phone as she rolled, feeling every inch of asphalt along her side. The air was driven out of her. Her head spun and she looked up, blinking her vision clear as the car continued its race away. She angled her phone, managed to tap her camera open and click as the car skidded and turned out of sight.

Footsteps sounded all around her, voices shouting, uttering commands. Gentle hands touched her arms, her torso, but nothing computed. Nothing made sense. She couldn't answer the questions she was asked, and didn't want to move. There was only one thing she could think to do. Hands shaking, she lifted her phone and called Cruz.

Chapter Eleven

"So you're a cop." Ty finally joined Cruz in the minuscule kitchen of his house, poured himself a cup of the coffee Cruz had taken the liberty of brewing. One a.m. didn't seem a great time for caffeine, but it didn't look as if he was going to be getting any sleep tonight anyway.

"I am." Cruz, seated at the small circular table by a window overlooking a backyard containing an old swing set and a collection of baseball equipment, toasted him with his half-full mug. "How are they?"

"Asleep. I think." Ty retrieved a container of leftover Chinese, held it up in question. "You hungry?"

"No, thanks." Thinking of the snacks Tatum had made for him, he found himself looking forward to eating them once he was on his way home. "So you're a grandpa."

Whatever suspicions Ty had of Cruz vanished beneath the flash of pride. "Two times over. My daughter, Deena, she works nights as a bookkeeper for a chain grocery store. Up until a few weeks ago she had a sitter come stay with them, but since Eddie got out—" he slipped two cartons into the microwave and set the timer "—she was afraid something like this might happen." In that moment, Ty looked exhausted. "I was never much of a father to her. Was in and out of prison for most of her life. Last time I got out I promised that was it, that I'd be here for her no matter what. When she asked for my help watching the kids at night—"

"You couldn't say no." Cruz nodded. "You don't have to explain taking care of your family, Ty. It's nice to know where you've been, though." It felt good to have his first impression about Ty confirmed. The man had turned his life around. He'd put family first.

"That sounds like relief to me."

"It is." He'd never been so grateful to be wrong.

"You going to tell me why you're working at True or do I have to guess?" The microwave beeped. After Ty dumped what looked like sweet and sour chicken and fried rice into a bowl, he sat across from Cruz and dug in. "Is Tatum being stalked?"

"Stalked? No. Why would you think that?"

Ty shrugged. "You seem to always be around when she needs you. And you certainly watch her every minute you're in the same room together. I thought maybe you started out protecting her and it's changed to something…else."

Cruz squirmed. Put that way, a lot of what Ty surmised seemed right. "I don't watch her that closely. Do I?" He'd never been that careless before and he didn't like the idea that he'd been so now.

Ty grinned and some of the tension melted away. "So whatever's going on between you two doesn't have anything to do with why you're working there. Tatum's pretty picky about who she lets work in her place. Richard's suggestions are always a hard sell. She likes giving people a chance, but sometimes they just don't work out. You, uh, haven't worked in a kitchen before, have you?"

"Does my mother's count?"

Ty shoveled in more chicken. "Not really. You're good at it, but it's not where your heart is. Knowing you're a cop?" He took an extra beat, seemed to be peering into Cruz's very soul. "That definitely makes more sense. You don't have to worry about me blowing your cover. Provided you're there to help Tatum and not hurt her."

Was that warning the True company motto or something? "I'm investigating the new influx of drugs to the area. Heroin in particular. You know anything about it?"

"Heroin?" Ty shook his head, but there was no deception in his expression that Cruz could find. "Only thing I know is that overdoses are up, and whatever people are using is as pure as you can get. That's one side of things I never got into. You need an example of why, you just have to look at Deena's ex. Kid was as strait-laced as they came in high school, then he went away to college and got hooked. Doesn't stop her from loving him. Thankfully, it does stop her from being with him. What does a drugs case have to do with Tatum?"

"My case puts True right in the middle of the distribution area."

"True?" Ty sat back in his chair, wiped his mouth. "Nah, man. You have that wrong. No way Tatum has anything to do with drugs."

"I didn't say she did. But someone who works there does." He was taking a chance, a big one, by coming clean with Ty, but there wasn't much more he could do on his own. He needed some extra cover, cover he didn't want Tatum to have to provide. "That knock on Tatum's head? She got that when someone broke in the other night. They shoved her in the freezer. Knocked her silly."

Realization dawned in Ty's eyes. "Well, that explains that. Never did buy she tripped. Woman's more graceful in the kitchen than Misty Copeland is on the dance floor. My granddaughter, Katie," he added at Cruz's blank stare, "she's taking ballet lessons. Misty's her idol."

"Right." Cruz's lips twitched. "Near as we can tell, nothing other than my employment file was taken. And then it was returned the next day."

Ty swore. "Meaning someone working at True, or at least with a working knowledge of True, was responsible. All right." He took a deep breath, resumed eating. "So what's the game plan? You getting a look at everything you need?"

"I'm examining the financials, but nothing's popping. Is there anything I should know, maybe something Tatum doesn't know, that you can share?"

Ty didn't answer for the longest time, and when he did, there was an odd determination—or was it resignation—in his voice. "I've never been one to snitch on anyone," he said finally. "If I thought it would help Tatum, I would. Keeping that in mind, I think you're wrong about this, Cruz. I've been around criminals most of my life. I am one. It'll be in my obit when I leave this earth. I know that world and it's not at True. Not that I've seen. Not that I've felt. You're wrong, Cruz. You're just wrong."

It wasn't something he wanted to hear; admitting

that meant he'd taken a wrong turn somewhere, wasted time and energy and promises to find the person who had shot Johnny. In a way it would be easier to admit defeat and walk away, go back and see where he'd gone wrong, but…there was something there, in the back of his mind, that wouldn't allow him to let go.

"I've got over a decade as a detective telling me otherwise." He didn't know how else to explain it. "But if you honestly believe there's nothing there…" Cruz's cell phone vibrated in his pocket. Used to late-night calls from the station, he pulled it out, glanced at the screen. Seeing Tatum's name pop up had him both smiling and wincing at Ty's snort of instant comprehension. "Stop it," he warned the older man, who held up his hands in surrender. He clicked to answer. "Tatum, you'd better be calling me from—"

"Car. Parking lot. Took picture."

"Tatum?" Cruz shot to his feet, held up a finger when Ty followed him. "Tatum, what's wrong? Where are you?"

"Car. Plate. Picture. On my phone."

He strained to hear, but all he could pick up were voices shouting and the sound of a siren. "Tatum?" He was yelling now and heading toward the door. "Tatum? Answer me."

"Hello?" Someone else's voice came on the line. "Um, I don't know who this is but the lady's passed out. She got clipped. Not sure how bad. We called an ambulance. I can hear it now."

"Tell me where you are," Cruz demanded.

"Parking lot of Barley and Bakes Market. It's on—"

"I know where it is. I'm on my way." Cruz disconnected, faced a worried-looking Ty. "Tatum's been hurt. I need to go."

"Yeah, go, go. Call me when you know something."

Cruz barely heard him as he was already running.

"FOR THE TENTH TIME, I don't want to go to the hospital. I want to call my sister!" Tatum didn't know how many more times she could repeat herself. "Please." She looked to the female EMT currently taking her blood pressure. Again. "Please just get me my phone."

"Ma'am—" The woman's partner had his hands locked around Tatum's ankles, attempting to keep her still on the stretcher. "You need to let us do our job." The stern tone of his voice reminded her of Cruz. Instead of the notion calming her, it only irritated her. The crowd that had formed in the parking lot wasn't huge; it wouldn't be this time of night. But there were enough people for her situation to be embarrassing. The manager from the market had come out with a bottle of water for her while they'd waited for an ambulance. Once she'd regained consciousness. She didn't remember passing out. She wasn't entirely sure she had. But she did have one whopper of a headache. Worse than the one after her freezer encounter.

"I'll make you a deal." Tatum stopped trying to kick her way off the stretcher at least. "You get me my phone and I'll let you haul me wherever you want."

The male EMT looked to his partner, who simply shrugged and moved the stethoscope from the crook of Tatum's arm to her chest. "Her vitals are okay. Not great," she added at Tatum's snort. "From what we've been told you bounced off a car and landed pretty hard."

She set the stethoscope aside and reached for a penlight, flashed it into her eyes. "We're going to take you in for a CT scan if nothing else. What's this?" The woman pressed her finger lightly against the bruise along her scalp.

"I bashed my head at work a few days ago."

That seemed to settle things. "Yeah," the woman said. "You're going in to check for a concussion. Ms. Colton... Tatum," she said when Tatum started getting restless again. "You need to be checked out, and fighting us isn't going to make this any easier."

"I need. To call. My sister." Humiliated tears formed in her eyes. She couldn't think beyond the idea that January was hurt in a hospital somewhere and she was here, being poked and prodded in a parking lot. "Please find my phone."

"I've got it." The male EMT returned, held up her phone.

Tires screeching into the lot had a scream forming in Tatum's throat. That sound. She'd never forget that sound for the rest of her life. The next thing she knew, Cruz's SUV pulled to a stop and he jumped out, heading straight for her.

"Cruz." She couldn't help it. She reached for him, and when she grabbed hold she instantly felt calmer. "I need to call January. She's been in an accident. I need to know if she's all right."

"Okay, we'll do that." Had he just patted her hand? "Just give me a minute."

"No, now!" Tatum blinked the tears free. "Cruz, please. If something's happened to her—" She couldn't finish the sentence. If January was hurt or worse...

Tatum could barely breathe around the terror threatening to strangle her. She couldn't lose anyone else she loved.

"Tatum." Cruz's voice gentled and intensified. He caught her face in his hands and forced her to look at him. "I'm going to check on your sister. I promise. But right now I need to know what happened and how you are." He looked to the female EMT. "Detective Cruz Medina. Tell me what you know."

Tatum could only imagine what the EMT thought about her, but she didn't care. She sat there, shaking, worrying, as the EMTs listed a litany of possible injuries and why she needed to be taken to the ER.

"You were hit by a car." Cruz's deadpan statement had her wincing. "For the love of… Tatum, why are you arguing with them?"

"I got a call from an Officer Pearson." She was so tired of explaining. "He said January was in a car accident and I should get to the hospital." She ground out each word as if it were glass under her frustrated foot. "Now let me call my sister!"

"Do you have her phone?" he asked the EMT, who handed it over. "Tatum, I'm going to check on January for you, okay?" He pocketed her phone, caught her face once more. "I want you to go to the ER in the ambulance. I'm going to follow you there and I'll let you know about your sister when I get there. All right?"

"You promise?" She hated that her chin wobbled. Hated that she sounded so…pathetic. "You said you wouldn't lie to me, so if you promise, I'll believe you."

"I promise." He bent down, pressed his lips to her forehead. "I'm glad you're all right." She reached up,

wrapped her hand around his wrist and felt the unsteady, frenetic pounding of his pulse.

"You were worried about me." The joke had him
smiling. A little. "I'll see you at the hospital."

She swore she heard the male EMT mutter "finally,"
but she chose to ignore it as they belted her in and lifted
her into the back of the ambulance.

"My purse!" she yelled at Cruz, who nodded and
retrieved it from an onlooker. The last thing she saw
as the ambulance siren sounded and the vehicle pulled
away was Cruz dialing his phone.

"Yeah, Ty, she's okay. As far as I know." Cruz started
the call before pulling his SUV into the emergency lot
of the hospital. He felt like he'd been on a roller coaster
of emotions ever since Tatum called. The abject fear
pulsing through him on the unending drive to the market was not something he was used to. Adrenaline, yes.
Anticipation? Of course. But not knowing what he'd
find when he got there, the idea she'd been seriously
hurt or worse... He swallowed and forced himself back
into cop mode. His feelings were going to have to wait.
"They're going to run some tests, I'm sure. She knocked
her head again and had some bruises and scrapes, but I
think she was lucky."

"Was she?" Ty's question wasn't anything Cruz
hadn't already thought himself. He'd been so focused
on everything around Tatum he hadn't considered she
was deeper in this than either of them realized. This was
twice someone had tried to hurt her, twice someone in
the shadows had struck out, the fear of whatever threat
she posed more powerful than their desire to stay hid-

den. He'd missed that and it had put her in danger. What else had he missed? "After what you told me about what you suspect, Cruz, this can't be an accident."

"No," Cruz said as he found a parking space. "It wasn't." She was supposed to be home, safe and sound. What had she been doing at the grocery store? He scanned the lot for the familiar face he'd called less than an hour ago, saw a pair of headlights turning in. He climbed out of the car, grabbed Tatum's purse. "Let me get a handle on this before we call anyone else from the restaurant. You're the only one I can count on right now, Ty. You up for it?"

"If it'll help you find whoever hurt Tatum, you bet. The restaurant's closed today. My daughter's going to pick up the kids around ten. With Eddie in custody, I shouldn't have them at night anymore. You tell me what you and Tatum need and I'll be there."

"We'll make it work. I need to go. I'll call when I know more."

"Okay. Thanks."

"Sean." Cruz hung up and approached the couple heading toward the emergency room doors. They looked as shaken as he felt. "Cruz Medina."

"Yeah, sure. Cruz." Detective Sean Stafford slipped an arm around the woman at his side. She was shorter than Tatum, a bit curvier, and looked significantly younger than her age, but her eyes were all Colton. "This is January Colton."

"Nice to meet you." Cruz gave a short nod. He almost said he was glad to see she was all right, but that would only raise more questions than Tatum's sister no doubt already had. "She'll be glad to see you."

"Thank you for calling." January's soft voice was controlled, but he could hear the worry nonetheless. He took the lead, holding open the door and then finding out what cubicle Tatum was in. When he drew back the curtain, the relief at seeing Tatum not only awake but very clearly irritated nearly drove him to his knees. It took him a moment to catch his breath and he stepped back as January raced around him to her sister's side.

"Jany?" In that one word, in that one moment, Tatum broke down. "Oh, thank God you're all right." She wrapped her cord-encased arms around her sister and nearly dragged her down onto the bed with her. "I was so scared…"

"Shhhh. It's okay, Tate. I'm here. I'm fine." January glanced back at Sean, a confused furrow on her brow. "Everything's fine now."

Clearly, Cruz thought as Sean led him away, January hadn't been told everything. "You didn't tell her."

"That someone told Tatum she'd been hurt? No. I wanted her to see Tatum was all right first." Sean didn't look one bit remorseful. "She'd only have worried and that wouldn't do anyone any good. She's where she needs to be. So." He straightened, shifted from concerned boyfriend to detective in the blink of an eye. Only an inch separated them in height, but Stafford's build dwarfed Cruz in a way. Sean's reputation as a stand-up, no-nonsense cop preceded him, and bolstered Cruz's opinion he'd made the right call. "Tell me what this is about."

It didn't take long to fill Sean in. The department gossip mill ran smoothly enough and fairly accurately that he could speak in common cop code. Hearing his girlfriend's sister's restaurant was under suspicion for drug trafficking didn't, however, apparently sit well with his fellow detective.

"You should have come to me," Sean said, an icy glint in his eyes that matched his tone. "I'd have told you you were off the mark on this one. No way is Tatum—"

"I know that," Cruz cut him off, probably more sharply than he should have, but darn it, why did everyone assume he thought Tatum herself was involved? Anyone who met her would know she wasn't capable of deception, let alone long-seated criminal activity. As it was, his cover at True wasn't going to hold much longer now that Tatum, Ty and Sean Stafford knew what he was really doing there. "And for the record, she was supposed to go home tonight. And stay there. What kind of person goes to the grocery store at one in the morning?" He glanced at the clock above the nurses' station. It was going on three, and Cruz was beginning to wonder if he'd ever calm down long enough to sleep again.

"A chef," Sean said simply. "January says she cooks at all hours, whenever inspiration hits. Shopping, cooking, eating. It isn't just what she does. It's who she is."

"Right." He needed to accept that. She wasn't a nine-to-five kind of woman. She didn't fit into any stereotype, let alone any box he might tag her with. And he wouldn't have her any other way. Not that he had her at all. But maybe… "Right. Okay, so." He pinched the bridge of his nose. "Since January is just fine and there wasn't any accident—"

"There's no Officer Pearson in the department."

Cruz stared at him.

"Not in patrol, not in any investigative unit. I figured you had enough on your mind," Sean offered, an almost friendly smile breaking across his face. "I made some calls while January got dressed. And before you ask, I had them check citywide. Whoever called Tatum wasn't a cop."

Cruz swore. Someone had purposely lured her out of the store. Right into the path of that car. So much for them being in the clear. His suspicions were proving correct. But beyond the drugs, someone wanted Tatum out of the way and that someone knew her routine and her habits. Given work was her life, that person had to be connected to True.

"Sean? Cruz?" January poked her head out. Her smile didn't quite reach her eyes, which flashed dangerously at Sean, as if warning him there would be a long discussion later. "Tatum wants to talk to you."

"Right. Good, thanks." Cruz returned to the cubicle and this time he was the one standing at Tatum's side. "You doing okay?"

"Mmm. Good now." She smiled and her head lolled to the side. "Nurse gave me a shot."

"Just to relax her," January clarified. "They want her conscious for the tests, just not so tense."

"Nice big shot." She made an injection motion with her fingers before she tapped them against Cruz's chest. "You're pretty."

Sean snorted. January smacked him. Cruz's face went hot. Even as he took hold of her hand and kissed the back of her fingers. "I don't suppose you saw the car that hit you?"

"Yep. Big. Big car. So big." She started to hum. "Got a picture. After it hit me. I clicked it with my phone."

She seemed to focus for a moment, just long enough for the fear she must have been feeling at the time to flash in her eyes. In that instant, Cruz felt such overwhelming rage he had to take a deep breath as he held on to her. "Do you still have my phone?"

"I do. I need your face."

Tatum laughed. "He needs my face," she said to her sister, who was clinging to Sean and clearly torn between laughing and lecturing. "Here you go. Cheese!" She grinned and tried to keep her eyes open as Cruz held her phone up to unlock it. Once he did, he quickly disabled that feature so he could access her call log and photos. "Okay, yeah, got it here. It's blurry." He winced. "But I'll get it to our techs. I can just make out a few of the..." He trailed off, the buzz of realization clouding his mind. Son of a— He recognized that car. It was the same SUV that had been parked outside the loading bay the night she'd been shoved in the freezer.

"They've got her scheduled for a CT scan," January said. "But it's going to be a while. If it comes back clear they'll send her home."

"No other injuries?" Cruz asked as Tatum continued to hum and wave her hand in the air as if she was conducting an orchestra. He pressed a hand against her shoulder, needing, wanting to feel the warmth of her body.

"She's a bit battered and will be sore for a few days. She'll need help at the restaurant."

"Can't keep her from going back, I suppose," Sean said.

Both Cruz and January snorted, and in that moment, seemed to bond. "She's got a bigwig food critic coming in on Friday night," Cruz said. "We'll be lucky if she isn't at True twenty-four seven until then. That said, I've got help on standby. True will be fine if she needs a couple of days off. Since she's going to be out—" he glanced down and saw Tatum playing Itsy Bitsy Spider with her fingers "—I'd like to run this car's info down."

"Why don't you two go and do what you do? I'll stay here," January said. "I'm going to wait until morning to call Mom and Simone. Neither will be happy about me waiting, but the ER wouldn't appreciate being taken over by Coltons. Go on." She patted Sean's shoulder. "We'll talk later."

"Okay." Sean tipped up her face and kissed her. "I'll be back soon and I'll bring coffee."

"And a bagel? I'd love a blueberry bagel."

"You got it. Cruz?"

"No bagel needed," Cruz joked as the two of them left. "But I'll take an assist with the lab."

Chapter Twelve

"Cruz is going to kill you when he finds out you helped me escape."

"Yeah, well, he's got work to do." January finished tucking Tatum into the corner of her sofa not at her condo, but at her ranch house in Livingston. "You know we should call Mom, right?"

"And tell her what exactly?" Tatum had been waiting for this ever since the ER doctor came in to tell her the CT scan was clear, but that she was to take it easy for the next twenty-four hours at least and not overdo it when she did go back to work. "It was an accident and I'm fine. Let her and Aunt Fallon keep decorating. I can't deal with either of them hovering right now."

"You're mostly fine and it wasn't an accident," January retorted from the kitchen behind Tatum. "Stop pretending like it was."

She wasn't pretending exactly. She just wasn't in the right frame of mind to deal with the fact someone had tried to kill her. Tatum didn't respond to January's comment. Her sister was puttering in the kitchen. Her kitchen. She gnashed her teeth. She didn't like anyone in her space.

Space was one thing in abundance in this place. As cozy and practical as the condo near True was, the ranch house was her refuge, where she went to rejuvenate and relax and tune the rest of the world out. Her family knew this, which was probably why when she'd been discharged from the hospital, January had driven her here.

She loved the open floor plan of the old house. She'd had it completely remodeled before she'd moved in, eliminating the walls between the living room, kitchen and dining area, and replacing walled-in windows with big plate glass ones. The front third of the house was now one big open space outlined with glass and overlooking the drought-resistant and low-maintenance landscaping. She didn't get here as often as she liked, but when she did come out, she didn't want to spend what time she had puttering in the yard.

Besides, other than herbs, she wasn't the greatest gardener.

"Maybe we should compromise and call Simone," January said right before a clatter of pots and pans had Tatum's nerves fraying. "Oops. Sorry. I'll just…" Crash. Bang. Cursing followed by a triumphant "aha!" had Tatum shaking her still sore head. Maybe she should have accepted that prescription for painkillers after all. "I got it."

"Got what?"

"Never mind. You just stay there and relax."

Having someone in her kitchen was not relaxing. In any way.

"Did you let Sean know where we'd be?"

"Considering I absconded with his car, I didn't have

a choice. Not that he deserves me telling him anything right now. Oh, good. You have milk. And bread! Score."

"I haven't been here in over a week, so if you're looking for produce—"

"Being run down in a parking lot does not call for salad. And you changed the subject."

"Yes, I did." It was bad enough January had been brought into the situation; she didn't want her sister or mother anywhere near what was happening with True. She'd tell them. Once she was on the other side of things. When January started humming, a signal to Tatum that she was done talking for the moment, Tatum snuggled down in the corner, tucked her feet in and gazed into the dormant fireplace.

Strange. An odd pang struck, and she realized, as his face flashed in her mind, that she missed Cruz. Seeing him in the parking lot had erased a lot of the rising fear, and when he'd finally arrived at the hospital, the anxiety and worry had faded, as well. She'd seen the concern in his beautiful eyes, felt the worry in him when she'd clung to him. There was a gentleness she didn't particularly accept, and seeing it on full display had broken away whatever pockets of resistance still dwelled inside of her. In the space of a few days he'd managed to slip into her world, into her life, into her thoughts, and—she dared to think—into her heart.

She jerked herself awake, unaware she'd dozed off. The very idea she may very well be falling in love— with a cop, no less—might just keep her awake for months.

"Spooked?" January was standing over her, a steaming mug in one hand and a plate of bread in the other. "What's wrong?"

"What's that?" Tatum sat up and accepted the mug, sniffed at the contents. The familiar combination of chocolate, cinnamon and cardamom soothed her senses and her thoughts. "You remembered."

"Your cure-all? Of course. Both Simone and I are experts at it now." January sat on the other end of the sofa and set the plate down between them. "How many broken hearts, broken dates, failed exams and late-night gossip sessions have we had over your hot chocolate and Simone's cinnamon toast?"

"Too many to count." Tatum sipped, swallowed and sighed. The warmth slid down her throat and spread through her body. "Thank you."

"Yeah, well, after this your cupboards are bare." January drank her own cocoa and took a piece of toast. She grinned and laughed. "I used way too much butter." She licked her fingers.

"Nothing wrong with that." The sound of crunching bread and the aroma of hot, spicy sugar had Tatum claiming her own piece. Definitely too much butter. And it was delicious.

"So." January rested her arm along the back of the sofa. "You and Cruz. What's going on there?"

"He's working a case. He needed my help."

"Uh-huh. Not what I meant. I mean you *and* Cruz. Am I right in thinking the Colton sisters might have a type?"

Tatum continued eating her toast, crust first, saving the buttery, sugary goodness for last. "I like him. A lot. I also like to think the attraction is mutual."

January kicked her with her foot. "You don't have to think. I saw it. He cares about you. I'm not sure he's happy about it, but he cares."

Tatum shrugged. "He's got a lot riding on this case." She had to remind herself of that. The case was important to him. His partner's life—and impending death—was important to him. She could only hope he understood how important True was to her. She'd certainly told him enough times. "We'll see what happens once it's over."

January frowned. "You mean you two haven't—"

"No, we haven't." Now it was Tatum's turn to kick, and when she did, she felt a twinge of pain in her leg and hip. "It's complicated."

"You do know complicated sex is the best kind of sex, right?"

"I've been hit by a car, Jany. I don't need a sex talk from my baby sister."

"Obviously you do. You want to know what I've learned being with Sean?"

"In the entire month you've been with him?" Tatum fluttered her lashes. "Oh, do tell."

Her teasing didn't elicit a smile, not much of one anyway.

"There's no guarantee of tomorrow." January's eyes shifted and it seemed as if a curtain she'd been keeping in place dropped away. "Being a cop…it's scary for the people who love them. The people they love. I never know if when my phone rings it'll be his CO telling me he's been hurt." She swallowed hard. "Or worse. And I get that there are plenty of people in the world who feel that way about their loved ones, for various

reasons. Nobody ever knows, but I don't take one minute I have with him for granted, Tate." She held up her
hand and with her thumb, spun the ring Tatum hadn't
noticed until now on her finger. "That's why I'm going
to marry him."

"Seriously?" Thoughts of hot chocolate and toast
abandoned, she grabbed her sister's hand with both of
hers to get a closer look. "Oh, January. It's beautiful."
Tears misted her eyes as she looked at the delicate collection of smaller diamonds circling a solitare. Unpre-
tentious, simple and perfectly suited.

"He found it in an estate sale. The woman who had it
before was married to her first love for over sixty years."
January sighed. "Beneath that cop heart lies a romantic." Tatum's brow lifted and her sister laughed. "Maybe
deep down. But my reasoning stands. I'm not going to
waste one single second and I plan to take advantage of
him being crazy about me every chance I can."

"Translation, you jump him when he walks in the
door." Despite her sister's obvious joy, there was still
a trace of concern. It wouldn't be evident to everyone,
just to those who knew January Colton best. Wanting
to ease her sister's worry, she reached out her hand.
"Sean's a good guy, Jany."

"He really is. And from what I can see, Cruz is, as
well. You could have died, you know."

Tatum drew in a deep breath. "Jany—"

"You're sitting here worrying if his job might be too
dangerous for you to deal with when he was the one
who got the call last night you'd been hurt. None of us
gets a pass on the future. We've learned that the hard
way. If we can lose Dad in the blink of an eye, anything

can happen. If you want to be with Cruz, if you want to take that chance, that swing at happiness, take it."

"You think?"

"I really do." January drank more cocoa. "You know what else I think? Pretty soon the Chicago PD is going to be overrun by Colton women."

Tatum laughed and finished her toast. There were definitely worse things to have happen.

"THANKS FOR DOING THIS, Ty."

Cruz stepped through the doors to an eerily silent True. The older man had met him across the street at O'Shannahan's, where they'd waited for the last of the cleaning crew to leave the restaurant. Now, at nearly noon, Cruz was finally able to put some of his frustration to work. The fact his frustration stemmed from not being where he really wanted to be—with Tatum—was something he was trying not to think about.

"What is it you're hoping to find?" Ty followed him up to Tatum's office where Cruz took a seat, and after a few keystrokes and work-arounds, found himself in the business's system.

"Remind me to educate Tatum on the importance of passwords and a firewall. After I'm done," he added at Ty's chuckle.

"What do you think is on here that—"

"It's not just Tatum's computer on this network. Don't worry." He flashed Ty a grin. "It's all covered by a warrant."

"It's not legalities I'm worried about," Ty said. "It's Tatum. When she finds out what you're—"

"If it saves her business she won't care how I did it. That's at the top of my list."

"What else is on that list?"

"Taking a better look at the storage area and loading bay. The intruder the other night went in and out like he knew the place. That tells me they're familiar not only with True but also with that section of the building. The way it's set up, you have to know where you're going, to get to the kitchen."

"But why use True in the first place?" Ty's annoyance mirrored Cruz's. "What possible good could a restaurant be for moving drugs? Especially one that's been in the spotlight like True?"

Cruz had his suspicions, but nothing concrete enough to share. Yet. "Pretty much everything I've learned about how this place works is that privacy is pretty much impossible. There's always someone around." One of the reasons he'd had a difficult time getting away to search various spaces of True. "It's been more of an elimination of ideas rather than proving myself right." Anger popped like tiny bubbles of fire in his blood. He may have been convinced he was wrong if Tatum hadn't been nearly killed. "Why go after her now?"

"She must have set them off. Did something, said something."

"Inadvertently, yeah." He scanned through files and folders, clicking open anything that didn't look like it fit or made sense. "She's made someone nervous, if not before, then by hiring me."

"What put you onto True in the first place?" Ty asked and took a seat across the desk from him.

"GPS. We've been looking at GPS and phone locations for drug arrests in the past year. There's a lot of overlapping area they cover, but there are two sections in the city they have in common. The warehouse district a mile and a half south and the four-block radius around True. You and Sam have worked here the longest, right?" Click and copy. His flash drive hummed.

"Yeah." Ty's brow furrowed. "Quallis came on board a few months later. She's had wait and bar staff come and go, and there's high turnover for the dish room, no surprise. But no one who stands out as a criminal mastermind."

"And you can't think of anything that happened in say the last year that seems strange in hindsight?"

"Other than Daria quitting out of the blue, no."

"Daria." Cruz stopped, mentally flipping through the employment records Tatum had given him. "She was the manager before Richard, wasn't she?"

"Yeah. Daria Naughton. She helped Tatum open this place. Of course, back then Tatum was still a control freak. She didn't really let Daria do much more than manage the front of the house and consult on staff. Some of us wondered if that's why she quit. Tatum wouldn't let her do a lot of what she could or should be doing. She resigned and that weekend she and her husband were killed in a car accident."

Definitely horrible. And another coincidence Cruz didn't buy into. "When did this all happen?"

"Seven, eight months ago?"

Around the same time the drug distribution kicked into high gear.

"Tatum didn't give us any details," Ty went on. "She just said Daria resigned unexpectedly and that she was going to be hiring a new manager. A couple days later we heard about the accident. Tatum was devastated. I think she thought Daria was upset with her about something and they could never clear the air. Probably why she's let Richard take over so much of what she used to do. She didn't want to make the same mistake."

"Do me a favor." Cruz gestured to the filing cabinet. "Go through those and see if Daria's file is still in there?" He remembered coming across the name, but because her employment period hadn't seemed connected, he'd moved on.

"It's locked."

Cruz reached to the narrow table behind him and flipped the photo of Tatum and her sisters around. The key was wedged into the back. "Here."

Ty's brow went up. "I guess Tatum really does trust you."

While Ty rummaged for the file, Cruz quickly accessed the network settings, clicked on remote-connected computers and…yeah. He clicked to upload files from the other laptop on the system. The light on the flash drive started blinking like crazy as it downloaded.

"Here it is." Ty handed over Daria Naughton's file, flipped it open as Cruz took it. "She was a sweetheart. Enthusiastic. Excited about being in on a restaurant from the ground up. Smartest woman I've ever known. Tatum included."

Cruz glanced down at the photo. The woman was older than he expected. Forty-four at the time she'd started at True. Degrees in business and hospitality services. Married. No kids. Chicago… "Daria Naughton." There was something familiar about her. Something he couldn't quite… He checked the file again for her husband's name. "I remember this." He plucked out the resignation letter dated seven months earlier, then pulled out his phone and called Sean. "Hey, can you look up a name in our database? Daria and Nathan Naughton?"

"Sure thing. When you're ready, can you give me a lift to Tatum's? January took her home in my car and I'm stuck at the station."

"She's out of the hospital?" Why wasn't he surprised?

"You've met Tatum, right?" Sean asked slyly over the sound of clicking keys. "The CT scan came back clean. Doctors cleared her to be released. January took her to the ranch house. Figured she'd take it easier there. Also Tatum didn't want to take the chance of running into her mother. Also I should have the info on the SUV by the time you get here."

"Okay." Cruz shook his head. "I'll pick you up as soon as I'm done here. You find anything?"

"Yeah. Daria and Nathan Naughton. Killed in a one-car collision seven months ago. It was ruled accidental death, mechanical issues with the car. I remember this one. They hit a power junction. Knocked power out to a couple thousand homes and businesses for half a day."

"What's the date of the accident?"

"September 17. Why? You find something?"

"Yeah. I think I did." He handed the letter to a curious Ty. "I'll see you in a bit."

"What?" Ty asked when Cruz hung up. "I don't see it."

"The date." Cruz pulled out the flash drive and pocketed it, then turned off and disconnected Tatum's laptop to bring with him. "How many people do you know quit their job after they're dead?"

"WHY AM I not surprised to find you in the kitchen?"

Cruz spoke in what Tatum now called his "I surrender" voice.

"Because I'm going stir-crazy in my own house and this is the only thing that helps. Here." She waited for him to set the grocery bags on the counter and held up a sauce-covered spoon. "What do you think?"

"And by what do you think, she means tell me you love it," January instructed as she started unloading.

"No lie, it's delicious." Cruz grabbed hold of the spoon and brought it back to take another taste. "Spicy."

Tatum grinned. "That's the sriracha powder. You hungry?"

"Starved." Sean clapped his hands together. "When do we eat?"

"When we get home." January abandoned her task and quickly retrieved her purse and jacket. "I'll call you tomorrow, Tate. Sean, we're leaving."

"But I just got here." Tatum laughed at Sean's little-boy whine. "And I'm sorry, babe, but your sister is a much better cook than you are."

"You aren't in enough trouble?" January asked and dragged him by the arm. "Save us some leftovers!" The door slammed behind them.

"How are you feeling?" Cruz set a gentle hand on her shoulder and squeezed. The sensations rocketing through her, the emotions swirling as if they couldn't grab hold, nearly overwhelmed her.

"Better than I should." She got a new spoon and

stirred the sauce. The pasta dough was resting in the fridge and the breadsticks were doing a final proof before baking. Imperishable staples had saved her sanity this afternoon as she waited for word—any word—from Cruz. Reducing the heat, she took over her sister's unloading. "I see you got my list."

"Might have been easier to tell me what not to get." They reached for the fresh basil at the same time, his hand covering hers.

She glanced up, heart pounding, as he tugged her close and slipped his arms around her. "I'm glad you're all right." He brushed his lips over her forehead, across her mouth. "All I wanted was to be with you today."

"That's all I wanted, too." Emotion clogged her throat. "I'm feeling a bit unsteady, Cruz. I don't know what's going on."

"I know." He smoothed her hair away from her face, his palm caressing her cheek. "I'm working on it and I think I'm making progress. But before we get into that, there's something you should know."

"Okay." She swallowed hard, braced herself.

He kissed her. Slow, deep, a kiss filled with such promise she cried out when he lifted his head. "Until this is all over I'm moving in." He inclined his head toward the oversize duffel by the front door.

"Oh." She blinked, tried but for the life of her couldn't come up with an argument. "All right. Just one problem." She lifted a hand, tapped a finger against his lips. "I never got around to furnishing the guest room, so you'll have to share my bed." Her smile was slow, deliberate, and filled with as much promise as she'd felt in his kiss. "That work okay for you?"

"That works just fine."

"Good. Now here's a beer." She stepped out of his arms, pulled a bottle out of one of the bags and handed it to him. "Go sit down and relax while I finish dinner."

It was, Tatum thought as he wandered off with his beer into her living room, a routine she could most definitely get used to.

THERE WAS LITTLE that made Tatum happier than a full fridge, a warm sauce simmering on the stove and a pile of fresh pasta awaiting its baptism by boiling water. The aroma of fresh-baked garlic breadsticks wafted through the air, along with the sounds of classic Hollywood soundtracks drifting from her television. Cruz was stretched out on her sofa, arms crossed over his chest, beer by his side, sound asleep.

Suddenly the full fridge, et cetera, didn't hold the appeal it had moments before. She lowered herself to the sofa, careful not to touch him for fear of waking him. Given what had happened last night, she couldn't fathom when he would have slept, and while she had certain plans for the evening, she couldn't bring herself to wake him.

Dinner would wait. Her plans would wait. Wanting nothing more than to wash the day away, she headed into her bedroom suite to shower and change.

By the time she emerged, damp hair clipped to the top of her head, towel wrapped around her wet body and knotted between her breasts, the sun had dropped low enough to cast the garden outside her window into the prettiest of shadows. She'd seen the bruises forming along her side, on her hip and torso, felt the aches fade beneath the pulsating hot water. She was lucky, she told herself. Things could have been, could be, so much worse.

"And here I was thinking you should have woken me up."

Tatum smiled, keeping her back to him. "You needed to sleep."

"I'm not complaining." He stepped into her room, moved in behind her, rested his hands on her bare, damp shoulders. "I'm glad I didn't miss this." His lips brushed away the droplets of water on her skin and made her shiver. "I missed you today."

She lifted a hand to cover one of his. "I missed you, too." She turned, tilted her chin up to meet his eyes. "Are you hungry?"

"More than I have been in a long time." His thumbs caressed her shoulders before his fingers trailed down her arms. With one hand he pulled the clip in her hair free. The damp tangles dropped over the backs of his fingers.

"I meant for dinner."

"Did you?" He dipped his head, placed a whisper of a kiss on her mouth. "I've never been less interested in food. How about you?"

"I—"

His smile told her he was teasing. "Why don't you get dressed and we'll—"

"How about I don't?" She reached down and released the knot and let the towel drop to the floor. She was already reaching for the hem of his T-shirt when he stepped back to admire his view. "You're severely over-dressed for what I have in mind, Detective Medina."

"Tatum, I—" The words seemed to catch in his throat. He caught her hands as they slipped beneath the fabric of his shirt. "You were nearly run over by a car just hours ago."

"Nearly." She'd expected the protest, the concern. But as much as it touched her, she wasn't in any mood to add another frustration to her life. She could deal with the bruises and aches. She couldn't deal with waiting any longer to be with him.

She tightened her hold on his hands, made certain he was looking at her when she spoke. "The gift almost being killed gives you is you realize how much you want to live." She slid one hand up his chest, her fingers tingling at the feel of his taut form. She curved it around his neck, drew his face down and to her. "I know what I want, Cruz. I want you."

When she kissed him, it was with all the passion and attraction she'd felt since he'd first stepped into her restaurant. She'd thought of, dreamed of this moment to the point of distraction. There had never been another man who had stoked desire to the levels he did simply by walking into the room. His beard scratched gently at her skin, heightening her senses as her mind fought to keep up with her body.

If he had any reservations, they seemed to evaporate the moment his lips captured hers. She couldn't get enough of him. While her lips pressed and pushed, her tongue seeking and tempting, her hands shifted and moved down his back and under the edge of the fabric so she could flatten her palms against his back. Her bare breasts tightened against the roughness, and when he lifted his mouth for the mere moment it took to pull his shirt over his head, she cried out.

A fraction of a second was too long to wait. For him, too, and he locked his hands around her waist, turning her toward the bed as he lifted her against him. The moment her breasts met his bare skin she gasped, tore her mouth free and dropped her head back to expose her throat.

"This isn't going to be slow." She heard more determination than seduction in his voice. Even if she'd had the compulsion to slow things down she couldn't have. Her mind could no longer function beneath the intensity of sensation sparking through her. Everywhere their skin touched, every step he took closer to her bed left rational thoughts spinning into oblivion.

She felt the mattress brush against the back of her legs before he lowered her to the bed. They stood there, in the barely-there light, the only sound in the room their ragged breathing. "You're still overdressed." She brushed the backs of her fingers against his cheek, drew her fingers down the tight brown skin of his throat, his shoulders, around to his chest.

He was hers. She saw it in the dazed passion of his dark gaze, felt it in the restless, exploring touch of his hands. Felt it beat against her palms as she pressed her hands flat against where his heart resided.

She slid her hands down, lower, to the waistband of his jeans, made quick, determined work of the zipper and button that kept them separated. His breath hot against her face, she lifted her chin, found his mouth waiting and dived in. Tatum felt the hard length of him straining, throbbing behind the jeans she couldn't help him discard fast enough. "Cruz." She murmured his name and the answering moan she received as she wrapped her hand around him had whatever reason she had left shattering.

His hips moved, pushing him more firmly into her hold. His breathing came in short, determined gasps as she adjusted her hold, moved up and down his hot arousal.

"Enough," he growled and reached down to catch her hand. "You keep touching me like that and I won't be able to wait."

"Maybe I don't want you to wait." She pressed her lips against his throat, gently nipped with her teeth. "Maybe I want to see exactly what I do to you."

"Tatum." He released her hand, caught her face between his palms and, after kissing her so deeply she lost her breath, pressed his forehead to hers. "I left the condoms in my bag."

She smiled, slid her hands down his sides and pushed his jeans down over his muscular thighs. He kicked them free and sucked in a breath that echoed through the room as she grasped him once more and brought him to her mouth.

It only took one open-mouthed kiss on the most sensitive part of him to have him reaching down and hauling her to her feet. "When I come, I want it to be inside you. Not before." His mouth took hers again, his tongue doing now what she had only dreamed of. "Let me go get—"

"Nightstand drawer." She locked her hands around his wrists when he started to set her away. "You aren't the only one who planned ahead."

He stood there, his hands deep in her hair, looking down at her in a way that made her heart skip a beat. "I love you, Tatum."

"Because I bought condoms?" she teased.

"No." Another kiss, one that all but melted her bones. "Because you're you."

"I also opened the box," she prodded. "I didn't want to waste time…" She'd barely uttered the words before he had the drawer open, the foil packet ripped and the condom in hand. She couldn't tear her eyes away as he covered himself, yet another form of protection that had love swelling inside of her.

She sat on the edge of the mattress, moved back as he moved over her. Tatum lay back, reached up her arms to encircle his neck as he stretched out above her. She opened for him, her legs falling apart and he settled as if he'd been made for her. "Now," she whispered and arched her back. She could feel him, hard, covered and ready, against the part of her that was waiting and wanting. "Cruz, please."

She slipped her foot up the back of his leg, wrapped herself around him as he pressed into her, full, throbbing and thick. She moaned, absorbing both him and the sensations rippling through her as he joined their bodies. Her hips moved in time with his thrusts, slow at first, giving her time to adjust to him, adjust to them.

"Look at me, Tatum." His rough order had her blinking through the stars in her eyes, and when she gazed into his eyes she knew that this was where she belonged. In this moment. With this man. "Tatum?"

She lifted her hand, touched his cheek. He was hers. All hers. "Take us over." Her other leg came up, her thighs locked around him, pulling him in deeper as his breath moved out in a rush. "Take us over together."

She wanted to keep them here, in this moment, but she could feel the pressure and passion building, her body igniting under his touch and invasion. She met him, move for move, thrust for thrust, and when he fused his mouth to hers and erupted inside of her, she crested that final edge and soared with him.

The orgasm tore through her, locking her around him as she hovered in that perfect moment of ecstasy. Her cries caught in his mouth as he held her and she rode it out. When she came down from the high, when he lay in her arms pressing light butterfly kisses along her jaw, she smiled. He was hers. This man was, and always would be hers.

"Cruz." She murmured his name, drew her fingers through his hair. "I love you, too."

"Yeah?" He shifted, keeping them linked as he drew the sheets over them.

"Yeah." She snuggled into him, feeling herself begin to drift. "Most definitely yeah."

EXTRICATING HIMSELF FROM Tatum's arms, Cruz reached over and lifted his vibrating and buzzing cell off her nightstand, careful not to wake her. The message from his LT acknowledging that he had enough to keep him moving forward with the case should have eased his mind.

Instead, he turned his phone over and lay there, in the dark silence, unable to sleep.

Tatum let out a sigh and shifted, her still damp hair spilling over her shoulders and across his chest. He dropped a hand down, took a moment to appreciate the feel of it sliding through his fingers.

This wasn't supposed to happen.

Moonlight streamed through the skylight above, casting its gentle shadows at the sliding doors into the garden beyond her house that, growing up, was a dwelling he could barely have imagined.

He'd found paradise, a sanctuary he hadn't known existed within the confines of the city he called home. He'd liked her condo, the practical, convenient space, but this place removed from their real lives felt almost like a mirage in the middle of a crazy, whirlwind desert. He'd known, well, he'd hoped they'd end up right where they were, wrapped up with and in each other to the point of distraction.

But falling in love?

That wasn't supposed to happen.

He trailed his fingers up and down her arm and a surge of masculine pride shot through him when she moaned in her sleep and snuggled closer. He turned his head, closed his eyes and inhaled the floral fragrance of the shampoo she'd used only moments before he'd seen her standing at that window, glistening, beautiful and perfect. It was in that moment, before he'd touched her, before he'd made love to her, that he realized it fully.

He was in love with Tatum Colton.

Not only in love, but in serious like. She made him laugh. At life, at himself. She made him think. She drove him nuts. And she made him worry. He'd never been as afraid as he'd been last night when he'd gotten that call. He understood now why some people believed love made you weak. How could he function, how could he do his job knowing one wrong decision, one wrong step, could take him away from her? And he was bound to, wasn't he? Something was bound to come between them, no matter how hard he worked to stop it.

Was it selfish to want this to last? To want to stay here, in this place, hidden from everything out there, where the two of them could live off her cooking and each other? Of course it was. But he could still dream it.

This moment couldn't last. Not with what he had to do. But he'd draw it out as long as he could. He'd do whatever it took to keep her safe, sacrifice whatever he needed to. He had hours, maybe days before he confirmed who was behind True's involvement with the drug cartel that had its hooks in the city. Until that time, until he had to do what needed doing, he'd take what he had now and embrace it. Enjoy it.

He'd love her.

And hope, when all this was over, that she'd forgive him.

Chapter Thirteen

Tatum couldn't remember the last time she slept so late. Or so well. When she opened her eyes and looked at the bedside clock, she had to take an extra beat to compute what she was seeing. And…she sniffed the air. Ahhh, coffee and…

She rolled over, stretched and let out a very satisfied sigh before she sat up. The bedroom doorway suddenly filled with a very sexy, very shirtless, and barefoot detective. No one man should ever look that good in a pair of unbuttoned jeans. Even as her cheeks warmed and she tugged the sheet up to cover herself, she smiled. "Good morning. What's this?" She scooted back against the brass headboard as he approached with a tray. When she looked down, tears misted her eyes. "You made me waffles." She inclined her head. "In the shape of a heart."

"I did." He sat on the other side of the tray, scooted it closer so she could get a look at the berry-laden syrup spilling over the crisp, golden cakes. "I heard somewhere they're your comfort food. Which explains your fetish for waffle irons."

She picked up a knife and fork, cut, and took a bite,

her starved palate singing in response. "Oh, wow." She took another bite, swallowed and sighed. "These are amazing. What's this?" She scraped her fork over the white melted into the grooves. She tasted, frowned.

"The Medina special ingredient." He leaned forward and kissed a drop of syrup off the corner of her mouth. "Marshmallow fluff."

Tatum gaped. "I, um. Okay." The laughter bubbled up from her toes. "I guess I've neglected to test that particular ingredient's superpower. Consider me a convert." The light, sweet, ultra-crispy texture definitely deserved closer inspection. "I need to eat quick and get going. I'm already late."

"If you mean for the fish and farmers market, it's already taken care of." He nudged her coffee forward. "Ty and Sam have already headed over. You're taking the day off."

"I most certainly am not." That she could declare that even as her body throbbed like one large bruise was a minor miracle. "Do you know what this week is?"

"I know about Friday and I know how important it is." He sat back as if he'd mentally rehearsed this conversation. "I also know you were nearly killed the night before last and are lucky to be alive. I think you can take one day off to recover."

She shook her head, unable to stop shoveling waffles into her face. "Can't. I don't even know what I'm going to serve Friday night yet. I need time—"

"You need time to focus and create and make this the best dinner service True has ever offered. This seems the perfect place to do so."

"I need my people around me. I need to tell them what's going on."

"You can do that on a video call later this afternoon, once everyone's in. This isn't a discussion, Tatum. You aren't leaving here today. Tomorrow is another story, but for today, I need you safe and protected. And by protected, I've got two officers outside keeping an eye on things while I go to work."

"You really think someone's going to try to get at me again? Cruz, if I don't turn up—"

"They'll think they succeeded in putting you out of commission, which is precisely what they hoped to do. Just be grateful it wasn't permanent. You've got the best people working for you, Tatum. If you can't trust them for one day…"

That he trailed off and seemed to be waiting for her to finish the thought had her grumbling around her breakfast. Previous conversations pushed back on her, and as she swallowed, her mind cleared. "You've put your faith in Ty. That must mean you don't think he's a suspect anymore."

"No, I don't." He quickly filled her in on Ty's situation with his daughter and grandchildren.

"I knew he had a daughter, but he never talks about her. Or them." Tatum sat back, coffee clasped in her palms. "I supposed I should have." Maybe if she'd been paying attention to other people's lives as much as she did her own, she would know a lot of things. "Are they okay?"

"Yeah, they're fine. And Ty's going to be our go-to until the case works itself out. I told him everything I could. And he won't say anything until we're on the other side of this. And we will be soon, Tatum." He lifted a hand to her face and she leaned in to his touch. "I promise."

"You're making progress, then." She turned and pressed her lips into his palm. "Tell me. Please."

"The license plate you caught belongs to the same car I saw that night at the restaurant. We've traced it to a company here in town. A company we suspect is a shell company for the drug cartel. We have an all-points out for it, but I'm betting it's been ditched."

"Ditched?"

"I'd be surprised if we don't find a burned-out shell in the next couple of days. They want you out of the way for some reason. We won't get lucky a third time."

"All right." As much as she hated to surrender, the idea of spending the day alone in her kitchen, with her cookbooks, sounded more appealing by the minute. "Will you still be working at the restaurant?"

"I will. I'm going in around one. Ty's going to have you call in on video chat around three. He'll have told them you're taking an inspiration day. His suggestion. He said they'd understand that once you let them know about Constance Swan's reservation."

"You two just thought of everything, didn't you? Oh! We have a catering job tomorrow." She snapped her fingers. "Sam and Quallis—"

"Sam's on top of it."

"He'll need to get the final details from Richard—"

"Yep. He knows. They all know. You've trained them well, Tatum. Now let them do their jobs."

Tatum flinched, his words hitting too close to a target she'd closed off months before. "I'm a control freak, I know." She pulled her knees in as Cruz moved the tray, wrapped her arms tight and locked herself in. "Since you've been going through the files, you probably know about Daria." Even now, all these months later, the thought of her friend could still make her heart weep. "She quit because I didn't let up. It was a hard lesson to learn, losing her that way."

"Then don't learn it again." He leaned forward and kissed her. "I need to go into the station, catch up on a few things before I head to True."

"Okay." She grabbed hold of him and hung on, deepening the kiss. "Did you already shower?"

"I did." His mouth lingered, lightly trailed down the side of her throat. "But I can always scrub your back?"

"Now that—" she kissed him again "—sounds like the perfect start to the morning."

IT HAD TAKEN him a while to form his plan of attack when it came to convincing Tatum to stay home for the day, but the time had been worth it. She was safely ensconced in her house, a pair of patrol officers securely in place and on watch, and a grocery delivery system on call should his shopping run last night not have provided her the appropriate supplies. He had a good four hours before he needed to get over to True and back up Ty during their video conference call between Tatum and the rest of the staff.

He'd barely taken a seat at his desk when his LT appeared. "Progress report?" She stirred a steaming cup of what could loosely be called coffee and blinked as if trying to stay awake.

"Ah, right. Here?"

"In my office." Luce headed down the hall before Cruz could reply. He found his commanding officer slouched in her chair looking completely exhausted. "Took Sheryl to the hospital last night." She smothered a yawn. "Braxton-Hicks contractions."

"False labor?"

"Four hours' worth. When your time comes, save up your vacation time because you're going to need it."

"Do you know something I don't?"

Luce looked at him, gaze narrowed. "It looks like maybe I do. You and Tatum Colton seem to have set off some sparks from what I've heard. That going to be a problem?"

"No, ma'am."

"Cut the ma'am crap, Cruz, and sit down. Don't be snippy. If your relationship with Colton is going to complicate the case—"

"It won't," he repeated. "Did the warrant for Richard Kirkman's financials come in?"

"Pending. Should be late tomorrow, Thursday morning at the latest."

Cruz cursed. He needed that information now. "Why the delay?"

"The bank is playing hardball. Sicced their lawyers on the assistant DA assigned to the case. The woman's already juggling four big cases, so her attention's a bit divided. We'll get it, don't worry."

"There's a catering job being run tomorrow. I'm hoping that'll give us the last of the evidence we're looking for."

"Pretty sneaky, using the catering service."

"But it makes sense. Talking to Ty and Tatum, I

found it was Kirkman who brought up the idea after Tatum had True cater her father's funeral reception. The timing lines up. Distribution in the neighborhoods around True increased in the weeks following. They only have one continuous customer, so I'm going to check that out on my way in today. I was able to access the delivery schedule. They have a big one coming in right before this job. That has to be it."

"Move carefully," Luce advised. "I know you're anxious to get this case behind you, but we need it closed clean with as many big fish in the net as we can catch."

"That's the plan." He already had Ty working on a way to conceal his presence in the loading bay so he could observe the delivery. "Kirkman's the inside guy. He's been the point person from the jump. Whether he had Daria Naughton killed or not, he was certainly there to help pick up the pieces. Not that any of that will matter if we don't get into his financials."

"Agreed." His LT nodded. "And what about Tatum Colton? How much have you told her?"

"About Kirkman? Nothing. She still thinks I'm looking." He hated, no, he loathed lying to her, but he didn't have a choice. "Whatever buttons we've pushed, they see Tatum as the threat, not me." That was the only thing that still nudged at him. "I'll know more tomorrow. Then once we have what we need to use against Kirkman, we can bring him in, flip him on the cartel and finally shut them down." *And Johnny will be able to rest in peace.*

"Draw up the arrest warrant so it's ready to go the second you need it," Lieutenant Graves said. "I'll get you a backup team for when you need, and yes, before you ask, I put out the alert on his name. He tries to make a break for it, we'll be ready. Surveillance on his residence will be in place by tonight. He makes some weird move at True, you phone it in, understood?"

"Yeah." He let out a long breath. "The fallout from this, it's going to be bad." He hadn't meant to voice it. Didn't want to. "Even if everything goes right."

"You knew that going in," Luce reminded him. "It's your call how much you think Ms. Colton needs to know. You sure you don't want to fill her in?"

"I'm sure. She's a terrible liar." He managed a quick smile as if he'd made a joke. He'd do what he had to in order to protect her. As for protecting her business? He couldn't let himself dwell on that. "I need to catch up on some stuff before I head in to the restaurant. Hope Sheryl has that baby pretty soon, LT. You look beat."

"Spoken like a true man," Luce said with a strained smile. "Just for that I'm putting you on the babysitting list. Go on. Get going." She waved him out. "And Cruz?"

"Yeah?" He glanced over his shoulder.

"Be careful."

He supposed she meant with the case, with his safety. But as he returned to his desk and dug into the mounting evidence against Richard Kirkman, he had to wonder if maybe she was referring to his heart.

KIRKMAN'S USE OF True's catering service as a decoy was the inspiration for Cruz's surreptitious visit to Belma Trade, located, according to their website, on the sixth floor of a high-rise half a mile from True. The small business district housed multiple financial investment and law firms, as well as one well-known hole-in-the-wall pizzeria.

Cruz called in and paid for an order for three large and loaded pies, gave Belma Trade as the delivery address, then parked across the street from the building and waited.

Less than a half hour later, he spotted the delivery person, familiar blue visor on his curl-encased head, heading toward the office building. When he ducked inside, Cruz waited a good few minutes, then got out, tugged his shirtsleeves down and straightened the tie he'd donned. The next second, the delivery guy emerged, a confused, anxious look on his face. He turned, looked to the number on the building and rechecked his phone.

Cruz jogged over. "Hey! Are those for Belma Trade?"

The kid practically sagged with relief. "Yeah, that you?" He pointed to the spinning glass door. "You know your offices are empty, right?"

"No one up there?" Cruz pulled out his wallet.

"Place is a ghost town. Name's on the directory, but it's all dead space. They move without telling you?" The kid laughed but didn't seem convinced it was funny.

"Not exactly." Cruz held a fifty up between two fingers. "Anyone asks, the delivery went fine. No surprises. You get me?"

"I got you, yeah. You want these?"

"Absolutely." Cruz hefted the pies out of the kid's hand, and the kid took the money and walked away.

He had the pieces. All the pieces, as well as the framework, and finally, he could see the complete picture. A picture he was almost reticent to finish. Whatever happened now, he'd done what he'd set out to do: he'd have a major supplier of narcotics off the streets and soon he'd have leverage to find out exactly who pulled the trigger and shot Johnny. Nothing else, nothing else, he told himself firmly, mattered.

He didn't believe that for one flat second.

When he walked back into the station, he dropped off one of the pizzas to the front desk, carried the other two up to Narcotics, where the best group of detectives had helped him get to this point. Those detectives gave him a bit of a cheer when he left the pies in the break room, but he didn't stop until he reached his LT's office. He wasn't hungry. He wasn't sure he'd ever be hungry again. He rapped his knuckles on the doorframe, ducked his head inside. "Hey, LT?"

"Yeah?" She glanced up from her computer. "Well?"

"We got them."

THE COMBINATION OF ADRENALINE, anticipation and potential triumph made for one powerful fuel that catapulted Tatum through the week. Armed with a plethora of new menu ideas and riding high on the positive benefits of excellent and mind-numbing sex with one seriously hot cop, she had True and its employees buzzing like serious worker bees determined to please their Queen.

Word that Constance Swan would be dining with them on Friday had been the injection they'd all needed and everyone was on board to present the best food, the best experience of their careers.

Friday morning, do-or-die day, she was up and moving well before the sun, unable to sleep. But Cruz was out, sprawled on his stomach in her bed, black hair a stark contrast against her daisy yellow sheets. The sheet currently riding low across his narrow and quite agile hips. As the barely-there rays of the morning sun peeked through the skylight, she sat for a moment, tempted to trail her fingers down and along the toned, taut, tempting sight of him. It wouldn't take much. This she'd learned fairly quickly. But he'd been wiped out last night, and not, funnily enough, because of her.

She curled her hand into a fist, resisting the urge, and grabbed her yellow robe before padding into the kitchen, where she put on the coffee and set to work.

A little over an hour later, coffee in hand and the homemade cinnamon buns she'd made last night after getting home from work securely in the oven, she sat at the table with her computer and notebook, and got to work.

When she sniffed the air a while later, she set a mental clock, and sure enough, not ten minutes after, Cruz wandered in, nose first. "Woman, you are magic to wake up to, you know that?" He stopped long enough to capture her mouth with his, his hand massaging the back of her neck as she leaned into his kiss. "That said, if you don't stop baking I'm going to have to get my butt back to the gym." Cruz grabbed what was now his coffee mug off the counter and filled it.

"I think we're managing just fine with our own workout routine, don't you?"

"We're getting by. So." He took a seat. "You ready for tonight?"

"As ready as I can be." Nerves were taking hold; she could feel their tiny catlike talons creeping around inside her, leaving marks in their track. "I keep telling myself it's all going to be fine. Even if she hates us, there's no such thing as bad publicity, right?" He didn't laugh with her. He barely smiled as he sipped his coffee. "Hey." She reached out, closed her hand over his. "Everything okay?"

"Yeah, of course." His lips quirked up. "I just feel like we haven't stopped for a while."

"That's because we haven't. Last night you said you had something you wanted to talk to me about. I assume it's the case?"

"Yeah." He nodded, caught her hand when she pulled away. "Yeah, it's about the case. You have some time now?"

"Sure. Oh, wait a second. Hold that thought." She practically bounced out of her chair when the oven timer went off. She nearly swooned when she pulled the pan of fluffy, springy, fragrant rolls out. "Are you a gloopy icing kinda guy?" She set the pan on the counter and retrieved the batch of cream cheese icing off the back counter.

"Isn't everyone, with cinnamon rolls?" He stood, walked over and, coffee in hand, watched her slather the still steaming buns. When she started to lick her finger, he reached out, took hold and brought her fingers to his mouth, kissing and licking the icing clean.

"These are just as good warm as they are hot," she murmured, shifting and moving closer to him.

"I have no doubt." He brushed his sugarcoated lips across hers and she wondered if she'd ever tasted anything so completely wonderful. "But about that conversation."

"Right. The case." Because she knew it had to happen sometime, she put some distance between them and slid a knife around the edge of the pan. "I've been assuming no news is good news."

"We found the car that ran you down in the parking lot. It hadn't been burned out, but it was stripped. Registration information shows it was reported stolen three weeks ago. The plates were from another car altogether, so I'm afraid that's a dead end."

"Meaning?"

"Meaning whoever this is, they still have you in their sights."

"And you're here." She focused on the buns because there wasn't anything she could do about the other. "I've been back at the restaurant for days. Nothing's happened. Everyone's been great and as normal as usual."

"Yeah. That's what's worrying me."

"Well, I can't let it worry me." She took a deep, controlled breath. "Today is literally the biggest day, the biggest opportunity of my career. It can and I'm hoping will set up everything that comes next. So unless you're going to tell me to cancel dinner reservations tonight—"

"I'm not."

"But you did consider that, didn't you?" She may have only been sleeping with him for a few days, but there wasn't any doubt in her mind he was hedging that answer.

"I did. Things are…moving fast. Faster at this point than I think I can stop."

Her throat tightened, frustrated and disappointed tears pressing for release. "If that's your way of telling me you were right and I was wrong, congratulations."

She locked her jaw, refused to look at him, and the iced buns wavered before her eyes.

"Tatum—"

"You're choosing to tell me this now, today of all days." She finally found the courage to look him in the eyes.

"I…" He seemed to be struggling.

"Give me today." She could feel herself begin to shake. "Tomorrow we can sit down and hash it all out, but please, Cruz." She lifted a hand to his face. "Please just give me today."

He turned his head, kissed the inside of her palm, in the same way she'd done to him days before. "This isn't going to go away, Tatum. No matter how much you want it to."

"I know that." Did she? Everything about the last few weeks had been almost surreal, from being suspected of being a drug trafficker to having an undercover cop in her kitchen who then ended up in her bed. There wasn't anything about the days since she'd met Cruz Medina that weren't completely out of the ordinary for her, so why wouldn't she be able to keep pretending everything was fine? "Tell me one thing." She tried to keep her voice steady. "Did you mean it the other night when you said you loved me?"

"I did. I do. I wouldn't have said it if I didn't believe it."

"Then that's enough for today. You won't hurt me, Cruz. I believe that as much as I believe I've never loved anyone the way I love you. This matters." She caught his hand and clasped it between hers. "We matter. If we both acknowledge that, if we both accept it, we can tackle whatever happens. Together, right?"

His free hand came up and brushed her cheek, tucked a loose tendril of hair behind her ear. He smiled, a sad, resigned smile that didn't exactly make her heart leap. But at least it kept beating. "Together. Now." His gaze flicked to the counter. "Are you going to keep torturing me or am I finally going to get one of those cinnamon rolls?"

"This is a sign." Tatum was talking to herself again. Talking and pacing and examining each and every nook and cranny of True hours before they were scheduled to open. "This new seafood vendor is already exceeding my expectations." She lifted a fresh head-on prawn to inspect it. "Sorry little fella, but you are getting star billing tonight." She set it back on the ice on the plastic-wrap-covered tray and waved Colby to the refrigerator.

"How's she doing?" Ty's question had Cruz glancing over his shoulder. "She's been like a spinning top for the past two days. I don't think she's stopped to breathe."

"She has. It's called crashing," Cruz said, then offered a sheepish grin. "Sorry. That was a bit crass, I suppose."

"Only a bit. What's going on with Kirkman? You get what you need yesterday when you followed him on the catering job?"

"I think so." Cruz angled his head and urged Ty to follow him into the break room. Never in his wildest dreams would he have considered Ty his partner in all this, but the man had proven a worthy one, working with him to gather information and keep an eye on people

Cruz couldn't. A quick check of the locker rooms confirmed they were alone. "Kirkman accepted a delivery yesterday afternoon. Had them load it right into the catering van. I couldn't get anywhere near it."

"So you don't know what was in it?"

"I only know Sam and Pike helped load up the van with the food orders and Richard headed out. When he came back, the van was empty."

What he had managed to do earlier in the week was put a tracking device on the van. His people knew everywhere that van had gone in the past three days and it hadn't gone near any of the addresses listed on the delivery invoices.

"Bastard really is using Tatum's place to distribute drugs. There won't be a hole deep enough for him," Ty said. He started to say something else, but Cruz held up a hand, motioned to Ty to look busy.

Ty shifted to the coffee machine and pushed Brew.

"You two going to join us or not?" Sam sounded more stressed than Cruz had ever seen him. "No main entrée pizzas tonight, Cruz. Tatum wants you working prep with Chester."

"Understood." Cruz nodded and straightened his jacket.

"Ty, you've got pastries. Remember not to overdo it on the saffron."

"Right." Ty nodded. "It's going to be fine, Sam. We all know what we have to do."

"Good, good." Sam let out an uneasy laugh. "Sorry. I guess I'm wound tight. Tatum called me into her office earlier. After this weekend she's going to put me in charge of the catering side of things. Including the menu." He straightened and beamed with pride. "She says she trusts me with it. Best news I've had in a long time. One step closer to my own place. Catering for True. Can you believe it?"

"You're going to do great," Cruz assured him. "And yes, I can. Once we get through this weekend, we'll celebrate. Maybe even get Tatum to join us."

"Yeah, well, we all know who has an inside track on that happening. You guys get to work, okay? We've got food to prepare."

"What's going to happen?" Ty asked when they were alone again. "After?"

"I don't know. But I plan to do everything I can to minimize the fallout." He offered a tight smile and together they returned to the kitchen to help make Tatum's dreams come true.

Chapter Fourteen

"T-minus thirty minutes to open!" Colby yelled out as she rinsed a huge colander of mussels under running water. "Let's get it done, people!"

"Look at her, all cheerleader." Susan, tablet in hand, paced in front of the serving area where Chester and Pike were busy loading dishes onto the shelves. "Front of house looks good. Everyone's pressed and polished. Don't worry." She held up her hand when Tatum started to comment. "They don't look like they're trying too hard. Everything is just tip-top. Promise."

"Good, okay." Tatum glanced at the clock, which at times seemed to jump into warp speed. "We've got two and a half hours before Constance is due to arrive. Just do what we've been doing and everything will be fine."

"I've got you coming out to greet her shortly after eight thirty. That still work?"

"Yep." Tatum tightened her apron band. "But feel free to remind me. Where's Richard?"

"He had to take a call. He should be…yeah, here he is. You ready?"

"Absolutely." Richard smoothed a hand down the front of his suit jacket.

"Everything okay?" Tatum recognized one of his nervous twitches.

"Yeah, fine. Just had a call from Nancy. Nothing to worry about." He slapped his hands together. "Tonight is going to be one for the books, I don't have any doubt. I'm going to head out, do one last check. Good luck, Tatum."

"You, too." Relieved to know the space beyond the kitchen was in good hands with both Richard and Susan, she felt a little bubble of apprehension burst. They'd spent the last two days rearranging some of the kitchen equipment to make room for the large paella pans she'd purchased, enough for one per table. She'd gone back and forth between single-serving plates, single-serving pans and family-style. Given the inspiration for tonight's menu had been Cruz and his Spanish heritage, she'd taken the chance and gone with family. The rest of the meal, appetizers, salads, and desserts, would be served in their normal way, but the paella, when ordered, would steal the show.

Which meant it was time to start. Paella done the right way took dedicated time, and that was where Tatum was putting her energy. Everything was at her fingertips, from pans to rice, seasonings and seafood. Spicy chorizo they'd made fresh in-house was ready to be cooked, organic chicken was cut up and undergoing its precook treatment of salt and pepper and a hint of smoky paprika. She could already smell and taste the herbs and spices permeating the steamy air of the kitchen.

She took a deep breath, let it out and found her gaze shifting to Cruz. He was watching her, those dark eyes of his so penetrating, so piercing. So perfect. He gave her that smile she'd come to love, the one that said so much without a word, that she touched a hand to her heart, absorbing the support, confidence and approval.

Embracing all the encouragement he sent her, she turned to her stove and got to work.

WRIST-DEEP IN CHOPPED onions and peppers, Cruz felt his phone vibrate against his hip. He glanced up at the clock. The doors had been open for over an hour. Orders were brisk and constant. Constance Swan was set to arrive any second.

He swore. No cell phones were allowed in the kitchen, but he didn't have a choice. Not with the case about to burst wide open. Stepping to the side, he turned his back on Chester and the prep area and pulled out his cell. Seeing his LT's number did not make him feel better.

"You got this for a few, Ches?" Cruz asked his fellow prep chef. "I have to take this."

"Tatum sees a phone in here she'll skin you like a chicken." But Chester nodded. "Be quick."

"Right." Nothing like having a twentysomething kid tell you what to do. He ducked into the hall and hurried into the storage room. Ignoring the voice mail she'd left, he quickly called Luce back. "What's going on, LT? I'm up to my neck—"

"Kirkman's booked a one a.m. flight for two to Mexico. Saw his name pop on the alert we set up. He's running, Cruz. He's running tonight. And he's running scared, because he didn't even try to hide this."

"Why now?" It didn't make sense. Or did it? The

chaos of the night, the frenetic energy spinning in and around True. What better time to disappear when people would be too busy to notice. "Only reason to do that would be if he was running scared, but I don't think he is. I watched him on those deliveries yesterday, LT." He'd barely seen a hint of nerves on the man as he conducted a drug handoff as easily as one might cash a check.

"We can ask him why in questioning. We're out of time, Cruz. You need to make a decision."

"What decision? We pick him up when he gets home."

"We just took his wife into custody. She was on her way to the airport, two suitcases and passports with her. She had instructions to meet him at the gate. If we want him, we'll have to grab him at the restaurant."

No. Cruz felt the blood drain from his face. No, not here. Not tonight. He glanced over his shoulder. "LT, I can't do it to her. Tonight means—"

"We have one shot at this, Cruz."

"Then grab him at the airport!" Anywhere but here.

"There's a workers' strike, remember? The logistics would be a nightmare and we risk the chance of losing him. We have a clear shot at him right where he is. I warned you this could happen. You want to close your case or protect your girlfriend?"

Cruz's mind raced. *Girlfriend* seemed such an inadequate descriptor for what he considered Tatum to be. She was…well, she was just it for him, wasn't she? It hadn't taken long for him to understand he didn't see—didn't want—a future that didn't include her in it and yet…

And yet Johnny was lying there hooked up to machines thanks to someone lurking in the shadows of this case. Tatum could be everything to him but Johnny would never have that chance. And Cruz couldn't let the people responsible get away.

"Ticktock, Medina." Luce's voice snapped him back. "What's it going to be?"

"Do it." As he said the words he could all but feel the connection between him and Tatum snap. "But I'll take lead. Have the team meet me around the corner."

"It doesn't have to be you, Cruz."

Yes, it does. "It's my case." He wasn't going to shirk the responsibility just because of his feelings for Tatum. Once he started down that slope, it wouldn't stop. "We go in fifteen."

When Cruz hung up and turned around, he found Ty standing in the doorway. Arms crossed over his chest, eyes cool as a freshly honed blade. "What are you doing, Cruz?"

"What I have to." He tried to move past, but Ty stopped him with a solid hand on his chest. "Let me by. I need to talk to Tatum."

"It's too late. She's out on the floor."

Cruz steeled his jaw, clenched his fists. "Richard's skipping town. There's nothing I can do about this, Ty."

"Sure there is." Ty's voice turned cold. "You just don't want to. No." He pushed Cruz back, took a step toward him. "If you're going to walk out on her you go out the back." He pointed out the loading bay door. Unwilling to take on another fight for the evening, Cruz acquiesced and walked away. "You disappoint me, Cruz."

Cruz froze at Ty's statement. "I thought you understood what was really important. I guess I was wrong."

Nausea rolled thick and slippery through him. He did understand. He understood more than Ty could imagine. But he'd made a promise, and Cruz was nothing without his word. Tatum of all people would understand. Cruz reached up and unbuttoned his chef's jacket as he walked. He turned down the alley, tugged it off, wadded it up, and as he passed, tossed it into the dumpster. "Someday she'll understand."

TATUM MADE IT a point to greet a number of other guests before making her way to Constance Swan's table. Everyone in True was always given the same service, the same quality food and the same attention. As anxious as she was to connect, she slowed down, took her time. *Make it count.*

"Ms. Swan, it's lovely to meet you." Tatum shook the offered hand of the woman who could put True on the culinary map. Petite and far more slender than any food critic had a right to be, Constance Swan introduced her fellow dining companions. "Welcome, all of you." Tatum looked to each of them, Constance's publicist, her web designer, and her daughter Margaret, who looked to be about Tatum's age but had far more polish and presence than Tatum could ever hope to have. "I hope you're enjoying your evening at True so far."

"It's been sublime, and it's Constance, please."

Tatum gave Susan a glance that had her hostess moving away. "We were thrilled to hear you were interested in dining with us," Tatum continued. "I admit to taking advantage of the privilege and using the opportunity to stretch my cooking wings a bit." She motioned to the paella.

"It was a nice surprise," Constance told her. "I went to Spain on my honeymoon and had the best paella. I've talked about that trip and that meal often over the years."

"Spain was my father's favorite vacation spot," Margaret clarified.

"What you've given us here is as close to that experience as I could ever hope to recreate," Constance said. "Especially now that he's passed."

"My condolences," Tatum offered. "But I'm glad I could bring back some good memories. That's what food should be about, isn't it? Connecting with our emotions, our pasts. Our experiences. That's what I strive for every day I'm in the kitchen. Connections."

"Well, from where we are sitting you're accomplishing that perfectly."

Not wanting their food to get cold while they chatted, Tatum stepped back. "I'll leave you to your meal, then. Please, if you have any concerns or questions, I hope you won't hesitate to let Susan know. We'll do our best to accommodate you."

"I wonder." Constance caught her hand when she began to walk away. "If a tour of your kitchen would be possible? I would love to meet the staff who helped prepare such a wonderful meal."

"Absolutely. Only—" Tatum hesitated, glancing around the filled dining room "—would you be willing to wait until closer to the end of service? I'd be happy to send over another bottle of wine, on the house of course. Once we've caught up with orders I'd be pleased to give you a tour."

"That would be fine." Constance nodded. Tatum stole a look at the others seated at the table. Given their approving expressions, Tatum wondered if she'd just passed some kind of test.

"I'll have Susan bring you back as soon as…" Tatum trailed off at the unexpected flash of movement at the entrance by the bar. Uniformed officers flanked the glass doors outside. And three men with polished badges hanging around their necks stepped in.

Two of the men were utterly unfamiliar, but the third? That glossy hair, the neatly trimmed, thin mustache and beard. The determined spark in dark eyes that didn't miss a single thing. "Cruz." She hadn't realized she'd spoken out loud until she noticed Margaret turn her chin up.

No, this wasn't possible. She tried to swallow but couldn't. He wouldn't… He was supposed to be in the kitchen, working prep with Chester. It wasn't possible he'd…and yet it clearly was.

Tatum's breath caught in her chest. She reached out and grabbed the back of Constance's chair to stop her legs from folding. Cruz spoke to Susan, who, from behind her podium, turned her head and locked wide, disbelieving eyes on Tatum. Her gaze instantly shifted behind Tatum, to where Tatum had seen Richard moments before.

Richard.

A million questions flew through her mind in an instant, spinning around each other, too fast for her to even attempt to find an answer.

Of course. It was the only answer that made sense, wasn't it? Richard, who had access to her books, who had the run of the place whether she was here or not. Richard, who had been so solicitous and caring when her father had been killed. It had all been a ruse so he could get his claws deeper into the restaurant that may as well be her beating heart.

Cruz had told her this morning, warned her that he'd found the connection, but she hadn't wanted to listen. She hadn't wanted anything marring her perfect day, but she never, not in a thousand years, would have believed Cruz would use it against her. Not tonight.

"He wouldn't." Recalling that first night he'd come here, with that self-assured I'm-not-wrong attitude that had somehow slipped through whatever sense she might have had, she thought he would. *When someone first shows you who they are, believe it.* Her father's voice echoed in her mind.

But as he walked toward her, she looked at his face and knew. He pointed to the kitchen doors, and the two men with him took up position there, turning and holding up their hands when Ty, Quallis and Sam pushed their way out. Pike and Colby emerged as well, but were held back by Ty. Pike quickly ducked inside, and seconds later Chester and Bernadette joined their fellow employees; all shared the same dumbstruck, confused expression Tatum could only dream of wearing.

Her world moved into slow motion. Nothing made sense. And she could hear the ever so faint sound of her future beginning to crumble. She was peripherally aware of people grabbing their cell phones, recording every torturous moment, cementing True's reputation in online scandal even before she could remember how to breathe.

Cruz made his way through the tables as effortlessly as he'd slid into her heart. Conversation stilled as he came closer, as if muting customers as he passed.

"What's going on?" Richard's tight-throated question had Tatum's hand clenching around the back of Constance's chair. "Tatum, what's your sous-chef doing?"

Tatum couldn't stop herself. She stepped between them, planted a hand on Cruz's chest, her fingers brushing against the badge he wore, and lifted pleading eyes to his. "Don't do this now, Cruz. Please. Not tonight. Not here." Didn't he see? Couldn't he feel anything other than blind obligation and duty?

"I'm sorry, Tatum. I don't have a choice." While he kept his voice low, in the graveyard silence of True, everyone would hear. "There's nowhere for you to go, Richard. We have your wife in custody along with your passport. You need to come with me."

"You're a cop?" Richard's relief might have been comical if the entire situation wasn't so… Shakespearean. "You're a damned cop? Tatum, what the…you let an undercover cop into your kitchen?"

"Please," Cruz tried again. "Don't make this worse for Tatum."

Tatum went cold inside. There wasn't an ounce of warmth, not in her blood. Not in her body. Not in her heart. This was the man from the bar, the man she'd refused to believe. Not the man she'd fallen into bed with. And certainly not the man she'd fallen in love with.

"Worse than you're making it?" Richard scoffed. "Like that's possible."

"Are we really going to do this this way?" Cruz challenged Richard.

"Richard, please, just go with him," Tatum urged. "If it's a mistake—"

"Of course this is a mistake! What are the charges? I demand to know what I'm being charged with." Richard turned gleaming, if not defiant, eyes on Tatum. "Tell me why you're arresting me. I want witnesses." In that moment she knew exactly what he was doing. And she wasn't going to let him get away with it. "I want everyone to know."

"He's arresting you because you're a drug dealer," Tatum said before Cruz could find the words. He reached out for her, but she stepped away. The last thing, the very last thing she could deal with right now was Detective Cruz Medina touching her. "You've been using my business to distribute drugs in the city, Richard. You've been using me. Using all of us. Was it you who tried to run me down the other night? Did you try to kill me?"

"No." Richard blinked as if coming out of a trance. "No, Tatum, I swear, that wasn't me. That was—"

"Doesn't sound like a denial on the rest of it." Cruz spun Richard around and slapped handcuffs on him. That clicking sound as they tightened would haunt her for the rest of her life. "Since you wanted witnesses, how about they hear me read you your rights. Richard Kirkman, I'm arresting you on charges of…"

Tatum didn't hear the rest. Would that she could have melted into the floor and disappeared, but that wouldn't happen. She walked behind them, more than aware of every single eye on her. She stopped at the podium when Cruz stopped at the door.

"Tatum," Susan whispered and then stopped, as a middle-aged woman stepped forward, her cool, controlled cop expression aimed at Tatum.

"Ms. Colton. Lieutenant Luce Graves. I'm sorry, but I'm afraid I need to ask you to close your restaurant immediately."

"Why?" Susan demanded, but Tatum shook her head and looked to Cruz.

There it was. The final nail in the coffin.

"Because it's a crime scene," Tatum said softly. When she continued, she did so with her gaze firmly on Cruz. And she waited until he met her eyes. "I'll take care of it, Lieutenant. On one condition. You make certain I never see *him* again."

Cruz winced.

"Ms. Colton—"

"That's the condition." She didn't want the sympathy she heard in his boss's voice; she didn't want platitudes or explanations. He'd lied to her. Over and over. From the moment he'd sat down at the bar all the way up to when he'd said he loved her. He didn't. It wasn't possible he did, when he'd just blown up her entire world. "Do we have a deal?"

"Yes." Lieutenant Graves nodded and motioned for her cops, including Cruz, to leave. "I'll be sending in a team—"

"Can this wait a few minutes?" Tatum cut her off. She'd never felt so in control and yet so detached in her life. "Susan, show the lieutenant to the bar and help her with anything she needs." She didn't wait for agreement or understanding before she faced her customers. "Ladies and gentlemen, I apologize for..." She cleared her throat. "It's with my deepest regret that I ask you all to leave. There will be no charge for your meals. I can't offer any explanation at this time. I hope to in the near future. Please." She stepped up onto the bar stair, stood with her hands clasped behind her back and willed them all away. Slowly, silently, people gathered their belongings and did as she asked.

She stood there, chin up, eyes dry, heart pounding a staccato in her chest, as they filed by, one by one. The tears would come later, much later, when she was alone and could scream them free. She nearly lost control when Constance Swan stopped and reached out her hand. Tatum clasped it and found only warmth.

"I'll take a rain check on that kitchen tour," the older woman said.

It was no doubt an offer made out of pity, but Tatum managed a small smile and nod. When the last customer stepped out and the door closed behind them, Tatum walked slowly through her empty restaurant. She heard Ty's and Sam's outraged voices echoing against the glass, but she couldn't talk to them. Not now. Not yet.

She made her way around the scattered tables and chairs, casting tear-filled eyes upon the partially eaten meals and half-filled wine glasses. Tatum climbed the stairs, one by one, slowly, deliberately, until she reached her office.

And closed the door behind her.

Chapter Fifteen

"It's all over the internet." The declaration shot at Cruz from across the squad room like a bullet, hitting him square in the heart. A heart he couldn't afford to listen to at the moment if he was going to do his job.

And he would do it. Not following through would mean he'd betrayed the woman he loved for nothing. He would never, for the rest of his life, be able to erase the image of Tatum standing there, in the middle of her beautiful restaurant, looking utterly and completely defeated. And yet…

And yet she'd stood. She'd done what she had to do, because she was Tatum Colton and anything less would be utterly unacceptable.

As much as she loathed him now, he'd never loved her more.

To top it all off, he was an internet star, which meant his days as an undercover anything were officially over.

"Medina, you ready? They've got him in interview three."

He didn't answer. Instead he pushed to his feet and went to the break room to distract himself with some coffee.

"Cruz." Luce leaned in the doorway and crossed her

arms. "You did what you had to do. You did the job. I know it wasn't easy—"

"No," he said, not wanting to discuss it with anyone, but especially his boss. "It wasn't. But it's over and done." He dumped a crap ton of sugar into his coffee, prayed the combination of sugar and caffeine would get him through the next few hours. "I'm letting him stew. A couple of hours should do it."

"Hours? You sure?"

He looked at her. "Has he asked for a lawyer? Even once? Asked to see his wife? Asked for anything?"

"No." Luce inclined her head.

"It won't take much of a push to get him to talk. He's already scared, and the longer he's in here, the more worried his partners will be. I want him shaking when I go in there." He took a sip of coffee, winced, and accepted it as appropriate punishment. "Maybe then I won't choke the life out of him."

"Cruz, it'll blow over. You'll talk to her. You'll work it out."

"Is that what you'd do if you destroyed Sheryl's career? Any hope she has of advancement? How do you think she'd react if you made her a social media sensation for employing a drug dealer?"

Luce didn't answer. She didn't have to, because they both already knew the truth.

"Sometimes what we have to do seriously sucks, Cruz. I'm going to head back, see how the team's coming along with their search. Anything you want me to tell her?"

Tell her I'm sorry. Tell her he wished there was another way. Tell her if he could, he'd turn back the clock and tell her everything that morning when she'd waved him off. "No." There were no words that would fix or change what had happened. The only thing he could do now was close the case and lock Richard Kirkman and his partners up for the rest of their lives. "Just watch out for her for me, will you?"

Beyond that, there was nothing else he could do.

WHO KNEW A police search could take so long? She should have asked Ty or Quallis or Sam about that, but she waited it all out, opening her door only once when Lieutenant Graves came up to give her an update.

"The restaurant will have to remain closed for at least the next few weeks."

"You can't be more specific than that?" Tatum asked, wondering if this situation could possibly get any worse.

"I'm afraid not."

"Don't plan things out very far, do you?" She had yet to remove her chef's jacket; it felt like the ultimate surrender, but the fabric was beginning to feel more like a straitjacket than her uniform of choice.

"I'd say I'm sorry," the lieutenant said. "But I have the feeling you wouldn't appreciate it."

"You're right. If you and your team are finished, I'd like to lock up and go home." She gathered her purse and jacket and led the older woman downstairs. She waited until the lab techs and officers walked out her front doors, then turned out the lights and locked up. She dug into her purse for her set of spare keys and handed them over. "In case anyone needs access and I'm not here."

Lucille Graves looked down at the collection of keys. "About Cruz—"

"I'm sorry." Tatum held up a hand. "When I said I didn't want to see him again, that included I don't want to talk about him."

"He cares about you, Ms. Colton."

"All evidence to the contrary. I'd say thank you, but I wouldn't really mean it. Good night, Lieutenant."

"Good night."

Tatum couldn't stop swallowing on her way to the parking lot. Her car felt a million miles away, but the tears were just beneath the surface, waiting for one tiny crack in her control to flow free. She lifted her face into the cold wind, let the chill take care of them. She stopped when she saw her car was surrounded by her employees. By her friends.

Sam and Quallis and Colby and Chester. Bernadette and Susan clung to each other. Every server, every bartender, every bus-person and Ty. All of them stood there in the cold March air waiting for her.

When Ty stepped forward, she couldn't stop herself. The tears spilled and she held up her hand, shook her head. "Don't," she whispered. "Please." But he did. He moved in and wrapped his arms around her, drew her in to an embrace that reminded her so much of the ones her father had always provided that her knees buckled.

The sobs nearly choked her as she clung to him, the cold fading as the others encircled her, rested their hands on her shoulder, on her back.

"I'm sorry," she managed between sobbing breaths. "I'm so sorry. This is all my fault. I never should have let—"

"You have nothing to apologize for," Ty assured her. "If you want to blame someone, blame me. I helped him. I trusted him. Should have known better than to trust a cop. Especially a cop who lies for a living."

"We're going to fix this," Susan insisted. "Somehow, someway, we are going to get True back on track."

"You can't really think there's any hope of that." But it meant the world to her that they at least pretended. She'd seen the videos online. They were trending on Twitter and had been splattered all over Facebook. The food world would be next, especially once Constance Swan added her two cents. "We're closed. Indefinitely. I'll pay you all through the end of the month at least. After that, I don't know when or if…" There was every real possibility she might never open those doors again.

"Come on, boss," Sam urged when she stepped back and got herself under control. "Let's go get a drink across the street."

She wanted to. Tonight of all nights, but she couldn't. She was exhausted and the last thing she wanted to do was rehash it over and over. "Another night. I'm going home. I'll call you when I know something," she insisted and made her way to her car.

Tatum didn't look at them as she drove away. She couldn't bear to. She drove by rote, heading for the ranch house only to pull over to the side of the road halfway there. Her home, in the last week, had somehow become theirs. Everywhere she looked she'd see him, hear him. Smell him on her sheets. Imagine him lounging on her sofa while she cooked or acting as taster as she experimented. There wasn't a part of that place that wouldn't haunt her tonight.

She turned the car around, headed for the condo. She barely remembered getting there, parking, taking the elevator up. All she wanted was a shower and her bed and to sleep until she could forget.

But when she stepped inside, all those wants vanished. Her mother, her aunt and January all got to their feet. The space looked new, with its pale Wedgwood blue walls and elegant, gold-accented brocade draperies. Her furniture was rearranged into a more practical pattern, but most of all, they'd left her kitchen alone. It was beautiful. It was, she thought, perfect.

"Guess you finished just in time for me to move out."

When she buckled this time, her other family was there to catch her.

"How do you function on so little sleep?"

January stumbled out of the bedroom and somehow managed to perch on the barstool without tumbling to the floor. Her sister had never done particularly well with all-nighters, whereas Tatum thrived on them. Her mother and Aunt Fallon had finally headed home sometime after one, having given Tatum just enough time to wallow and wail before the anger set in.

Now, five hours, three loaves of bread and a vat of beef stew later, that anger was on a full-blast-boil.

"Coffee," January groaned. "For the love of all that is holy, coffee."

Tatum smirked and abandoned her puff pastry to do her sister's bidding. She waited to speak until her sister had had her first sip, then dived in.

"Somewhere between the sourdough and *fougasse*, I made a decision."

"Hmm." January looked doubtful. "Usually your best decisions are made over waffles. I say hopefully," she added, eyeing the waffle iron cabinet.

"Not today." That she now resented waffles only added to her mood. "Today, I take a stand. I'm not giving up."

"Well, duh." January rolled her eyes. "You're a Colton. It's literally a gene defect. We fight to the death. But, for clarification, are we talking about Cruz or True?"

"What do you think?" She had Cruz Medina solidly in her rearview mirror. Mostly.

"Ummm." January pressed her lips into a thin line. "Maybe we need Simone for the rest of this conversation."

"Mom said she didn't answer her phone last night when you all called her, but she did text."

"Whoopee!" January waved a finger in the air. "Such support she's showing you."

Because of her own issues with compartmentalizing, Tatum wasn't going to blame Simone for not being there with the rest. The longer the investigation went into their father and uncle's killer, the more determined Simone became. "She's having trouble dealing with Dad's death. You know this. Let her be."

"I'll remind you you said that at a later date. So, what's this plan of action you've come up with?"

"First—" Tatum brushed off her hands "—I'm going to call one of the local news stations and offer to give an interview, clear the air, so to speak."

"Can you do that?" January frowned. "I mean, will the police let you?"

"Let me?" Had she heard that correctly?

"Legalities and all. Due process and blah-blah-blah. Just…" January crinkled her nose. "And don't take this the wrong way, but you didn't like it when Cruz interfered with your career. Blindsiding him might not be the best idea. He has arrest powers."

Oh, he had a lot of powers. "The irony was not lost on me." Tatum folded her pastry, turned it and wrapped it in plastic wrap to set in the freezer for a half hour. "And don't worry. I'll clear any statement I make with Lieutenant Graves. I'm also thinking of writing something up for social media."

"Nah." January shook her head. "Let this ride out. Things like this burn out in days, replaced by some other attention suck that make people feel superior. The more you contribute to it, the longer the fire will burn. Trust me on this, Tate. Just focus on getting True's doors back open." She sat up, frowned. "I think that's my cell."

"Probably Sean again. He's been texting you all night. Don't worry," Tatum assured her when she got the glare. "I only answered once to let him know I was okay and that you were asleep. Call him back and tell him you're on your way home."

"Am I?" She looked down at the borrowed set of pink bunny shorts and matching tank. "I don't look like it. I don't like the idea of you being alone today."

"I won't be." She was already heading into her bedroom to get dressed. "I'm never alone at True."

CRUZ MANAGED TO wait until dawn before interviewing Richard Kirkman. He wouldn't have made it that long if he hadn't taken a call from Jade and had a long, decision-making discussion with her about Johnny. It was time, she'd told him, only a short time to go. Cruz glanced at his watch, at the date below the time. Today was Johnny's thirtieth birthday. It was fitting, Jade insisted. To let him go on the day he'd been given to the world.

He'd sat there at his desk, multiple coffee cups lined up on the table. In hours he'd say a final goodbye. All that was left was to close this case and tell Johnny, before he was gone, that he'd kept his promise. Except…

He hadn't. Not yet. But he had managed to destroy the one good thing to come into his life. Tatum Colton had, in a very short amount of time, carved a permanent place inside of him. He'd never understood the idea of finding the person who fit, something Johnny had lamented for him on more than one occasion.

"Once you find her, man, you will never, ever want to let her go." Johnny's bright blue eyes and Hollywood-blond hair all but shone whenever he spoke about Jade. "It'll happen. One day. And I'll be there laughing my butt off even as I plan your stag party."

But there wouldn't be a stag do. For either of them. And that, Cruz thought as he scrubbed a hand down his face, was perhaps the greatest tragedy of all of this. Both their futures had disappeared in the blink of an eye, or, in Johnny's case, the flash of a muzzle.

The clock tick-tick-ticked its way to eight o'clock.

By this afternoon when he walked into that rehab facility, he'd have Richard Kirkman locked down as a witness against one of the biggest drug cartels in the state. And that would be his parting gift to his partner.

He stood up, stretched, and, catching his LT's eye, headed down the hall to interrogation. Cruz popped his head into the observation room, glanced toward the two-way mirror as Luce came in behind him. "He ready, you think?"

"Oh, yeah." The plainclothes detective sitting at a computer monitor, ready to record whatever happened, nodded. "He's about worn a trench in the linoleum. And he definitely should have to pee by now."

"Seems a good place to start. I'm going in."

"Cruz." Lieutenant Graves held out her hand. "Forgetting something?"

"Not really, no." But he handed over his sidearm anyway. When he stepped into the interview room, he knew instantly his instinct to let Kirkman stew had been right on target. The room smelled like sour sweat, guilt and desperation. His favorite combination. He motioned for the monitor officer to leave, murmured his thanks and closed the door.

Kirkman stopped his pacing and all but launched himself at Cruz. "Kept me waiting long enough. Where's Nancy? Where's my wife?"

"She's safe." Cruz held up his hands, pointed to the mirror. "You put hands on me we're going to have to add to your list of charges, Richard. I don't think you can afford any more."

Richard backed off, resumed pacing. "You don't know what you've done, Mendoz..." He stopped, whirled around, eyes narrowed. "That's not your real name."

"Close. Detective Cruz Medina. Mendoza was

Tatum's idea. Keeping things as close to the truth as possible."

"Your admiration won't get you far anymore." Richard had the gall to smirk. "She won't have anything to do with the man who ruined her business."

"Then I guess we have something in common. Sit."

Richard ignored him. "You got this all wrong, Cruz. I've been protecting Tatum. For months! I'm the only reason she's still alive. Hell, I'm still protecting her!"

"Really?" Cruz pulled a chair closer, spun it around and sat. "Do tell."

"First you tell me where Nancy is. What are you charging her with?"

"Nothing. For now. She's being held for questioning. If she doesn't know anything—"

Richard scrubbed his hands down his face. "She only knows I screwed up. Cruz, she's innocent. You have to give her protection. You have to give it to both of us."

"Convince me. Tell me about Tatum and this fantasy you have about having saved her. You were a plant at the restaurant. You work for the Nacio drug cartel."

Richard sat, dropped his head into his hands. "I grew up with Javier Nacio. He was my best friend all the way through college. His father...his father considered me a second son. I didn't know what the family was about until it was too late. He paid for my college, bought my mother a house, made sure she moved into a safe neighborhood. And then I was in deep. So I went where they told me."

"Try again." Cruz shook his head. "No way Nacio Sr. would have had True on his radar." Cruz wagged a finger at Richard. "You should take credit for your ideas, Richard. That was all you."

"Okay, yeah, it was. I might have mentioned using a high-end restaurant like True would be a good cover for distribution, but I didn't know, I had no idea they were going to kill Daria Naughton to get me in the door."

That was one. Cruz made a mental note. "But once you were, you started pushing the catering idea."

"Yeah. It didn't get me very far until Tatum's dad was killed. That reception was the opening I needed. From there it was just a matter of creating the right client with the right system in place. In one month I managed to triple their supply."

"By accepting deliveries of drugs at True and transporting them in catering orders to Belma Trade."

"Yeah. Yeah, and it was all going okay until she hired you. I had someone all picked out. One of Nacio's lieutenants was ready for the sous-chef job and then there you were."

"And since Tatum hired me herself, you needed to get a hold of my employment file."

"I was ordered to. Nacio wanted to know who you were. He doesn't like coincidences."

Great. He had something in common with a drug lord.

"You didn't have to lock her in the freezer. You could have just gotten it during the dinner rush."

"Her office is all windows. She'd have seen me and I didn't have time to think about it. He had Nancy under surveillance. He probably did last night when you picked her up."

Cruz hoped his boss picked up on that. If Nancy Kirkman was being watched by the cartel, then they knew she was in custody. Not being able to reach Kirkman himself was probably adding to their concern. "We'll take care of Nancy, Richard. I promise. What did they do when you gave them the file?"

"They told me you couldn't be trusted and that meant Tatum couldn't be, either. She needed to be taken care of, but I said I could do something without hurting her. That's when I had Nancy approach Constance Swan. Nothing distracts Tatum like potential to grow True. I just needed her to focus on something that didn't involve you and whatever you were looking for."

"And when it didn't work, you tried to run her down with your car."

"Not me, man. That was Nacio's deal. He put one of his best men on it. Cruz, you have to listen to me. This isn't over. Getting me, that's nothing. You want me to flip, great. Fine, yeah, you put me and Nancy somewhere where they won't find me, WITSEC, whatever, I'll take whatever deal you guys offer. But you have to get to Tatum and keep her away from True."

"But you're here. What threat—"

"You really think I'm the only one Nacio had working at True? It takes two people to drive those catering deliveries, Cruz. Man. Oh, man, this has all gone wrong. I told him this wasn't going to work. They always find out." He sagged forward, burying his face in his arms. "This has all gone wrong."

"What has gone wrong? Your last delivery—"

"The last drop-off didn't make it to the suppliers. He

took it, Cruz. He's stashed it to sell on the side. My cut was supposed to be enough to get me out of the country, but I felt things going wrong and planned to get out."

"Stop whining and tell me who else Nacio had working at the restaurant." His mind was already flipping through the employees. Susan, Sam, Chester, Colby... half a dozen servers, just as many bartenders. Ty, Bernadette and... "Pike. Was Pike driving that car that went after Tatum?"

Richard's head snapped up. "Yeah. He said she wasn't distracted enough. She needed to be taken out. He was furious when she walked back into True."

"Son of a... Pike is behind all this. Lieutenant!" He was on his feet and out the door. She popped out into the hall at the same time, held out his weapon. "Richard's low man on the ladder."

"But Pike's record came up clean."

"I'm betting that's not his name. Run a deeper background check. Talk to him." He pointed into the interview room. "I need to find Tatum."

"Wait, Cruz!" Richard tried to step clear, only to be stopped by the officer standing outside the room. "Pike's not giving up that stash. He's been ripping them off for months. He needs a scapegoat, someone to blame, someone to give Nacio as a trade-off."

"Tatum." Cruz felt the blood drain from his face. "He's going to turn Tatum over to Nacio. Luce?" He didn't even try to quell the panic spinning inside him.

"Go!" his boss yelled. "Take backup with you to the restaurant. I'll send a car to her house."

"And the condo." He yelled out the address as he ran through the squad room.

Please, please, he prayed as he raced to his car. *Don't let me be too late again.*

Chapter Sixteen

It took all Tatum's focus not to do the math as she emptied True's refrigeration units of the leftover and unused food from last night. On the bright side, things had blown up on a Friday night, so she hadn't purchased food for next week yet.

She'd been able to cancel her standing order, and, having spent the past two hours on the phone with various vendors, assure them that payment was on the way and that there would be no outstanding invoices by next week. Only when she was caught up could she take a serious look at the accounting to see what other damage Richard had wrought on her restaurant.

"Not only Richard," she muttered and tossed multiple heads of lettuce into a plastic bin. She was just as responsible. She'd been mired in grief and all too happy to let someone else take control of what she should have been paying close attention to. She'd find a way, some way, to drag True back; she hadn't worked this long and hard to give up. She certainly wasn't going to give Cruz Medina the power to destroy her life.

True would be the phoenix of restaurants and rise from the ashes of scandal better and bigger than before.

As for the food she was left with, she would be spending her day making donations and deliveries to various food banks and homeless shelters. No way was she going to let any of this go to waste.

"Figured I'd find you here."

Tatum yelped, jumped back and pressed a hand to her racing heart. "Sam!" She all but shrieked at him. "What are you doing here?"

"Well, I was going to do what you've already started." He set his phone on the stainless steel counter beside hers. "Need some help?"

"I would love some."

Her phone buzzed for what must have been the tenth time in the past hour and she could tell by Sam's expression who it was. "Cruz?" she asked.

"Guy's got a set, I'll give him that. Man." He shook his head and joined her at the refrigerator. "A cop. Ty was right. I so should have seen that."

"If it matters, he never suspected you," Tatum said.

Sam hefted a box of produce, arched a brow at her.

"Okay, maybe before he met you, but not after." At least she didn't think Cruz did. Honesty wasn't exactly at the top of his list of positive qualities. The loading bay door rumbled. They stopped, looked at each other. "Someone come with you? Ty?"

"Nah. He has his grandkids today. Did you know he has grandkids?"

"I found out this week," Tatum said. "I've had a lot of information to process. Maybe it's Quallis."

"We need some more crates anyway. I'll go check." Sam set the box on the counter and headed for the loading bay.

Smiling for the first time in a while, Tatum resumed unloading the perishables from the walk-in. She heard voices, Sam and at least one other, muted. There was no way of telling who it was from here.

Curious, she closed the fridge and headed off to join them, clicking on the light in the storeroom.

"Sam?" she yelled. "Did you find who—"

Bang! Bang bang!

"Sam?" Tatum ran toward the sudden crash, skidding to a halt as she saw Sam lying on the ground, a thick pool of blood spreading under him. "Sam!" She raced forward, dropped to her knees and pressed her hand against his side, the only place she could see a wound. "Sam, what happened? Who did this?"

He blinked, his dark eyes wide with shock. "Tatum." Blood trickled out the side of his mouth. "Tatum, run."

"Run? No, you need help." She looked behind her but didn't see anyone around. The loading bay door was open, as was the van's back double doors. "I have to call an ambulance." She patted her bloodied hands against her shirt, over her pockets. "I left my cell. I need to go get it. I'll get help, okay?" She grabbed his face. "You stay with me, you hear me? I can't do this without you!"

"Go." He tried to sit up, but his face went ashen and he gasped, coughed up blood.

"Stay still. Sam, please, just don't move. I'm going to—" She turned to race back to the kitchen and slammed right into a solid form. She screamed, jumped back, and barely had a blink of a second to register what was happening.

He dived for her, grabbed her around the waist and threw her into the van. The doors slammed before she could scramble to her knees. She clawed for the handle, screaming for help. Two hands locked around her ankles and pulled her back. She slammed face-first onto the floor of the van. Dazed, she rolled onto her back, tasted blood in her mouth.

She pushed over onto her side as the engine roared to life and the van began to move.

"Tatum?" Cruz figured yelling his presence was enough of a warning as he pulled open the unlocked door of True. Irritation flickered. What was she thinking not locking the door behind her? If she wanted to strike out at him, fine, but he wasn't going to let her ignore him. "Tatum, I know you're here. I know you don't want me here but…" He slammed through the kitchen's swinging double doors.

Empty.

Crates and boxes of food were stacked around the kitchen, on the counters. The walk-in fridge was closed. Cruz pulled out his phone, dialed her cell again.

The buzzing from the counter had him walking forward. "Tatum!"

He picked up her phone, glanced at the second one lying beside it. He tapped the screen, saw an image of a laughing Sam with his mom appear. Of course Sam was here. Relief she wasn't alone surged through him, only to be stifled at the continuing silence. "Tatum? Sam?"

A crash exploded in the storage room.

Cruz raced down the hall, spotted the pile of boxes. The catering van was gone. Something moved beneath the boxes. Moved and groaned. He threw them to the side, uncovered a trembling, bleeding Sam. He swore, ripped off his jacket and wadded it up to push against the younger man's chest. "Sam, what happened? Where's Tatum?"

Sam blinked hard to stay awake. "Pike." Blood continued to trickle out the side of his mouth. "Couldn't stop him. Took her. Get her back." He grabbed hold of Cruz's shirt, hauled himself up. "Go get her back."

"I will." Panic and terror battled for control, but Cruz eased Sam back, kept pressure on the wound and pulled out his cell. "Detective Medina, Narcotics. I need an ambulance in the back alley behind True. I've got a single gunshot—what?" he asked when Sam shook his head, held up three fingers.

Cruz swore again, yanked up Sam's shirt, then hauled him onto his side. "Be advised victim has three gunshots to the torso. Two appear to be through and through."

Sam coughed. His eyes rolled back in his head. Cruz pressed two fingers against the side of his neck. The pulse was there—faint, but still there. "You hang on, kid, you hear me? I expect you to kick my butt for what I did to Tatum."

He could have sworn he heard Sam try to laugh.

Footsteps pounded behind him. Cruz looked up and found two uniformed officers headed his way. "Over here!" he yelled. "Ambulance is on its way. I want you to keep pressure on this wound here." He dragged the young woman down into his position. "You, call in an all-points for one Jeremy Pike. He's driving a white van, with True Catering on the outside."

"On it," the officer said.

Cruz raced back through the restaurant and out to

his car. He was pulling away as he hit Dial on his car's dashboard phone. Waited for his LT to pick up.

"Report, Medina."

"I was too late. Tatum's gone. Witness said Pike took her. I need you to access the GPS tracker I put on the True catering van." Thank God he hadn't had the chance to remove it yet. "I've got it bookmarked on my laptop."

"Give me a few."

Cruz drove mindlessly, uncertain where to head.

"Okay, Cruz, looks like he's headed to the warehouse area. I can get you a precise location in a bit."

"On my way."

"Backup's rolling. Ten minutes out."

Cruz hung up. Ten minutes. He had less than that before sirens rolled and all hell broke loose. Ten minutes to save the woman he loved.

"PIKE." TATUM'S VISION finally cleared enough for her to make out the driver's profile. Even if she hadn't seen his face, that tattoo was unmistakable. "Pike, what are you doing? What's going on?"

She pushed to her knees and dragged herself forward. Another headache pounded its way through her skull.

"Just stay back and shut up." Pike's order shot out like bullets. "We're almost there."

"Almost where?"

"You're the only one who can get me out of this."

"Get you out of what? Shooting Sam?"

"Stupid of him to get in the way. Stupid, stupid!" He slammed his hand against the steering wheel.

"Jeremy, tell me what's happening. Please." It

couldn't hurt to be patient, but something told her it would hurt a lot more to panic.

"They want their drugs." He looked at Tatum. "They think you have them. They want to talk to you."

Reality struck hard. He was taking her to the dealers working with Richard. No. The dealers working with him. "You're working with Richard."

"Richard was working for us! It should have been easy, should have been so easy, but then you had to bring in that cop. I knew, I knew I'd seen him before." He gripped the wheel, jaw pulsing. "Took me a while to remember, but when I did I knew, I knew he was a cop!"

"Where did you see Cruz?"

Pike laughed. "Like I'm going to confess everything to you. What do you think this is? A TV show?"

"I think I trusted you enough to hire you and I deserve an explanation." She looked at his hands, the way his knuckles went white as they tensed. The oversize gold ring on one finger. The same ring she'd seen flash in the glow of the grocery store parking lot. "It was you." She hadn't meant to say it out loud, but once she did, there was no taking it back. "You tried to run me down."

"You were supposed to be cooking! Supposed to be focused on the critic. But you couldn't be distracted. Not with that cop with you twenty-four seven."

That cop. Cruz. Hope sprung to life inside of her. He had Richard in custody. He'd probably questioned him. Was it possible...was there even a chance Cruz would know she was in trouble? She needed to stall, needed to give Cruz time to catch up with them.

"Pike, if you take me to these men, they'll kill me."

"Better you than me."

"You aren't going to get away. Not from Cruz."

"Cruz." Pike snorted. "Should have killed him that night I killed his partner. Then none of this would have happened."

She tasted bile in her mouth as nausea surged inside her. She pressed a hand to her stomach, willed the panic to subside. "His partner isn't dead."

Pike whirled in his seat, accusing eyes on her before he refocused on the nearly empty road.

"He's in a recovery unit," Tatum lied. "You haven't killed anyone yet, Pike. Please. There's still time to make something good come out of this. Don't do this. Don't take me to…" He turned into a fenced area of warehouses. All these buildings, all this space. There was no way Cruz would find her here. "Pike, please. I don't want to die."

"Too late." Pike hunched over the steering wheel. "We're already here. There." He pointed to the collection of cars just inside a wide-open door. "Don't worry. I've seen them do this before. It'll be quick. You won't know it's happening."

"Yes, I will." She spoke softly as her mind raced. Above the sound of the engine, she thought she heard sirens, but she had to be imagining it. Manifesting it. She needed to believe, even as she accepted the odds were against her.

These were the men, Pike and these cartel members, responsible for so much pain, so much suffering. So many deaths. The drugs they sold and dealt were only to line their own pockets, and their greed knew no end. This was what Cruz had spent his life trying to stop.

He'd taken an oath, promised his partner, dedicated his life to protecting people and stopping the same kind of criminals who in a matter of minutes would kill her. Forgiveness, she realized, wasn't so hard to manage, after all.

If she was going to die, she wasn't going to die a victim. She'd go out fighting.

It was what Cruz would do.

Tatum threw herself forward, grabbed hold of the steering wheel and slammed her foot hard over Pike's. The van lurched forward, speeding up to the point the entire vehicle began to shake.

Pike tried to get his arms free, but she pushed all her weight into him, elbowed him in the face when he nearly knocked her aside. She lifted her foot, slammed it down again and wrenched the wheel to the side.

The momentum tossed her into the passenger seat. Her shoulder cracked hard against the door as the van spun, lost traction and, for an instant, seemed to be flying. She grabbed hold of the seat belt strap and yanked it down as the tires caught and flipped, once, twice, too many times to count.

She squeezed her eyes shut against the sound of crushing metal and a scream that went suddenly silent. When the van skidded to a stop, the sirens blared louder. Shouts and cries were followed by gunshots. Tatum lay there, bathed and covered in shattered glass. Tiny pinpricks of pain dotted her face and arms. She sat wedged between the dash and seat, tried to catch her breath and assess if she could move.

More shouting. Pounding footsteps. Two more shots. Tatum opened her eyes and found Pike's dead-eyed stare. Blood covered most of his face as he hung suspended by his seat belt, his arms dangling toward her.

Tatum whimpered, kicked out, desperate to get free. She could climb out if she could just—

"Tatum!" Cruz's voice blasted through the ringing in her ears. "Tatum!"

"Cruz." She had to clear her throat. "Cruz, I'm here! In here!" She pulled with her arms, hoisted herself up only an inch before Cruz appeared on top of the van. He lay there, half in the shattered windshield. She smiled up at him, half laughing, half sobbing. "Would now be a good time to tell you you're forgiven?"

"I don't think there's a better one." He reached out his arm. "Take hold, babe."

She released the belt and reached up. The instant her hand locked around his she knew, without hesitation, without reservation, that this was where she belonged. With him.

Minutes later he was pulling her off the van and hauling her into his arms, holding on so tight she couldn't breathe. And she'd never been happier.

"I was afraid I was too late." He led her away from the van, toward one of the waiting ambulances. "I was so sure I'd lost you."

"No way that's happening now." As she clung to him she looked around at the chaos she'd wrought. "Did I do that?"

"A woman of many talents. Thanks to your stunt driving we've got the entire cartel. Including Javier Nacio Sr."

"Pike's dead."

"Yeah, I saw."

"He shot Johnny." She felt him tense, then his hold tightened. "He could have shot you, too, but he chose not to. I'm so glad he did. It was maybe the only good thing he's done."

Cruz set her back, caught her face in his hands. "You aren't going to fight me on going to the hospital are you?"

"The hospital." She gasped and felt the first twinge of pain. "Sam! He shot Sam! Oh, Cruz…"

"He's alive," Cruz said with a nod. "Last I heard he was still alive."

"I need to be there."

"Yeah." Cruz pulled her back into his arms. "So do I."

"I AM SO done with hospitals," Tatum groaned as she uncurled from the torture device of a chair in the waiting room. She accepted the mediocre coffee Cruz handed her. She'd been checked out and discharged, but only because Cruz had promised to monitor her injuries. She had bruised ribs, multiple lacerations and another crack on the head. She'd be out of commission for at least a week, the same amount of time True would be closed.

The Chicago Police Department had also released a public statement thanking Tatum and the employees of True for helping to bring down a significant narcotics ring in the city. With Richard Kirkman cutting a deal with the feds, True and Tatum were in the clear to reopen with the restaurant's saved and praised reputation.

Or so Cruz's lieutenant had told her when she'd arrived at the hospital to touch base with Cruz. She sat with them and Sam's mother, who had been brought to the hospital by Ty. The rest of True's employees filed in to wait for word on their friend.

Hours ticked by. Tatum dozed, her head tucked into Cruz's shoulder, the sound of his deep voice lulling her into a fitful sleep. By the time he shook her awake it seemed as if forgiveness, while not completely earned yet, was soon to come from the staff. Sitting among her friends, her family, peace settled over her corner of the world.

"Doctor's here," Cruz murmured as she sat up.

"Right, okay." She steeled herself. "Dr. DeSantis, how is he?"

"Very lucky." The female surgeon removed her surgical cap and gave an encouraging smile. "We removed his spleen and repaired some internal damage. He must have turned at just the right time. The other two bullets missed any vital organs. It'll be a while before he's on his feet again, but I expect he'll make a full recovery."

Sam's mother let out a relieved sob that brought tears to Tatum's eyes. "Thank you so much."

Dr. DeSantis left them alone.

Cruz swore when his cell rang.

"What?" Tatum wasn't sure she could take any more unsettling news today.

"It's Jade." He flinched, glanced at his watch. "I need to take this." He held up a hand at Tatum's curious expression. "Jade. Don't worry. I haven't forgotten. I can be there in—what?"

"What?" Tatum couldn't remember ever seeing him so shocked. "What's happened?" He reached for her hand, squeezed so hard she had to move in to ease the pressure.

"Okay, yeah. I'll be there as soon as I can. Tell him…" Cruz's eyes misted. "Tell him I'm bringing someone with me." He cupped Tatum's cheek. "Someone special. Yeah. I'll see you soon." He hung up. "It's Johnny." He backed up, looked between his LT and Tatum. "He's awake."

"But…" Tatum couldn't process. "Is that even possible? I thought you said—"

"I told you what the doctors told me. They don't have a prognosis yet and he's definitely got a long road, but he's alive. And he's awake. He's talking."

"Well, don't sit around here," Sam's mother insisted. "Get going already. My boy's in good hands."

Tatum hugged her. "I don't want you to worry about hospital bills," she whispered to the older woman. "I take care of my family. That includes you and Sam."

"Your parents did a right good job with you, young lady." Sam's mother kissed both her cheeks. "My boy's blessed to have found you."

A few minutes later, Cruz and Tatum walked to his car. "It's been quite a day," Tatum sighed. "One I won't soon forget." Not that she wanted to. Well, maybe some of it. "What?" She asked when Cruz didn't respond.

"What are you doing Monday evening?"

"Considering my restaurant won't be open for business for a bit yet, I think my schedule's pretty clear. Why? You have something in mind?"

"Yeah, actually." He pulled open the passenger door, and as she sat, he said, "I'd like you to come to dinner with me at my parents'. It won't be anything fancy, but my mom's a pretty darn good cook. I want you to meet them. So you know what you're getting into."

She caught his face between her hands, pressed her mouth to his. "I would love to go."

Tatum laughed when his cell went off again. "What now?"

"Better get used to it," he teased. "Such is the life of a cop." He glanced at the text. "Well, what do you know." The smile that broke across his mouth sent a zing of pleasure rippling through her. "Looks like the Narcotics division is getting a new member of the family. The LT's wife just went into labor."

"So we'll come back once you see Johnny," Tatum said even as she smothered a yawn. "You do know how to show a girl a good time, Detective Medina."

"And I plan to keep doing that." He bent down and pressed his lips to hers again. "For as long as you'll let me."

* * * * *

COMING SOON!

We really hope you enjoyed reading this book.
If you're looking for more romance, be sure to
head to the shops when new books are
available on

Thursday 4th March

To see which titles are coming soon, please visit
millsandboon.co.uk/nextmonth

JOIN US ON SOCIAL MEDIA!

Stay up to date with our latest releases, author news and gossip, special offers and discounts, and all the behind-the-scenes action from Mills & Boon...

 millsandboon

 millsandboonuk

 millsandboon

might just be true love...

MILLS & BOON

HISTORICAL

Awaken the romance of the past

Escape with historical heroes from time gone by. Whether your passion is for wicked Regency Rakes, muscled Viking warriors or rugged Highlanders, indulge your fantasies and awaken the romance of the past.

MILLS & BOON

MODERN

Power and Passion

Prepare to be swept off your feet by sophisticated, sexy and seductive heroes, in some of the world's most glamourous and romantic locations, where power and passion collide.